UNDER A TELL-TALE SKY

DISRUPTION - BOOK 1

A Thriller By

R. E. McDermott

Published by R.E. McDermott

Copyright © 2015 by R.E. McDermott

For more information about the author, please visit
www.remcdermott.com

Layout by Guido Henkel, **www.guidohenkel.com**

Printed in the U.S.A.

Acknowledgments

With each new book, the ranks of supportive people to whom I owe thanks grows.

As always, my wife, Andrea, was my first reader and sounding board, saving readers from any number of less than wonderful turns of phrase.

Longtime friends and former classmates Captains Ken Varall and Seth Harris once again lent their combined seventy-plus years of sailing experience to the cause, reading the shipboard scenes and making valuable suggestions to improve both their technical accuracy and plausibility.

Also from the fraternity of sailormen, Captain William Heu of the Wilmington, North Carolina, pilots gave generously of his time and helped me avoid putting the fictional *Pecos Trader* aground. I appreciate his efforts and also thank Captain Jorge Viso for introducing me to Captain Heu.

I have no trouble ensuring sailors talk like sailors, but longtime reader (and now friend) First Sergeant David Schoettle of the 101st Airborne (aka *The Screaming Eagles*) made sure the dialogue between soldiers rang true. I thank Dave for both his help and service to our country.

Beta reader extraordinaire Barbara Elsborg read the manuscript multiple times, making terrific suggestions with each iteration. Our son Chris and daughter-in-law Jennifer read the final draft, which as it turned out, wasn't quite so final. Many thanks to them for catching multiple errors which had eluded me. Our son Andy through-hiked the Appalachian Trail from Georgia to Maine in 2011, and serves as my resident expert on all things related to the AT. A special thanks to him for keeping my Appalachian Trail scenes accurate and realistic.

On the publishing front, Pauline Nolet turned her eagle eyes to purging all remaining errors. I've come to rely on her completely as the best proofreader I've ever used. Guido Henkel jumped in on very short notice to do his normal excellent job of formatting the ebook, and Jeroen ten Berge once again blew me away with yet another astounding cover. I say this each time, but I think this is his best one yet.

Over two hundred readers of my previous books volunteered to read the advance review copy of *Under a Tell-Tale Sky*. Space prevents me from mentioning each by name, but you know who you are and you have my profound thanks.

And last but far from least, the character Laura Hughes is named for Laura McKinney, and I thank Allyn and Laura McKinney for allowing use of her name. Laura's role in the Disruption series is far from over.

Any errors made, despite all this excellent help and support, are mine and mine alone.

To the men and women of
The U.S. Coast Guard
Past, Present, & Future

Semper Paratus

THE EVENT

The world ended on a Wednesday.

Not physically, of course, but the world as most knew it. The Big Blue Marble continued to spin on its axis and orbit the sun, and neither the indigenous people of the Amazon River Basin nor the Papuan tribes of New Guinea noted anything amiss. But the 'civilized' world, the modern world of cheap abundant electrical power and all the wonders it provided, regressed a century and a half in the blink of an eye.

It was fitting Wednesday was also April Fool's Day. As if on cue, world governments responded foolishly, dithering over the wording of last minute press releases on the eve of the Apocalypse, sending mixed signals to an oblivious public. Don't panic. Everything is under control. Business as usual. Communications went down before most advisories were transmitted.

A few warnings did get through, but the unfortunate timing and muted official response led many to conclude it WAS an elaborate April Fool's Day prank. Witty anchor people cocked eyebrows and shared the joke, accompanied by a clip dug from the archives, featuring a rustic gentleman with a single tooth and a tin-foil hat, discussing The End of The World as We Know It (to say nothing of his recent colonoscopy at the hands of extraterrestrials).

But events would prove the gentleman with dental hygiene issues and aluminum head wear to be right after all. The world would never be the same again. But what would it become and who would rule it? An open question, it seemed, but if bureaucrats the world over had been shortsighted in regard to disaster preparation, guns and ammunition were available in abundance. They might not understand preparedness, but they certainly understood power and control.

Desperate times call for desperate measures, and extraordinary circumstances produce heroes and villains in equal measure. Sometimes it's difficult to tell the difference.

CHAPTER ONE

M/V *Pecos Trader*
Buckeye Marine Terminal
Wilmington, North Carolina

Day 1, Impact

Dan Gowan stood bent at the waist, forearms resting on the ship's rail. The lightening eastern sky was bringing the first hints of the coming day. The terminal was a vivid contrast of light and dark shadows as powerful dock lights reflected off enormous stark white storage tanks. He shifted a plug of tobacco from one cheek to the other and squirted tobacco juice over the rail to arc into the dark shadows between the ship and the dock. Beside him, Captain Jordan Hughes shook his head.

"Damned engineers. If it's not grease, it's tobacco juice," Hughes said. "Get that nasty stuff on my nice clean deck, you're gonna clean it up."

Gowan looked over with a lump-cheeked grin. "Don't worry, Cap, I always hit what I aim for." The engineer straightened and glanced down the deck toward the cargo manifold. "And when we gonna start pumping? We've been hooked up over two hours."

Hughes looked at his watch. "It's just after four. These third-shift guys won't get in too much of a hurry. I'm betting they'll drag things out to make sure they don't get stuck with the disconnect at the end of the discharge. They'll likely screw the pooch a few hours before they let us start pumping, just to make sure." He shrugged. "No skin off our ass. We gave them written notice of readiness, so any delays are on them." He paused. "Besides, what's it to you? Why aren't you in your bunk sleeping instead of worrying the hell out of me about something that doesn't concern you?"

"I just kept tossing and turning. Figured I might as well get up."

Hughes grinned. "Short-timer fever, huh? Don't worry, Chief, we'll be back in Beaumont this time next week. You'll start your vacation on time."

"We better be, or Trixie's gonna have my ass."

Hughes cocked an eyebrow. "I thought the divorce was final."

Gowan reddened. "It is, but we're trying to… to work some things out."

"Uh, didn't you already try to reconcile a couple of times already?"

"It's complicated," Gowan said, changing the subject by nodding toward a slightly built black man approaching from the deckhouse, a backpack slung over one shoulder. "Looks like Levi is headed home."

Hughes turned. Levi Jenkins was a qualified member of the engine department, or QMED for short, and had been on the ship longer than anyone else except Hughes himself. Even-tempered and a hard worker, Jenkins was universally liked and generally known as a 'good shipmate.' There was no higher accolade.

"Evenin', Capt'n, Chief," said Levi, focusing his gaze on Gowan.

"Chief, if it's okay with you, Jimmy's gonna cover for me today so I can go home. I already cleared it with the first engineer, but he said to double-check with you before I left."

"No problem as long as your job's covered, and the First runs the engine room, so that's his call. Just make sure you get back before we sail." Gowan grinned. "But there is the usual condition."

Levi grinned back. "Peanut butter or chocolate chip?"

"Some of each would be nice," Gowan said.

Levi laughed and nodded toward the distant parking area, where they could just make out a figure leaning against the front fender of a vintage Ford pickup. "I expect Celia's already got the cookie dough mixed up."

Gowan shook his head. "Now that, my friend, is outstanding. Trixie stopped picking me up at the dock about six months after the honeymoon, and she NEVER showed up at four in the morning."

Levi shrugged. "We want to get through Wilmington traffic before rush hour. We don't call at Wilmington often, and when I got less than a day to spend with the family, I don't want to spend any of it tied up in traffic."

"And we're keeping you," Hughes said, "so take off and enjoy your day, Levi."

"But don't forget the cookies," Gowan added.

"I won't. Anyway, Celia knows if she was to send me back aboard empty-handed there might be a mutiny." Levi laughed and moved toward the gangway.

Gowan called after him, "And when are you going to get rid of that old beater and get a decent truck anyway? Celia deserves more dependable transportation."

"Celia's just fine with that truck," Levi called back over his shoulder, "and they don't get more reliable than Old Blue. If it ain't broke, don't fix it, Chief."

"Good man," Hughes said as he watched Jenkins' departure.

Gowan nodded. "The best unlicensed guy I have in the engine room. I've been bugging him forever to take the license exam, but I can't convince him. Says he's happy right where he is. He does have a few strange ideas, though," Gowan added quietly before turning back to Hughes. "Now when the hell are they gonna let us start pumping?"

Hughes rolled his eyes. "Soon, I hope. Otherwise I'll have to go ashore and start opening valves myself, just to shut you up."

***

An hour later, Hughes and Gowan were in the officers' mess when they heard the familiar whine of the cargo pumps.

"Finally!" Gowan said, checking his watch. "I thought maybe they'd all gone home. This'll put us finishing when, mid-morning tomorrow?"

Hughes nodded. "Give or take, even with a delay we should get out of here on the evening tide."

"It won't be soon enough for—"

The radio squawked, "Captain Hughes, Captain Hughes."

Hughes put the mike to his mouth and pressed the transmit button. "This is Hughes. Over."

"Cap, you might want to come out on deck," said the chief mate.

"On my way," Hughes said, rising from his seat with Gowan close behind.

They arrived on the open deck to stare in wonder. The predawn sky in all directions was awash with shimmering colors, vivid greens, reds, and blues and all shades in between, dancing across the sky from horizon to horizon.

Gowan's mouth hung open. "What the hell—"

"It's… it's the Northern Lights," Hughes gasped.

"In friggin' North Carolina?"

"I saw them once in Alaska," Hughes said. "Trust me, this is them. And enjoy them while you can. It'll be sunrise in half an hour, and they'll fade with full daylight."

They stood mesmerized, soon joined by others of the crew, both working and non-watch seamen, wakened by their shipmates to see the spectacle. As Hughes predicted, the light show began to fade with the dawn.

"Well, I guess the show's over," Hughes said as the last curtain of shimmering green disappeared. "Time to get back to—"

He was interrupted by a thunderous bang and a flash as a transformer on a utility pole ashore exploded, followed by more explosions in the distance along utility lines, one after another like a string of firecrackers. Lights on the dock winked out in response to the explosions, while on board *Pecos Trader*, the hydraulic cargo pumps continued their high-pitched whine.

"They've lost power ashore!" said Hughes. "We have to stop pumping!"

Just as he spoke, the ship lost power as well, and they heard the telltale sound of the pumps winding down.

"Well, that takes care of the pumps," Gowan said.

"What the hell is going on, Chief?" Hughes asked.

"Damned if I know, Cap, but it's not good."

"Go check—" Hughes began, but he was already talking to Gowan's back as the engineer rushed across the deck toward the deckhouse and the engine room below, tugging an ever-present flashlight from his pocket as he ran.

US HIGHWAY 421
NORTHBOUND

Levi Jenkins gripped the wheel tightly as they sped north on US 421. His headlights bored a tunnel through the darkness at ground level as a dazzling display of shimmering colors lit the upper reaches of the predawn sky.

"It's so beautiful." Celia stared into the sky a moment longer, then turned back to him. "Do... do you think this is really it? One of those big solar storms you've been worried about?"

"I can't be sure," Levi said. "I've never seen the Northern Lights, but this can't be anything else, and everything I've read says they're caused by solar activity. If we're seeing the Northern Lights in North Carolina, I'm thinking it's a LOT of solar activity."

Celia gestured to their right at the lights of Wilmington. "The lights are still on."

Levi shook his head. "We're turned away from the sun now, so the lights in the sky may just be from the solar storm, kind of washing around the edges. But it'll be sunrise soon and we'll be taking the full force of the blast. If anything is gonna happen, it'll happen then." He moved into the left lane and passed a slow-moving truck before continuing. "I'm just glad traffic is light. I don't know what's going to happen, but I don't feel good about this and I damn sure want to get across the bridge at Peter Point before sunrise. Even with light traffic, it doesn't take much to jam that bridge. If we get stuck south of the river, it will be tough to get home anytime soon."

"Will all the cars stop working?" Celia asked.

Levi shook his head. "I don't think so, not from a solar flare, anyway. But it really doesn't matter. If the power grid goes down and stays down, there won't be any way to refine and distribute fuel anyway." He glanced at the colors dancing across the lightening sky and increased speed. "A worry for another day. Right now, we just need to get across that bridge."

Celia leaned over and looked at the speedometer. "You're going twenty miles an hour over the limit now. If we get pulled over, we may not make it across the bridge at all."

"Calculated risk," Levi said, but eased off the accelerator a bit.

Ten minutes later they crossed the bridge. Levi heaved a relieved sigh and slowed to the posted limit as he drove northwest through a mixture of woodlands, vacant fields, and industrial development along US 17/421. It wouldn't do to get pulled over at this point. Traffic was getting heavier as he encountered the first of the morning commuters headed into work. Levi looked once again at the lightening sky.

"The kids with your folks?"

She smiled. "You know they are."

It was a standard ritual. Whenever Levi made port in Wilmington with an anticipated nighttime arrival, Celia arranged for their two children to sleep over at her parents' house next door. Thus, they were never alone when she went to collect Levi, and the adults could enjoy some 'private time' before the kids woke up.

"You think your folks are up yet?"

Celia laughed. "Are you kidding? They'll be mostly through a pot of coffee by now. Why?"

"Better call your momma. Tell her if the lights go out, to wake up the kids and start getting ready to move to the river."

"You really think that's necessary? Shouldn't we wait a bit—"

"We've talked about this, Celia. If we lose power after these lights in the sky, I'm thinking this is the real deal. We need to get out of harm's way while everyone else is confused."

"I know, but then it just seemed... I don't know... theoretical."

Levi shot another look skyward. "Well, we're about to find out just how theoretical it is, so you better make the call now while we still have cell service. Another five miles and we'll be in a dead zone."

Celia nodded and dug her phone from her purse. Levi listened as she made the call. It was obvious from Celia's side of the conversation her mother wasn't particularly receptive to the idea.

"I know, Mom, I know. But you don't have to do it unless the power goes out. Yes, I'll tell him. Love you too. See you soon."

"Tell me what?" Levi asked as Celia put her phone away.

"That she loves you, but you irritate the hell out of her, scaring everybody with all this 'end of the world stuff,'" Celia said.

"But she's gonna do—"

KA-BOOM! Sparks cascaded into the roadway as a transformer exploded on a utility pole, followed immediately by similar explosions all along the power line in the distance. Levi flinched and jerked the wheel, inadvertently sending the old truck into a skid. He fought the truck back under control, but two hundred yards ahead of them, a startled motorist veered from the northbound lane into the path of an oncoming car with a resulting thunderous crash. Similar events happened along the length of the highway, and Levi stood on the brakes to bring Old Blue to a shuddering halt at the side of the road, only a few feet away from the wreckage of the nearest collision. He and Celia jumped from the truck and rushed to help.

The northbound vehicle causing the crash was older, either without an air bag or with one that failed to deploy. Nor had the driver been wearing his seat belt. He'd gone through the windshield head first and was draped across the smashed hood of the car like a bloody and boneless rag doll. There was no doubt he was dead. Levi rushed to the other mangled car, where Celia was tugging frantically, and unsuccessfully, at the driver's side door. Inside the vehicle, two young women slumped in their seat belts, deflated air bags lying across their laps. Both were dazed but conscious, and he ran around to try the passenger-side door as Celia continued to jerk frantically on the driver's door.

"Hurry," Celia yelled. "I smell gas!"

Levi's nose was assaulted by the pungent smell as he tugged at the passenger door. It was locked.

"Unlock the doors," he screamed, beating on the window, but the only response from the passenger was a glassy-eyed stare.

He searched the ground and spotted a fist-sized rock in the grass just off the road. It was too small to hold and use as a hammer, so he backed off and threw it at the passenger window with all his might. It produced a crack but little else, rebounding off the glass to fly out of sight into the tall grass. The gas smell was almost overpowering now. Levi weighed his chance of finding the rock, just as the woman passenger began to scream. Levi moved back to the window.

"Unlock the door," he screamed, but the woman was in hysterics.

Desperate now, he leaned his back against the cracked window and hammered the weakened glass with his bare elbow. It yielded on the third blow, showering the screaming passenger with glass. Levi whirled and thrust his hand through the broken window to unlock the door and jerk it open. Still screaming, the terrified and confused woman fought Levi as he attempted to unfasten her seat belt.

"Easy, easy." Levi groped one-handed for the belt buckle, fending off her attacks with the other. "You've been in a car wreck. I'm trying to get you out. Don't fight me!

Finally it registered. The woman allowed Levi to help her from the car. Celia was there now, and Levi passed the woman to her.

"Get her away from here and over by our truck. I'll get the driver out."

"Hurry, Levi! The gas—"

"I know, get out of here, now!" Levi dug in his pocket and handed her the truck keys. "And back the truck away from here as quick as you can."

Celia started toward the truck, dragging the rescued woman along in a stumbling run. Levi dived through the passenger door to reach across the now lucid driver and unlock the driver's side door. He reached for her buckle, but she beat him to it.

"I'll get your door open—" Levi began, but she was already tugging at the door handle.

"Jammed!" she cried and clawed her way from behind the wheel and over the center console as Levi backed out of the car to give her room. He helped her scramble out the open passenger door.

"Can you walk?" Levi asked.

"I can run. Which way?"

Levi grabbed her arm and ran toward where Celia had backed the truck fifty yards away. They were halfway there when the wreckage ignited with a whoosh.

The first victim was sitting on the open tailgate, obviously in shock. Levi helped the driver sit beside her friend. He retrieved two bottles of water from behind the truck seat and carried them back to the women. The driver accepted both gratefully, but the passenger continued to stare off into space.

"You're bleeding, Levi," Celia said.

Levi looked at his bloody right elbow. "Must have done it on the window."

"I'll get the first aid kit."

Celia moved to the cab and returned with the small box and another bottle of water to wash the wound. She got it as clean as possible before she smeared it with antiseptic cream and bandaged it.

"That'll have to do for now." She lowered her voice. "What are we going to do about them?"

Levi's face hardened. He looked down the road. There were two more wrecks in the distance and it was obvious cars were still moving, but traffic was beginning to back up.

"We leave them. We can't wait for help. Emergency services will be totally maxed out, even assuming there's any way to contact them. If we don't get through this mess fast and make the turn onto Route 1114, we'll be stuck here for hours. And between the Northern Lights and all these transformers popping, it's obvious something is wrong. If we're lucky, it's localized, but we have to assume the worst. We have to get the family to safety, now!"

"We can't just leave them here, Levi! One of them is in shock. She may have serious internal injuries."

"She might, but what can we do about it? We saved their lives, but now we have to worry about our own family." He nodded toward the women on the tailgate. "They're on their own. You know I'm right, Celia."

Celia hesitated, then gave a reluctant nod. Levi hugged her, then fished more water and some protein bars from behind the truck seat and moved back to the tailgate.

"I'm sorry, ladies, but we have to leave. Our kids are home alone. I expect with all the accidents, the police and EMTs will be here shortly," he lied. "We'll leave you some more water and protein bars, but then we have to leave."

The driver stood and helped her friend stand as well. Levi set the meager supplies at their feet.

"I understand," the driver said as Levi closed the tailgate. "And thank you so much. We'd both be dead if not for you."

"No problem," Levi said, "I'm sure you would have done the same for us."

They all stood in awkward silence until Levi nodded and moved towards the driver's door. Celia hesitated a moment and then nodded and moved toward the passenger side. Levi opened his door, muttered a curse under his breath, and called back to the women.

"Where do y'all live?"

"About seven miles north, in a subdivision a half mile off 421. We were on our way to work," the driver said.

"Is that before the turn for Route 1114?" Levi asked.

"Yes. Our road is about a mile before the turn."

"Well, we're going that way, so we can give you a ride home," Levi said.

"But my car... and that... that other car... is the driver..."

"I'm sorry, ma'am, but he's beyond help," Levi said gently, moving back toward the tailgate as Celia matched his movements on the other side of the truck.

"It's really best if you let us take you home," Levi said.

"But... I can't leave the scene of an accident, and Brenda's not right. She needs to go to a hospital, I think... I just can't..."

Levi and Celia were both by the women now.

"Ma'am, despite what I said, I'm pretty sure no one's coming, at least any time soon. Y'all need to get off the road," Levi said.

"But the police... I mean isn't it a crime to leave the scene of an accident..."

"The other car isn't burning," Celia said. "I have some paper and a pen in the glove box. Leave your name and number on the other car and the police can contact you when they arrive. How's that?"

"I guess so," the woman said.

Celia retrieved an old envelope and a pen from the truck and scrawled a note. Levi trotted over and jammed it under the wiper on the intact passenger side of the windshield, doing his best to avoid looking at the corpse draped across the crumpled hood. Moments later they were all squeezed into the cab of Old Blue as Levi wound through wrecks and cars that had stopped to help. Twenty minutes after that they helped the women into the driver's house and were back on US 17/421 headed north.

"I'm glad we helped them, Levi," Celia said softly. "It was the Christian thing to do."

Levi didn't respond immediately.

"I'm glad we could help too," he said finally, "but I expect the world's just become a crueler place, Celia, and it's likely charity, Christian or otherwise, may not have much of a place in it. And my family will survive, no matter what I have to do."

CHAPTER TWO

The Honorable Theodore M. Gleason, President of the United States of America, glared down the long table at the Secretary of Energy. The man didn't meet his gaze, but continued reading, tension in his voice.

"Between 0500 Eastern Daylight Time on 1 April and 1700 Eastern Daylight Time yesterday, 2 April 2020, a solar storm of unprecedented magnitude released a series of massive coronal mass ejections, all of which struck Earth. The number of impacts is unknown, as the first events destroyed measuring instrumentation. Global damage is severe."

The Secretary paused. A glance at the President was met with a stony stare. He quickly continued.

"Damage assessment of the North American power grid is ongoing, but in excess of sixty percent of the two thousand one hundred high voltage transformers are confirmed damaged beyond repair. Percentages for medium voltage transformers are similar. Damage to millions of smaller distribution transformers to residential and commercial service drops is more difficult to assess, but sampling suggests a failure rate over seventy percent. Power is out across all of North and Central America. Though the transformers were a known vulnerability—"

"Then why weren't they addressed?" The question was quiet, for all its career-killing potential.

The Secretary of Energy stalled. "Excuse me, Mr. President?"

"It's a simple question, John. If these transformers were so damned vital, why wasn't the issue addressed?"

"With respect, Mr. President, everyone in this room knows why. Those transformers are forty-five feet tall with a footprint of over two thousand square feet—larger than most single-family homes. We have to close roads to move even one of them. And they're custom built for each site, so it's not just a matter of keeping a few interchangeable spares on hand; 'addressing the issue' requires one hundred percent spares. Even if the government mandated one hundred percent spares, the private utilities would have to raise rates by three hundred percent or more to pay for it, and neither the utility industry nor their various regulators have ever deemed rate increases of that magnitude politically feasible. Both parties have been kicking this particular can down the road for a long, long time, Mr. President. Time has run out."

Gleason visibly struggled to contain his rage, and the room grew silent, awaiting his outburst. It never came.

"Very well," he said, "there'll be time enough to get into causes later. What's important now is restoring power. How long are we looking at, bottom line?"

The Secretary of Energy took a deep breath. "Bottom line, Mr. President? Years. Spares to recover in the short term simply don't exist, nor does the capability to produce or ship them. Most are, or I should say were, manufactured in Germany and South Korea, and even if limited manufacturing capability is restored, global demand will be tremendous. Every country that restores or develops manufacturing capability will undoubtedly restrict exports until domestic needs are met, which means we have to develop our own capability in the midst of this chaos. There are only five manufacturing plants in all of North America even capable of manufacturing HVTs, and three are in Canada. Our current most optimistic estimate is power restoration to forty to fifty percent of the US within a decade—"

BANG! Coffee cups jumped in their saucers as Gleason slapped the table.

"UNACCEPTABLE! Don't sit at this table and tell me what CAN'T be done! Get off your ass and start finding me solutions to this problem." Gleason looked at his watch. "It's a bit after nine. We'll reconvene at three and I expect a plan from you for getting power back in months, not years. Is that clear?"

"Yes, Mr. President," the Secretary of Energy said, stuffing papers into his briefcase.

Gleason nodded at the rest of his cabinet. "All right, ladies and gentlemen, this meeting is adjourned. Be back here at three p.m., prepared to update us in your various areas of interest." He looked at his Chief of Staff and the Secretary of Homeland Security. "Doug, Ollie, stay back please."

The pair nodded and kept their seats while the rest of the cabinet members rose and filed from the room. When the door closed behind the last to leave, Gleason turned to Oliver Crawford, Secretary of Homeland Security.

"How bad is it, Ollie?"

"It's bad, Mr. President. Within forty-eight hours every major city in the US will be ungovernable. We need to get you up to Camp David Compound and soon. The First Family will go via chopper, of course, but the others will go by motorcade with armed escort. If we wait much longer, they may have to fight their way out of the city."

Gleason nodded and turned to his Chief of Staff. "Okay, Doug, work with Ollie's people to start the move but not until we finish our meetings today."

Doug Jergens nodded and scribbled on a legal pad.

"Mr. President, we should go ahead and get the Vice President and his group headed toward the NORAD Complex in Cheyenne Mountain, in accordance with the Continuity of Government plan," Crawford said.

"Good idea," Gleason agreed. "How about the Mount Weather complex? Is FEMA ready to open for business?"

"It'll be tight, but we can accommodate senior military, members of Congress, and their families and staff. Not all underground, but the surface complex is huge too. We'll manage, providing we can round them all up."

Gleason shot him a questioning look.

"Easter recess, Mr. President. It was to start today, but there were no major votes scheduled in either house, and a lot of legislators took off last weekend. No telling where they all are now, and with comms down, they might be tough to locate."

Doug Jergens nodded. "Most of them probably wanted to get some campaigning time in."

Gleason snorted. "Elections! We'll be lucky to have a friggin' country in November."

"Ah… about that, sir," Secretary Crawford said, "have you thought about the way forward."

Gleason's eyes narrowed. "What do you mean?"

Crawford took a deep breath. "The only way I see surviving this with any sort of national government intact will likely require using the Constitution as toilet paper, something damn near impossible without a cooperative legislature. We both know there's a pretty fair chance we might not be holding elections in seven months. If that happens, whoever shows up here and now is going to be in power a long time. We have some control now, and we'd be foolish not to use it."

"You're suggesting I just abandon any legislator who might present future problems?"

Crawford shook his head. "Not at all. If a legislator is in town, we put them, their family, and staff on the bus for Mount Weather, regardless of their party or perspective. But I'm betting that will be a minority. And if they're NOT here, or don't contact us, I see nothing wrong with restricting use of our very limited resources to finding and transporting those members of Congress we believe to be most beneficial to the country's recovery. It's all about the national interest."

"As dictated by us?"

"Well, yes, sir, but I'd probably avoid that particular verb," Crawford said.

"Point taken. Both points taken, actually." Gleason turned to his Chief of Staff. "Doug?"

"Yes, Mr. President?"

"Draw up a priority list of our favorite legislators and render all possible aid in getting them up to Mount Weather."

THE WHITE HOUSE
SITUATION ROOM

3:00 P.M.

Gleason walked into the room, motioning his cabinet secretaries to keep their seats. They stood anyway and waited for him to settle into his own seat before they sat back down.

"All right, folks," Gleason said, "let's get started. I want a brief, and I stress brief, overview of the situation from the viewpoint of your particular problems and challenges. Is that clear?"

There were nods around the table.

"All right, we'll start with State." Gleason gestured to a woman sitting to his right. "You're up, Dot."

Dorothy Suarez, Secretary of State, nodded. "Thank you, Mr. President. All of our embassies have hardened backup generators and radio stations. We've heard from all of them. In brief, the global situation mirrors our own, especially in the northern hemisphere. Civil unrest is accelerating. Our facilities are all on high alert. Our foreign counterparts are, like us, currently assessing the way forward. Initial indications are the southern hemisphere may have escaped the brunt of the impact. Specifically, the southern portions of both Chile and Argentina, all of Uruguay, Paraguay, much of Sub-Saharan Africa, Australia, and New Zealand are reported to have electrical power. Rio Grande do Sol, the southernmost state of Brazil, may also have escaped relatively unscathed."

"Threats?" Gleason asked.

"I've consulted with both the Agency and Defense." She nodded toward the Secretary of Defense. "Secretary Ballard will touch on that as well, but our consensus is there are no immediate foreign threats. Frankly our biggest concern at State right now is getting our people home."

"Understood. Sounds like we should hear from Defense next." Gleason nodded toward the Secretary of Defense.

"No one is in a position to launch a conventional attack," the Secretary said, "and the consensus is a nuclear attack would be pointless, as we would meet it with an overwhelming response from our submarine-based nukes. However, long-term viability of our overseas bases is dependent upon the infrastructure in the host country, and that's impossible to assess. After consultation with the Joint Chiefs, our recommendation is the repatriation of US military personnel by the most expeditious means, leaving behind only a skeleton force to maintain and secure the bases pending our eventual return. We can start repatriation of both military and State Department personnel and dependents via navy ships."

"How about equipment?" Gleason asked.

The Secretary of Defense grimaced. "Anything we can't fly or sail home will be at risk, Mr. President. We will bring away all our forward-deployed tactical nukes and as much other equipment as possible. But we'll have to leave a lot. Armor, missile batteries, or other equipment will be pre-rigged with demolition charges so the 'stay behind' force can destroy them quickly if necessary to keep them from falling into the hands of those who might use the equipment against us."

"How are you going to resupply the stay-behind force?"

"The numbers will be small, Mr. President, and we'll leave them enough resources for several months. We'll reassess sixty days down the road and decide whether to pull them out or resupply them. We didn't feel we could in good conscience abandon our entire overseas infrastructure with incomplete intelligence and seventy-two hours of study."

Gleason nodded. "It sounds like a prudent approach, so proceed. But you said use the navy ships to 'start' repatriation. Does that mean you don't have sufficient transport capacity?"

"That's correct Mr. President. Accommodation space is tight on navy ships already, and we'll have to make multiple trips. Quite frankly, I doubt things will hold together long enough to allow that. My next suggestion was to authorize military commanders on scene to charter commercial vessels and purchase food and stores. The question then becomes payment and what to do if ship masters or bunker suppliers refuse our offers."

Gleason reflected a moment. "Payment will be by voucher, guaranteed by the full faith and trust of the US government. Should anyone refuse to accept vouchers, use all necessary force. Just try not to piss off anyone with nukes."

The Secretary of Defense nodded, and the President looked across the table. "Agriculture."

"Domestically, this couldn't have hit us at a worse time, Mr. President," said the Secretary of Agriculture. "We have limited stocks of recently harvested winter wheat and barley, but less than five percent of this year's grain crop has been sown. Getting the rest of the crop in and cultivating it all is going to be tough with fuel shortages. Internationally, things look better. It's just past harvest in the southern hemisphere, and there are substantial crop surpluses in southern Latin America, Southern Africa, and Australia/New Zealand. We're trying to get grain purchase contracts in place. The big unknown is cost."

Gleason shook his head. "I won't be gouged. Stick to Latin American stocks and buy all they have, paying in gold from our reserves, and at the market price prevailing the last day international commodity markets were open. If they won't accept that, we'll take the food by force if necessary." He looked at the Secretary of Defense. "I want nuclear carrier battle groups off both coasts of South America. Any food cargoes leaving South American ports will be bound for the US or no place at all."

The Defense Secretary nodded and Gleason turned back to the Secretary of State. "Before we evacuate our embassies in Russia and China, have our ambassadors assure those governments we have no designs on any surplus food stocks in Africa or Australia/New Zealand."

"Yes, Mr. President," Secretary Suarez said.

Gleason nodded and turned to the Secretary of Energy.

"Okay, John," Gleason said, "your turn. And I hope you have something better to offer than you did this morning."

"Ahh... yes, sir, I believe I do." He cleared his throat. "While our capacity to produce electrical power remains largely intact, the lack of transformers severely limits our ability to efficiently distribute that power. The key word being 'efficiently.' Even without the transformers, we can still use the power within a limited distance from the source. By designating certain nuclear power plants as manufacturing hubs, we'll dedicate remaining resources to converting nearby facilities to manufacture transformers. Simply put, we will bring the manufacturing facilities to the power. With nuclear, fuel supply won't be a problem. As we produce transformers, we'll rebuild the grid outward from the nuclear plants." He hesitated.

"Go on," Gleason said.

"There are... significant challenges, Mr. President. Not only will such an accelerated effort require a tremendous share of our remaining labor force and industrial resources for the foreseeable future, but it will require nationalization on an unprecedented and massive scale—the national electrical grid, all power plants, all related manufacturing facilities, as well as all private assets within a designated radius of each plant will become government property. It's never been done before, sir, and quite frankly, I question the legality."

"Well, the world never ended before, John, so I suppose an unprecedented disaster requires an equally unprecedented response. And starting three days ago, it's legal if I... if we... say it's legal. Now. How long before we get the lights back on?"

The Energy Secretary set his jaw. "Unknown, Mr. President. And it will still be unknown, even if you demand a time. I simply do not know, nor does anyone else. We'll work just as hard as possible to make this happen, but I still believe it will be years and not months. You may replace me with someone who'll tell you what you want, or demand, to hear, but that won't change facts."

Gleason had been leaning forward in his chair, but he slowly sat back, the glare on his face dissolving. After a moment, he nodded. "You're right. But I want a timetable. I'll give you thirty days to begin implementation and then we'll reassess and set deadlines. Deadlines you will meet. Are we clear on that?"

"Yes, Mr. President."

"Good," Gleason said, nodding at Oliver Crawford. "Let's hear from Homeland Security. All right, Ollie. Bring us up to date on the unrest."

"It's not good, Mr. President. The blackout overwhelmed first responders. Rioting and looting is widespread in all major cities. It's the typical blackout scenario, focusing on looting of consumer goods, but that will change. The average city has less than a week's supply of food on hand. Escalation of violence is inevitable as people begin to compete for dwindling but vital resources. Our most optimistic estimate is millions of deaths in the next six months, from violence and other blackout-related causes. The elderly and the chronically ill requiring maintenance medication are the most vulnerable. Hunger, polluted drinking water, and disease will take the rest."

There was silence around the big table, broken by the Secretary of Defense.

"My God," he said. "We have to try to get ahead of this. Call out the National Guard—"

Gleason raised a hand to cut him off. "First we have to fully understand our options." He turned back to Crawford. "How many millions?"

"Unknown, Mr. President, but perhaps as much as half the population."

The room grew quiet again. Gleason shook his head.

"That can't be right! I understand violence and casualties among the 'at-risk' population with the medical infrastructure overwhelmed, but half the population? Mass starvation? What about FEMA stockpiles? We've spent a lot of taxpayer dollars on disaster preparedness, are you telling me that bought us nothing?"

"On the contrary, Mr. President, we're well prepared for disasters, but not an apocalyptic event. Our models call for stockpiles sufficient for three separate but simultaneous regional disasters, each of thirty days' duration. They further assume impacted regional populations of twenty-five million, since a disaster would not impact all regional inhabitants. Thus we have supplies for seventy-five million people for thirty days distributed among regional FEMA warehouses, with the bulk prepositioned near the coasts. The military maintains its own emergency stockpile, and the figures above are for FEMA stockpiles only. However, it's likely FEMA stockpiles might be needed to support military personnel at some future point."

"Sounds like a lot," Gleason said.

"The population is over three hundred thirty million, Mr. President. Even supposing we could meet the enormous distribution challenges, FEMA stockpiles wouldn't last more than a week, ten days at most. The previously mentioned stores of winter wheat and barley could help, again assuming we seize that grain in the national interest." Crawford paused. "There is no realistic scenario that sees us feeding the majority of the US population long enough to harvest a crop in the fall, or even hold out until the arrival of the foreign grain shipments we've been discussing."

The President looked around the room, studying the shocked faces of his cabinet secretaries. He wasn't encouraged.

"All right," Gleason said. "We obviously have to give this more thought. We'll adjourn now and I'd like you all to begin immediate implementation of the plans we've discussed so far. We'll reconvene here tomorrow at—"

Doug Jergens, the Chief of Staff, cleared his throat. Gleason shot him an annoyed look.

"Ah. Sorry to interrupt, sir," Jergens said, "but the transfer…"

"Oh, right," Gleason said. "We'll meet tomorrow morning at seven o'clock at Camp David."

The White House
Oval Office

Same Day, 6:00 p.m.

Gleason slumped in the armchair, staring into his glass as he swirled the amber liquid. Oliver Crawford sat on the sofa across from him, sipping from his ever-present bottle of water. Gleason wondered for what must have been the thousandth time whether or not he really trusted a man who wouldn't take an occasional drink.

"How many?"

"Approximately ten million, Mr. President," Crawford replied, "not counting the military and assuming we have to sustain our civilian core group no longer than six months, eight at the outside. I figured in a small contingency in case the harvest is worse than average or the foreign grain imports are inadequate."

"Will that be enough?" Gleason asked.

"It will have to be. It's the most people we can keep fed, sheltered, and productive, and the absolute minimum we'll need to keep the power-restoration project going forward until we get a crop in, along with government workers to administer it all," Crawford said.

"What's the breakdown?"

"Approximately two hundred thousand government administrative employees and twice that number of security personnel. Everyone else will be dedicated to either power restoration or agriculture, the bulk of them agriculture. There'll be a lot of manual labor needed there."

Gleason nodded and stared into his drink.

"If I may ask, Mr. President, why are you assigning me these various tasks? I'm happy to take them on, but a lot of them rightly fall under the responsibilities of the other cabinet members. There may be… problems."

Gleason looked up. "Because this can't be run by a goddamned committee, that's why. I could sense it this afternoon, and I'm sure you could as well. We've both been reading people a long time, Ollie, and despite all the 'Yes, Mr. Presidents,' I sensed a great reluctance to make the hard choices demanded of us. You're the only one who seemed to immediately appreciate what we're up against. I need someone to help me run things."

"The Vice President—"

"The Vice President is on his way to a hole under Cheyenne Mountain, and there he'll stay."

"Yes, Mr. President," Crawford said, his face impassive.

Gleason drained his glass and held it out. Crawford leaned over and accepted the glass and rose and walked to the sideboard, where he replenished the President's drink. He returned and handed the drink to Gleason before resuming his seat.

"Thank you, Ollie," Gleason said, "and you know I'm right. How do you think Agriculture will react when he hears we're nationalizing all grain and seed stocks and all agricultural holdings and farm equipment, or Labor when she hears we're recruiting our migrant farmworker force out of state refugee camps on a 'no work—no food' basis? What's that name you came up with? The Civilian Agricultural Initiative?" Gleason snorted. "We can pretty it up all we want, but I doubt we'll fool anyone."

"We're not nationalizing ALL land," Crawford temporized, "only holdings larger than five hundred acres. Family farmers on smaller holdings will produce fruits and vegetables on the truck gardening model. We'll even provide starter seed and fertilizer if available, as well as providing labor—"

"And take ninety percent of their crop in return."

"Which will still likely leave them more food than most people," Crawford said. "I KNOW we could sell the whole program to Secretary Jackson—"

"That's the damned point, Ollie! I don't have to SELL programs to anyone, especially someone who works for ME! This isn't a debating society, we just don't have the time. YOU understand what's necessary and are on board with the program, so I'm putting you in charge. That's that. Now, what's your plan on lodging the workforce?"

"My initial thoughts are to quarter the power workers on site in redevelopment zones centered on each of the nuclear plants we're bringing back on line. The agricultural workforce will have to be more transient with the crop and the season. I'm thinking a dozen semipermanent regional camps with temporary satellite camps as and when needed. We'll need perimeter security on all of them. We don't want to lose trained workers at peak labor periods."

Gleason nodded. "What about the administration workers?"

"Staying in the cities is a nonstarter. I was thinking cruise ships, maybe anchored off Annapolis. They'll be self-contained offices and living quarters with plenty of amenities and a lot easier to defend at anchor. And we can move them around if we need to set up regional HQs," Crawford said. "And what's more, they'll mostly be out of sight of the general population. There's bound to be resentment, and there's no need to advertise the fact that government workers are living in decent conditions."

"Good idea," Gleason said. "Actually a damn good idea. They should be thick out of the Florida ports and the Caribbean this time of year. Try chartering them on payment guarantees like we're doing overseas, but if that doesn't work, just seize them by force. And speaking of force, how do you think our friends in uniform are going to take all this?"

Crawford didn't answer immediately, but when he did, it was obvious he'd already considered the question.

"It's my greatest fear, actually. The worst-case scenario is for the military, either collectively or individually, to decide these very necessary steps are unacceptable. If we send them out to put down civil unrest, I think there's a good chance they'll turn against us. No one's going to be happy firing on starving refugees. The last thing we need is a bunch of disaffected military personnel deserting and taking their weapons and training with them," Crawford said.

"What choice do we have? I can't see how any of this works without them."

"First, we get rid of any potential troublemakers. I'd say anyone who wants to leave, we grant an immediate discharge. Let them leave with their personal possessions and maybe a few days rations. Not only do we lose a lot of problems, but also extend military food and water reserves, at least in the longer term. Service personnel with families on base will likely stay, and we can beef up security around the base perimeter and also take in as many dependents of remaining troops as possible. We clear a quarter-mile security perimeter around all bases, both to provide clear fields of fire and prevent refugee camps from springing up next to the bases. And finally, we have to discourage fraternization with the civilian population completely, and immediately discharge any military personnel caught doing it. To the degree possible, we need to build a psychological wall between the troops and the civilian population. The civilians will grow to resent those inside the wire, and the troops will feel doubly protective of both the base and their families the base is sheltering. In six months, possibly less, the military will be with us completely—presuming we don't drive them away in the short term."

"Just great, Ollie, but what do we do in the interim? Use the National Guard—"

Crawford was already shaking his head. "The Guard's too close to their respective communities, and for the same reason, we shouldn't let Defense mobilize the reserves. We're trying to sever connections between the civilians and the military, not build them." Crawford paused. "I have another idea."

Gleason cocked an eyebrow. "Mercenaries?"

"Private security contractors," Crawford corrected. "Most are very experienced in chaotic conditions in third world countries. They'll have no problem doing whatever needs to be done. We can use the regular military for overseas missions like the South American thing, or maybe duties not likely to be challenging, like guarding the power plants. But if something looks likely to be domestic and messy, we'll use the contractors. They'll be the tip of the spear."

"We can't just send in armed thugs," Gleason said.

"They'll all be members of a FEMA Special Reaction Force, something I've been working on for a while. I can have it up and running in forty-eight hours."

"You'll have enough merc... contractors?"

"I'll have enough to form the backbone of the unit and get things started. They'll set the tone; then we'll fill the unit out by selective recruitment from the regular forces," Crawford said. "We'll restrict it to single individuals and then station them in SRF units far from their regular units and in places where they have no former ties to the civilian community. They'll be isolated, and the SRF will become their home—and if they fail to adapt, we'll strip them of weapons and equipment and 'discharge' them into the civilian population."

"How are you going to recruit them in the first place?" Gleason asked. "I can't see too many of our regular troops being eager to join a 'contractor' force set up to keep the lid on civilian unrest."

Crawford smiled. "I'm going to lie, of course."

Crawford glanced at his watch. "It's almost time for you to be off, Mr. President. I think the chopper is—"

"Going to leave when I'm ready to leave, Ollie, and there's one more thing I'd like to set in motion ASAP."

"Yes, Mr. President, what did I miss?"

"Spin, Ollie. Any of our citizens who survive on their own over the next months are going to be mad as hell. So if we end up with a nation of say fifty or a hundred million angry citizens, we have no chance of governing even if we restore electrical power. We have to make sure we give them someone other than us to hate."

Crawford nodded. "Makes sense, but how?"

"By making state and local officials the face of a failed relief effort. I want your folks on the horn, assuring governors and other state officials that stores are tight, but we can meet the near-term requirements and that distribution will begin immediately. Tell them we're not calling out the National Guard at the federal level, because we don't want to 'panic the population' or some such excuse. Make up something plausible, you're good at that sort of thing. Then tell state officials FEMA is going to take a secondary and supportive role and encourage the governors to call their own Guard out for state service to set up state-run shelters and distribute the FEMA-supplied stores. Invite the governors and other state officials to join the appeal for calm and make sure they get plenty of airtime on the Emergency Broadcast System to do it. I think those guys will all jump at the chance of being heroes."

"So THEY'LL own the relief effort when it goes belly up?"

"Exactly," Gleason said. "I also want you contacting all the 'administration friendly' news anchors and entertainment celebrities you can reach. Give them jobs at DHS Public Affairs Office, and find places for them and their families on those cruise ships. Got it?"

Crawford nodded again, impressed. "You're thinking when we need to get the word out on something, we use spokespersons the public already trusts? But what happens if they come aboard and then develop journalistic conscience?"

Gleason shrugged. "Then we terminate their employment and evict them from their cushy new quarters. I'm sure we can arrange to establish some brigs on these cruise ships. They'll fall in line, trust me."

Gleason continued. "When public outrage boils over at the incompetence at the state level, FEMA will supply the worst trouble spots with a few days' supply of water and food. Package the whole affair as state and local government missteps corrected by the prompt FEMA intervention. Have our celebrity spokespersons on hand to report on FEMA saving the day via the Emergency Broadcast System. The narrative will be the feds were doing their best, but state and local governments screwed up. Then we refuse the state governments any access to the Emergency Broadcast System so they'll have no means to counter our story."

"It makes sense," Crawford said. "People always want a focus for their anger. If we can direct it elsewhere, we're ahead of the game."

"This recovery effort's going to take years," Gleason said, "and if we have a hope in hell of getting continued cooperation, we have to spin the inevitable famine in such a way to legitimize the federal government in the minds of the survivors. And who knows? If the governors are convincing enough, they might even help keep things calmed down a bit for a few days so it will be easier to start getting the rest of the programs in place."

Gleason finished just as Doug Jergens stuck his head into the Oval Office.

"Marine One is standing by on the helipad at your pleasure, Mr. President," Jergens said.

Gleason nodded and rose. "All right, Ollie. You've got your work cut out for you. See you at Camp David tomorrow morning."

CHAPTER THREE

5 April 2020

RECIPIENTS' EYES ONLY

From: POTUS
Distribution: All Cabinet Members
Secondary Distribution: PROHIBITED

Subject: Disruption of National Power Grid - The Way Back

First let me say how relieved I was to learn most of your family members made it to Camp David or otherwise found shelter in secure government facilities. Gina and I are keeping those still unaccounted for in our hearts and prayers, in hopes all will reach safety soon.

By this time, I know all of you have had time to absorb the assessment of our situation Secretary Crawford shared with us Friday and then discussed in more depth at yesterday morning's cabinet meeting here at Camp David. I feel sure you found it as disturbing as I did. The situation seems bleak and the actions necessary are beyond frightening, and all things I would reject out of hand in most circumstances. That said, I can see no real alternatives if we are to survive as a nation, and after prayerful deliberation, I have concluded we have little choice but to implement the initiatives presented by Secretary Crawford. I have issued executive orders directing full implementation of all such measures. Also, given the overall role the Department of Homeland Security must play in our recovery efforts, I'm sure you all understand why I've delegated oversight and management of that effort to Secretary Crawford. Please consider any requests or directions from Secretary Crawford as carrying the full weight and approval of the Office of the President.

On a slightly related subject, while I know a number of you disagree on constitutional grounds with some or all of the actions we're taking, your full cooperation is expected and appreciated. For those of you who indicated an intention to resign as a matter of conscience, I respect that decision and harbor no ill will. I will ensure Presidential Transport places helicopters at your disposal to return you and your dependents to a location of your choosing.

For those of you staying the course, you have my profound thanks, as the road ahead will be anything but smooth. As you all know, both the Speaker of the House and the President pro tempore of the Senate are currently sheltering with their families at FEMA Headquarters at Mount Weather, and I had a conference call with them this morning. As expected, both Congressman Tremble and Senator Leddy objected vociferously to our planned action, but neither offered viable alternatives. At the conclusion of the conversation I had little choice but to direct Secretary Crawford to have FEMA security personnel confine both Speaker Tremble and Senator Leddy to their quarters to be held incommunicado. My fervent hope is, in time, they'll recognize the necessity for my actions.

May God have mercy upon us all.
Theodore Gleason
President of the United States

***

PRESIDENTIAL QUARTERS
CAMP DAVID COMPLEX
MARYLAND

DAY 5
5 APRIL 2020

"Are any of them giving you trouble?" Gleason asked.

"Nothing I can't deal with, Mr. President," Crawford replied. "The three secretaries making noise about resigning had a change of heart. I'd say your memo did the trick."

"Well, watch them. If they aren't contributing, we may have to replace them anyway, and if they do leave the facility, it goes without saying they know a bit too much. We'll have to consider that," Gleason said.

"As cabinet members, they all signed National Security nondisclosure agreements—"

Gleason snorted. "Seriously, Ollie? And you really think that's sufficient under current conditions?"

Crawford flushed. "No, sir, obviously not. But I want to be clear. You want me to…"

"I want you to be aware of the potential problem and take care of it should it arise. I've placed you in charge, so take charge. And don't bother me with the details. That isn't the sort of thing I need to know. I've given you a great deal of power, Ollie, and power comes at a price. Clear enough?"

"Yes, Mr. President. I'll handle it."

CHAPTER FOUR

Day 5

Johnson looked up from his crossword and pulled cotton out of his right ear. "What's a five-letter word for 'occupied, as a table,' beginning with s?"

Broussard threw the paperback on the desk and pulled out one of his own earplugs.

"What?" he asked.

"I said, what's a five-letter word for 'occupied, as a table,' beginning with s?"

"How the hell should I know?" Broussard turned his head toward the cell block. "God, can't those assholes shut up for even a minute? They've been howling twenty-four hours straight."

Johnson shrugged. "Animals being animals ain't surprising. They been locked down five days straight and it must be a hundred plus in there. Whatever genius designed a building for south Texas with no natural ventilation and a crappy little backup generator too small to run air-conditioning was obviously some fat-ass politician's not-too-bright nephew or something."

"Well, it's not like it's much better in here," Broussard said, nodding at the cheap box fan laboring in the corner of the control room. "That damn thing's just blowing around hot air; it's probably ninety in here. And you could use a shower."

"You're no damned petunia yourself," Johnson responded. "Now go make a round."

"I went last time!"

"And you'll go next time if I say so. That's why I got these here sergeant's stripes on my sleeve," Johnson said.

"The toilets are starting to back up. It's getting really nasty in there. On my last round one of the assholes threw shit at me. Son of a bitch almost hit me."

Johnson nodded. "After Hurricane Rita it was like this for a month." He nodded toward the cell block. "I was new then, and they started doing the same stuff, hollering and moaning and throwing crap. But ole Sergeant Thompson, he just walked out calm as you please and told 'em there'd be no food or water for anyone for two days. They calmed right down." He paused. "Which reminds me, what did that food services guy say when he brought the food yesterday."

"He said they're down to baloney sandwiches on stale heels, and not much of that," Broussard said.

"Well, whatever," Johnson said, "when you only got baloney, you don't want to lose it, so go over to food services and tell them not to bother for a couple of days, then see how those animals in there like it."

Broussard hesitated. "Only one problem, Sarge. From the smell of the sandwiches yesterday, I doubt that baloney's gonna last two days."

CHAPTER FIVE

M/V *Pecos Trader*
BUCKEYE MARINE TERMINAL
WILMINGTON, NORTH CAROLINA

DAY 6

Jordan Hughes contemplated the three senior officers clustered around the seating area of his day room, half-finished cups of coffee on the low table in front of them. The last days had taken their toll, and all looked worried and sleep deprived; Hughes knew he didn't look any better. He directed the first question at Gowan.

"How're things looking down below, Chief?"

Gowan shrugged. "We're keeping the lights on. Other than the initial blackout, all the machinery seems to be okay, but I'm getting a few intermittent faults in the electronic controls. It could be totally unrelated to this whole solar-flare thing. I mean, we've had control problems before. However, this is WAY outside my experience, and under the circumstances, I'm concerned."

He shook his head. "I just don't fully trust the automation yet. We're running everything in manual mode and I've got us on the emergency generator for now." He nodded toward Rich Martin, the first engineer. "Rich and I will be going through all the systems, but we're stretched thin. The automation was designed to reduce manning, and if it's not working reliably, we just don't have the manpower to compensate. I'd rather find that out alongside the dock than in the middle of the ocean."

"We're on the same page there," Hughes said. "Do what you have to do."

He turned to the chief mate. "Any movement ashore, Georgia?"

Georgia Howell shook her head. "No change. Not a soul in the terminal."

Hughes nodded. The dock foreman came aboard about four hours after the blackout to report almost none of the day shift had showed up for work, and those that did went home after confirming there was no power in the terminal. The man was obviously worried about his family and conflicted by a pressing need to get home and a reluctance to leave the terminal unmanned. Concern for his family prevailed. He'd assured Hughes he'd return and left, not to be seen again.

"How're the fires?" Hughes asked. Shortly after the blackout, smoke rose across the city, likely fires caused by massive electrical surges. They burned out of control as the sheer number of blazes overwhelmed the city's firefighting resources. Intermittent rain over several days had dampened but not completely extinguished the fires, and based on the growing columns of smoke now billowing in the distance, they were raging once again.

"Tex is keeping an eye on them. They're not any closer and the wind has them traveling in the other direction for now, but—"

She was interrupted by the sound of sustained gunfire in the distance.

"Damn! That's beginning to sound like World War Three," Gowan said.

"And it's getting closer," Rich Martin added as the others nodded agreement.

"Which brings up my next point," the chief mate said. "Bob and I walked up to the street this morning, and the main gate's standing wide open. It's on a drive chain, and the security guard probably couldn't close it without power and just headed for the hills."

Hughes nodded. "Good point. When we finish here, take some guys and tools and manhandle it closed. Bust the drive linkage if you have to, but get it closed. And take some chain and a padlock too. We're off the beaten track in an industrial area, and we can't really be seen from the streets because of the terminal tanks, but better safe than sorry. I don't like the sound of things and the radio traffic isn't very encouraging either."

"What's the latest?" Gowan asked.

"Confused," Hughes said. "There was the national alert about a solar storm on the NOAA Weather Radio frequencies, but it kept breaking up, and reception was crap until earlier today. I'm thinking since the Northern Lights didn't start fading until last night there was still a lot of atmospheric interference, but communications are improving. I've been scanning all the frequencies and picking up bits and pieces. Best I can tell, what's happening here in Wilmington is being repeated everywhere. Scumbags are seizing the opportunity to do whatever they want, and desperate people are just trying to make sure their families survive. The police are losing control, if they ever had it. There's no cell service and not much on the marine frequencies, though it sounds like the Coasties at Oak Island Station are still in business. They answered my call but told me to get off the air unless I had an emergency. I tried the pilots too, but I couldn't raise anyone." Hughes shrugged. "Basically, I think we're on our own."

"It's all over the country?" Georgia Howell asked.

Hughes shrugged. "I think it must be."

The group grew quiet until Rich Martin broke the silence. "I wish there was some way to contact our families."

"I'm sure we all do, First," Hughes said, "but we just have to have faith they'll be okay and figure out what to do next."

"Well, one thing's for sure," Gowan said, nodding towards shore. "We're a hell of a lot better off than those poor bastards out there. We got power and hot showers and at least a few months of food and water."

"Yeah, and I'm thinking someone might figure that out," Hughes said. "It's only a matter of time. We can't be seen from the street and the locked gate might discourage the curious, but we can be seen from the river, so starting immediately we're going to set blackout discipline. I want all blackout curtains closed on all windows. We don't show any lights at night. None. Is that clear?"

"Absolutely. Good idea," Gowan replied.

"What about noise?" Rich asked. "With power down and no traffic, you can probably hear the emergency genny running a long way."

"We're quite a ways from the gate," Georgia said, "so I doubt the street's a problem, but sound carries pretty far over water. I'll set an extra security watch and tell them to keep a sharp eye on the river, especially upstream toward downtown Wilmington." She sighed. "Then I guess we just have to hope none of the looters decide to become river pirates."

"And if they do," Gowan asked, "just exactly how do we discourage them?"

"They'd have difficulty from the river side, so they'd probably land at the dock and come up the gangway," Hughes said. "Georgia, when you get back from locking the gate let's take in the gangway. If they can't get on board, they may just go away."

There were nods around the table. Captain Hughes rose. "Okay, folks, time to get back to work."

The others stood and moved towards the door, but Gowan held back a bit.

"Uh, Cap?"

"Yes, Chief?" Hughes asked.

"I'm thinking the looters might be after easy pickings now, but sooner or later one of them is gonna be smart enough to think of all the fuel in these shore tanks, not to mention the thirty-five thousand tons of diesel and gasoline we're hauling." Gowan paused. "To say nothing of the problem of being tied up next to a terminal full of gasoline and diesel if those fires shift direction."

"That already occurred to me, Chief, but one way or another, I don't plan on us being here much longer."

Levi Jenkins' Fishing Camp
Black River, North Carolina

Day 6

The ax bit into the wood with a satisfying thump and Levi Jenkins grinned to himself as the log separated cleanly, the pieces clattering down on either side of the chopping block. Moisture gleamed on the hard muscles of his ebony torso in the warmth of early spring, and he set down the ax to swat away a drop of sweat forming on the tip of his nose. It was liberating to lose himself in the mindless work and put aside the constant worry of the last few days.

He looked at the wood scattered around the chopping block and judged he had enough. He nodded to Little Tony, his nine-year-old son, who leapt from where he was standing to one side and began gathering the wood to carry it to the neatly stacked woodpile beside the outdoor kitchen. Though 'kitchen' was a bit of a stretch, Levi thought.

Basically it was an open-air structure with a rough wooden floor and a shingled roof supported by four stout corner posts. From the roof protruded the stovepipe for the enormous wood cookstove, and each of the four corner posts was fitted with tie-down points so sides of the structure could be either enclosed by roll-down tarps to block the wind or left open to take advantage of a cooling breeze. A sink with running water with counter space down two sides completed the layout, and a simple wooden worktable graced the center of the structure to provide more work area. It was rough, but functional, and during the warmer months avoided the necessity of heating up the main house while cooking. An additional wood stove in the 'regular' kitchen of the main house got a good workout in the colder months when it was too cold to cook outside, and when the heat was a welcome addition to the small home's interior.

Levi heard footsteps and turned to see his father-in-law approaching from the direction of the river. Anthony McCoy looked past Levi to his grandson and namesake stacking the wood, and beamed.

"Well, looks like you got a hardworking helper there, Levi," Anthony said. "That is one fine woodpile. Good job, Tony."

"Thanks, Grandpa. And guess what? Dad says when I finish all my chores, we can go fishing. Wanna come?"

The old man looked upward, as if concentrating on something, and stroked his neatly trimmed goatee, its snow-white stubble a stark contrast to his face. "Well, let's see, now that I think about it, I don't believe I have any prior engagements, so yes, I believe I will go along." He looked back at the boy and smiled. "And if you promise not to tell anyone, I'll show you my very favorite place to dig night crawlers."

"Okay, deal," the boy said, returning the smile.

"And that would be AFTER chores, and I believe there are a few left on the list," Levi said.

"Yes, sir," little Tony said, and started toward the chicken coop.

"Where you going?" Levi asked. "I thought gathering the eggs was on your sister's chore list."

"It was," Tony said, "but Sally claims she's afraid of the chickens, so I switched with her. She's making my bed instead." The little boy rolled his eyes so expressively Levi had to stifle a laugh. "Besides," Tony continued, "she don't wanna do nothing since she got here but mope around and gripe about how dumb it is to be here, but I think it's awesome."

Levi laughed. "Well, thank you for your support. Now get those eggs in to your mom and grandma."

Tony nodded and hurried away, and Levi turned back toward his father-in-law.

"See anything on the river?" Levi asked.

"Not a thing," Anthony responded, "and I took the kayak a mile in each direction. There wasn't any activity at either of the camps you can see from the river, so I don't think anyone's moved into them yet. Likely they won't now, so I suspect we're the only ones around for several miles. I also had another look at our inlet from the river. Those willows you planted a few years back are perfect. They hang right down to the water like a curtain, and you can't even tell the inlet is there. And we're so far back off the river, as long as we mind how we show lights at night, I don't think anyone will know we're here."

The older man gave an involuntary shudder. "My only problem with that willow curtain is thinking about a big ol' cottonmouth laying up in the branches when we're going through, just ready to drop on my head."

Levi shuddered as well. "Damn. I hadn't thought about that. I must've been through there fifty times without a care, but now I'll be nervous as hell every time." Levi paused. "What say we hide one of those long cane poles somewhere on either side of the willows so we can poke in ahead of us and shake it around before we go through? That should scare any sunning snakes into the water."

"Damn good idea," Anthony agreed. "I do hate snakes."

Levi nodded and looked back toward the neat little homestead, surveying his handiwork of many years. A wisp of smoke rose from the stovepipe of the outdoor kitchen, no doubt from the remains of the fire the women had kindled to cook breakfast, and Levi's face once again took on the look of worry he'd had so many times since the blackout.

"You got your worry scowl on again," Anthony said. "What you worried about now?"

Levi sighed. "Everything, Anthony. But just now I was thinking about smoke. If we keep the wood dry and learn to control the air, we can keep it pretty clear, but I reckon it will still have a wood-smoke smell. I was just wondering if it's likely to give us away."

The older man shrugged. "These woods are thick as hell and stretch at least ten miles in every direction, with poor roads. Maybe a small plane or helicopter could pinpoint the smoke, but that would be about the only way. And if anyone is flying over, they'd see the clearing and maybe a reflection off the solar panels anyway. But I don't think anyone's gonna find us coming overland. Even if they smell smoke, it could be coming from anywhere. Hell, you got that twisty road coming in here camouflaged so well I can't hardly find it myself, and I helped you build it."

"I know, I know. But I still worry," Levi said.

"I know you do, but you need to stop. You've done a wonderful job here. We got a tight, snug house, as much electricity as we need, and hot and cold running water. In a month's time, there's not going to be many folks can take a hot shower and use a real toilet. You got food laid by for us all for a year and extra to boot, seeds and a good garden spot, and with the rabbits and chickens we brought from the house, we'll have meat and eggs, even if huntin' an' fishin' is poor." He paused. "Hell, you hit a home run in my book."

"If someone doesn't try to take it all away from us," Levi said. "There's just me and you to protect the family and there's gonna be a whole lot of really desperate folks out there, Anthony. I wish there were more of us, not only for defense, but for the social side of things. Little Sally already thinks I ruined her life, and truth be known, Celia and Jo aren't really happy to be here either. I mean I know they UNDERSTAND why we have to be here, but I can tell the isolation is already starting to get to them."

Anthony nodded. "It's a fact women are social creatures. I think men can be much more content in isolation. But what exactly were we supposed to do? We couldn't go blabbing around about our plans, and no one trustworthy seemed interested. You got no family to speak of but us, and Celia's our only living child. And I SURE as hell don't want to be spending the apocalypse with none of my no-account relatives, nor Josephine's either."

Levi hesitated. "That prepper group over at Bryson's Corners. We might still hook up with them if…"

Anthony was already shaking his head. "There's good people and bad people, black and white," he said, "and you know I'm not one to be hollerin' 'racist' every time some white man opens his mouth before he engages his brain. Black people say pretty dumb stuff sometimes, and for sure, no race has a monopoly on stupid. I go mostly by how I see folks actin' more than what they say. I suspect most of the members there are good folks, but there's a few of them who make me uncomfortable, no matter how friendly they might seem. I don't want to be the only black family in that group. At least not yet." He paused. "We gotta play the hand we've been dealt. I expect we'll do just fine as hidden river rats."

Levi nodded and grew pensive.

"What?" Anthony asked. "I've seen that look before. C'mon, out with it."

Levi hesitated. "There are some people I trust completely, not far away."

"The folks on your ship?" Anthony asked, and Levi nodded.

"You sure you can trust them? And why would they want to come here anyway? And what about food, will ours stretch?"

"First, yes, I trust them completely" Levi replied, "most of them, anyway. And I'm not sure any would want to come here, but some might, at least the single folks might come temporarily. There's food aboard, so we could probably barter for a bit extra if any of the guys come back with us, and even if we don't, I think we can stretch what we have over at least two or three more people, especially if hunting and fishing are even marginal."

"You sure you've thought this out, Levi?"

"Actually, I've been thinking about it since we got here. It didn't seem right to desert the ship, but the family came first. And this has possibilities, even if they are a bit remote. These folks are used to operating independently and they all have practical skills we can use. There aren't any repair shops at sea. Anybody I invite here will be able to pull their weight."

Anthony looked skeptical. "How do you know the ship's even there anymore, it's been six days?"

"I don't for sure," Levi said, "but the radio's getting clearer. I didn't want to transmit, but I can risk a quick call to see if they're still docked in Wilmington."

"And if they are, what then?"

"One thing at a time, Anthony. One thing at a time."

LEVI JENKINS' FISHING CAMP

DAY 6, 8:00 P.M.

Levi and Anthony stood beside the flat-bottom aluminum boat, surveying their handiwork in the fading light. The sun had just dipped below the tree line and would be fully set in half an hour. The pair were going over everything one last time. They both had sidearms and holsters, along with an AR-15 and Anthony's old Model 12 Winchester shotgun. Two pairs of night-vision goggles lay on the boat seats.

Levi always planned on the river as their main access. Water didn't leave tracks and he could move on the river stealthily. Mounted on the boat's stern was a twenty-horsepower outboard, the model and brand chosen for its quietness rather than speed or power. At Anthony's suggestion, Levi muted the motor even more with a layer of adhesive Ensolite insulation under the cowling. A large bow-mounted trolling motor powered by two deep-cycle marine batteries completed the propulsion options. He'd had to compromise, as the older model outboards wouldn't meet his noise requirements and none of the newer models were completely free of electronics. Nor did the older trolling motors have near the power he needed. He'd solved the problem by opting for the newer models and shielding both the outboard and trolling motor in makeshift Faraday cages made of old oil drums lined with plywood. Overkill, as it turned out, since Levi had planned for the worst-case scenario of an electronics-frying EMP, and the damage from the solar storm was largely confined to the power grid. Better safe than sorry, he thought, as he looked at the outfitted boat.

Anthony broke Levi's reverie. "That about it?"

"Almost," Levi said. "I'm bringing a thirty-eight revolver and the old twenty gauge, along with ammo. We don't have much for those anyway and they're mismatches to everything else we have. I figure they'll need some protection, and other than maybe a thirty-eight in the Old Man's safe, there are no guns aboard."

"Gettin' kind of generous, aren't you? Guns and ammo will be more valuable than gold about now, I expect."

"I'm not GIVING them away. I'll be looking for a fair trade. Besides, if we bring back recruits, it might make Captain Hughes a bit more willing to send along some extra food with them."

"Fair enough," Anthony said. "They expecting us?"

Levi nodded. "I got a light signal arranged so they don't think we're river pirates and try to drop something on our heads when we come alongside. We'll leave here just after midnight. If there's anyone along the river between here and there, I want to give them plenty of time to get to sleep. My biggest concern is downtown Wilmington. I'd like to pass there in the wee hours, when folks are likely to be sleeping the soundest."

"How long you figure?"

Levi shook his head. "I've never run the river at low speed in the dark with night-vision goggles, so your guess is as good as mine. I'm figuring four hours max."

"It'll be longer coming back against the current, and the boat will be heavier." Anthony paused. "Well, hopefully it'll be heavier."

"Yeah, but even at that, if we start back at midnight tomorrow night, we should still make it back here before daylight."

Anthony nodded. "Well, I guess you've thought of everything. Make that almost everything. I'm gonna go get a long cane pole and put it in the boat. And by the way, stealth or no stealth, when we're going out through those damned willows we WILL have the spotlight on high beam. I'm not dancin' with no snake in the dark."

M/V *Pecos Trader*
Buckeye Marine Terminal
Wilmington, North Carolina

Day 6, 8:00 p.m.

Hughes called the senior officers together again that evening to announce his intentions. He tried to suppress his anxiety as he glanced around the coffee table, awaiting their reactions. Gowan spoke first.

"You'll get no argument from me," the chief engineer said. "I live in the area."

"All of us here do, or at least we live closer to Beaumont than here," Georgia Howell said, "but the problem is how it will play out with the rest of the crew. We might not exactly be a democracy, but I believe there'll be some push back." She looked at Hughes. "How you planning on selling this, Captain?"

Hughes ran a hand through his hair. "Well, I won't lie. I want to get home like everyone else, but Beaumont is our only logical destination regardless. I can't reach anyone in the company, and I doubt I will. Things here are generally going to hell, and Beaumont is the closest company terminal. I'm still responsible for the ship and cargo. If we eventually have to leave the ship, I want to at least leave it secured to the company dock."

"Things might not be any better in Texas," Rich Martin pointed out.

Hughes shrugged. "They're probably not, but at least it's worth a shot and will get most of us closer to home."

"I think the 'most of us' is key," Dan Gowan agreed. "It'll get the majority of the crew near home, but what do we do if some refuse. We're stretched pretty thin in the best of circumstances, and with the automation down, we really can't afford to lose anyone."

"Well, I can't force anyone to go," Hughes said. "This isn't the navy. Legally, we're in a US port and anyone can sign off at any time; all I can do is shake his or her hand and pay them off. I figure sooner or later all this uncertainty is going to get the better of folks, and they'll strike off for home on their own anyway. If we wait too long, we won't be able to move the ship." He paused. "Any thoughts on who we might lose?"

"Of the deck officers, probably only Tex," Georgia said. "Her folks live in western New Jersey and she's very close. I doubt she'll sail in the opposite direction. Among the unlicensed guys in the deck department, a couple are from somewhere here on the East Coast, but they've only been aboard a few weeks, so I don't know much about them. I think everyone in the steward's department lives close to Beaumont, so that won't likely be a problem. I'll let Rich speak for the engine gang."

"We'll lose Bill Wiggins, the second engineer, for sure," Rich Martin said. "He lives in Maine with his wife and kid and another on the way. In fact, he was about to get off on vacation to be home for the delivery. No way he's heading south voluntarily. On the unlicensed side, Jimmy the pumpman lives in Virginia, but I don't really know which way he'd lean. The rest of the engine department would be okay with the trip south." He paused. "Except, of course, for Levi. He's home, and not likely to be going anywhere else. And speaking of Levi, when is he supposed to be here?"

"He was a bit vague on the radio," Hughes said, "but I expect him in the wee hours." He turned to Georgia Howell. "The watch straight on the light signal?"

She nodded. "Two longs, one short, three longs."

"All right, I guess that's it. We'll deal with being shorthanded if and when the problem arises. I want to hear what Levi has to say, since he's been out in the world. Let's tentatively plan on calling the whole crew together tomorrow after breakfast."

The others nodded and rose, and Hughes followed them towards the office door and closed it behind them before walking back to his desk. He picked up his favorite picture of his wife, Laura, smiling out at him, her long auburn hair framing a beautiful face accented by lovely brown eyes, and her arms around their twin daughters, one on either side of her, mugging for the camera. He set the picture down gently and mentally sent up what must be the thousandth prayer for their safety, then walked slowly toward his bedroom, knowing even as he did so sleep was unlikely to come.

HUGHES' RESIDENCE
PECAN GROVE
OLEANDER, TEXAS

DAY 6, 11:30 P.M.

Laura Hughes held Jordan's picture and murmured another short prayer for his safety. He'd called from Wilmington as he always did if he had cell service and the hour wasn't too late. This time he'd called from anchor as they awaited a pilot, knowing she'd likely be fast asleep by the time the ship docked. He was considerate like that, though she'd told him repeatedly that hearing his voice was worth being awakened.

She gazed at the picture, her favorite photo of him. He was totally camera shy, and she joked in posed family pictures he always looked like his underwear was a few sizes too tight. This was a candid shot on the bridge of his ship, Jordan's dark hair flecked with just the right amount of gray and a bit mussed by a breeze, his slight squint as he stared into the far distance unable to obscure his clear blue eyes. He looked tan and fit and in charge; she called it his 'captain's' picture. She'd received it out of the blue in an envelope with Dan Gowan's return address and with a sticky note reading, "Thought you might like this picture of Cap I took when he wasn't looking. It's the only one I've seen where he doesn't look like he has a stick up his ass. Best, Dan." She laughed every time she thought of it.

A small desk lamp kept the dark at bay, and she could hear the low throb of the generator in its enclosure behind the garage. Jordan had installed the generator after one too many hurricanes left them without power for three weeks. It was a compromise between capacity and fuel consumption: big enough to run limited lights, the well pump, and the fridge and freezer. On hot southeast Texas nights, she temporarily diverted power from the freezer to two small window air conditioners in the master and guest bedrooms. She smiled, the guest-room unit was another 'compromise,' as the twins each wanted the unit in their own bedrooms. Jordan had issued a Solomon-like decision and installed the unit in 'neutral territory.' The girls were informed they could double bunk in the guest room during power outages or sweat. He called it a 'compromise,' but the twins characterized it as a 'decree.'

She looked at the pile of unpaid bills and sighed. Oh well, with power down, there was likely no one at work to pay anyway; not a pressing problem in the scheme of things. Truthfully, other than Jordan's absence, they had no major concerns. Water was no problem as long as she could run the well pump, and the generator ran on propane. She'd just had the tank filled last week to take advantage of low off-season prices. They were always prepared for hurricanes, and the ample kitchen pantry was well stocked. And if push came to shove, they could always eat pecans until the garden started producing more.

The sturdy old farmhouse built by her great-grandparents sat well off the blacktop, nestled in a grove of ninety-year-old pecan trees from which the property took its name. Laura thought naming property was pretentious in the extreme, and the practice always conjured up visions of yuppie assholes named 'J Something the Third' with overpriced McMansions built on one-acre lots in trendy suburbs. Houses the owners named 'Long Ridge' or 'Beechwood' prior to adding ostentatious driveway entrances suggesting Camelot lay within.

But unlike those efforts to fabricate a past that never was, Pecan Grove was a name bestowed not by the owners, but by area inhabitants. A name arising over time as the towering pecan trees grew to a landmark of note in the otherwise flat pastures and rice fields of Southeast Texas. A point of reference, such that 'out by the Pecan Grove' or 'about a mile past the Pecan Grove' became common directions. So common, in fact, Laura's ancestors finally adopted the term as the name for home, without the least bit of pretension or posturing. It was always just 'home' to them, with 'the' omitted for convenience and 'Pecan Grove' becoming a place instead of a feature of the landscape.

And those old trees still produced a bountiful crop each year, a small side business to Laura's large animal veterinary practice. All the proceeds of bulk pecan sales went into the girls' college funds, and the ten-acre pecan grove in most years provided sufficient surplus for a seemingly never-ending supply of pecans for home consumption and gifts to family and friends. Laura's honey-glazed roasted pecans were a coveted Christmas gift.

No, they weren't likely to starve, regardless of the length of the power outage, and her only real concern was Jordan. Was he safe, and when would he get home?

CHAPTER SIX

The best-laid plans, thought Levi, as he watched the river in front of the boat, the landscape a dull green in the NV goggles. Dull green but clear as day, thanks to a full moon. He'd counted on moonlight, and though a trial night river run had been on his 'preparation to-do list,' like many things, it had remained undone. He hadn't really appreciated just how much visibility the moonlight reflecting off the water would provide. It made things much easier—and much riskier. The moon was so bright, the NV goggles made the trip like navigating in broad daylight, and they'd made much better time than he'd planned. They quickly reached the point where the Black River became the Cape Fear, and the Peter Point highway bridge loomed across the river in the distance ahead. Levi cut the outboard and the muted muttering died, leaving only the sounds of the river around them.

"Let's switch to the trolling motor," Levi said softly. Sounds carried a long way over the water.

"Isn't it a little early," Anthony whispered back. "We're still a half mile from the first bridge."

"With this moon, anyone looking can see us, and I don't want to take a chance the noise will get them looking," Levi said.

Anthony bobbed his head and lowered the trolling motor.

They moved more slowly on the electric trolling motor, but still at a respectable clip with the current behind them. Soon they glided silently under the first bridge and a few minutes later saw the old battleship USS North Carolina on their right in her permanent berth. On the east bank, scattered fires burned in the distance in Wilmington proper, and much closer, Levi detected movement in the upscale shopping district lining the river's edge.

Well, so much for everyone sleeping. Evidently looters didn't keep regular hours. Ahead of him at the trolling motor controls, Anthony cast nervous glances to his left—he'd seen the movement too. Levi looked astern. They moved silently at three or four knots, leaving a wake visible in the moonlight, pointing at them like a telltale arrow. He glanced at the eastern shore again and then ahead to the Cape Fear Memorial Bridge towering above the river's surface. Downstream of the bridge, the restaurants and trendy businesses of the Wilmington riverfront gave way to industrial areas, and Eagle Island on the west bank held nothing but a dredge spoils area where the US Army Corp of Engineers dumped years' worth of muck dredged from the river bottom. If they could make it past Memorial Bridge unseen, they'd have smooth sailing to the *Pecos Trader*.

It seemed to take forever to reach the bridge. Just as they started under the span, a large heavy object fell from the sky, striking the water with a tremendous splash, narrowly missing the boat and soaking both men.

"What the hell—" Anthony gasped as he flinched away from the impact by reflex, inadvertently pulling the trolling motor tiller hard over and radically altering the boat's course—a chance event that saved them. The boat exited the shadow of the bridge several feet off her original course, and the assailant waiting on the downstream side was unable to adjust in time. The heavy steel pipe he released speared the water just aft of the boat, soaking Levi a second time as he cranked the outboard.

"Pull up the trolling motor, Anthony," Levi yelled. "They know we're here."

Above him he heard shouted curses and loud arguing as the assailants blamed each other for the failed attack. The little outboard coughed to life, and Levi ran it up to full speed, such as it was, and immediately started zigzagging downstream as he heard semiautomatic gunfire above and behind him. Fortunately, their attackers' marksmanship was no more accurate than their makeshift bombardment, and the thunderous assault resulted in multiple splashes around them, but none seemed to hit the boat. It was over in seconds, and Levi swallowed his heart.

"You... you okay, Anthony?" he called when they were out of range.

"I might have to clean out my pants, but other than that, yeah, I'm okay," the older man replied. "You?"

"Yeah, I'm okay. I just... damn!"

"You hit?" Anthony called, concern in his voice.

"Not me. But there's water in the boat. They hit us somewhere."

"What are we going to do?" Anthony asked.

"Haul ass and pray. We're only a couple of miles from the ship. You take the flashlight and see if you can find the leak and plug it with something. If we start taking on water too badly, I'll run the boat to the bank and we'll continue on foot if we have to."

"This is a fine how do you do," Anthony said. "If the boat sinks, how the hell are we going to get home?"

"We'll cross that bridge when we come to it," Levi said.

"Huh," Anthony muttered. "If you don't mind, I'd just as soon steer clear of bridges from now on."

M/V *Pecos Trader*
Buckeye Marine Terminal
Wilmington, North Carolina

Day 7, 3:05 a.m.

"There it is," the sailor said, pointing.

His watch partner followed his pointing finger.

"That's the signal all right. Flash him back, then help me get the pilot ladder out," the second man said, as his shipmate moved to comply.

Minutes later, an aluminum boat with two men aboard pulled into the beams of their flashlights and moved sluggishly to press its length against the ship's hull, just below the dangling ladder. The men in the boat were standing ankle deep in water.

"Damn, Levi," one of the sailors said, "you're damn near sunk."

"Obviously," Levi said, "get us lines down here so we can tie her off bow and stern to the ship's rail. We can save her if she doesn't sink!"

The sailors ran to grab rope from the nearby deck locker and, minutes later, had the boat safe from immediate danger. They threw down additional lines to allow Levi to tie off gear in the boat to be hoisted aboard. When satisfied they'd done all they could, Levi took a last look around and nodded, and both newcomers climbed the swaying rope ladder to the main deck. They reached the deck just as the chief mate arrived, summoned by radio.

"Good to see you, Levi," Georgia Howell said, offering her hand. "Who's your friend?"

"Thanks, ma'am," Levi said, returning her handshake. "This is my father-in-law, Anthony McCoy. Anthony, this is Georgia Howell, the chief mate." Levi grinned and nodded at the two sailors. "And these two deck apes are Charlie Lynch and Pete Sonnier."

Anthony shook hands all around as Levi turned back to the chief mate.

"Ma'am, someone upstream shot some holes in us," Levi said. "I'd like to hoist her aboard with the deck crane as soon as possible. She's our ride home."

"Okay," Howell said, "but we'd have to put on the deck light, and the skipper doesn't want us showing any more lights than necessary. It'll have to wait until daylight, but we'll make sure she's not going anywhere."

She turned to the two sailors. "Pete, Charlie, get some extra lines on that boat and make sure they're snugged up good and tight. And check the other lines while you're at it. You know these engine-room pukes couldn't tie a knot to save their own ass."

Levi smiled to himself at the familiar banter as the two sailors laughed.

"Yes, ma'am," said the two sailors in unison as they set off to get more rope, and Howell turned back to Levi and Anthony.

"Let's head up to the Old Man's office. He told me to wake him as soon as you arrived."

M/V *PECOS TRADER*
BUCKEYE MARINE TERMINAL
WILMINGTON, NORTH CAROLINA

DAY 7, 3:30 A.M.

"They fired on you for no reason?" Hughes asked.

Anthony answered before Levi got a chance. "I expect it was because they missed with the stuff they tried to drop on our heads."

Hughes chuckled in spite of the situation, taking an instant liking to Levi's father-in-law.

Levi gave Anthony a 'shut up' glare and reasserted control of their side of the conversation.

"No reason I can think of, Captain," he said, "but it pretty much squares with what I've been hearing on the radio. Most of the cities are becoming war zones, and Wilmington's no different. The gangs are out of control and the police and National Guard are overwhelmed, along with everyone else. I mean, let's face it, the cops were hard-pressed to control certain sections of the city even when everything was working, so they got no chance now.

Nobody really knows what's happening for sure, but it's nothing good, I know that, and I don't see it getting better."

Hughes nodded. "I'd already come to the same conclusion. That's why I've decided to sail back to Texas."

Levi nodded. "I figured you might. That's really why we're here."

Hughes raised his eyebrows in an unspoken question, and listened as Levi explained the reason for the visit.

M/V PECOS TRADER
CREW MESS ROOM

DAY 7, 10:30 A.M.

Hughes held the meeting in the crew mess to accommodate the entire crew, with the exception of two sailors he instructed Georgia Howell to leave on security watch. He told her to make sure she chose people likely to have no problem with the trip south. He wanted anyone likely to have objections to have an opportunity to speak their piece in the open meeting.

With the crew assembled, he rose and briefly outlined the current situation, told them he intended to sail the ship to Texas and his reasoning for doing so, and opened the floor for comments. No one spoke for a moment, until Jerome Singletary, one of the new sailors in the deck department, raised his hand. Hughes nodded, and Singletary stood, his attitude hesitant at first.

"My people all live in Baltimore. What if I don't want to go to Texas?"

"No one can force you to sail with us," Hughes said. "You can sign off and I'll give you as much cash advance as I can out of master's cash. Your full pay will have to come from the company later, but to be honest, I can't say for sure when that will be." He refrained from adding, 'if ever.'

Singletary processed that for a moment before responding, his initial hesitance rapidly disappearing. "Sign off to do what, exactly? Get capped by a bunch of gangbangers trying to get home? Seems to me like the company owes me transportation to my home of record. SAFE transportation, and that's to Baltimore."

Hughes hesitated a moment. "I can certainly include airfare in your payoff—"

"That's bullshit, Captain, and you know it! Ain't no planes flying. My contract says you owe me transportation home. If y'all are going to Texas, then you can just turn north first and take me up to Baltimore—"

"Not happening, Singletary. First of all," Hughes said, his voice rising with his blood pressure, "by contract, you're not owed transportation if you sign off of your own free will. Second, this isn't a taxi cab, and even if I was willing, which I'm not, there's no way I'm running a fully loaded forty-thousand-ton tanker up Chesapeake Bay without a pilot. Third, if Wilmington's a war zone, I can't imagine what Baltimore…"

Hughes reined himself in, but Singletary glared at him. "I'm sorry, Singletary, but no, we won't be taking this ship to Baltimore. You're welcome to come with us, and if you don't want to do that, I'll do everything I can to leave you here in good shape, but you'll have to make your own way home, and I truly hope you make it there and find your family safe."

"Ain't right," Singletary muttered, looking around the room in search of support. Finding none, he sat back down, defeated.

Hughes looked around the room, inviting more comments.

"I'll be signing off, Captain," said a petite brunette sitting at the table nearest Hughes. Shyla Texeira or 'Tex' as she was inevitably called, was small in stature but long on competence. She was a consummate mariner, as would be expected from someone descended from five generations of Portuguese seafarers. Her departure would leave a hole and Hughes was sorry to lose her. Nonetheless, he nodded.

"I figured," he said. "We'll miss you, Tex."

"I'll be signing off too," said Bill Wiggins, the second engineer, looking at Dan Gowan. "I'm sorry, Chief. I don't want to leave you shorthanded, but —"

Gowan held up his hand. "It's okay, Bill. We hate to lose you, but I'd be doing the same thing in your position. I just hope you make it home safe to your family."

Wiggins nodded and fell silent, looking down as if he were shamed by the thought of deserting his shipmates.

Hughes looked around the room. "Anyone else?"

No one spoke up, and just when Hughes was saying a silent 'thank you' they hadn't lost anyone else, another voice broke the silence.

"I reckon I'll get off," said Jimmy Barrios, the pumpman.

Seeing his engine room gang being reduced by yet another experienced man, Gowan couldn't restrain himself. "Why, Jimmy? I know you live in Virginia, but I thought you told me you didn't have any family left there."

"Just my ex-wife," Jimmy said, "but I ain't hanging around because of her, Chief. Matter of fact, if you looked up 'bitch' in the dictionary, there's a picture of her."

The room erupted in tension-easing laughter and Jimmy let it die before he continued. "No, and with all due respect to you folks from the Gulf Coast, if this is the Apocalypse, I'd just as soon not spend it in plus ninety percent humidity, and with skeeters that can stand flat-footed and rape turkeys. Every time I get bit by one of those damn Texas mosquitoes, I swell up like a balloon, and I got a feeling Deep Woods Off is gonna be in short supply pretty soon. I think I'll try to find me some place to lay low here in North Carolina and ride it out."

Hughes glanced across the room and saw Levi struggling to suppress a smile, and he in turn suppressed a spark of irritation. It dissipated as quickly as it arose. Levi had agreed not to offer options until the crew had made up their own minds, and he'd kept his part of the bargain.

M/V Pecos Trader
Captain's Office

Day 7, 11:30 a.m.

Levi sat across from the captain, nursing the coffee Hughes had pressed on him and feeling a bit nervous. As laid back as things generally were on merchant ships and as long as Levi had been a valued member of the crew, an unlicensed crewman being invited up to coffee with the Old Man was still something outside his experience. But then again, nothing was ever likely to be 'normal' by 'old world' standards again. That said, he'd still rather be out on deck with Anthony, seeing to the repairs of their boat. He looked over at Hughes as the man heaved an audible sigh.

"Looks like you were right about all this 'prepper' stuff you've been preaching the last few years, Levi," Hughes said. "This really looks bad, and I suspect it's going to get worse before it gets better."

If it ever does, thought Levi. "I take no satisfaction in being right, Captain. I could have happily lived my whole life being prepared for something that never happened."

"Well, be that as it may, it looks like you WERE right and, you've got at least one recruit. I have to say we really hate to lose Jimmy too."

"I understand, Captain," Levi said, "but he did make up his mind without any influence from me. Fact is, I don't even know if he'll ultimately decide to stay with us or not. I just have to put it to him and see what happens." Levi paused. "But we need to talk about resources. I don't think you can rightly just send these guys off empty-handed, so how do you see this playing out?"

Hughes smiled wanly. "Something tells me you already have some ideas along those lines."

Levi nodded. "I'm willing to take Jimmy, Tex, and Wiggins to our place. Jimmy can look things over and decide whether he wants to stay or go off on his own, and I'll help Tex and Wiggins figure out the best route to where they're going and supply them as well as I can. Thing is, you can't just give them their share of the payoff cash and say goodbye. If cash isn't already completely useless, it likely will be in a week anyway. I can give them all the water they can carry, and some hiking gear, but you're going to have to kick in some food. I can't afford to be depleting my own family's stores."

"Ahh… aren't you forgetting someone?"

Levi shook his head. "I'm sorry, Captain, but we're not taking Singletary. We won't have room in the boat."

"I suspect that's bullshit, Levi," Hughes said, "but on the off chance it's not, we can solve that problem. I'll have the mate tow you upriver with the fast rescue boat and carry the extra load. From the chart it looks like you can take the Brunswick into the upper river system and bypass Wilmington. I expect she can have you where you're going in no time."

Levi looked doubtful. "I considered coming down the Brunswick, but I've never run that section of river and I've heard there are a lot of side channels. I was concerned we might get lost or delay—"

"The harbor chart shows the river system and side channels, even though they're not navigable by ship. I'll give you a copy. I've got an old one aboard."

"Thanks, I'd appreciate that, but I'm still not taking Singletary. I don't really know him and he seems to have an attitude. I'm not going to risk it. Sorry, Captain."

"C'mon, Levi. He just wants to get back to Baltimore. He'll be out of your hair in a day or two, just like Tex and Wiggins. He IS a shipmate after all. We can't just dump him ashore and abandon him."

Levi sat silently for a moment. He had a bad feeling about this, but he didn't think he could refuse in good conscience, and he had already been thinking of how to mitigate the risk of letting other people know about his hideaway.

Levi sighed. "All right, I'll take him if he wants to come."

"Good," Hughes said. "Now about the food—I suppose you'll want can goods and the like?"

"Negative," Levi said. "All the steward's canned stores probably come in cans the size of five-gallon buckets. That's okay when you're feeding twenty people and have plenty of refrigerated space for leftovers, but it sucks when you're traveling or have a small group with limited refrigeration capacity. We'll want dry stores, pasta, rice, and dry beans."

"All right, how much of each?" Hughes asked.

"A hundred pounds a person, four hundred pounds total, more or less evenly split between the various commodities," Levi said without hesitation.

Hughes just looked at him. "That's a little much, don't you think? I still have to feed the rest of the crew."

"And you'll still have plenty of dry goods and all the canned goods and refrigerated food to do it," Levi said. "We took on ninety days' stores ten days ago in Texas, so you should be in pretty good shape. And you know as well as I do how much food normally gets wasted or thrown overboard, you can stretch it, especially with a reduced crew."

"So you're sending Tex, Wiggins, and Singletary off with a hundred pounds of food strapped to their backs? C'mon, Levi, Tex probably doesn't even WEIGH a hundred pounds," Hughes said.

"No, I'm going to send them off with the best mix I can find, including small packages of meat, jerky, and other calorie-dense stuff from our own stores, but I have to replace the CALORIES with something we can store long term and eat later. I'm also going to be taking other supplies out of my stores, like guns and ammo, medicine kits, etc. and I need to get that back somewhere." Levi paused. "It's a tough new world out there, Captain, and it's going to get a lot tougher fast. You get nothing for nothing."

Hughes blew out an exasperated sigh and shook his head, and Levi reached down and began to dig in the pack sitting beside his chair. He had his hand on the vintage .38 revolver but hesitated. If he was going to have to take Singletary, getting the travelers equipped for the road might bite into his stores a bit more than he planned. He left the pistol in the backpack and pulled out the disassembled halves of a broken-down shotgun with a shortened stock and barrel and placed it on the coffee table, then dipped back into the bag for a full box of 20-gauge shotgun shells and placed it on the table beside the shotgun.

"I figure you're short on firepower, so I'll throw this in to sweeten the deal," Levi said.

Hughes looked at the gun. "You know you just broke a bunch of federal laws bringing that aboard?"

Levi smiled. "Why, you going to turn me in?"

Hughes shook his head. "No, I'm going to take your deal, on one condition."

"I've already agreed to take Singletary, so this would be two conditions. What is it?"

"Stay until we leave," Hughes said. "Dan is slammed trying to troubleshoot everything and make sure we're seaworthy, and now almost half the engine gang is leaving, all of you experienced. You can spare us another day or two, at least."

Levi shook his head. "Celia is expecting us back tonight. She'll worry."

"Given how well you've obviously planned everything else," Hughes said, "I suspect you have some contingency plan in place for notifying her of changes. I'm happy to let you use the radio."

Busted, thought Levi.

"All right, Cap. Point taken. We'll stay two more days, three max, but if you're not ready to leave then, we're taking off regardless," he said.

"Done," Hughes said, "and I'm sure the chief will be—"

Levi held up his hand. "I'm not quite done. If I get word from Celia they're having problems, I want the fast rescue boat and that chart you were talking about so we can get back home in a hurry."

"All right," Hughes said, nodding slowly, "I can do that. What else do you need?"

"Just access to the radio. I have our handhelds, but they don't have the range. Celia will be listening for an update at nine p.m."

"Done," Hughes said, and Levi nodded and stood.

"Where you headed now?" Hughes asked.

"To check on the repairs to our boat," Levi said, "and then track down Jimmy and the others and see if they're okay with my plan. And if they are, I probably need to give them a little guidance as to what to take with them to make sure we don't sink the boat, given everything else we'll be hauling. I've found folks have some pretty liberal interpretations of the term 'traveling light.'" He paused. "And then I'll find the chief and see how we can help him before we get out of here."

CHAPTER SEVEN

DAY 8, 9:30 A.M.

Dan Gowan, clad in sweat-stained and grease-smeared coveralls, sat perched on the edge of the upholstered chair on a piece of cardboard Hughes kept handy for just such impromptu visits. There was a streak of grease across the engineer's forehead, and he wasn't exactly sweet-smelling, but if his presence wasn't a treat to the senses, he did bring welcome news.

"It's looking better," he said. "The First and I isolated most of the problems to the governor on the number one generator, and we replaced it with the spare. We've still got more systems to check out, but we're getting there, and Levi will be a big help."

"Thank you and your guys for all the hard work, Dan," Hughes said.

Gowan just nodded. "How are things topside?"

"If you think the power's reliable now, we can restart the gyrocompass and let it settle. Everything else seems to be okay except the satnav, which appears to be down for the count. I guess the solar storm took out the birds." He grimaced and nodded at a thick book on the coffee table, "I'm just brushing up on my celestial navigation."

Gowan grinned. "Been a while since you cracked that book, I expect."

"Yeah, like not since I took my third mate's license exam. I'll have to blow the cobwebs off the ship's sextant, presuming I can find the damn thing," Hughes said. "But that's not the hard part. I'm having nightmares about taking this beast downriver without a pilot or tugs. Those guys make it look easy, but this is starting to feel like driving a forty-thousand-ton tanker through a mud puddle, except a mud puddle doesn't have a current. Truthfully, I'm terrified."

"You'll make it," Gowan said, then added practically, "Besides, what choice do you have?"

Hughes sighed. "None, really, which is the only reason I can convince myself to even consider it."

Both men looked up at the soft rap of knuckles on the open office door.

"Sorry to bother you, Captain," Charlie Lynch said, "but the mate sent me up to tell you the Coast Guard is coming up the river."

"About friggin' time," Gowan said, as both men rose at once.

M/V *PECOS TRADER*
MAIN DECK

Hughes and Gowan arrived on the main deck to find Georgia Howell supervising the deployment of a rope pilot ladder down the offshore side of the vessel as a US Coast Guard patrol boat stemmed the current fifty feet from the ship, its engine emitting a low rumble as it held the boat in place against the current. The boat was forty to fifty feet long, with a crew of six, all with sidearms and body armor, and one manning a bow-mounted machine gun. The gunner wasn't pointing the gun at them, but his tense stance left no doubt he could and would do so quickly if threatened. In fact, none of the men in the boat looked particularly friendly.

Kenny Nunez, the bosun, looked over at Howell and nodded, and she beckoned the boat alongside. The coxswain eased the boat alongside the ladder expertly, and four Coasties boarded the *Pecos Trader* . When the last man was on the ladder, the boat eased back into the river, where the machine gunner resumed his watchful vigil.

First up was a stocky man of middle age, his eyes scanning for threats as soon as his head cleared the deck level. He stepped to one side quickly to clear the way for the man behind him as, hand resting casually on his holstered handgun, he completed his survey of the crew of the *Pecos Trader* , now assembling in force, drawn by the news of the visitors. When all four Coast Guardsmen were on deck, the leader relaxed slightly and he walked across the deck towards Hughes. Beneath his body armor, the man's blue coveralls bore the insignia of a senior chief petty officer.

"I'm looking for the captain," the man said.

"You found him," Hughes said, extending his hand, "Jordan Hughes."

"Matt Kinsey," the man said, taking Hughes' hand. "I'm the CO of the Coast Guard Station at Oak Island."

"Nice to meet you, Chief," Hughes replied, and inclined his head towards his two officers. "Georgia Howell, chief mate, and Dan Gowan, chief engineer."

"Ma'am, Chief," Kinsey said, as he exchanged handshakes with Howell and Gowan in turn.

"We're glad to see you guys," Hughes said. "We were starting to get a little concerned about the lack of any sort of governmental response. How can I help you?"

Kinsey looked around uneasily at the crew crowding around and Hughes took the hint.

"Okay, folks," he said. "Show's over. Get back to whatever you were doing and give our guests a little breathing room."

With muted muttering, the crew moved away, some rather slowly in obvious hopes of gleaning a bit more information. Hughes waited patiently until they'd all dispersed.

"Can I offer you some coffee up in my office, Mr. Kinsey? We can talk a bit more privately there," Hughes said.

"No, thanks, to the coffee, but yes to the office," Kinsey said.

Hughes nodded and turned to the chief mate. "Georgia, I'll be in my office with Chief Kinsey. Would you escort our other guests to the crew mess and see they get some coffee?"

"Sure, Captain. No problem," Howell said, and walked over to introduce herself to the other Coasties.

Hughes inclined his head to indicate Kinsey should follow and started across the deck, belatedly realizing Gowan was following.

"Chief," Hughes said, "please let me know when we can start the gyro."

Gowan looked confused. "What? You can start it any... okay, right. I'll let you know," he said, and changed course towards the entrance to the engine room. Hughes was sure he heard him muttering as he walked away.

Minutes later, Hughes waved Kinsey to a chair in his office and settled down across from him.

"So what's up, Mr. Kinsey?" Hughes asked. "This doesn't strike me as a courtesy call."

"It's not," Kinsey said. "We came upriver to check on our other guys. We haven't been able to raise the command center in Wilmington for two days. We had intermittent contact at first, then nothing. Our second objective is to check out the situation along the river. We knew you were here, so I figured we could dock here at the product terminal and kill two birds with one stone, so to speak."

"The command center? Is that anywhere near the Marine Safety Office over off Medical Center Drive?" Hughes asked.

"Yeah, they're all in one big building, why?"

"Ahh... there's been a lot of smoke over in that area, and about two days ago there was a lot of gunfire. Sounded like World War Three."

Kinsey lapsed into silence, obviously troubled by the news.

Hughes broke the silence. "Any idea exactly what's going on? From what I could piece together from the radio traffic, a solar storm knocked out power. How widespread is the problem?"

Kinsey shook his head. "Not one storm, at least two and maybe three or four. They hit spread out over twenty-four hours or more, and I hear the impact was global." Kinsey paused. "That basically means no one's likely to be giving or receiving international help. But on the bright side, I guess it also means none of our enemies can come in and kick us in the balls while we're down."

"But surely there's an emergency plan? What are your orders?"

"The last one I got was to get as many of my people on station as possible and sit tight, but I'm thinking twiddling our thumbs isn't the wisest thing to do right now," Kinsey said. "We're low on resources, and things have been screwed up from the get-go. The storms hit before the normal workday, and everyone off duty was caught off station. I know the sector CO and a few other officers made it in to the command center, but communications were really spotty at first. Then two days ago, everything went dead up my chain of command, so I decided to take some people and try to establish contact."

Hughes nodded. "What about your larger vessels? Isn't a cutter home ported here? I recall seeing it tied up downtown during a previous port call here. I figured y'all would probably be running things from the cutter by now."

Kinsey nodded. "The captain of *Diligence* probably would have inherited this shit show if she were here, but the *Diligence* went on dry dock up at our Maryland yard last week for emergency propeller repairs. I doubt we'll be seeing her steaming upriver anytime soon." Kinsey paused. "So everything is on me unless I can find someone who outranks me. Which is why I desperately want to find someone further up the food chain with some semblance of a plan."

"Anything we can do to help?" Hughes asked.

"Any ideas on transportation? It's only a couple of miles to the command center, but I'd like to get there and back as quickly as possible. Any kind of vehicle would work. Do you know if anything is working in the terminal?"

Hughes shook his head. "All the terminal folks hauled ass, and the parking lot is empty. The only thing I know of is a couple of golf carts parked up by the office near the gate. The dock supervisors used them to ride around the terminal."

Kinsey didn't look impressed. "Ahh… thanks for the suggestion, Captain, but I can't really get my head around riding into what might become an armed confrontation in a couple of golf carts."

"Suit yourself," Hughes said, "but there aren't very many of you and we've been hearing a LOT of gunfire ashore. If you have to haul ass back here, it would be a lot faster than running, and might work if your opposition is also on foot. And if you do run into any opposition in vehicles, you can always take cover and work your way back on foot. You won't be any worse off than you are without ANY transportation, and at least you'll have a ride one way."

"What about keys?"

Hughes thought a minute and shrugged. "I can't recollect I ever saw the supervisors take the keys out. I mean, they're behind a locked gate, and the carts are in use around the clock by one supervisor or another. Who would steal them?"

Kinsey stroked his chin. "Good point. I guess it won't hurt to have a look."

"Which brings me to another point," Hughes said. "If you do run into trouble, I'd really prefer it if you break contact and not lead an army of bloodthirsty gangbangers back on your heels. The only thing keeping us fairly safe is no one knows we're here."

Kinsey nodded. "Understood. How about this? On the way there, we have to pass the main gate to the container terminal upstream anyway, and we'll make sure it's passable. I'll move our boat upstream to the container dock and if we're coming out with bad guys on our tail, I'll radio ahead and the boat can be standing by to haul ass as soon as we reach them. I might not be able to prevent leading any bad guys back to your neighborhood, but maybe I can avoid leading them right to your front door."

"You do realize if they look downstream from the container docks, they may see us sitting here anyway?"

Kinsey shook his head. "The container dock is really long, so we'll board as far upstream as possible then head farther upstream and across the river to keep their attention focused away from you. We'll hang out just in sight across the river until sundown and then move downstream under the cover of darkness. That's the best I can do."

"Better than nothing," Hughes said, "but let's just hope you don't meet any bad guys."

EAST BOUND ON SHIPYARD BOULEVARD
WILMINGTON, NORTH CAROLINA

DAY 8, 1:00 P.M.

Senior Chief Boatswain's Mate Matt Kinsey, USCG, was conflicted as he sat in the golf cart rolling down the deserted street at a blinding ten miles per hour. It was infinitely preferable to walking and they'd get to their destination much faster, but four men in full body armor and carrying automatic rifles looked a bit ridiculous perched in golf carts. Oh well, maybe if they did encounter opposition, they could take them out while they were still laughing.

The number of burned-out buildings increased as they traveled east. Some still smoldered, and the stench of rain-soaked ashes hung heavy in the air. There were no moving vehicles, and the few pedestrians scouring the pathetic ruins scurried into hiding at the sight of armed men. The whole tragic scene reminded Kinsey of television newscasts from some war-torn third world country, not Wilmington, North Carolina; the improbable comparison made even more apt by the furtive actions of the residents. If civilians were already scattering at the sight of armed men, even four assholes in golf carts, it said a lot about what they'd endured in the short time since the blackout. It also made Kinsey increasingly uneasy about riding exposed down the middle of the street.

"It's the next left," he said.

Jeff Baker nodded. "I've been to HQ before, Chief."

Kinsey bit back a reply and nodded as Baker turned the wheel hard to make the sharp turn onto Carolina Beach Road, heading northwest. Another quarter mile on this road and then right on Medical Center Drive for a quarter of a mile, and they'd be there.

"What's that up ahead?" Baker asked, and Kinsey felt the cart slow.

"Stop," Kinsey said as he clawed a monocular from his pocket to glass the intersection ahead.

"Looks like a Humvee blocking the intersection," Kinsey said, sitting the monocular on the seat beside him and keying his shoulder-mounted microphone.

"Jackson, do you copy?" he said.

"Go ahead," came the reply from the following cart.

"Hold where you are. I think these are the good guys, but Baker and I are going to check it out. Copy?"

"I copy," said Jackson.

Kinsey nodded to Baker and they started forward. As they approached the roadblock, the gunner on top of the vehicle tracked them with an M2 .50-caliber machine gun. When they were a hundred feet from the roadblock, a soldier clad in body armor and carrying an M4 stepped from behind the Humvee, his hand raised.

"Stop right there," he called. "Exit your vehicle. Leave your weapons in your vehicle. Tell your friends back there to approach slowly and do the same. This is an order, not a request. Be advised you are covered from multiple locations and we will open fire if you fail to obey. You have ten seconds to comply."

Kinsey looked around and spotted the muzzle of another machine gun peeking through some low shrubs on the left side of the road just ahead, and he suspected there were more he didn't see.

"All right. Don't shoot," he called, and keyed his mike to call Jackson forward.

Three minutes later, all four Coasties were standing by their golf carts, awaiting further instructions, and the soldier at the roadblock called out again.

"All right. Approach slowly with your hands in the air. Do not make any sudden moves."

The four started forward, and when they were halfway to the roadblock, the soldier halted them and instructed Kinsey to approach alone.

Pretty smart, thought Kinsey, he's separated us from our vehicles and weapons and is keeping the majority at a distance while he questions one of us. It looked like the guy had danced this dance before.

The soldier waved Kinsey to a stop ten feet away and the two studied each other silently. Kinsey noted sergeant's stripes on the soldier's ACUs, and the man seemed to relax when he spotted the insignia on Kinsey's coveralls. The sergeant's face split into a grin.

"I heard you Coasties were on a tight budget," he said, "but golf carts? Seriously? Is the clown car in the shop?"

Kinsey returned the grin. "Small service, big job," he replied. "Wear it out, fix it up, make it work. That's our motto."

"I thought it was *Semper Paratus* —Always Prepared," the soldier said.

Kinsey's smile faded. "That too, though I don't feel very friggin' prepared for this."

"None of us were," the soldier said, closing the distance and extending his hand. "Josh Wright, North Carolina National Guard. Now, Chief, what brings y'all into our fair city. If you're looking for the golf course, you're headed the wrong way."

Kinsey took the offered hand. "Matt Kinsey." He glanced pointedly up at the machine gunner.

"Oh, right," Wright said, releasing Kinsey's hand. "Y'all can point those elsewhere, boys," he called to the gunners. "They don't appear to be hostile." He then waved to the other Coasties. "Y'all come on in."

Wright turned back to Kinsey as the other Coasties approached. "So again, Chief, what the hell are you doing running around Wilmington in golf carts?"

"We're from the Oak Island Station, and we're trying to get over to the command center. We got as close as we could on the river, and the golf carts were the only transportation we could find," Kinsey explained.

Wright hesitated. "You don't know?"

"Know what?" Kinsey asked.

"The Coast Guard building was attacked two nights ago. It burned to the ground."

"What? Who the hell would attack the Coast Guard HQ? And why? We HELP people, for Christ's sake! I can see if it was a food store or…" He broke off, unable to articulate his confusion. "This… this just doesn't make sense. What about our people? Was anyone hurt? Where did they set up?"

Wright just shook his head and looked at the ground, unable to meet Kinsey's eye. It took a moment to sink in.

"All… all of them? Are you saying they're all dead?" Kinsey demanded.

"As far as we know," Wright said. "We got a Mayday from your folks and saw the fire from the armory. We sent out a team immediately, but by the time we got there, the building was already completely engulfed and we couldn't get close. We found a dozen bodies in the ruins yesterday, but the building is unsafe and we couldn't search thoroughly." He hesitated again.

"They… they had their hands tied behind their backs. It appeared they'd all been killed execution style."

Red began to flood Kinsey's vision and his heart raced as Wright continued.

"The 'why' I can't answer, but as far as the 'who' goes, it was likely gangbangers. When the lights didn't come on by the second day and it became pretty obvious law enforcement and everything else was being overwhelmed, the stronger gangs saw an opportunity and took it. They have a 'command structure,' so to speak, and filled the power vacuum. And to be honest, they were a helluva lot more effective than the police. I mean, there's probably only three or four hundred police officers and sheriff's deputies combined, and with everything else going to hell, there's no way they could handle a gangbanger uprising too, so the gangs sort of took over. Let's face it, if you've got no problem murdering anyone that gives you any trouble right on the spot, it tends to get folks' attention. By the time the governor called out the guard and those of us who could respond mobilized, the police were already overwhelmed and were forted up in various places with their families and loved ones. We were already outnumbered and playing defense when we got here."

"But what's that got to do with the Coast Guard? Why were they attacked?" Kinsey asked.

Wright shrugged. "Who knows how these bastards think? I guess maybe the Coasties wore uniforms and represented governmental authority, and it's not like they were a hardened target. I mean, it was an office building with open parking lots all the way around it and multiple entrances. There wasn't even a damn fence! I mean, I know our CO was in touch with your CO and wanted him to move over to the armory since it's at least somewhat defensible, but your guy was reluctant."

"Why?" Kinsey asked.

"Well, it kind of makes sense in a way. I think your skipper was a pretty stand-up guy and he was trying to figure out some way to make a difference in an impossible situation. He apparently had pretty good backup generator capability and all his coms were concentrated there in the command center, so if he moved, he was sure to lose some of whatever capability remained. Also, with the media down and communications being as piss poor as they were, there was no way to spread the word if they moved, and more of your people were straggling in as they were able. If he moved, they likely wouldn't know where to report." Wright paused. "And I guess like you, he didn't figure anyone would be targeting the Coast Guard."

"Who the hell does this?" muttered Baker.

"The same stupid worthless assholes that torch their own neighborhoods and then shoot at the firefighters who come to put it out," Jackson said.

The men nodded agreement and then fell silent, processing what they'd just heard. Kinsey broke the silence.

"What's the status here? Are you guys making any headway?"

Wright shook his head. "Negative. We're forted up ourselves, back in the armory about a mile up the road. We push out patrols like this one up all the major cross streets every morning to show the flag and maybe give folks a bit of hope, but come nighttime, we'll be back behind the barbed wire. Most of us are fortunate enough to live outside the city, so at least we don't have to worry about our families facing gang violence. Some of the guys that live in the city brought their families inside. The CO said no at first, but it became pretty obvious the families stayed or the guys were leaving, so he eased up. We've got a storage tank with a couple of thousand gallons of drinking water and there are a couple of little lakes over by the armory. We suck water out of them with a tank truck for flushing toilets and taking outdoor showers. We got maybe ten days of MREs and twice that of diesel fuel, depending on how we conserve it. If we don't get resupplied before then, I guess it's game over."

"What do you hear from up the chain of command?" Kinsey asked. "Surely there's some sort of recovery plan?"

"Maybe on paper, but from where I'm standing here on the ground, it's not working," Wright said. "I mean, the governor's office screwed around over two days before calling up the Guard, but with communications being spotty and all the media down, very few of the notifications got through anyway. And even if they did, enough of them didn't that 'no notification' is a pretty good excuse and what person wants to go off and leave their family when all hell is breaking loose? I mean, I figured we'd be needed and left my wife and kids with my brother's family and reported on my own, but way less than fifty percent of my unit showed up, and to be honest, I'm starting to feel like a chump. It would be different if we could make a difference, but all we're really doing is trying to stay alive ourselves."

"How about the regular army," Kinsey said, "or FEMA?"

"Ah yes, FEMA," Wright said, spitting the acronym out like a curse word. "We had a visit from a FEMA official. He came in by chopper to 'brief us on the recovery effort.' His main concern seemed to be he couldn't get his laptop to boot up so he could show us his PowerPoint presentation. Apparently he couldn't answer any questions without his presentation, so he spent two hours telling us nothing in great detail then got on his chopper and left, never to be seen again. I wouldn't count on FEMA."

"And as far as the regular army goes," Wright continued, "that's way above my pay grade, but I do know they have to be called out by the President after he declares a disaster. I figure if anything qualifies as a disaster, it's this. But the thing is, where they gonna stage from? I mean, if there's a hurricane or flood or whatever, they stage from places that aren't impacted and move resources to the disaster. But what do you do if the friggin' disaster is EVERYWHERE? And part of the unwritten deal with soldiers is the security of their families. It's one thing to expect troops from Fort Campbell or Fort Bragg to deploy to the sandbox with their families safe and sound at home, and it's quite another to ask them to leave their loved ones in danger. And besides, the way I look at it, there's no need to deploy troops. There's plenty of disaster to go around. What would be gained by moving troops from one place where things are going to hell to another place where things are going to hell? At least if troops are providing relief services around their home bases, they're helping friends and family." He shook his head. "I'm thinking the cavalry isn't coming to the party."

"You're just a little ray of sunshine, aren't you," Kinsey said.

"Just realistic," Wright said. "If you'd seen what I've seen in the last few days, you'd feel the same."

Kinsey nodded and sighed. "I expect you're right. Well, I guess we need to get out of your hair."

"You headed back to your boat?"

Kinsey hesitated and looked at his men before responding. "We're only a quarter of a mile from HQ, and we all had friends there. I think we all want to at least go have a look."

Wright nodded. "Tell you what, it's not like we were accomplishing anything here. We'll run you over there."

"Thanks," Kinsey said, but Wright was already turning to speak into his radio.

"All Bird Dog units, this is Bird Dog Actual," Wright said. "Mount up, repeat, mount up."

Kinsey heard the Humvee rumble to life beside him and then another, and glanced over to see a second vehicle he'd missed parked across a parking lot in the shadow of a Bojangles restaurant. Meanwhile three soldiers emerged from the shrubbery on the west side of the street, one of them carrying the machine gun he'd noticed earlier and the other two armed with M-4s. The second Humvee just drove across the grass strip and sidewalk, and the soldiers started moving towards the two vehicles, but Wright called out last minute instructions rearranging them between the two vehicles as Kinsey and his men walked back to the golf carts to retrieve their weapons.

"Y'all can ride with me," Wright said from the open passenger-side door of his Humvee as they returned. "Plenty of room."

The Coasties mumbled their thanks and climbed into the vehicle. Less than a minute later, they pulled into the parking lot of their former headquarters. The building was a blackened ruin, one wall had collapsed in places along the top floor and portions of the roof were visible sagging in the gaps. The burned smell was almost overpowering and mixed with it was a sickly sweet odor that didn't bear thinking about.

"Don't try to go inside," Wright warned. "All the bodies we recovered were on the ground floor, but we had to get out when a section of ceiling and a piece of a support wall collapsed on us. One of our guys was hurt pretty badly."

Kinsey just stared at the building a moment. "Thanks for trying," he said quietly. "Can we have a moment?"

"Absolutely," said Wright, and the Coast Guardsmen all got out of the vehicle and moved closer to the building as Wright keyed his mike and ordered his two machine gunners to cover the street in opposite directions. The remainder of the soldiers dismounted and stood near their vehicles, covering the Coast Guardsmen from a respectful distance.

Kinsey stared into the ruins, his grief and his rage as black as the ravaged building. He had almost thirty years in the Coast Guard and it was a small service, almost like a large, extended family. If you stayed in long enough, it seemed like you knew, or at least knew of, almost everyone, and the men and women in that blackened ruin weren't just fellow service members. They were shipmates with whom he'd weathered raging storms, and rescue chopper crews, and veterans of arctic ice breakers, and rescue swimmers, and men and women of a dozen other specialties. They were people he'd worked with and played with, gotten drunk and been hungover with. He'd danced at their weddings and commiserated with more than a few when they divorced, their relationship unable to withstand the demands of the service. He'd toasted the birth of their children as they had toasted his. He'd shared their triumphs and defeats, and most of all a sense of purpose and quiet pride in their chosen calling. They were as tough as they had to be and wielded necessary force when appropriate, but mostly they were life savers and not life takers, and that's what they'd signed up for. They were his friends, and he felt their loss on a visceral level he was utterly incapable of articulating to anyone who wasn't a Coastie.

He dropped to one knee, grounded his weapon, and bowed his head in a silent prayer. When he rose, wiping his cheek with the back of his hand, he looked over to see Baker observing him with glistening eyes.

"You thinking what I'm thinking?" Baker asked.

Kinsey nodded. "You know how to do it?"

"We can manage," Baker said, and stepped toward the other two Coast Guardsmen and spoke to them quietly. Kinsey saw their heads bob in affirmation.

Kinsey looked back at the building a moment, then drew himself up to attention and executed a parade ground perfect right face toward the other men.

"DETAIL FALL IN!" he bellowed in his best parade-ground voice, as the three men snapped to attention in a straight line.

"READY."

"AIM."

"FIRE."

The movements of the first salute were clumsy and the volley a bit ragged, but the second was better and the third and last perfect as the men obeyed Kinsey's shouted orders.

"PREEE-SENT ARMS," Kinsey then bellowed, and the men brought their rifles to the salute position in slow motion while Kinsey performed a hand salute equally slowly.

"OOOR-DER ARMS," Kinsey continued, and the men slowly brought their rifles to order arms as Kinsey matched their speed in releasing his hand salute.

"DETAIL DISMISSED," Kinsey called and the men just stood a moment looking at the ruins.

He turned to find all of Wright's dismounted men standing at present arms. Kinsey returned the salute and Wright called his men to order arms. They all immediately glanced toward the two machine gunners, who were staring in opposite directions down the road, vigilant guards to the impromptu ceremony.

"Mount up!" Wright yelled, and the men began climbing back into the vehicles.

A minute later, they were back at the intersection where they met. Wright spoke from the front passenger seat.

"Well, unless y'all are really attached to your clown cars, I'll give you a lift back to your boat."

"That would be outstanding," Kinsey said, and his men added their thanks.

"Just point us in the right direction," Wright said.

Kinsey briefly considered going directly back to the *Pecos Trader* , but he had agreed with Hughes to avoid revealing his location. He didn't really think that would be a problem with Wright, but neither was it absolutely necessary.

"Head to the main gate of the container terminal on Shipyard Boulevard," Kinsey said. "Our boat's at the container dock."

The driver nodded, no further instructions needed, and Kinsey radioed the boat to tell them he was coming in with friendlies in a Humvee. Five minutes later, they were rolling through the container terminal. Wright's head was on a swivel and they passed row upon row of brightly colored shipping containers.

"Hmmm? I wonder what's in all these containers?" Wright said.

"All manner of useful stuff, I'd guess," Kinsey said. "The custody transfer is all computerized, but I suspect there are some paper copies of the cargo manifests somewhere in one of these office buildings."

Wright looked thoughtful. "Overall this isn't a bad location. Pretty good fence, river to your back, and it wouldn't take much to rearrange these containers into a defensive wall, presuming some of these container transporters are still running. Not much in the way of shelter or power, though."

"I don't know," Kinsey said. "I suspect there are tugs, ferries, tour boats, and maybe other abandoned craft up and down the river that might have generating capacity and berths, and you've got a damned long dock to tie them up. Some of the larger vessels might have water distillers as well."

"Yeah, if we just had the fuel to run them."

Kinsey hesitated, then thought what the hell, Wright was a smart cookie and he'd figure things out quickly anyway.

"Matter of fact, the product terminal just downstream has great big tanks full of fuel. Food for thought," Kinsey said.

Wright was still looking around. "Damn right it is," he said, just as they reached the river and saw the Coast Guard boat moving in to where a recessed ladder extended from the dock down to the surface of the water.

The men all got out of the vehicles and handshakes were exchanged all around before the Coasties moved toward the ladder.

"A word before you go, Chief?" said Wright as he moved down the dock away from both the vehicles with Kinsey in tow. When they were well away from the others, Kinsey spoke.

"What's up?" he asked.

"Just a little chat, NCO to NCO," Wright said, then hesitated as if choosing his words carefully.

"You just took a helluva sucker punch, right between the eyes, and you likely need to process that a bit. The thing is, you also have to make some hard decisions, and fast, and you don't have the luxury of time to grieve."

Kinsey bridled. "Look, Wright, I appreciate the help, but I don't need you to tell me—"

Wright raised his hand in a calming gesture. "Hear me out. I'm not trying to tell you what to do, but I want you to fully appreciate the situation, because as negative as you think I was before, I was actually holding back in front of the other guys." He paused for emphasis. "This is a complete and total shit show," he said slowly. "We got a Humpty Dumpty situation here. You know, as in an 'all the king's horses and all the king's men couldn't put Humpty together again' situation."

"Yeah, I got that," Kinsey said.

Wright shook his head. "Maybe, maybe not. What I'm telling you is the guys calling the shots on a national level couldn't find their own assholes with both hands and a mirror on a stick, and there ain't no way anything is ever going to be the same again. There just aren't the smarts or the resources to make this better at a national level even if everyone played nice, and as you may recall, the country was pretty polarized before this happened. It's unlikely to improve with folks starving to death and killing each other. Even if the powers that be do manage to mobilize the Army or the other services, what can they do but kill people to keep them from killing each other over a dwindling supply of food and water? And in the end, they'll be killing people to take the resources for themselves, because that's the only way they'll survive."

Kinsey nodded. "Okay, but what's your point?"

"My point is most people are going to die, and it's gonna be up to guys like me and you to survive and help as many other people survive as possible, and we have to use our own best judgment, right or wrong. If we wait for orders or follow stupid ones, more folks are going to die, and we might be among them. Also, if I'm gonna try to save anyone, my family's got to be at the top of the list. Until five minutes ago, my plan was to haul ass with those of my guys who wanted to go and two Humvees, to collect our families and make it up to my uncle's farm about twenty miles north of here." He gestured around the terminal. "But you got me thinking we might be able to establish a foothold here, so I'm going to at least put that plan to the major before I take off.

"But my real point is this," Wright continued, "I'm just a weekend warrior, so I might be more willing to head for the hills than you career types, but y'all all need to be thinking of yourselves and your families too. However you do that, you can always help as many other people as you can too. It's sort of like that Marine Corps general said back in Korea when he was surrounded by the Chinese, 'We're not retreating. We're attacking in another direction.'"

Wright fell silent and Kinsey just looked at him for a minute.

"Who you trying to convince, Wright?" Kinsey asked. "Me or you?"

Wright took off his helmet and ran his hand through his hair before giving Kinsey a sheepish grin.

"Both of us, I reckon," he said.

Kinsey nodded. "Definitely food for thought," he said. "Let's exchange radio frequencies and call signs. I suspect we might hook up again."

Wright nodded and produced a small notebook and pen from a shoulder pocket, and the two men exchanged contact information before Kinsey extended his hand.

"Good luck to you, Sarge," Kinsey said as Wright gripped his hand.

"And to you, Chief," Wright replied.

UNITED BLOOD NATION HQ
(FORMERLY NEW HANOVER COUNTY
DEPARTMENT OF SOCIAL SERVICES)
1650 GREENFIELD STREET
WILMINGTON, NC

DAY 8, 3:00 P.M.

Kwintell Banks, first superior of the SMM (Sex, Money, Murder) 'set' of the United Blood Nation, sat in the committee meeting and surveyed the small conference room attached to the director's office of the new HQ he now occupied by right of conquest. All in all, it was fairly shabby, and he knew they could and would do better in the future, but there was symbolism at play here, and despite his lack of a formal education, Kwintell was nobody's fool. People were already trained to come to the Department of Social Services to bow and scrape for the meager government handouts that defined their miserable lives, so why not take advantage of that? And what better signal to all concerned there was a new order—a new regime controlling their lives—than usurping the government's administration center? The only difference was, the new regime had teeth, and the populace could either fall in line—or die.

He shook himself from his reverie and refocused on Darren Mosley, his Minister of Information.

"... and then they rode off with the soldiers down to the river," said Mosley.

"That's it?" Kwintell demanded. "They just showed up at the building and shot their guns in the air? What kind of crazy cracker shit is that?"

"No, it wasn't just like poppin' off in the air," Mosley said. "It was like at a funeral, you know, a salute like."

Kwintell considered a moment. "Like for all them mofos we capped there two days ago?"

Mosley nodded. "True dat."

"And where we didn't get shit. You the Minister of Information, Darren, and you said there was some good stuff there, but we didn't get a dozen gats out of the whole deal, even after we started capping the mofos." He paused for effect. "Which ain't very good information."

Mosley shifted in his chair. "Straight up, Kwintell, I thought there was shit there. One of the Pee Wees be choppin' it up 'bout how his cousin in the Coast Guard and how they have all kinda gats at the HQ. Machine guns and grenades and shit. I—"

Kwintell waved Mosley silent. "Ight, ight, just don't be slippin' no mo. Now what up with the soldiers?"

"No change," Mosley said. "They go out in the morning and sit in the road and go back in at night."

"They messin' with us anywhere?"

Mosley shook his head. "We been leavin' them alone, they be leaving us alone. Ain't very many of them, but they got them machine guns and tanks. Why, you thinkin' we need to be bangin' them?"

Kwintell shook his head. "No. They run out of food and water and they'll leave. No point gettin' any of our soldiers shot."

"You think maybe the regular army be comin', or they might be sending supplies?"

Kwintell bit back his anger at having to provide 'intelligence' to his subordinate who was supposed to be providing it to him. It was early days, and Mosley still commanded respect in the set, more for his violent courage than his intelligence. Kwintell would have to be careful in replacing him. He shook his head again.

"Been eight days, and the radio say this happenin' all over. If they was gonna send help or supplies, they'd be here by now. I'm thinkin' this is how it's gonna be, and we need to move fast to make sure UBN take our share now."

There were murmurs of 'straight up' and 'true dat' around the small table, and Kwintell turned this attention to Keyshaun Jackson, his Minister of Food.

"What up with the food?" he asked.

"All good," Keyshaun said. "Most everything was stripped in the 'hood, but I got copies of the yellow pages so we could hit all the food stores and divided up the city, putting a lieutenant in charge of each section. We sittin' on most of the food in the city, but it's spread out, so I'm thinkin' we need to move it all to one place where we can guard it. The yellow pages gave me an idea too, and I started havin' them sit on the bottled water companies too."

Kwintell nodded approval and turned his attention further down the table.

"Desmond, help Keyshaun out if he needs more soldiers to sit on the food. Use baby gangstas if need be, just to sit on the stores 'til we get it moved. And use that yellow pages idea—but look for gas stations, gun stores, beer and soft drink distributors, shit like that, you know, anything we gonna need.

"And one more thing," Kwintell continued, "I see all you niggas smilin' when I said beer distributors, so let's be straight up here. I ain't playing around and I don't want nobody forgetting that! Last week we all seen people running around, acting the fool and looting liquor stores and stealing TVs that ain't never gonna work again. We in this for the long run, and if I see a UBN soldier doing that shit, I will cap his ass right there on the street and I expect you to do the same. Is that clear?"

The rest of the committee members traded hesitant looks, then one by one, nodded their concurrence.

"Good," Kwintell said, then turned to the last member of the committee. "Jermaine, where we at on recruitment?"

"Way more than we can handle," Jermaine said, "leastwise more than we can initiate anytime soon, and since we got a truce going on with the Crips and everyone else and the cops aren't out, they ain't really nobody for the recruits to take out to earn membership."

"How many you figure waiting to join?" Kwintell asked.

"Couple of thousand, easy," Jermaine said, "and probably anybody we want when the food runs out and we got all that's left."

Kwintell was silent a moment and when he spoke again, he addressed his question to Keyshaun Jackson, the Minister of Food.

"How many others have food?" he asked.

Keyshaun shrugged. "The Crips be sitting on the Food Lion over on Oleander and a bunch of convenience stores, and the Sure Shots and Gaza maybe got half a dozen convenience stores and gas stations between 'em. Ain't none of the other gangs big enough to matter. Mostly the gangs all just loot and leave, but the Crips and the others started trying to occupy places a couple of days ago, copying us, I think."

Kwintell nodded and turned back to Jermain.

"Okay," he said, "we gonna change the rules a bit. Accept every prospective member that come and make them all 'probationary recruits.' Divide them up in groups of at least fifty and put one of our baby gangstas in charge. Send a group against every rival gang location—that's the initiation, they have to take the location and cap all the rival gangstas there. The group succeeds or fails as a group, and if one group fails, have another standing by to go right in. This way we initiate the recruits and get rid of those other mofos without risking any experienced soldiers."

There was silence around the table.

"Wh-what about the truces?" Mosley asked.

"FUCK THE TRUCES!" shouted Kwintell as he pounded the table with his fist. "We got no time for truces! We got the advantage now and we gonna use it to wipe them out so we don't have to be looking over our shoulder all the time. This is a new world, homies, and we gonna be the kings!"

"What about the cops?" Jermaine this time.

"They'll slip away, just like the soldiers, we give them half a chance," Kwintell said. "Hell, most of them don't even live in the county, much less the city. We'll leave 'em be for now and concentrate on wiping out the other gangs and controlling all the food and water. After that, we take out all the crackers and toms. A lot of them are armed, but they're not organized, so we can overwhelm them. We'll use the baby gangsta swarms again. I'm sure we'll be getting more recruits that need initiation anyway."

"What if anyone surrenders?" Jermaine asked. "We gonna cap 'em anyway?"

Kwintell smiled. "Maybe not. I got my eye on a real nice place in Forest Hills, so maybe I'll keep the mayor around as my yard boy."

M/V *PECOS TRADER*
CAPTAIN'S OFFICE

DAY 8, 8:30 P.M.

Hughes once again sat across from Matt Kinsey, who was gazing down into the half-finished cup of coffee grown cold on the low table between them. The Coasties had accepted Hughes' hospitality, unable to resist the offer of hot showers, a good meal, and a bunk with clean sheets. Kinsey had radioed back to Oak Island to confirm they would return to base in the morning, and Hughes had bedded four of them down in the ship's hospital while two kept a security watch on their boat tied up alongside *Pecos Trader* . As an added benefit, they'd gone to dinner clad in the disposable Tyvek coveralls used aboard for tank cleaning and other dirty tasks, and Hughes had arranged for the steward to wash and dry their clothes, all luxuries hard to come by in their crowded base at Oak Island.

"That must have been hard," Hughes said, referring to Kinsey's just recounted visit to Coast Guard HQ.

"Yeah, it was," Kinsey said, and Hughes nodded towards Kinsey's half-finished coffee.

"Care for something a bit stronger?" Hughes asked.

Kinsey hesitated, then said, "Don't mind if I do."

Hughes rose and retrieved a bottle from his lower desk drawer and two short water glasses from the cabinet behind his desk. He walked over, set the two glasses on the coffee table, and poured an inch of amber liquid in the bottom of each.

"Purely medicinal, of course," Hughes said.

Kinsey grinned. "Of course."

As Hughes resumed his seat, Kinsey raised his glass and said, "Absent friends."

Hughes joined the toast, and both men took a swallow then settled back in their chairs.

"So where's home and family, Chief?" Hughes asked.

Kinsey shrugged. "Wisconsin originally, but when you've been in the Coast Guard almost thirty years, you find out pretty quick home is anywhere the Coast Guard says it is. I'm an only child and my folks passed, so I don't really have any strong connections to Wisconsin. My wife is... was from near Baton Rouge and has family there; they're pretty much my family now. That's where I'm planning... or at least WAS planning... to retire. Our son's in the 101st Airborne in Fort Campbell, Kentucky, so

80

there's no telling where he might end up in all this mess. Our daughter is a freshman at LSU in Baton Rouge, full boat scholarship for soccer," he added, pride in his voice. "School's out, but she was taking summer courses and staying with my sister-in-law, so I think she should be okay."

"So you're not married now?" Hughes asked.

"Widowed, two years now." Kinsey didn't elaborate and Hughes sensed it was a painful subject.

"When are... or were... you planning to retire?"

"I hit thirty years last week, and I already put in the paperwork. No clue what I was going to do for a second career." He took another sip and shrugged. "But I guess we're all going to be frigging farmers now—or dead."

Hughes smiled at the gallows humor. "So what now?"

"Damned if I know," Kinsey said. "But there are over fifty of us all told at Oak Island and I have to figure something out. I'm responsible for them."

"I wouldn't have thought so many," Hughes said.

"Well, we only had the duty section on station at the time of the blackout, but when it hit the fan, everybody who could make it in did so. Most of my guys live relatively close to the station. When it became obvious everything was going to hell, I let families on station as well. We're basically camping out in the office and support spaces. There's a limited solar system from a 'green initiative' the Coast Guard put in place a couple of years ago, and the water's still running, though who knows for how long. Everyone stripped their cupboards and brought their food, and we're fishing as well, but it won't last more than another week, two at most. I'm hearing rumblings people are going to take off, and I can't blame them." He shrugged. "To be honest, Cap, I've no clue what to do."

Hughes fell silent a moment, mentally parsing the possibilities.

"Come with us," he said finally.

Kinsey looked confused. "Come with you where?"

"Beaumont, Texas," Hughes said. "We're sailing day after tomorrow. Beaumont's close to Baton Rouge, or at least it's a hell of a lot closer than Wilmington. You and any of your folks are welcome to join us."

Kinsey rubbed his chin. "I don't know, Captain. I'm the unit CO and that kind of seems like desertion."

"Look, we're shorthanded, and we could really use the extra manpower," Hughes said. "And besides, isn't one of your missions protection of shipping? Well, we're shipping, and we sure as hell could use some protection. And besides, you're retiring anyway, so I suspect your relief, or at least someone qualified to relieve you, is probably already on station, right?"

Kinsey was mulling it over when he thought of Wright's comment about 'attacking in a different direction.' That tipped the balance. "All right," he said. "I can't speak for the others, but I'll come. We'll go downriver at first light and come back with anyone else who wants to come. When do you plan on leaving again?"

"Day after tomorrow. I want to leave the dock midafternoon at low slack water. That way I figure the incoming tide will mitigate the current in the river, especially down at the Battery Island Turn, and if we go aground between here and there, the rising tide will help us off. We should be at sea before nightfall," Hughes said. "Supposing I don't put her into the riverbank."

MAYPORT NAVAL STATION
JACKSONVILLE, FLORIDA

DAY 8, 11:00 A.M.

Lieutenant Luke Kinsey, formerly of the 101st Airborne and currently a member of the newly formed Special Reaction Force, squinted in the bright sunlight as he watched the UH-60 Black Hawk settle in the landing zone a hundred yards away, partially obscured by wavy lines of heat steaming off the tarmac. Near noon in north Florida always seemed like summer, even in early April. The T-shirt under his ACUs was already soaked.

"So when do we change to the black uniforms?" asked Sergeant Joel Washington, staring at a group of eight black-clad soldiers a short distance away.

Luke followed the sergeant's gaze as the third man in their group commented.

"I'm fine with our old uniforms," Long said. "They look like losers in a Johnny Cash look-alike contest. I don't want to wear that crap."

Luke stifled a laugh and managed to snarl at Long. "Knock it off, Long. We all volunteered and these guys are all part of our new unit. And when they get more of the new uniforms in, I expect you to wear yours without any bitching. Is that clear?"

Beside Luke, Washington laughed. "You're dreaming, LT," Washington said, pronouncing the title 'el-tee' in the typical verbal shorthand of an enlisted man for a lieutenant. "Long here was born bitching. Why, if he couldn't bitch, he wouldn't be able to talk at all."

Long reddened. "Oh, and I suppose you just love the Johnny Cash look, huh, Washington. And I did volunteer, LT, but I did it mostly 'cause I was tired of twiddling my thumbs in barracks and I wanted to do something to help people. Nobody told me most of this so-called 'Special Reaction Force' was just a bunch of damned mercs. I haven't met over a handful of regular troops since we've been here, and some of these 'private security' guys seem pretty shady."

"And we've been here, what, all of twenty-four hours?" Luke asked. When Long didn't reply, he continued, "So I expect you should crank it down a notch or two, Long. Just because some of these guys were previously private contractors doesn't mean they're bad troops. Private security pays well, and a lot of first-rate guys leave the service to go private."

"Yeah, well, these ain't those guys," Long muttered. "These are the assholes that used to be guarding drug shipments in Colombia and blowing up villages in East Shithole, Africa."

"Chill, Long," Washington whispered. "Here comes the captain."

Luke looked up to see their new commanding officer approaching. He was well over six feet and of indeterminate age, and moved with a grace made somehow sinister by the solid black battle utilities he wore. At odds with the strict grooming standards Luke was accustomed to as a member of the Screaming Eagles, his new boss wore a thick, but neatly trimmed blond goatee, which reminded Luke somehow of a pirate. The pirate illusion was enhanced by the ropelike welt of scar tissue emanating from the outer corner of the man's eye, obscuring most of his left cheek and marring an otherwise handsome face. Captain Rorke exuded a quiet menace that signaled in no uncertain terms he was not a man to be crossed.

As he approached, the three former Screaming Eagles came to attention and Luke saluted crisply. Rorke looked surprised. A derisive smile tugged at the corners of his mouth before he responded with something between a wave and an aborted high five.

"We don't do much of that, Kinsey," Rorke said, "but it is kind of refreshing. Maybe it'll rub off on the rest of the boys."

"Yes, sir," Luke said, dropping his salute.

Rorke looked them over. "Sorry we couldn't get you a uniform issued just yet, but the mission comes first and we're way understaffed. Today it's a 'come as you are' party."

"Not a problem, sir," Luke said.

"Okay," Rorke said, "this is your first time out, so just follow my lead. We're flying to Miami to board a cruise ship the government has chartered. The passengers are refusing to leave, and our job is to clear the ship. We did one here in Jacksonville yesterday, and one in Charleston the day before."

"Cruise ships? What's the government... oh, I get it, housing," Luke said. "But can they do that? Just kick the people off, I mean. Don't they have some sort of obligation to the passengers or something?"

Rorke glared. "That would be both well outside your 'need to know' and also way above your pay grade, Kinsey. Now, do you have any questions of an OPERATIONAL nature?"

Luke said nothing for a moment, then responded, "Yes, sir. Did you have... ah... any trouble with the other boats?"

Rorke shook his head. "Nothing substantial. When well-armed operators show up in full battle rattle, it tends to put a damper on any opposition. We did have a few loudmouth assholes with hero complexes yesterday, but that turned out to be beneficial." He smirked. "You'd be surprised how a couple of publicly administered beat downs and a little blood speeds people toward the exits."

Over Rorke's shoulder, Luke saw Washington and Long exchange concerned glances as Rorke continued.

"Shouldn't be a problem this time, though, our orders are to lighten up. We're going with a charm offensive. Matter of fact, it looks like the head charmer just arrived."

Luke turned to follow Rorke's gaze across the tarmac.

A woman approached at a fast walk. She was slim and even at a distance it was apparent she was attractive, with long dark hair swaying from side to side. The dark lightweight FEMA coveralls she wore did nothing to conceal her femininity, and as she drew nearer, Luke thought she looked vaguely familiar. Apparently he wasn't the only one.

"Is she famous or something?" Washington asked. "She looks familiar."

"Maria Velasquez," Rorke said. "She's a local news anchor in Miami, but her reports get picked up nationally. That's probably where you saw her. She is, or was anyway, a rising star. Now she works for FEMA."

The woman reached the group and studied them a moment before spotting Rorke's rank insignia.

"Captain Rorke?"

"That would be me," Rorke said, extending his hand. "Nice to meet you, Ms. Velasquez, I'm an admirer."

She favored Rorke with a dazzling smile and he continued without bothering to introduce Luke or the others.

"I presume you've been briefed?"

"Oh yes," she said, "and I have a script committed to memory. I'm sure we can resolve the situation without unpleasantness."

"Excellent," Rorke replied. "Let's be off, then. Sit next to me and we can discuss the situation more fully on the flight down."

She bobbed her head and Rorke rested an unnecessary hand on her waist to guide her toward the chopper, leaving the other three to trail behind.

"Secondary mission objective," Luke heard Long whisper to Washington, "getting into *chiquita*'s pants."

Luke's attempt to communicate his displeasure via a hard look was somewhat defeated by his inability to suppress a grin.

An hour and a half later, they were hovering over the Port of Miami on Dodge Island, gazing down at almost empty docks and little movement except aboard a large white cruise ship at one of the cruise terminals. Rorke directed the pilot to land, and the chopper flared over an empty parking lot and settled to the pavement. They were scrambling out before the blades stopped turning, moving behind Rorke and Velasquez toward the cruise terminal.

They passed empty shuttle buses in front of the terminal and found the terminal itself practically deserted except for a scattering of people in FEMA T-shirts and a few terminal personnel pressed into service to tie up the ship and deploy the gangway. Luke wondered where they got the power to deploy the gangway, then heard the muted throb of a generator somewhere in the near distance. He almost bumped into Rorke's back as his new boss stopped and watched one of the FEMA people hasten toward them.

"So what's the story?" Rorke asked. "Any change?"

The man shook his head. "Not really. The captain and crew are cooperating. I mean, the captain's pissed we're basically confiscating his ship, but he agreed to sign the charter on behalf of his company after I assured him we wouldn't kick the crew off if they don't cause trouble. The problem is the passengers. It was a seniors' cruise with several veterans' groups, mainly from the Korean and Vietnam wars, and a scattering of World War Two vets. Hell, a couple of the old farts look like they might have survived the Civil War." He paused. "Anyway, they were in St. Thomas when the blackouts hit, and I guess things got nasty there in a hurry. A shore excursion was surrounded by a mob and they were all robbed at gunpoint and verbally and physically abused. Several of the old guys who attempted to defend the group were beaten for their efforts before local police intervened and got the group back to the ship. They've heard a lot of conflicting reports since and they're confused and scared and not inclined to believe anything I tell them."

He shook his head. "The captain managed to convince them to leave their luggage outside their staterooms this morning, and the crew went around and gave them all baggage claim checks, but that's where things bogged down. I guess a lot of them figured out no matter how anxious they are to get home, conditions on the ship might be a lot better than they are anywhere else. They'll be a pretty tough sell, I'm afraid."

Rorke nodded. "Understood. Is there any place where Ms. Velasquez here can address all the passengers in person?"

"Not in person, at least where everyone can see her directly," the man said, "but I had the captain ask all passengers to gather on the embarkation deck for an update on the situation ashore. That area runs most of the length of the ship, and there are large flat-screen TV monitors every few feet. Ms. Velasquez can address everyone from the ship's communications center. If she gets them moving, we'll funnel them right down the gangway and across the terminal to the buses."

Rorke nodded again and turned to Luke. "I'll accompany Ms. Velasquez to the comm center. You take the rest of the men aboard and space them out along the embarkation deck to keep things moving after they start. Spread six of them out evenly along the deck, but pick three men to stay with you near the gangway. That's the potential bottleneck, so keep it moving. Do NOT let things back up there, is that clear?"

"Yes, sir," Luke said, and Rorke turned and started toward the ship.

Once aboard, Rorke and Velasquez disappeared into the crowd and Luke picked six of Rorke's men to spread out along the deck, retaining both of his own men and a private named Grogan to stay with him near the gangway. When he was satisfied everyone was in position, he surveyed the crowd. As the FEMA man indicated, they were seniors, and while most seemed reasonably fit, there were many canes and walkers, and not a few wheelchairs, as well as scattered passengers with oxygen tubes clipped in their noses. The mood was tense and subdued. Suddenly the undercurrent of hushed conversation stopped as the TV monitors all sprang to life with the identical images of a handsome blond man of late middle age whose shirt displayed the four-stripe shoulder boards of a captain.

"Good day, ladies and gentlemen. As I'm sure you know by now"—he showed perfect white teeth in a smile—"I am Captain Larson. I apologize for what I know has been a frustrating lack of information, but in truth we have had very little information to share. I know you all have questions regarding the situation ashore. So, I'm very pleased we now have on board representatives of the US Federal Emergency Management Agency, or FEMA, who can address your various concerns."

The captain stepped to one side, and Maria Velasquez took his place, somehow managing to look professional while favoring her viewing audience with a radiant smile. From the murmurs rippling through the assembled passengers, it was obvious to Luke many recognized Velasquez and were informing their less-enlightened shipmates of her identity.

"Hi, folks, I'm Maria Velasquez, and some of you might recognize me from my work on both local and national news teams. However, today I'm here on behalf of FEMA. As I'm sure you've figured out by now, most of the media infrastructure was badly damaged by the recent disaster, so when FEMA reached out to media professionals and offered us a way to serve our viewers, or perhaps I should say former viewers, most of us gladly accepted the opportunity to do our part.

"First, the situation. Eight days ago a massive solar storm released a series of what are called 'coronal mass ejections' at earth. Without going into too much technical mumbo jumbo, the bottom line is there were blackouts, not just across the US and Canada, but the world. Obviously, there has been chaos and confusion, but the good news is, here in the US anyway, the authorities have control of the situation. Food and water is going out to folks who need it, even as we speak, so don't worry about your loved ones."

Washington looked over at Luke, who merely returned his puzzled look and shrugged his shoulders.

"But the bad news," Velasquez continued, "is the power is still out. However, all of the utilities are working on the problem, with the full assistance of the federal government, and they are confident they can restore the power within the week in some places, but perhaps two to three weeks in most." There were groans from the audience and evidently the comm center was close enough for Velasquez to hear them, because she responded with a sympathetic smile and allowed the groaning to dissipate on its own.

"Now," she said, "as far as your situations go, it's another big mixture of the good news/bad news thing, I'm afraid. The bad news is air travel is disrupted, and gasoline and fuel of all kinds are currently in really short supply—again both things the federal government is working on

87

correcting—but that doesn't help you folks much in the near term. The good news is we're working on charter flights to get you where you need to go, but the bad news is it's going to take a few days. More good news is you'll get to extend your vacation a few days at government expense because we're going to put you all up in some of Miami's great hotels. The bad news is they're not so awesome these days, because most are operating with limited power on backup generators."

There was grumbling from the crowd now, but a few chuckles as well, as the information gave the listeners a greater sense of understanding, and Velasquez's earnest but somewhat light-hearted delivery seemed to make the situation more tolerable. Though Luke doubted the veracity of some of her claims, he figured they were at least partial truths, and having the crowd disembark voluntarily was a hell of a lot better than the alternative.

"More good news," Velasquez said, continuing her monologue, "is all of your food and drink will be taken care of, but the bad news, I'm afraid, is it will be in the form of FEMA emergency provisions. However, even that's good news in a way, as the many veterans among you will be able to satisfy what I'm sure is your curiosity as to whether the new meals ready-to-eat, or MREs, are superior to the old rations you may remember from your own gallant service." She paused for effect. "The bad news is current soldiers refer to the MREs as 'meals, rarely edible.'"

The laughter was spontaneous and widespread this time, mixed with good-natured groans, and Luke had to admit Velasquez was a pro when it came to winning over a crowd. The tension in the crowd was significantly lower than when they'd arrived. Velasquez waited for the laughter to subside, and continued.

"So here's the deal, folks. We have buses standing by outside to transport you to your hotels. You don't have to worry about your baggage, as the crew will collect it and we will transport it to your hotel. We have crew members standing by to assist those of you who require assistance in disembarking —"

"Why can't we just stay here until the flights are ready? The chow's a hell of a lot better and we got power," yelled a voice from the crowd. There was another voice of agreement followed almost immediately by a chorus of noisy agreement, drowning out Velasquez's words as she continued to speak on the screens. She continued to speak for a while and then stopped and looked a bit confused, as if she'd heard the noise but not the specific question. She then looked off camera and it was obvious she was listening to someone; then she turned back to the camera and made calming gestures. Eventually, the crowd noise subsided.

"I understand some of you have asked why you can't just stay aboard," she said. "That's a reasonable question and I apologize for not addressing it first. The fact is, the captain informs me there is less than a day's food left on board, so we are reduced to emergency rations regardless of where you are quartered. As far as staying here, the ship is also almost out of fuel, and it will be a long time before any more is available. With no power, the ship will be even less pleasant than the hotels ashore, so it's better to leave now while we have resources in place to accommodate the transfer." She paused. "And I have to stress here, folks, there are a lot of people needing help, not only people on other cruise ships like this one, but other people in the community at large. We are here now and ready to help you, but if you turn down our offer, you will be completely on your own as far as getting back to your homes."

Luke doubted the last assertion. The government wasn't 'chartering' a ship to leave it sitting at a dock empty and without fuel. However, he couldn't help feeling relieved as he saw heads nod here and there in the crowd, his disgust at the blatant manipulation mitigated by the rising hope he wouldn't have to participate in a forcible eviction of a crowd of senior citizens. Velasquez gave her announcement a moment to sink in and then continued.

"Now as I was saying, we have crew members standing by to assist those of you who need help disembarking. Unfortunately we only have the single gangway in use, so we ask crewmen assisting wheelchair-bound passengers to stay to the right during disembarkation to allow walking passengers to pass to your left. Thank you for your cooperation, ladies and gentlemen, and I wish you all a safe journey to your homes."

Velasquez's face blanked from all the screens and Luke saw ship's officers around the embarkation deck begin to dispatch Filipino crewmen into the crowd to assist wheelchair-bound passengers. Like magic, other crewmen arrived with folding wheelchairs, encouraging passengers with walkers or canes to accept a wheelchair ride to the buses. A few seemed resistant, but in the end all accepted the assistance.

Somewhat unsure of his role, Luke positioned himself on one side of the gangway entrance with Long and nodded for Washington and Grogan to take the other side as the crowd converged on the gangway entrance. It wasn't a line exactly, but it was orderly, as people at the front of the pack politely waited their turn to move onto the gangway, generally making way for the wheelchairs pushed by the Filipino seamen to move on the gangway and start down in a slower moving line, hugging the right rail as faster walking passengers filled the left side of the gangway.

As the gangway filled, two wheelchairs moved on to the gangway side by side, obviously an elderly couple, with the woman clinging to her husband's hand. When the seaman pushing the woman's chair tried to move ahead to form a single line, his passenger grew visibly agitated and refused to release her husband's hand. The Filipino seaman relented and it became obvious they intended to transit the gangway abreast.

"Shit!" muttered Grogan as he shouldered the little Filipino aside and shoved the woman's chair forward, the unexpected move breaking her grip on her husband's hand as Grogan pushed her chair to the right.

"Frank! Frank!" the old woman screamed, terror in her voice.

But Grogan hadn't counted on the husband behind him, who grabbed the cane stowed upright between his knees and propelled it forward between Grogan's legs, crooked end up, then jerked back savagely, hooking it into Grogan's crotch, to stop him in mid-stride before the old man lost his grip on the cane.

"Jesus," gasped Grogan as he released the wheelchair and stumbled to the rail. The cane clattered to the gangway at his feet. Grogan straightened and whirled, face red with rage and fist raised—to face Washington, who had swiftly inserted himself between Grogan and the old man.

All the while, the old woman's piteous screams continued.

"Stand down, Grogan!" Luke shouted, then motioned the seaman pushing the old man's chair forward so the couple could be reunited.

Grogan glared at Luke. "But he—"

"I said stand down and get off the gangway, now!" Luke said, and after a moment's hesitation, Grogan complied and Luke stepped forward toward the reunited couple as Washington scooped the old man's cane up off the gangway.

The woman was calmer now, though still agitated, and her husband was holding both her hands and speaking to her softly. "It's fine, sweetheart. I'm right here and I'm not going anyplace. You're safe now."

"Is she all right, sir?" Luke asked.

The old man looked up, his eyes moist. "She gets… confused sometimes and doesn't know where she is. When that happens I can't be out of her sight without her getting upset. It was only happening once in a while, but all this stress made it worse."

Luke nodded, and when the old man disengaged his left hand from his wife's grip in order to accept his cane from Washington, Luke notice the man's baseball cap for the first time. It bore a Screaming Eagles patch over the logo 101st Airborne, with a small enamel pin depicting sergeant's stripes. Another small circular pin said "Charter Member" in the center, with script around the outside reading "The Battered Bastards of Bastogne."

Luke saw Washington do a double take when he noticed the cap. On the front of the old man's shirt was a temporary name tag, likely one he'd neglected to remove after some previous shipboard gathering. Written in a spidery, old man's hand was the name Frank Hastings.

"Sergeant Washington," Luke said, "would you and Private Long be good enough to escort Sergeant Hastings and his lady to the end of the gangway?"

"It would be our honor and privilege, sir," Washington said, and motioned Long over to help.

Luke watched them start down the gangway, his men pushing the wheelchairs abreast as the old couple held hands and the attending seamen trailed along, as if unsure what to do. He turned and walked the few steps back to the ship where Grogan waited. As soon as he stepped off the gangway, Grogan motioned the waiting passengers forward.

"Disregard that," Luke said to the waiting passengers, raising his hand. Then he turned to Grogan. "Let's let them get far enough along that people aren't breathing down their necks."

"But the captain said—"

"As you were, PRIVATE," Luke said, and Grogan glared at him.

When the couple was halfway down the gangway, Luke nodded at Grogan and motioned the waiting passengers forward. As they passed him, the other veterans who'd seen the incident on the gangway favored him with nods or murmured words of approval, making him feel even guiltier given his role in the con job. He took some comfort in the fact at least they were getting the people to their homes, however bad the situations might be when they got there.

He kept a watch down the gangway and saw Washington and Long release the Hastings into the care of the Filipino seamen at the bottom of the gangway, and watched the couple roll out of sight, still hand in hand. Via hand signals, he directed Washington and Long to remain at the bottom of the gangway.

The rest of the disembarkation went without incident, and his other men trailed the shrinking crowd to the gangway, so when the last of the passengers moved off the ship, Luke had all his troops together with the exception of Washington and Long. Rorke made a brief appearance and indicated he had 'matters to attend to on board' and Luke should take the rest of the men and wait for him at the chopper.

At the chopper, Luke put the men at ease, and they broke into groups of two or three to talk, segregating themselves based on past friendships or shared experiences, with Washington and Long together near him. Not good, thought Luke, knowing if they were to develop any sort of unit identity they had to start integrating themselves on all levels. He saw Grogan wander even further afield to bum a smoke from one of the FEMA drivers, and Luke watched as the two chatted like old friends while passengers boarded the last bus. The FEMA driver dropped his cigarette and ground it out underfoot, to board the bus himself just as Luke got a radio call from Rorke, directing him to board the chopper and have the pilots start their preflight checks for departure in ten minutes.

Washington and Long sat near him in the chopper, looking subdued as the pilots ran through their preflights.

"It's a bad situation," Luke said, "but at least they're headed home."

Washington and Long nodded as across the chopper, Grogan tried unsuccessfully to stifle a snort.

"You got something to say, Grogan?" Washington asked.

"Seriously? You didn't buy all that happy horseshit she was spouting, did you?"

"What are you getting at? It sounded legit to me," Washington said.

"Except there ain't no flights, man, and there hasn't been a hotel with emergency power in Miami in three or four days, except the ones currently occupied by bunches of gangbangers," Grogan said. "And you might not have noticed, but things are frigging grim, and I'm thinking FEMA's not wasting any food on those people. I mean, let's face it, they're all likely to be dead in a month no matter what happens."

"Bullshit," Long snorted. "How could you know that? Does FEMA consult you about their relief plans?"

"Because my cousin's driving one of those FEMA buses, genius," Grogan said, "and he says they're only pumping out bullshit to get the passengers away from the dock and out of the way. Randy told me this was his second trip today, and his orders are to ride at least twenty minutes and then pick out someplace that looks reasonable from the outside. He just dumps them in front of whatever hotel he wants, and by the time the old farts hobble into the lobby and find it deserted, or maybe full of gangbangers, he's already hauled ass back here to the terminal."

Luke sat in shock as Washington and Long turned to him, seeking assurances he didn't have.

Finally Washington spoke.

"This is messed up, LT! Like REALLY messed up!"

Luke could only nod.

CHAPTER EIGHT

Day 9, 4:00 p.m.

"That was fast," Hughes said, standing on the deck with Howell and Gowan staring downstream at the approaching flotilla.

There were two of the forty-five-foot patrol boats they'd seen earlier as well as two smaller boats that appeared to be semirigid inflatables, each about twenty-five feet long, and all carried the distinctive markings of the US Coast Guard. Following them, and setting the somewhat sedate pace of the flotilla, was a much larger barge-shaped vessel with a cube-like deckhouse and a large flat deck dominated by a large crane near the bow. Numerous people were visible on both the larger patrol boats and the barge.

True to his word, Kinsey had left at first light and raced downriver. He'd radioed back to the ship that he'd be returning with his group of volunteers the same day, as soon as he'd 'arranged a few things.' Hughes glanced at his watch and then looked to the west. The early spring day promised at least four more hours of daylight. His only concern was the noise and activity might invite unwelcome attention.

"More people than we figured," Georgia Howell said. "We might be hard-pressed to accommodate them."

"We'll make it work," Hughes said somewhat absently as he gazed downstream. "Why in the hell did they bring a buoy tender barge?"

"Beats me," Dan Gowan responded, squinting downriver himself. "There's a pile of stuff on deck. Maybe they brought us a present."

"We'll find out soon enough," Hughes said, turning to Georgia Howell. "Mate, that's a lot of folks and they'll probably all have baggage, so the pilot ladder will be a bottleneck. Would you please deploy the accommodation ladder?"

"Right away, Captain," she said, "and I'll get some lines out over the side so the boats can tie off while they wait to unload. No point in having them waste fuel holding station against the current."

"Good idea, Georgia," Hughes said, and she started across the deck, calling for the bosun as she did so.

***

Kinsey was first aboard, followed up the accommodation ladder by six other men in Coast Guard coveralls. He waved to Georgia Howell where she was supervising the welcome of his little flotilla, then looked around and moved toward Hughes and Gowan, his men following close behind.

"Welcome aboard," Hughes said as Gowan nodded his concurrence. "That's quite a crew. They all signing on?"

Kinsey grinned and shook his head. "No, some are just here to help. However, these guys"—he inclined his head toward the men with him —"are your new shipmates. They're from Corpus Christi to Mobile, and all of them want to get a bit closer to home."

"We're glad to have you," Hughes said. "I'm Jordan Hughes, the captain, and this is Dan Gowan, the chief engineer."

The men all nodded and Kinsey introduced each along with their occupational specialties. When the group turned out to be all petty officers, including two machinery technicians and one electrician's mate, Gowan's face split into a wide grin.

"Out-fucking-standing!" Gowan said, and Kinsey cocked his head at Hughes.

"It takes so little to make engineers happy," Hughes deadpanned, "and apparently new playmates are high on the list." He grinned. "Seriously, gentlemen, we're pleased to have you all, and as soon as you've settled in, we can surely use your help." He glanced over at Gowan. "Though for those of you unfortunate enough to be engineers, I'm not sure the chief here is willing to wait that long."

One of the men, a petty officer second class whose name Hughes hadn't yet committed to memory, spoke directly to Dan Gowan. "We're ready to turn to right away if you need us, Chief." He shifted his gaze to Kinsey. "That is, presuming Chief Kinsey can get by without us and see our gear and families get aboard okay."

"Done," Kinsey said. "Go help Chief Gowan."

"REALLY out-fucking-standing!" Gowan said.

"And I assure you," Hughes added, "he really does have a much larger vocabulary."

Gowan turned red, grinned as everyone else laughed, motioned for the newest members of his engine gang to follow and headed toward the deckhouse. Kinsey detailed the remaining Coasties to assist with the boarding of the families and loading of gear, then turned back to Hughes.

"How many altogether?" Hughes asked.

"Seven men, counting myself, five wives, and nine kids. Twenty-one in all," Kinsey said.

Hughes nodded. "We're tight on accommodations. I can double up some crew, use the hospital and the owner's room, and probably put some cots in the public spaces like the officers' lounge. It won't be the most comfortable accommodations, but you'll all have a place to sleep, access to toilet and showers, and three meals a day." He paused. "But speaking of food, did you bring any with you? This more than doubles our head count and effectively cuts our rations in half. We're probably all right for eight to ten weeks, but after that, we got nothing."

Kinsey shook his head. "The accommodations are no problem, and we have inflatable mattresses if they're needed, but the food's a different story. I'm leaving over thirty people here, without much food to start with, so I didn't feel right taking any. Our leaving will double their food supply, but that's maybe three weeks at most." He hesitated. "Besides, I've got an idea regarding provisions, which may solve everyone's problems, but I'd like to hold off discussing it for a bit, if you don't mind."

Hughes raised an eyebrow. "That's a bit cryptic," he said, gesturing at the various vessels alongside. "Does it have anything to do with your little fleet here? If you're just bringing people and baggage, I figure you could have crammed them into the two bigger patrol boats and saved a lot of fuel."

"I didn't say we came empty-handed." Kinsey pointed past the accommodation ladder where Georgia Howell was greeting new arrivals and sending them with crewmen to get settled.

Hughes followed Kinsey's finger to the buoy tender barge. Stacked on the open deck were boxes and cases of various sizes along with an empty boat trailer. Hughes looked back at Kinsey, obviously confused.

"Okay, I see a boat trailer and some boxes. What's in the boxes and what good is a trailer going to do us?"

"The trailer by itself, nothing," Kinsey said. "But we're going to hoist it on board, tie it down securely, and use it as a transport cradle for THAT!"

Again Hughes followed Kinsey's pointing finger to one of the smaller patrol boats.

"Which is not, as you might think, a nice little inflatable boat, but a Defender-class Response Boat, with an aluminum hull and a rigid foam-filled flotation collar, and with a range of one hundred seventy-five nautical miles and a speed of forty-six knots," Kinsey said. "And we're taking her."

Hughes seemed stunned and Kinsey continued. "And those boxes contain, among other things, two M240 machine guns, along with ten M4 carbines, and of course, ammunition for all of the above."

Hughes just stared at Kinsey, wide-eyed.

"Well, say something, dammit! You look like you're about to have a stroke," Kinsey said.

Hughes burst out laughing. "All I can think of," he said when he'd recovered, "is out-fucking-standing! I guess... guess I've been sailing with Dan too long."

Then Hughes cast an appraising eye at the stack of boxes down on the barge.

"But all those boxes can't be just guns and ammunition," he said.

"Oh, I almost forgot," Kinsey said, "the big boxes are solar panels."

"All of them? There must be a dozen boxes there?"

"Fifteen, actually," Kinsey said. "Station Oak Island is, or was, I guess now, home to an Aids to Navigation Team maintaining buoys and lights up and down a sector of the Intracoastal Waterway. Most of those navaids are solar powered, and we received a big shipment of the latest model solar panels right before the blackout." He paused. "Given the situation, I suspect navaid maintenance isn't going to be very high on anyone's list of priorities anytime soon."

"What are we going to do with them?" Hughes asked.

Kinsey shrugged. "I don't know, but something tells me they'll come in handy. They're reliable as hell and meant to work unattended in the salt air and in the middle of nowhere, to say nothing of being covered with seagull droppings—that stuff is corrosive as hell, you know."

"I'll say one thing, Kinsey, when you commit, you go all in," Hughes said. "The guys you're leaving behind all right with you taking all this stuff? You know if things start getting back to normal in a few months, this is all going to look like a very bad idea."

"If things get back to normal, I'll take the heat for any decisions I make, and be thankful to do it," Kinsey said, shaking his head, "but I honestly can't see that happening. And as far as the other guys, they agreed to a fifty-fifty split on resources, as long as they kept the food and we documented everything." He smiled. "I haven't been in the service this long without learning how to cover my ass when necessary. Mike Butler is the chief in charge of the Aids to Navigation Team, and he's taking over as CO of the Oak Island Station. We filled out the paperwork and had a short 'change of command' ceremony this morning. Me and the other guys going with you all officially requested transfers to the Marine Safety Unit in Port Arthur, Texas, which in his role of commanding officer, Mike provisionally approved since we aren't in contact with anyone to say no. We followed the time-honored concept it's better to apologize than ask permission."

Hughes grinned appreciatively. "Pretty slick, but what about all the stuff?"

"We're one of the first units to receive our allotment of the new solar panels, and it would be selfish of us not to share them with our unit in Port Arthur during this time of scarcity," Kinsey said piously. "Nor can we in good conscience see valuable government property or, for that matter, this private vessel, which we have an obligation to safeguard, sail unprotected in this increasingly lawless environment. Therefore, we have drawn sufficient armaments and resources to execute that protective mission. Further to the execution of the mission, and in the US Coast Guard's best tradition of making maximum use of limited resources, we are pursuing those multiple missions efficiently, by cost effectively transporting personnel, equipment, and dependents to their new duty station while simultaneously conducting said protective mission."

Hughes shook his head, still grinning. "I gotta hand it to you, Chief, you're full of surprises."

Kinsey grinned back. "Oh, you haven't seen them all yet, Captain. Matter of fact, I think we can expect visitors any time—"

Kenny Nunez, the bosun, shouted across the deck from where he was standing at the ship side next to the terminal. "Captain, there's some sort of armored car with a machine gun on top coming this way through the terminal!"

"I was getting to that," Kinsey said. "Now about those provisions…"

M/V PECOS TRADER
CONFERENCE ROOM

DAY 9, 5:00 P.M.

Hughes' chair squeaked a bit as he leaned to his left and whispered to Georgia Howell, "Any word from Tex?"

She shook her head and whispered back, "No, but it shouldn't be long. She'll either find something or she won't, and I told her to call me on the radio, either way."

Hughes nodded and turned his attention to the group crowded elbow to elbow around the rectangular table that nearly filled the small conference room. He sat at the head, nominal host to the impromptu meeting, and opposite him at the far end sat a man of early middle age with chestnut hair shot with streaks of gray Hughes suspected weren't there a week earlier. Dark circles under the man's eyes gave testimony to lack of sleep. His ACUs bore the insignia of a major, and he was flanked on one side by a younger black man wearing lieutenant's bars and on the other by a sergeant.

On Hughes' end of the table sat his three senior officers, and in the middle on either side were the two senior Coast Guardsmen, Kinsey representing the group sailing with the ship, and Chief Boatswain's Mate Mike Butler as the new CO of Station Oak Island. Also summoned to the meeting at the suggestion of Dan Gowan (and looking decidedly ill at ease) was Levi Jenkins.

Major Douglas Hunnicutt shook his head. "It's a good location, but there's no way we have enough people to secure it. We're down to fifty combat effectives, maybe seventy-five if we multitask support people, and between the container terminal and oil terminal, there's just too much perimeter fence. And we've still got over three hundred civilians depending on us." He sighed. "I'd like to save those people at least. I'm thinking the wisest course of action is to get out of the city while we still have the means, and hope FEMA resupplies us."

"But we don't really have to defend it all, sir," Sergeant Josh Wright countered. "It's ten feet high topped with razor wire, so we just have to control the gates and patrol the rest, while we use the containers to build an interior strong point if we need to fall back. If the Coasties move up and join us like Chief Kinsey and I discussed," he added, warming to the argument, "we'll have our back to the river and they'll be protecting that. Besides, I'd rather take a chance on whatever is in these containers than FEMA. There must be a thousand containers here, and there's BOUND to be some food in some of them."

"You don't know WHAT'S in those containers, Sergeant," the major countered, "and we don't have the manpower to start a treasure hunt. And as far as moving the containers, we don't even know if any of the equipment in the terminal is operable or if we have anyone who can operate it even if it—"

"Sorry to interrupt, Major," Hughes said, "but there are at least SEVERAL thousand containers in the terminal, and I suspect the sergeant's right about the food. The US imports a lot, and it just makes sense some percentage of these boxes contain canned goods." The major glared at him for interrupting and was about to cut him off when Hughes raised a hand. "But we'll know soon enough. Our Coast Guard friends here were kind enough to ferry our third mate to the terminal. She's sailed container ships and she'll search the terminal offices for cargo manifests. We should know pretty quickly what's in each box and exactly where it's located in the terminal. There won't be any need for a treasure hunt."

Hunnicutt sighed and settled back in his chair, then looked back and forth between Hughes and Wright. "Even presuming we identify useful resources, what you're suggesting is looting, the prevention of which is one of our primary missions. The contents of those containers doesn't belong to us, and I have no authority to appropriate private property. My orders are to prevent looting with any force necessary."

The room fell silent for a long moment until Dan Gowan spoke from Hughes' right.

"How's that 'looting prevention' thing working out for you?"

Hunnicutt glared at the chief engineer and was about to reply when Hughes cut him off.

"Look, Major," Hughes said. "I understand your position, but when did you last receive any orders you have even a remote chance of successfully executing?"

Hunnicutt shifted uncomfortably in his chair. "I haven't gotten any orders that made sense since this whole fiasco started"—his face hardened—"but that doesn't mean we should quit trying to execute our—"

"*Pecos Trader* , *Pecos Trader* , this is Tex. Do you copy?" squawked Georgia Howell's radio.

"We copy, Tex," Georgia said into her own unit. "Find anything?"

"The mother lode," came the reply, "but you really need to see this for yourself. I'm on the way back, be there in ten. Tex out."

***

Fifteen minutes later, the group watched impatiently while Georgia Howell leafed quickly through a thick stack of paper brought in by Shyla Texeira, the third mate. Tex retreated to the corner and leaned against the bulkhead, her arms crossed as she waited and watched.

"Dammit, Mate," Hughes said, when Howell was about a third of the way through the thick stack, "what's the deal?"

"Oh, sorry," said Howell, looking up. "There's tons of stuff here. I'm only scanning for food, but so far I'd guess at least a hundred containers, maybe more. Canned seafood of all sorts, pine nuts, water chestnuts and other Asian veggies… it's just… a lot," she finished, unable to articulate the sheer magnitude of their discovery.

Hughes looked at Hunnicutt. "Well, Major, there's obviously food here. What now?"

Hunnicutt nodded. "Under those circumstances, I suppose it does make sense to secure this area as our new base of operations. We'll use what we need to sustain ourselves and distribute food to the civilian population until FEMA can get its act together and the power is restored—"

"The power's not coming back, at least not for a long time. Maybe never."

Everyone turned to where Levi sat, looking nervous at the sudden attention.

"And how do you figure that?" the major asked, then looked back and forth between Levi and Hughes. "And who the hell are you, exactly? I can understand the role of everyone else here, but I can't quite figure out what qualifies you to be in this meeting."

Levi opened his mouth to respond, but Hughes beat him to it.

"Mr. Jenkins is a trusted member of my crew," Hughes said. "And of all the people here, he's the only one who's been consistently right about what to expect since this whole mess began." He paused. "So to answer your question, Major, he's likely the only guy in this room with a clue, so my advice is to listen to him. Go ahead, Levi."

Levi hesitated, looking back and forth between Hughes and Hunnicutt. He took a deep breath and started to speak.

"I'm no expert," he said, "but I've been reading about this stuff a long time. Solar storms are sometimes accompanied by coronal mass ejections, or CMEs for short, which generate power spikes in the electrical distribution grid. In this case, we've been hit by multiple CMEs. The way I understand it, the long transmission lines act like antennas to collect power, and it pretty much burns out anything connected to them, specifically the big transformers. Those transformers are big and expensive, and there are minimal spares. If the solar storm smoked even ten or twenty percent of those big transformers, power could be down for months or even years.

"So ask yourself, where are they going to get those spares if there's no power to the plants that make them? And supposing they did miraculously get spares, who's going to install them? It's not like a hurricane, where linemen from Maine or Nebraska or Washington State roll in to help out. This disaster is everywhere, and even supposing there was enough fuel in the right places to get repair crews on the road, all those linemen are trying to make sure their own families don't starve. No one is going to voluntarily leave their family in danger or their own community in the dark to go help restore power somewhere else."

Levi shook his head again. "It took a century for electrical distribution to reach the stage it's at now, or was a week ago anyway, and right now, we're back to 1900. I think the power grid's down for the count, and the quicker everyone accepts that, the better off they'll be. Waiting for the lights to come on is right up there with waiting for Santa Claus, in my opinion."

The room fell silent.

"That's a pretty grim assessment," Hunnicutt said at last, "and with all due respect, I'm not particularly inclined to base my actions on the theory of some random seaman. But supposing for the sake of argument you're correct, what do you propose?"

Levi shrugged. "We all saw those transformers exploding like a string of firecrackers, and we all saw the Northern Lights, so believe what you want, Major," he said. "And I'm not proposing anything, because all this is way above my pay grade. I'm going to take care of me and mine, and that's all I can really do. I just want y'all to go into things with your eyes open, that's all."

Mike Butler spoke for the first time, nodding at Levi, "I just met most of the people in this room an hour ago, Major, but for my money, this guy makes more sense than anything else I've heard since this whole mess started. The way I look at it, we've got nothing to lose by assuming he's right and acting accordingly, as in 'plan for the worst, hope for the best.' And speaking for the Coast Guard, we don't have enough people to maintain a presence down at Oak Island and one here to guard what is apparently our only source of supply, so I'm moving my people and their dependents up here and forting up somehow, whatever you decide to do. There's more than enough here to last us, all of us, for the foreseeable future, no matter what happens."

"Don't think all these goodies y'all found are going to last forever," Levi interrupted, "not the fuel in this ship and the terminal tanks, or the food in the containers. All of it has a shelf life."

"He's right about the fuel at least," Dan Gowan added. "This gas and diesel will last a year or two without stabilizer before it starts degrading, and there isn't any way you're going to come up with enough additive to stabilize it all. It will be useless in three years at the outside." He shrugged. "I don't know about the canned food, but I doubt it would last much longer."

"I can't speak for anyone else," Georgia Howell said, "but I'm not particularly thrilled about eating anything processed in China anyway, even if it was canned last week."

Laughter rippled through the group, easing the tension somewhat.

"All right," Hunnicutt said. "I'm not sold on this, but it does seem to be the only sensible plan at the moment." He turned to the lieutenant beside him. "Lieutenant Arnold, set up a guard rotation for the gates both here at the oil terminal and also for the container terminal next door. One Humvee with a fifty caliber and two troops at each gate at all times. Knock a hole in the fence between the two terminals and keep two extra men and one of the civilian vehicles as a reserve force to support either location or respond to threats elsewhere on the perimeter. There are no apparent threats for the moment, so we'll forgo full perimeter patrols until we get everyone inside and some sort of routine established. Also set up a schedule to ferry our troops and civilians here. I'd like everyone inside and things buttoned up by"—he looked at his wristwatch—"twenty-two hundred."

Arnold nodded. "Yes, sir, but that's pretty quick. There'll be some bitching from the civilians."

"Let 'em bitch all they want, but make sure they understand we're moving, and if they want to move with us and be protected during the move, they better be ready. If not, they get left behind and make their way here the best they can."

"Yes, sir," Lieutenant Arnold said, and Hunnicutt turned to Sergeant Wright. "Sergeant, since this was all your idea, I suggest you start looking at the office buildings in both terminals and figure out how we're going to turn them into accommodations." He looked over at Mike Butler. "And since we're sharing space with the Coast Guard, I suspect you need to coordinate with Chief Butler here."

"Yes, sir," Wright said, "about that. It's going to be pretty tight. However, there's that RV dealership down Carolina Beach Boulevard. I bet there are a hundred RVs and trailers just sitting there, and a lot of them even have their own generators. Since fuel's no longer a problem, I think they could be real useful."

Hunnicutt glared at him momentarily and then sighed.

"What the hell. I guess if we're going to be looters, we may as well be thorough," Hunnicutt said. "Take what you need from wherever you find it, under one iron-clad condition. Under no circumstances are you to take anything occupied or actively claimed by civilians, even if you suspect they may have acquired it by less than legal means. We're not in the confiscation business. All those poor bastards out there are having it hard enough without us adding to it. Are we clear on that?"

"Crystal, sir," Wright said.

"There is one more thing we need to discuss," Mike Butler interjected. "We haven't talked about water. We've still got water at Oak Island, but I suspect that's only because there's a pretty big water tower for a fairly small population. However, we checked the buildings in the terminal and it looks like everything is drained here in Wilmington. I suppose we can boil and filter river water if we have to, but it will take some time to jury-rig some means of filtering and sterilizing water on a sizable scale." He looked at Hunnicutt. "Y'all have any water to spare?"

Hunnicutt looked at Wright, who shook his head. "A week or ten days drinking water for our own group. I don't know—"

"I think we can help you out there," Hughes said, nodding toward Dan Gowan. "How about it, Chief? Can we spot our friends here some water?"

"Sure," Gowan said. "We came in almost full, and I'll be able to make some more on the way down to Texas. I could probably let you have two hundred tons with no problem."

"Ahh... how much is that in gallons?" Wright asked.

"A bit more than fifty thousand," Gowan said, "though I don't know where you're going to put it all."

"Don't worry about that," Wright said. "You pump it and we'll find a place to put it."

CHAPTER NINE

Day 10, 4:00 p.m.

Gowan leaned his elbows on the ship's rail and squirted tobacco juice into the void between the ship's side and the dock.

"Damned if he didn't do it," Gowan said, watching a mixed group of North Carolina National Guardsmen and US Coast Guardsmen wrestle a heavy hose into an aboveground swimming pool erected on the dock near the stern of *Pecos Trader* . Two identical filled swimming pools rested in line with the pool currently filling, covers in place to protect the precious drinking water. Two Coasties were adding a fourth pool to the line, erecting it rapidly with a practiced ease gained from assembly of the first units.

"Sergeant Wright is nothing if not resourceful," Hughes said. "Will he be able to take the whole two hundred tons?"

"He found a whole damned container full of those pools," Gowan said, "and he wants to erect two more. That'll give him capacity for almost two hundred and fifty tons, and I've a mind to give him the extra if you have no objection, Cap? I can distill almost that much on our southbound passage, and these guys are going to have their plate pretty full without having to immediately solve the water problem. Besides, it's not like we're not making out on the deal."

Hughes nodded and looked down the deck where the bosun was sitting in the cab of the hose-handling crane, watching Georgia Howell at the ship's side and waiting for her hand signals to lift a load aboard. On the dock below the dangling crane hook, two sailors were rigging a twenty-foot container for lifting. Other partially filled twenty footers stood open on the dock nearby, across from several open and densely packed forty-foot containers. Chief Cook Jake Kadowski, aka 'Polak,' scurried between them all, directing sailors from the deck and steward's departments in transferring stores from the forty-footers and stuffing the twenty footers with the most useful provisions.

They'd found the empty twenty-foot containers in the terminal, a fortunate find since they could be handled with the limited capacity and reach of the ship's hose-handling crane. Hughes was hoping to get six or even eight of the smaller containers aboard. Far more food than they could conceivably use, but in the new world in which they found themselves, something told him there was no such thing as too much food.

"That was good thinking on shifting over to this dock, by the way," Gowan said. "We had the main engine all set to go, but I'm glad we didn't need it."

Hughes grinned. "The first law of wing-walking. Never let go of one handhold until you have a firm grasp on another."

When they'd decided to move upstream the short distance to the container terminal, the Coasties helped them out by running a mooring line over to the container dock with one of their patrol boats, and a long line of National Guardsmen had taken the end and heaved the massive rope up on the dock and put the eye on one of the mooring bits. Hughes had pulled the ship forward by heaving in on the line with the ship's mooring winch, keeping the bow off the container dock during the approach by using his bow thruster. He'd made the move 'dead ship' without using the ship's main engine.

"And speaking of shifting," Gowan said, "when do you think we'll get out of here?"

"Tomorrow maybe, the day after at the outside," Hughes said. "Later than I wanted, but worth the delay, considering how much better off we'll be when we leave."

Hughes looked out over the bustling terminal, the National Guardsmen had moved in camping trailers and RVs parked in neat rows, and elsewhere erected large tents to serve as field kitchens and a mess tent. Several container transporters worked feverishly, rearranging those containers identified as having food to where they were all at ground level and accessible.

"It's amazing how much has been accomplished in twenty-four hours," Hughes said.

"Thanks to Tex for a lot of that," Gowan said, nodding down to the dock where the slender third mate held a clipboard and was now conferring with the chief cook. "Bringing in the terminal guys was frigging brilliant."

"That it was," Hughes said, smiling at the memory of Tex speaking up just before yesterday's meeting broke up, pointing out she'd found the contact list with the names and addresses of terminal personnel when she was searching for the cargo manifests, and that all those terminal employees were likely 'scared shitless' just like everyone else. Everyone had shrugged, until she suggested those with homes within easy reach of Major Hunnicutt's Humvees would likely be amenable to joining the group with their families, trading food and shelter for their knowledge of, you know, how all this stuff actually worked. Everyone jumped at the idea, and she'd further pointed out there was probably a similar list in the offices of the product terminal. A quick search proved her correct.

So Major Hunnicutt had 're-tasked some assets,' and by the following morning the little group of Coasties, National Guardsmen, and assorted civilians was joined by nine container terminal employees and two product terminal employees, with their families, five dogs, three cats, and a goldfish. Major Hunnicutt had a rather loud discussion with Sergeant Wright concerning the arrival of the pets, whereupon Sergeant Wright suggested perhaps the major might like to explain to the various children why their pets were being abandoned. The major dropped the subject. The point soon became moot in any event, as before the day was out, one of the cats ate the goldfish, then ran off along with both the other cats, and everyone liked the dogs.

"How about Levi?" Gowan asked. "You think he's going to stay with these folks? I'm sure they could use him."

Hughes looked across the deck where Levi and his father-in-law, Anthony, stood examining their aluminum boat.

He shrugged. "I know Chief Butler and Sergeant Wright are trying to talk him into bringing his family in, though I think Major Hunnicutt's not a big Levi fan just yet. However, Levi's gonna do what he thinks is best for him and his family, and you can't blame him."

***

"A hundred things can happen," Anthony McCoy said, "and ninety-nine of them are bad. I'm for keeping our distance."

Levi nodded. "I feel the same, but what if these folks do make a go of it? We wouldn't be so isolated and Celia and Jo and the kids would be part of a community. There's something to be said for that." He paused. "And besides, we don't have to worry about being the only black folks in the group. Between the Coasties and the National Guard and their families, it looks like almost a third of the group is black."

"I'll grant you it's tempting," Anthony said, "and it looks like food won't be a problem for a while anyway, but they're not exactly low profile, and guns or not, I reckon someone, or a lot of someones, is gonna take a shot at taking what they have. Our whole idea was to be invisible, and they're just the opposite."

"I know, I know," Levi said, then fell silent.

"All right, boy, what's eatin' you? Seems like this is bothering you way more than it should."

"It's just there are a lot of things they haven't considered," Levi said. "I mean, they just can't go handing out food without a plan. Yes, they need to help folks because a lot of stuff is likely to go bad before they can eat it anyway, but if they set up a feeding station, it needs to be some distance away or else they'll have a huge refugee camp right on their doorstep. And all those folks attracted by the food are going to be a sanitation nightmare, completely aside from the fact the folks here in the terminal haven't even considered the sanitation issue for their OWN group. And what about water? *Pecos Trader* probably left them enough for three months, but by then, they need to have some sort—"

"And you think you're gonna solve all the problems for them, huh?" Anthony asked. "All these folks looking up to the great Levi after you been hearing folks giggle up their sleeves about your 'prepper ways' all this time. Think maybe there might be a little bit of ego involved here, Levi?"

Levi bristled and started to reply; then he relaxed and nodded. "Yeah, maybe a little."

"Understandable," Anthony said, "but you can't let that get in the way of taking care of the family."

"I won't, but I do think I could help these people."

"I think you could too," Anthony said, "but how about this. We help them on a 'commuter' basis. We can stay in our hidey-hole but keep in touch with them on a regular basis by radio. If we use the Brunswick, we can get here fairly quickly and avoid passing through Wilmington. When we learn all the cutoffs and shortcuts, I think it might be not much more than an hour's run with the outboard. You come down here and help them out a couple of days a week, and maybe get paid in food. When hunting's good, we can also bring them in deer and pigs to trade. If everything seems to be safe, we can bring the family in maybe once every couple of weeks, just like farm families went to town in the old days. Difference is, we don't let NOBODY know where our home place is.

"In time," Anthony continued, "we may even decide it's safe enough to move into the group, but we ALWAYS keep our bug-out place stocked and ready, so we can take off if need be. How's that sound?"

"Sounds like a plan," Levi said.

CHAPTER TEN

M/V *Pecos Trader*
Starboard Bridge Wing
Wilmington Container Terminal

Day 11, 2:00 p.m.

Hughes paced the bridge wing and stared down at the main deck, where his crewmen and their new Coast Guard shipmates swarmed over the containers, securing them for sea under the watchful eye of Georgia Howell. Despite his nervousness, he had to suppress a smile when he saw Polak approaching her, arms waving. The chief cook was known for his excitability, and 'getting Polak spun up' was a favorite pastime among the unlicensed crew. Hughes heard a footstep on the deck behind him and turned to find Matt Kinsey standing there, a sympathetic look on his face.

"Nervous, Cap?" he asked.

Hughes sighed and ran a hand through his hair. "As a whore in church," he admitted. "I've practically memorized the damn chart, but I don't mind telling you I'm terrified. I never thought I'd make my debut as a harbor pilot taking a fully loaded tanker downstream with no tugs and a following current. I'm beginning to wonder if this is such a good idea."

"Well, at least you're timing the tide right. Besides," Kinsey said, "it's either this or stay here, right?"

Hughes nodded and was about to reply when his radio squawked.

"Mate to bridge. Over," came Georgia Howell's voice over the radio.

"Bridge, go ahead, Georgia," Hughes replied.

"Captain, Polak says one of the twenties he had marked didn't get loaded aboard—"

"What the hell is he talking about? He supervised the stuffing of those containers himself," Hughes demanded, and then belatedly added, "Over."

"This was a twenty he found on the inventory that didn't need re-stuffing," Georgia replied, "but I guess the terminal guys got overwhelmed and didn't bring it to the dock. He wants to hold up until we can get—"

"Absolutely not," Hughes said. "We have to leave here within the hour to hit the Battery Island turn at full flood tide, and it's going to be hairy enough at that. Nothing is important enough to delay that, so tell Polak to suck it up and figure something out. He's got eight containers full of extra food. Over."

Hughes turned back and looked over the wind dodger as he spoke, gazing down to where Polak was standing in front of Georgia Howell, arms waving. He saw the mate raise the microphone to her mouth again.

"Uh, Captain," said Howell, "Polak says it's not food. Over."

"Okay, what's so critical we can't live without it?"

"Uh, toilet paper," came the reply.

Hughes cursed under his breath. He heard a strangling sound behind him and turned to see Kinsey struggling unsuccessfully to keep from laughing. He snarled into his radio.

"You tell Polak to get his ass ashore and organize getting that container alongside. This vessel is leaving the dock in forty-five minutes and not one minute later, container or no container. Is that clear? Over."

"Yes sir," Howell replied, and Hughes saw her speak to Polak, who then raced for the gangway.

"Toilet paper!" Hughes muttered as he resumed pacing the bridge wing.

M/V *PECOS TRADER*
BRIDGE
WILMINGTON CONTAINER TERMINAL

DAY 11, 2:40 P.M.

"You okay down there, Dan?" Hughes asked into the telephone.

"Ready as we'll ever be," Gowan replied, adding after a short pause, "Don't worry Jordan, you can do this."

"Your lips to God's ear, friend," Hughes said. "Should be any time now."

Hughes hung up and turned as Levi Jenkins and the other three departing crewmen came through the stairwell door. He smiled and nodded.

"Looks like this is it, folks," Hughes said. "I'm sorry to lose you all, but I understand your decisions, and wish you all good luck and Godspeed getting back to your families."

"Same to you, Captain," Levi said, extending his hand.

Hughes shook first Levi's hand, then Bill Wiggins, the departing second engineer's. He turned to Singletary, but before he extended his hand, the man gave him a curt nod and Hughes didn't press it. When he turned to Shyla Texiera, she brushed his hand aside and took him off guard by folding him in a fierce hug before stepping back, her eyes glistening.

"Captain, if it wasn't for my folks—"

He held up a hand to stop her. "We know that, Tex. We're going to miss you, but no one faults you for leaving." He included them all with his glance. "Any of you. Family comes first."

Levi pulled a folded piece of paper from his pocket and handed it over. "I don't know what's going to happen, Captain, but here are radio frequencies I'll be monitoring and the days and times I'll be listening if you ever want to establish contact. I'd like to keep in touch if we can."

"As would I, Levi," Hughes said and slipped the paper into his pocket.

The group stood quietly for a few moments until Hughes broke the awkward silence.

He smiled sadly. "Well, folks, all ashore that's going ashore. Otherwise you'll be taking a trip downriver."

With more murmured goodbyes, the group turned for the stairwell door, and when the last one was through it, Hughes took a brief moment to compose himself and then moved forward to gaze out the wide wheelhouse windows as the last container dropped into place on deck under the watchful eye of the mate. He called her on his radio and saw her raise her own mike to her mouth.

"Bridge, this is the mate. Over."

"Georgia," Hughes said, "our departing folks are headed ashore. Please take the gangway in as soon as they're off. Leave the Coasties to secure the last container and gangway, and have our deck gang turn to fore and aft. I want you and Boats on the bow during transit and both anchors backed out ready to drop if necessary. Attend to that first and let me know when you're done, please. Then stand by to single up lines on my order. Over."

"Understood, Captain," she replied, looking back up at the bridge window. "I'll let you know when we're ready. Mate out."

Hughes nodded, and he saw her head bob in an answering nod far below.

111

"Just a suggestion, but you might want to have her rig the pilot ladder on the offshore side," said a voice behind him.

He whirled to see Kinsey standing there grinning.

"What the hell are you talking about?"

Kinsey's grin widened and he jerked his head toward the port bridge wing and started that way, a confused Hughes on his heels. When they got to the bridge wing, Kinsey pointed downstream to where one of the smaller Coast Guard patrol boats was approaching at top speed, with three people aboard.

"So? Who are those people?" Hughes asked.

"Well, two of them are Coasties," Kinsey said, "but the third, well, the third is Captain Randall Ewing, retired Wilmington harbor pilot and fishing buddy of my good friend Chief Butler. Mike convinced him, via some inducement that shall remain confidential, to come out of retirement for one last transit."

"What? Why the hell didn't you tell me, Goddamn it!" Hughes demanded. "I've been sweating bullets here."

"Because Mike didn't even know if Captain Ewing was still at his house on the river, and we couldn't spare the guys to go look until this morning." Kinsey paused. "We've been sort of busy if you'll recall?"

Hughes nodded, unable to speak.

"Anyway, we didn't even want to mention the possibility until we were sure it was going to happen, as we figured you were pretty stressed as it was, and it might really screw with your head if you thought you might get a pilot and then found out it wasn't happening at the last minute. Mike called me about ten minutes ago and said they were headed upriver." Kinsey grinned again. "So like I said, we better get the pilot ladder rigged."

"Kinsey, I could kiss you!" Hughes said.

The Coastie took a step back. "I'd just as soon you didn't, if it's all the same to you."

DAY 11, 5:00 P.M.

Captain Randall Ewing glanced ahead to starboard, squinting in the bright sunlight at a substantial concrete wharf along the western riverbank.

"That's the northern wharf of the Military Ocean Terminal," he said, nodding toward the riverbank, "and this is where things start getting a bit tricky. The channel narrows from six hundred to four hundred feet soon, and the current picks up quite a bit, even on the incoming tide."

Hughes only nodded, a tight-lipped frown on his face.

Randall Ewing's eyes never left the river, but a slight smile tugged at the corners of his mouth.

"You can relax at least a little, Captain Hughes," Ewing said. "This isn't my first transit, or even my first transit without tugs. I'll get you to the sea buoy all right."

"Sorry. Is it that obvious?"

Ewing chuckled. "You're as nervous as a nine-tailed cat in a room full of rocking chairs, and I suspect your fingerprints are probably permanently pressed into that rail."

Hughes laughed, the tension easing a bit. "Well, I'd be a hell of a lot more nervous if you hadn't turned up, I can tell you that. I'll bet you didn't figure you'd be coming out of retirement like this."

Ewing shrugged, eyes still on the river. "Didn't figure on coming out of retirement at all. I've got a nice place along the river and I was happy as a clam—until the power went out, anyway."

"What are you going to do now?" Hughes asked.

"Survive, I guess," Ewing responded. "We don't have it too bad, at least compared to most folks. I've got a nice place on the river, up in a little cove, actually, secluded like. Our two kids and grandkids made it there, so at least the immediate family's okay, and that's a blessing. We're on a well and have a septic system, and there's also an older well on the place with a hand pump. I kept it as a curiosity, really—our kids and then our grandkids liked to pump the handle and watch the water come out. Damn glad I got it now. My wife's always been into gardening and canning, so we're pretty well stocked up for a while." He smiled. "And it looks like we'll be eating a lot of fish.

"And as far as power goes," he continued, "I got a small generator after the last hurricane scare, and the Coasties"—he nodded to starboard where the Coast Guard patrol boat was moving along with the ship—"are hooking me up with some of those solar panels of theirs. That was my pilotage fee for getting you out of here."

"Cheap at several times the price," Hughes said.

Ewing grinned. "Glad you feel that way, because I'm looking for a little contribution from you too. How about a case of coffee? We can't grow that."

"Done," Hughes said.

Conversation lapsed as they both studied the river ahead, the silence broken only by occasional helm orders from Ewing. Then the pilot walked out to the bridge wing to study the bank a bit more intently and returned to the wheelhouse.

"Okay," Ewing said, "it's going to get a bit hairier from this point on. In half an hour we'll be going into Battery Island Turn, which means a ninety-five-degree turn to port, and I have to keep enough speed on her to maintain steerage way or the current will set us hard into the bank."

Half an hour later, Matt Kinsey stepped on to the bridge to find Fort Caswell to starboard as *Pecos Trader* cleared the channel, her bow pointed toward the open sea.

"Thank God," he heard Hughes say as Captain Ewing nodded in obvious agreement.

Kinsey looked toward the open sea and his mouth dropped open. Spread out in the nearby anchorage were a dozen ships of various sizes and types. "Damn, would you look at that," he said.

"Make's sense," Ewing said. "The port's been closed, what, eleven days now. It was unusually empty when the blackout hit, but there had to be inbound traffic, and here it is."

"Tanker outbound, tanker outbound," the radio squawked, "do you have a pilot aboard? This is the container vessel *Maersk Tangier* . We urgently require a pilot—"

"Tanker outbound, tanker outbound, any pilot aboard tanker outbound. This is the container vessel *Hanjin Wilmington* ," broke in a Korean-accented voice. "We at anchor and I claim priority—"

"US Coast Guard vessel with outbound tanker," said a Greek-accented voice, "this is the bulk carrier *Sabrina* , inbound with thirty thousand metric tons of wheat. I have a fuel emergency with less than twenty-four hours of fuel remaining. I must proceed to berth or have a bunker barge immediately."

The chaotic calls increased as more of the ships at anchor spotted the outbound tanker and pressed their claims for attention. Hughes reached over to turn down the volume on the VHF radio, then shook his head in amazement.

Wheels turned in Kinsey's head.

"What do you think about that?" Hughes asked.

"I think," Kinsey said, turning toward Ewing, "Captain Ewing here just started the first successful 'post blackout' small business, and Chief Butler and Major Hunnicutt just got several shiploads full of early Christmas presents. We just have to sort out what's waiting out here and pass the word back so they can tell Captain Ewing here what they want first, and where. You okay with that Captain Ewing?"

The old pilot shrugged. "I don't know what's in the containers, but I see another tanker and also at least two bulkers, and they're likely full of grain. I can't see leaving stuff out here that might feed or otherwise help people. It'll take a few days, 'cause we can only do daylight transits, but with the Coasties help, I can likely find at least a couple of other pilots. We can probably get all this stuff inside in a week or so." He paused. "Thing is, I expect at least a few more ships will show up, especially northbound grain cargoes from South America, as they're normally two weeks or more in transit."

Hughes nodded. "Well, we'll leave that for you and the guys in Wilmington to figure out."

Ewing returned his nod as a slow smile spread over his face.

"What are you grinning about, Captain?" Kinsey asked.

"Just realizing I won't be running out of coffee anytime soon," Ewing replied.

An hour later, after a rough assessment of the ships at anchor and a radio exchange with Wilmington, Kinsey and Hughes stood on the bridge wing and watched the Coast Guard patrol boat pull away from the ship's side, bound for the Greek bulk carrier *Sabrina* .

"Distributing raw grain is going to be challenging," Hughes said.

"They'll figure something out," Kinsey said, "and it's a lot better problem to have than trying to figure out how you're going to survive with nothing."

Hughes nodded, seemingly distracted.

"Why so glum?" Kinsey asked. "The river transit's behind us and we're ready to head south."

"Just thinking ahead," Hughes said, "because when we get to Texas, we're going to be the one's out at the mouth of the river with no pilot."

MAYPORT NAVAL STATION
JACKSONVILLE, FLORIDA

DAY 11, 1:00 P.M.

Sergeant Joel Washington squinted against the midday sun and looked out across the growing ranks of temporary shelters rapidly transforming the former golf course into a sizable town. Mayport had been tight on housing anyway, and with families of the shipboard sailors now required to live within the base perimeter—also in temporary shelters—there'd been no choice but to expand the base, and the adjacent country club had been the logical choice. They'd set up portable toilets and shower facilities as well, with a pump providing salt water from the inlet in unlimited quantities anytime but with a three-minute fresh water rinse available twice a week. Most of the members of the newly formed Special Reaction Force preferred to combine the two, so twice weekly showers had become the norm. Combined with the heat and humidity of north Florida and the increasing stench of the portable toilets, personal hygiene (or lack thereof) contributed greatly to the growing 'ambiance' of the camp.

Washington flicked a bead of sweat off his forehead. It didn't help that the new black uniforms could double as solar collectors, and he wondered for the hundredth time what genius had decided black was a good color for operations in the southern US in the summer, or anytime for that matter? Then again he strongly suspected the color was chosen to intimidate rather than conceal, for despite the recruitment pitch about 'serving the nation in time of crisis,' there was growing awareness among the newly recruited that the SRF were meant to be shock troops—insurance against civil unrest. The recent word the assignment was permanent rather than temporary as promised hadn't been well-received among the 'volunteers,' but no one had chosen the 'honorable discharge' option, or at least any 'takers' had been removed quietly. The consequences of being disarmed and dropped into the growing refugee population, far from friends or former comrades, didn't bear thinking about.

He heard distant whoops and laughter and turned toward a yet to be developed area of the golf course, where several men had stripped to their skivvies and were using one of the former water hazards as a swimming hole. That was technically against standing orders, but discipline was considerably more relaxed in the SRF than it ever was in the 101st Airborne and he was quickly learning to pick his battles. Maybe an alligator would eat their asses, he thought, and turned a blind eye to the swimming hole before he ducked into a shelter. He stood in the comparative gloom, waiting for his eyes to adjust. Corporal Neal Long was bitching as usual.

"I been eatin' this garbage five days now, and I haven't had a decent crap in three," Long said, staring down morosely at the contents of an MRE spread before him.

"Meals-refusal-to-exit, dude," said the man seated next to Long, with a shake of his head, "and it ain't gonna get any better unless you can score a few of those chili mac meals. Those things will set you free."

"And they distribute them like one in ten or twelve and every swinging dick in this camp is gonna hoard them, Gibson, so the 'chili mac exit strategy' isn't exactly a workable solution. And besides," Long said, "this is bullshit. In a camp this size there should be a kitchen and dining tent. Even you jarheads are that civilized."

Gibson shook his head. "When I left Lejeune, they were already running out of regular chow and switching to MREs, and it's the same thing here. I talked to some of the fleet Marines on the ships here and they told me the same story. Only difference is the galley squids heat up all the packages at once and set 'em out for the guys to grab when they go through the chow line."

"And you should be glad you have it, Long," Washington said from his spot near the entrance, "so quit your bitching. There are a lot of folks out there going hungry."

Long sighed and looked back down at the food packets. "I know, Sergeant, but some of this stuff is just nasty."

"Washington's right," said Grogan from where he sat on the opposite side of the shelter. "Save all the nasty stuff. Just give it a couple of more weeks for reality to set in good and you'll be able to trade it for all the 'fugee pussy you want." He grinned at the men on either side of him. "Ain't that right, boys?"

Washington crossed the floor to loom over Grogan and glared down at him.

"That's SERGEANT Washington, Grogan, and leaving aside how despicable that statement was, you seem to forget there's a 'no fraternization' policy in effect. You stay the hell away from civilians except in the line of duty. You got that?"

Grogan rose to his feet and looked Washington in the eye with an expression just short of a sneer. "Well, 'Sergeant,' I believe if you'll check, you'll find that 'no frat' rule is for regular troops, not us. And since the only pay we're likely to get in this wonderful new world is a place to bunk and these crappy MREs, I reckon we have to take our fringe benefits where we find them. And FYI, 'Sergeant,' me and the boys here"—he nodded at his two companions—"have been with Rorke through a lot of shit shows, and I can tell you from experience he don't sweat the small shit as long as it keeps the troops happy."

"Yeah, well, you take orders from me now, and I take mine from Lieutenant Kinsey, so you better get used to it," Washington said.

"And you better tell that prick Kinsey to lighten up," Grogan said, "or someone might roll a surprise into his quarters some dark night."

Washington's face hardened and he shoved his nose an inch from Grogan's.

"Did I just hear you threaten an officer in front of witnesses, Grogan?"

Grogan shrugged. "Just sayin' we live in dangerous times," He grinned. "But if you'd like to bring me up on charges, go ahead. I'm pretty sure I know how that would play out."

Washington stood dumbstruck by the blatant insubordination, and Grogan took a step back and moved toward the shelter exit.

"Come on, boys," Grogan said to his two companions, "let's go take a swim."

QUARTERS OF CAPTAIN QUENTIN RORKE
MAYPORT NAVAL STATION
JACKSONVILLE, FLORIDA

DAY 11, 9:00 P.M.

First Lieutenant Luke Kinsey closed his eyes and sighed as the breeze from the room air conditioner washed over him, then opened them to look at the remains of what was the best meal he'd eaten in a week—or maybe ever—spread out on the table in the flickering light of half a dozen candles.

"That was a fantastic meal, thank you, Maria," he said, as across from him, Maria Velasquez beamed at the compliment. As always, she looked as if she were about to step in front of a camera, and Luke marveled at her ability to maintain her appearance in the chaotic hell the world was becoming.

Beside Maria, Rorke reached over and covered her hand with his on the white linen tablecloth. "My Maria is a woman of varied and remarkable talents," he said, and Maria's smile widened.

"And," Rorke said, as he grinned and disengaged his hand to top off Luke's wineglass, "notwithstanding Maria's outstanding culinary talents, I suspect the air-conditioning added to our enjoyment."

"How'd you manage that, by the way? Friends in high places?" Luke asked.

Rorke laughed. "Or low places. There are two units, actually, and they were already here when we moved in, one in each bedroom. We just relocated the one in the second bedroom here to the living/dining room area. The generator's big enough to run one of them at a time and still keep the refrigerator cool, as long as we opt for candlelight."

"Which is more romantic anyway," Maria added, leaning over to nibble on Rorke's ear.

Rorke turned his face toward Maria's for a light kiss, then turned back to Luke.

"An unanticipated benefit of taking over navy enlisted quarters. We have AC and the regular officer's housing with big central units don't," Rorke said. "I was also able to scrounge a big propane grill for the garage. We just crack the garage door when we're cooking."

"So these units were empty?"

Rorke shrugged. "Rank has its privileges, Kinsey. You know that. The enlisted dependents who lived here were relocated to the temporary structures closer to the docks. It's been decided Mayport's going to be the main SRF base for the Southeast, so things have to be restructured a bit. We'll need officer's quarters, and housing inside the wire is tight. These units are now designated as housing for captains and above, which brings me to why I asked you to dinner. One of them is yours if you want it."

Luke said nothing as Rorke gazed at him in the flickering light.

"I'm not a captain," Luke replied.

"You will be if I say so," Rorke said. "We're growing daily and will be at brigade strength within two weeks. I've been given the brigade and a promotion to lieutenant colonel." He smiled at Luke's expression. "Yeah, we're going to do things a little differently in the SRF. I'm skipping the whole 'major' thing.

"Anyway," Rorke continued, "I'll need company commanders. I want you to be one of them."

"Why me?"

"Because you're smart, and you follow orders, most of the time anyway. You have a natural leadership ability. So presuming I can make sure you understand the new realities, I think you'll be an asset," Rorke said.

"What new realities?" Luke asked.

"That it's not getting any better, ever, and in fact, it will get a whole lot worse," Rorke said. "That the only ones who will prosper, or even survive, are those strong enough to take what they need and defend what they take. People are beginning to see this as The End of the World as We Know It, but that's not quite correct. It may be the end as far as YOU knew it, or as most people knew it, but it's pretty much business as usual for me and the men who currently form a big part of this force. We've been soldiering in shit holes all over the world for a lot of years. Places where we make the rules. We made large sums of money and then came back to civilization to enjoy it, but it turns out that was all just a dress rehearsal for the real thing." He grinned. "I've been training for this my whole life, I just didn't know it."

"I don't know," Luke said, after a long pause. "I'm not sure I accept your 'realities,' and even if I do, I signed up to help people, not exploit them."

Rorke's face hardened. "But you did sign up, and as you've probably figured out by now, this is a bit like the French Foreign Legion, only your hitch is forever. The only way you get out is being stripped of weapons and dropped among the 'fugees to fend for yourself. And if you stay, I can not only promote you to captain, I can also bust you back to private. So it's up to you to decide what kind of life you want."

Rorke motioned to the remains of the meal as he continued. "Where do you think that chicken and the fresh vegetables and the tomatoes for the salad you just ate came from? And what about the wine, and the generator running that air conditioner, and the gasoline running it? I've had a dozen of my guys out scrounging from the beginning, and I don't care where they find stuff or who they take it from. They take a share and pass on half to me, no questions asked. Then as long as they follow my orders, I protect them, no matter what they do. And as long as I meet the objectives set out for the SRF, FEMA doesn't give a damn either."

Luke said nothing.

"Well, what's it gonna be, Kinsey? I only make an offer once, and there are plenty of people to take the job if you don't. So you don't get to ponder it or think on it or sleep on it. I want your answer now. In or out? Captain or private?"

Luke sighed. "I guess I'll go with captain."

Rorke's face split into a grin. "Excellent choice," he said, turning to Velasquez. "This calls for a celebration. Break out the good stuff."

She nodded and moved to a sideboard, bringing back a cut-crystal decanter full of amber liquid and three squat glasses, then poured an inch of whiskey into each glass and set them within reach.

"A toast," Rorke said, raising his glass, "to Captain Kinsey."

"To Captain Kinsey," Velasquez echoed, and raised her glass.

It was the first of many toasts—one of Luke's new duties was apparently to be Rorke's drinking buddy. The decanter was quickly drained and replaced by a full bottle of whiskey of equal pedigree. By the second hour, Rorke was starting to slur his words a bit and Velasquez was openly groping him beneath the table, as well as occasionally stretching her leg out to run her toes along Luke's calf. They were both outdrinking him two or three to one, but he was definitely feeling the alcohol.

"...couldn't believe they could be so frigging stupid," Rorke said. "I mean, it's like a mercenary leader's wet dream. FEMA collects all the trained single guys motivated enough to volunteer and then just gives them to me. I get to decide to keep them or not, and anyone I can't turn into a follower gets a one-way trip to 'Fugeeville, courtesy of FEMA Air. It's a brigade now, but I'll have a regiment in two months, and in a year, an army. I'll be unstoppable, and all I gotta do is make nice with FEMA while they build, equip and feed my army."

"So what then? You set up your own kingdom?" Luke asked. "The regular military is a thousand times stronger, and they have air power. They'll crush us like bugs if we desert or go rogue."

Rorke's face split into a drunken lopsided grin. "But, Captain Kinsey, why would we ever desert or go rogue? Perish the thought! We'll do everything our FEMA superiors task us with, and they'll continue to build and support our force. And in two years or so the gas will start going bad, and spare parts will be in short supply..." He stopped and looked at Luke as if sidetracked by a random thought.

"Do you know how many friggin' spare parts and maintenance people it takes to keep those jets and choppers flying, Kinsey?" Rorke asked, his slur becoming more pronounced.

Luke shook his head.

"Me neither," Rorke said, whiskey slopping from his glass as he took a drink. "But it's a load, Kinsey. A SHIT LOAD! In two years, three at the outside, there ain't gonna be any 'air power,' and in ten or fifteen years, we'll be transitioning to horseback for most of the force."

"We'll still be outnumbered by regular troops," Luke said.

Rorke snorted. "You think so? FEMA's terrified to use them to do the dirty work, so they keep them close to base. Just sitting there with their dependents, sucking up resources and getting stale and less capable as we siphon more and more troops from them. Sooner or later FEMA's gonna cut 'em off, and they'll just dissolve or 'go rogue' themselves. Then we'll be the government's only 'enforcers,' with no counterbalance." Rorke smiled, "And we'll see who really cares about 'accountability to civilian authorities' then. Here's a hint—it won't be me. Time is on our side, Kinsey, no matter how you slice it."

"A military coup, then?" Luke asked. "But what if the government's plan is successful, and FEMA does succeed in a partial restoration of power and gets food production going? Then they can keep supporting the regular forces and there WILL be a counterbalance. What then, civil war?"

Rorke shrugged. "They may have some partial success, but even if they do, so what? It's a big country, Kinsey, and even if they have some success, they won't have the resources to control it all without us. If we can't take over what they manage to build, we'll just leave and establish our own operation outside of their control. It's all about options. And as far as civil war goes, that's inevitable, isn't it? You don't seriously think I'm the only 'ex-private security contractor' in the SFR who's figured this out, do you?"

Luke didn't answer immediately, sobered by the implications of Rorke's drunken revelations.

"So you're saying the government and FEMA are essentially creating a whole bunch of warlords," Luke said at last, "and you figure sooner or later it's going to be rival warlords fighting over whatever is left."

Rorke nodded. "For want of a better term, yes. My plan is to grow faster than the rest by becoming FEMA's fair-haired boy. After all, I've already got my own public relations department." He gave Velasquez a lascivious grin and she melted against him for an open-mouthed kiss.

The pair broke from the kiss, and Rorke turned back to Luke.

"It's like this, Kinsey," Rorke said, reaching for his glass. "If you think things are screwed up now, wait a year or two. We'll be talking medieval Genghis Khan shit, and I plan on being on top of that pile, whatever it takes. Are you with me?"

Luke hesitated and then raised his glass toward Rorke in a toast. "All hail the Great Khan!"

Two hours later, Maria Velasquez lay in bed, propped up on an elbow as she pressed her naked body against Rorke and stroked his chest hair, watching her lover in the moonlight washing in from the window.

"Do you trust him?" she asked.

"Trust is relative, my sweet. No one is trustworthy unless their interests align with my own. In Kinsey's case, I'm trying to make that happen, because I need him, and men like him."

"Why not just promote Grogan or any of the others you already know and trust?"

Rorke laughed. "I don't TRUST Grogan or any of those other idiots any more than I would trust an attack dog. I've already promoted the few who possess any leadership skills at all, and the rest are just barbarians—blunt instruments I manage and control. They're useful enough on the front line, and fine for controlling and terrorizing helpless fools in some Third World backwater, but sooner or later we may have to confront disciplined opposition, and when that happens, I'll need an officer corps. No, I need Kinsey, and men with his skills."

"Still, it seems a risk," she said. "How can you be sure of him, or anyone?"

"By starting slow," he replied. "I'll make sure each unit is a mix of my longtime mercenaries and new recruits, and send them out on nearby 'foraging' missions. If Kinsey and others like him can rein in the barbarians a bit, I have no problem with that, but my thinking is the influence will be in the opposite direction. Moral standards decline in chaos, and power corrupts—in six months, any high ideals our new recruits may have held will be long gone, and any who haven't adapted will be obvious and can be 'honorably discharged' in accordance with the guidelines our FEMA friends have so thoughtfully provided."

"What if they just leave?"

"Ahh, but that's the beauty of it," he said. "They have nowhere to go, now do they? They're all far from any support network and the FEMA guidelines ensure no organized command still functioning will take them in. If they strike out on their own, they'll be branded rogues and deserters and cut off completely, without a continuing source of food and water, to say nothing of ammunition and fuel—unless they scavenge and steal from the civilian/refugee population. So, they're going to be 'takers' in any event, because there isn't any other way they can survive. The intelligent ones like Kinsey will realize that, whether they like it or not. As much as they may be repelled by the idea, they will also come to realize if they're going to be 'marauders,' doing so with 'official' sanction is the least objectionable option."

CHAPTER ELEVEN

Bridge of M/V Pecos Trader
Atlantic Ocean—Southbound
East of Mayport Naval Station
Jacksonville, Florida

Day 12, 11:00 a.m.

"Are you sure disabling the AIS was a good move?" asked Hughes, staring westward through the binoculars. "Won't it look kind of suspicious if anyone sees us and we aren't transmitting a signal?"

Hughes lowered the glasses and turned toward Kinsey, who stood beside him on the bridge wing. The Coastie shrugged. "Maybe. Maybe not. The solar storm did weird and unpredictable things, so knocking out your Automatic Identification System transmitter isn't that far-fetched. At least, it won't be dismissed as an immediate lie. Given our cargo, it's best to keep a low profile."

"You think the government would commandeer the ship?" Hughes asked.

Kinsey shrugged again. "Right now a tanker full of fuel will be mighty tempting. We might find ourselves drafted into becoming floating storage for the navy or FEMA. That may happen in Texas anyway, but at least we'll all be closer to home. We won't have a problem if we can just get past Jacksonville and Key West.

"Mayport Naval Station at Jacksonville is home port for more than a dozen navy ships, and I'm sure they can use the fuel. If they pick us up, we can probably expect a visit. But we're well offshore, so we have at least a shot at slipping past. I'm more worried about Coast Guard Station Key West. We'll have to come close inshore to transit the Florida Strait, and our cover story is a bit thin."

Kinsey had just finished speaking when they heard a familiar drone. They scanned the skies, searching for an approaching aircraft.

"And speaking of our navy friends at Jacksonville," Kinsey said, "apparently we aren't quite far enough offshore. I believe that will be them now."

"Will they board?" Hughes asked.

Kinsey shook his head. "Doubtful, at least for now. It's a fixed wing so they'll circle and take pictures, or maybe hail us and report back. If they're interested, they'll send a chopper for a closer look, but we're at extreme chopper range, so they won't be able to hang around. If they decide to board, we're screwed anyway."

Both men stared as the P-3 Orion dropped lower into a long looping orbit above the ship. On the third pass, the VHF squawked.

"Southbound tanker, southbound tanker, this is the US Navy aircraft over you. Do you copy? Over."

Hughes stepped inside and lifted the mike.

"US Navy, this is the tanker *Pecos Trader*. We copy, go ahead. Over."

"*Pecos Trader*, state your destination and cargo. Over."

"We are bound for Beaumont, Texas, under command and control of the US Coast Guard. I repeat our destination is Beaumont, Texas, and we are under command and control of the US Coast Guard. Do you copy? Over."

"*Pecos Trader*, we copy. What is your cargo? Over."

"Off specification diesel rejected by receiving facility to be pumped to slops and reclaimed. Over."

"*Pecos Trader*, say again. Over."

"Off spec diesel, repeat, off spec diesel. We experienced an internal pipeline leak and our entire cargo was contaminated with gasoline and rejected by the receiver in Wilmington, North Carolina. Our last orders prior to the blackout were to return the cargo to the refinery for reclamation. Over."

"Affirmative, *Pecos Trader*, we copy. Please let me speak to senior Coast Guard officer aboard. Over."

Hughes passed the mike to Matt Kinsey.

"US Navy, this is Senior Chief Petty Officer Matt Kinsey, US Coast Guard. Over."

"Chief, we have no information on your vessel, please state your mission. Over."

"We are transferring personnel and equipment from Oak Island Station, North Carolina, to the Coast Guard MSU in Port Arthur, Texas. Our orders are to proceed by most expeditious means. *Pecos Trader* was the only ride available. You can see our patrol boat on deck. Over."

"Affirmative, Chief. Why have you disabled the vessel AIS? Over."

"Negative, Navy. I say again, negative. We did not disable the AIS. Captain reports it malfunctioned during the solar storm, exact cause and extent of damage unknown."

"We copy *Pecos Trader* . Wait one. Over."

"What now?" Hughes asked.

"They'll run this all by Jacksonville for orders," Kinsey said. "If they order us in, I hope that contaminated diesel story holds up."

"That's the beauty of it," Hughes said. "It can't be confirmed one way or another. I doubt any testing labs are operational these days, so it's just my word against anyone else's opinion. It's like putting a poison sign on a water hole; no one's likely to want to take a drink to check it out."

Kinsey nodded but looked uneasy.

"What's the matter, Chief?" Hughes asked.

"I've spent thirty years following orders, so this 'make stuff up as you go along' operation is pretty stressful."

"I understand," Hughes said, "but there's no shortage of people needing help, and you can help just as many people where we're going as you could where you were, and *Pecos Trader* is our only ride home. After we get there, we can decide what to do with the fuel."

Kinsey was about to reply when the VHF radio cut him off.

"*Pecos Trader* , *Pecos Trader* , this transmission is for Chief Kinsey. Do you copy? Over."

"We copy, Navy. This is Kinsey, go ahead. Over."

"Chief, when did you receive orders to deploy to Texas, and is your chain of command aware you are en route? Over."

"Four days ago, repeat, four days ago. My chain of command is aware of transit plan, but we lost comms prior to departure, so they do not know current status. Over."

"*Pecos Trader* , we copy and you are cleared to proceed as we have no orders to supersede your current ones. However, be advised two days ago, the US Coast Guard was subordinated to FEMA for the duration of the current emergency and is now the cognizant authority controlling coastal and inland marine traffic. When you transit the Florida Strait, please check in with US Coast Guard Station Key West for any updates to current orders. We will alert them to expect you. God speed, *Pecos Trader* . US Navy out!"

"Thank you, Navy," Kinsey said into the mike. "*Pecos Trader* out."

He cradled the mike, looking as if he'd just been slapped.

"What's the problem, Chief?" Hughes asked.

"The problem is the Coasties in Key West now have over twenty-four hours to check out my little fairy tale, and they know we're coming. A bigger problem is there are several patrol boats and a cutter at Station Key West, and a balloon-borne radar at Cudjoe Key covering the entire strait and its approaches. I've no doubt they'll want to have a little chat 'up close and personal,' all of which boils down to us being screwed."

TERMINAL OFFICE BUILDING
WILMINGTON CONTAINER TERMINAL
WILMINGTON, NORTH CAROLINA

DAY 12, 12 NOON

The battered office chair squeaked as Levi shifted his weight, the high-pitched noise filling the small office he and his father-in-law shared as quarters since the *Pecos Trader* sailed.

"We've got to get back to the river camp today, Anthony," Levi said. "We've been here five days now, which is three days longer than I told Celia we'd be gone. Despite radio updates, I'm sure she's fit to be tied."

The older man nodded. "I expect Jo's right there with her, holding the rope. Like as not it'll be us that's tied when we get back to the river." He paused. "What about the others? Who's going with us?"

"I think just Bill Wiggins and Tex." Levi said, "Jimmy the Pumpman decided to stay here in Wilmington now that the Coasties and National Guard guys are setting up shop. I'd been counting on him to join us, but I don't feel too bad about it, considering the possibilities of them making a go of it here in the terminal. Anyway, he'll be close by and we can invite him to join us if things go to hell here."

"What about Singletary?"

Levi shook his head. "I promised Captain Hughes I'd get him started to Baltimore, but that was when he'd have no place to go when the ship sailed. Now that we're not leaving him on his own, I have no intention of taking him to our place. Anyway, his best chance of getting back to Baltimore is grabbing an abandoned boat from one of the marinas and heading up the inland waterway. That's what I'll advise him to do, though what he's likely to find in Baltimore is anyone's guess. I doubt it's going to be pretty."

"That's a fact," Anthony said, "and I'm glad you said that. There's something off about the guy. I don't trust him any further than I could throw him. Maybe not that far."

"Me neither," Levi said. "I'll go get Bill and Tex, and I think we need to keep the Coasties in the loop because we need their help. Will you see if you can find Chief Butler and then meet us in that little conference room down the hall?"

"Will do," Anthony said.

A half hour later, Levi had most of the attendees gathered in the conference room, awaiting the arrival of Anthony and Chief Mike Butler. The group awaiting Butler was larger than Levi had intended. With lodging space tight, Bill Wiggins was sharing an office turned bedroom with Jimmy Barrios and Jerome Singletary. The two had tagged along to the meeting, and Levi could think of no graceful way to 'uninvite' them. He looked up as Anthony entered the room with a haggard Mike Butler.

"Thanks for joining us, Chief Butler," Levi said. "I know you're busy. I'll try to make this quick."

"No problem, Mr. Jenkins," Butler replied, "you've been a big help to us and I'm glad to return the favor. What do you need?"

"Maybe just some extra fuel and some logistical support if you can handle it," Levi said, "but I'll get to that in a minute. Right now I need to make sure we're all on the same page."

Butler nodded, and Levi turned to the others.

"Bill, Tex, first off, Anthony and I have stayed here as long as we can. I'm assuming you're both anxious to get headed back to your folks, and if you want our help, now is the time."

They both nodded, and Levi spread a road map on the table.

"Okay then, we need to take you both to our place on the river by boat and you can leave from there. That'll let you bypass any possible problems getting out of Wilmington. Anthony and I've been talking it over, and our family has four cars between us, which is about three more than we need now. We left a later model SUV in our barn at home. It runs, or it did when we left it, anyway. We can let you have that, and with the help of our Coast Guard friends here, enough gas to get you pretty far along your way, if not all the way to your destinations."

Wiggins and Tex looked shocked.

"I don't know what to say, Levi," Bill Wiggins said, "that's incredibly generous." Tex nodded agreement.

Levi shrugged. "Given how hard it's likely to be to get fuel and parts from now on, automobiles are back to being a luxury used only when necessary. Having four is an extravagance no one's likely to be able to afford, and the newer cars will only last until something goes wrong with the computers, then they're toast. We're keeping the old, reliable vehicles that are easy to work on, so it's really not all that generous—just realistic. We're not likely to use the car, so I got no problem helping shipmates get home."

"Still, thank you," Tex said.

Levi and Anthony seemed embarrassed by the thanks, so Bill Wiggins moved to break the uncomfortable silence.

"You said the car was in your barn, is that on the river too?" he asked.

Levi shook his head and bent over to point out a spot on the map. "No, the barn's at our old place, just outside of Currie. Anthony and I will take you to it in my old truck and you can leave from there."

"Look's good," Wiggins said. "We can cut across on secondary roads to I-40 and that'll take us right into I-95 North."

"Negative," Levi said, "way too many big cities and people along the I-95 corridor. You'll never make it through unharmed."

"I'm with Bill on this one, Levi," Shyla Texeira said, "95 North's the most direct route to both my folks' place in New Jersey and Bill's home in Maine. We can circle the cities."

Levi shook his head. "Even the suburbs have way too many people, and by now they're all starving. I'm sure the interstates are all jammed with abandoned cars as well, because by all reports, folks are fleeing the cities, and maybe not thinking too clearly. If you're running AWAY from a city on the interstate system, it means you're running TOWARD another one. If they abandoned their cars on the interstate when they ran out of gas, or just realized their error and moved off onto nearby secondary roads, there's likely a huge mass of desperate, hungry people not only in the cities, but spread out within corridors several miles wide along both sides of the interstate system. If you're driving by, winding your way through stalled cars, you might as well be carrying a big sign reading 'we got gas, we got food.' Trust me, you'll never make your destinations along major roads."

"How, then?" Wiggins asked, gesturing to the map. "The kind of roads you're talking about don't show up on a road map of the Eastern US, and we sure can't be stopping to ask directions."

Levi smiled and reached down into a backpack on the floor at his feet and produced a small paperback book and a thick stack of maps bound with a rubber band. He laid both on the table.

"The book's a guide to the Appalachian Trail, and the bundle contains state and local maps from here to Canada," he said.

"But how did you…" Tex began, looking confused, and Levi laughed.

"I'm one of those crazy preppers, remember," he said, "and one who spent half of each year far from home, mostly traveling up and down the East Coast." He nodded down at the backpack. "I kept my 'getting home' bag with me on the ship at all times, and I have a route home planned out in my head from every port between Corpus Christi, Texas and St. Johns, Newfoundland. You just reverse one of my planned routes."

"But the Appalachian Trail is a hiking trail. We can't drive on it. Are you saying I have to walk all the way to Maine?" Wiggins asked.

"Not unless you have to," Levi said, "but yeah, that's plan B. But let me explain; the AT runs within twenty or thirty miles of both of your destinations, and in most cases it's paralleled by nearby roads. Sometimes they're not much more than dirt or gravel tracks, but they're drivable and they'll keep you both close to the AT and more importantly, away from people and close to water sources. If for some reason, you have to abandon the vehicle, you can continue on foot along the trail. There are shelters every eight miles or so, and more importantly game and natural sources of safe drinking water, all marked in the guide. The guide also has information on the towns you'll pass, how far off the trail, how big they are, or were anyway, and services they had before the blackout. If you're afoot on the trail, that might give you the best idea about where it might be possible to pick up another vehicle, or at least a clue to what you might expect if you go into the town." Levi shrugged. "It's not perfect and it's still going to be a hard trip, but I think you'll have a much better chance sticking to the boonies than trying to transit the more populated areas."

Wiggins and Tex nodded, clearly impressed.

"Again, I don't know what to say, Levi," Wiggins said. "This is terrific, thank you."

"Don't thank me yet," Levi said. "It's gonna be harder than you've ever imagined, and I'm pretty sure you'll be afoot before it's all over. And remember, this is a plan and theoretical, so it's not like I've made the trip."

"Still," Tex said, "it's far better than we could have done on our own, and it's obvious you've given it a lot of thought."

"Speaking of which," Singletary said, "did you have a plan for getting home from Baltimore I can use in the reverse direction, hopefully something that doesn't involve walking through the woods, picking ticks off my ass?"

"As a matter of fact, I did," Levi said. "I figured if I was caught anywhere between Miami and Baltimore, I'd try to get a boat and head up or down the inland waterway to Wilmington, and up the river from here. It's all very populated, but I figure most of the traffic will be on land and not water. Even if you have to row or paddle, it's a helluva lot faster than walking with a pack on your back."

"Okay," Singletary said, "but where am I gonna get a boat?"

Levi looked at Butler. "This wasn't the reason I asked you to attend, Chief Butler, but since Singletary brought it up, can you help us out here? There are several marinas upstream, and any boats still there belong to owners who aren't likely to need them anymore."

Butler hesitated. "Yeah, okay," he said at last, "I suppose I could send the guys up to have a look around. There ought to be something up there he could use, and we can load him up with gas cans to extend the range if need be."

"I'll need a gun too," Singletary said, but Butler was already shaking his head.

"Sorry, but no way I'm giving up any of our weapons. We'll probably need everything we have at some point," Butler said.

"I have a thirty-eight revolver and half a box of ammo I can let you have before I leave," Levi said. "It's a snub nose and not very accurate, but it's better than being defenseless."

Singletary nodded, seemingly satisfied for once. Levi turned back to Butler.

"Which brings me to my last request, Chief Butler," Levi said. "We found some Jerry cans here in the container terminal, and there's plenty of fuel in the product terminal next door. I want to send Bill and Tex off with fifty gallons of gas. Between that, the four of us, the extra food for their trip, and the extra food and fuel for our own use, we'll have to make multiple trips in our boat unless you can help us out."

"No problem," Butler said. "Is there less than four feet of water anywhere you want to go?"

"No," Levi said. "We've got that much even in our inlet."

Butler nodded. "Then we'll use the forty-five. She can even carry extra if you need, and tow you up to your place if you want." He leaned over the spread-out road map. "You said it was what, on the Black River? Can you show me the approximate location on the road map?"

Levi hesitated for the slightest moment and glanced toward Singletary. "It's easier to see on the actual river chart, and I don't have it with me," Levi said. "I'll show you later."

Butler caught the hesitation and nodded. "What time do you want to get out of here?"

Levi glanced at his watch. "It's almost one. If we start packing up now, we can get out of here by five and make it home before dark."

MAXIMUM SECURITY UNIT
FEDERAL CORRECTIONAL COMPLEX
KNAUTH ROAD
BEAUMONT, TEXAS

DAY 12, 3:00 P.M.

"What we gonna do, Sarge?" asked Broussard, a note of accusation in his voice. "There's only two of us left here in Max. The warden said when they released the inmates over on the low security unit, those COs would come over here and spell us. That was three days ago, and we haven't seen a soul except the food service guy who came over with the crap they stripped out of the commissary."

"What do you want me to tell you?" Johnson asked. "I've been here with you, right from the time the warden showed up with the air mattresses and the 'help is on the way' pep talk. You think I got a friggin' crystal ball?"

Broussard sighed and settled back in his chair, and looked up to where the few security monitors still working displayed the unimaginable squalor of the various cell blocks. "Well, at least we're away from the stink except when we have to feed 'em."

Johnson grunted and nodded toward the dwindling stack of cardboard boxes full of snack food in the corner of the cramped control room. "Yeah, well, I reckon we won't have that problem much longer. Not that a daily ration of a package of snack crackers and a bottle of water is doing much but delaying the inevitable."

"Well, I suspect plenty of ordinary decent people are going hungry too," Broussard said, "so the way I figure it, these assholes got it coming. Besides, the MREs they gave us suck too. I'd almost rather eat stale crackers out of the commissary."

"Let's see how you feel when the MREs are gone in a—"

"Shit," Johnson said as he stared up at one working monitor showing the prison exterior. The camera was mounted over the main entrance and focused on the approach from the now mostly empty employee parking lot and the grassy circle in the center of the lot behind the entrance. On the ground in the grassy circle was a body, features indistinct, but definitely clad in a correction officer's uniform with dark stains on it.

"When the hell did he get there?" Broussard asked.

Johnson shook his head. "I wasn't watching, but he's definitely a CO, and that looks like blood."

"We gotta get help. Are the inside phones still working?" Broussard asked.

"They were this morning, but who knows?" Johnson said, reaching for the phone. He tried several presets before shaking his head.

"Anything?" Broussard asked.

"Negative," Johnson replied, hanging up the phone, "I tried the main admin building, the medium-security unit, and the main gate. The phones ring, but no one answers." He sighed. "I guess I need to go see if I can help him."

"Uhh... we're supposed to keep two COs here at all times," Broussard said.

Johnson sneered, "Well, maybe you missed it, but things aren't exactly normal, so I think maybe bending the rules a bit more is okay. Besides"—he nodded toward the monitors covering the cell blocks—"those bastards in there can hardly lift their heads, so I don't think they're planning a prison break."

"All right," Broussard said, "but be careful."

"Yes, mother," Johnson said, walking over to retrieve a shotgun leaning against the wall, one of a pair. Normally guns in this area of the prison were prohibited, but given the circumstances, the two officers had accessed the armory without asking permission, and armed themselves with both shotguns and sidearms.

"Keep an eye on the monitor," Johnson said as he moved toward the door.

"Yeah," Broussard replied, "I pretty much had that part figured out." He paused and grew serious. "And try not to get in trouble, 'cause it's not like I have any reinforcements to call."

Johnson nodded and exited the control room to move through the now nonfunctioning double-door mantrap separating the secure area from the administrative side of the maximum-security unit, disabled because

Johnson had no one to man the security checkpoint. He moved swiftly through the halls of the administration office area and exited the building to cross the open yard and enter the deserted receiving facility built into the stout prison wall. Here too, the mantrap was left open due to a lack of personnel—not that it mattered with the main entrance locked down. He crossed through the building, unlocked the heavy glass door, and pushed it open. There, across the perimeter road that circled the prison walls, lay the inert form of a corrections officer. The red smears in the bright sunlight confirming the stains he'd seen on the monochrome display were indeed blood.

"Shit," Johnson muttered, and looked around for any threat. Seeing none, he hurried across the road toward his fallen comrade.

Darren McComb, aka federal inmate number 26852-278, aka 'Spike,' doing a triple life sentence and captain of the Aryan Brotherhood of Texas, lay sweating in the grass, with growing concerns the sweat running down his arms would wash away the dead badge's blood he'd smeared over his tattoos. It was fate that had him in a holding cell in the medium-security unit when the power went out, awaiting transfer back to max security after extraction of an abscessed tooth. More good luck allowed him to take advantage of deteriorating security measures as fewer and fewer badges showed up for work. Feigning death and luring the inexperienced rookie into his cell had almost been child's play. Freeing the others and killing the few remaining COs in medium security had been easy as well, and then they'd fallen on the central administration complex like a pack of wolves. He smiled into the grass; dealing with the warden had been particularly enjoyable, and informative as well. It was good to know there were only two badges left in the whole of max security; all he had to do was get the heavy security door open at the main entrance, and it was a done deal.

McComb stiffened as he heard the sound of an opening door, and opened his eyes to thin slits to look down his body toward the badge rushing toward him from the building. He closed his eyes tight as the CO approached, the man's breathing labored from the exertion of the short run. The man knelt beside him and McComb felt a hand on his shoulder begin to roll him face up.

"Are you all righ—"

The badge's question died on his lips as McComb drove the concealed knife into his throat, spraying them both with bright arterial blood. The man collapsed on top of McComb, the shotgun in his free hand tumbling to the grass. McComb held the man close, savoring the kill as he waited for him to stop struggling. When the badge went limp, McComb rolled him to one side and grabbed the shotgun before standing and placing two fingers in his mouth to emit a long high-pitched whistle. Two dozen figures in convict khaki, armed with assorted weaponry from the looted armory of the medium-security unit, rose from behind cars scattered throughout the parking lot and began to converge on Spike's position.

Broussard sat sipping a bottle of tepid water as he watched the grainy monitor. Then Johnson collapsed over the fallen CO, and Broussard was momentarily confused as the man he'd thought dead or injured rose with Johnson's shotgun. Confusion was replaced by near paralytic fear as armed convicts entered the picture from off screen and converged toward the main entrance of the max-security unit. The water bottle slipped from his trembling fingers and water gushed out around his feet as he stared at the monitor in disbelief.

He knew he couldn't beat them to the main entrance security door, so in a panic, he scooped up his shotgun and a box of shells and went in search of a defensible hiding place. He had no illusion he could stop them; his only hope for survival was to hide where they couldn't find him or if they did find him, make it too costly to get to him. Faced with losses to dig him out of his hole, they might ignore him, free the others, and clear out.

But time was not his friend, and by the time he made it through the nonfunctional mantrap into the administration area, he heard them slamming through doors on the opposite end of the building, howling like a pack of wolves. Out of options, he ducked into a large storage closet, reaching up with his shotgun to smash the bare light bulb as he entered, then pulled the door closed and backed himself into the far corner, shotgun positioned to blast any target silhouetted in the doorway if it opened.

McComb was at the front of the pack, head on a swivel, alert for the presence of the last CO. The dying warden had told him the last two badges were in Central Control, but McComb figured the surviving CO had witnessed his partner's death and might be anywhere. He led his men through the open mantrap and slowed as he neared the glass-enclosed control room. There was no one visible through the glass, but the badge might be crouched down behind the waist-high solid wall. McComb nodded to his two closest subordinates to follow him, then burst through the door of Central Control, bringing his shotgun to bear on the previously concealed portion of the wall. He heaved a sigh of relief when he found the control room empty and more of his followers crowded into the space.

"Okay, the last badge ain't here, and I want to take care of him before we get out of here. So far no one's escaped to rat us out, and I want to keep it that way, so spread out and find him," McComb said.

The man closest to him gave a gap-toothed smile. "Shouldn't be too tough," he said, pointing to the overturned water bottle and the wet footprints on the floor.

McComb grinned back and pushed through the crowd, backtracking and following the water trail. The footprints were obliterated by the cons' own entrance, but the water was still there, pointing like an arrow to the closed door of the storage closet.

"Anybody bring any of them flash bangs from the armory?" he asked quietly.

Several men nodded.

"Okay," McComb said, still keeping his voice down and pointing at the men with the flash bangs, "you three get ready to chuck those in when the door is open. You," he said, pointing to another man, "snatch the door open and jump out of the way, quick like so these three can toss in their packages. He's probably in there laying for us, so all you knuckleheads stay out of the open door until the flash bangs go off, got it?"

There were head nods all around, and McComb continued, looking around and spotting a couple of men armed with shotguns. "You two jump to the doorway as soon as the flash bangs go off and sweep the room with your shotguns. Don't stop until you empty the magazines and cover every square inch of the room. It ain't nothin' but a closet and I want to make damn sure he don't survive. Got it?"

The pair grinned their understanding.

"Shock and awe, baby!" McComb said. "Now everybody get ready."

The men moved into position quickly and executed the plan on McComb's hand signals. Thirty violent seconds later, he stood in the half light of the storage closet, looking down at the bloody remains of the last CO. He gave a satisfied nod then returned to the hallway and gathered his men around him.

"Okay," he said, "same drill as in medium security. Let our guys out, and any other whites willing to pledge allegiance to the ABT, but make sure they understand what'll happen to them if they try to punk out."

There were grunts of approval as he continued, "Leave the niggers and greasers," he said. "No point in wastin' ammo when we can just let 'em starve to death."

There was laughter, followed by a question from his gap-toothed lieutenant.

"What're you going to do, Spike?" the man asked.

"Oh, I'm gonna pay someone a little visit," McComb said.

Five minutes later, McComb was squatting on his haunches, sipping water from a plastic bottle as he stared through the bars at Daris Jefferson, leader of the Gangsta Killa Blood set of the United Blood Nation.

"Just wanted to stop by and say goodbye before me and the boys go on jackrabbit parole," McComb said.

Jefferson glared back, his eyes two burning embers of hatred in an emaciated face. "I see yo keeping yo distance, cracker. Get a little closer, and I'll beat that smile off yo pasty-ass face."

"Oh, I wouldn't want you to get all tuckered out trying, boy. You need to save your strength so it takes a long, long time to die. And here's a little something to remember me by." McComb rose from his haunches and leaned in a bit. "I hear thirst is worse than hunger, so while you're in there dying of thirst, I want you to look at this bottle and think about me." He hocked up something from deep in his throat and theatrically dripped it from his mouth into the open neck of the half-filled bottle, then set the bottle on the floor out of reach. "In a few days, you'll be looking at this bottle and dreaming of drinking my spit, and when you do, remember I wouldn't piss on you if you were on fire." McComb grinned. "So enjoy the rest of your miserable life, Buckwheat."

Jefferson tried to spit in McComb's face, but he was so dehydrated he had no saliva, and the failed effort looked almost as if he were blowing a kiss. McComb's laughter echoed through the half-empty cell block as he walked away, eager to make his mark in what he knew would be a predator's paradise.

CHAPTER TWELVE

BOROUGH ROAD
SOUTH OF CURRIE, NC

DAY 13, 2:00 A.M.

Levi kept the lights off and avoided the brakes as he kept Old Blue at a steady forty miles an hour, the county road an eerie green in his night-vision goggles. Anthony road shotgun, literally, with his trusty old shotgun upright between his knees, squeezed against the passenger door by the presence of Bill Wiggins and Tex in the center of the bench seat. The old truck wasn't designed for four passengers.

They'd gotten back to the fishing camp just before dusk, and Levi was pretty sure only the presence of strangers had saved him and Anthony from a dressing-down from Celia and Josephine. Despite the women's restrained anger over the longer-than-promised absence, they were both far too gracious to make guests feel uncomfortable by venting their anger. And the kids had been excited and happy about anything that broke up what, for them, was becoming a very boring existence.

Levi and Anthony had debated the wisdom of bringing the Coast Guard boat all the way into their hideaway, but in the end, there was just too much cargo to be shifted to allow for any other solution. Concerned about giving offense, but more worried about security, they'd discussed their concerns with Chief Butler, who, to their relief, was not at all offended. He'd volunteered to pilot the Coast Guard boat himself and brought along his most trusted subordinate, assuring both Levi and Anthony the secret of their location was safe.

That only left Wiggins and Tex, and though he trusted them completely, there was always the chance they might run in with bad people and be forced or coerced into revealing the source of the ample supplies they were carrying. But they couldn't reveal what they didn't know. Levi glanced to his right, past his two ex-shipmates to where Anthony rode at the passenger door, looking insect-like in his own set of NV goggles.

"I'm sorry we only had two sets of night-vision glasses," Levi said, "but since Anthony's riding shotgun, I figured he needed them."

"No problem," Wiggins said, "though I have to say, riding down the road in the pitch dark is a pretty uncomfortable feeling."

Beside him, Tex laughed. "I'll say."

"We'll be there soon," Levi said.

True to his word, a few minutes later Levi pulled into the long gravel drive of the five acres he and Celia shared with her parents, and eased down between the two houses to the barn. As Anthony exited the truck wordlessly to open the barn door, Levi looked around the property in the green glow of the NV goggles and wondered again if the move to the river had been premature. After all, it had been almost two weeks since the power went out, and the place seemed undisturbed. Then he shook his head again. Country road or not, it was still a paved road that saw traffic, and the houses were just too visible and hard to defend. No, moving to the river was the right call.

"Are we there?" Tex asked.

"Oh, yeah, sorry," Levi said. "I forgot you guys can't see. Anthony's opening the barn door now, and when we get inside, we'll crank up a couple of lanterns."

Anthony swung the barn door wide, and Levi nosed the car into the barn beside an SUV.

"Everybody out," Levi said as Anthony closed the barn door and walked over to take down two lanterns from where they hung on nails in the wall. In moments, light filled the barn, accompanied by the soft hiss of the lanterns. Wiggins and Tex blinked in the light and checked out the SUV, a ten-year-old Toyota Highlander that looked showroom new.

"That's still some gift, Levi," Wiggins said.

"Don't worry about it," Levi said. "Like I said before, it's not really as generous as you think. Everything's running now, but when all these newer cars and planes and helicopters and what have you start breaking down, there won't be any fixing them, at least not easily. They're all just about impossible to work on without sophisticated diagnostic equipment. We're much better off keeping the old, simple cars we can work on ourselves. I've got no problem letting shipmates use something we're likely to have little use for anyway. That's all." Levi tapped the map with his finger. "Now, we got a lot to go over, and Anthony and I want to be back in the woods before daylight, so let's get to it."

Tex and Wiggins moved beside Levi as he pointed at the map. "You need to stay off the main roads and get near the Appalachian Trail as soon as possible. That's likely going to be the most dangerous part, because the AT doesn't start paralleling the Blue Ridge Parkway until just north of Roanoke, Virginia. I've traced out a route on the North Carolina map from here to Linnville, where you can pick up the Blue Ridge Parkway north. It's about three hundred miles, which you could make in six hours in normal times, but now, who knows? However, I figure if you leave at first light and given the lengthening days, you ought to get to the parkway before dark. I've tried to keep you on secondary roads, so they should be okay, but whoever isn't driving needs to be looking at the county maps I've included so if you find a problem, you can get around it. Always be thinking of a plan B before you need it, understand?"

Both the travelers nodded and Levi continued. "You'll intersect the AT the first time about two hundred miles up the Blue Ridge Parkway at a little place called Black Horse Gap. Then the two routes stay more or less together until the parkway ends about a hundred miles north at Afton, Virginia. It actually doesn't 'end,' though. It just turns into another scenic road called Skyline Drive that continues a hundred miles or so to Front Royal. The AT parallels Skyline Drive as well. After that, you'll have to pick out secondary roads, logging roads, etc., that parallel the AT." He paused. "And just to be clear, I use the term 'parallel' loosely. Actually the AT cuts back and forth across these and the other roads you'll use to head north, but in some places it might veer away from the nearest road by ten or twenty miles. So this is important, ALWAYS know where the access points to the AT are, and how far it is back to the last one you passed, and how far it is ahead to the next one."

"Uhh… isn't this a little overkill, Levi?" Wiggins asked. "I mean, striking off on foot into the woods is about the last thing I want to do. We just want to get home."

"And I'm trying to make sure you get there, Bill," Levi said. "If things are as bad as I think and y'all run into trouble, hoofing it into the woods might be your only option. Also, that little AT guidebook lists locations where you can find good water, which may be like liquid gold, and all of the land the AT traverses is mostly state or national forest, which means there will be plenty of game if you end up needing it, 'cause you sure as hell will need to avoid grocery stores, assuming there are any that haven't been stripped."

"Is that even legal?" Wiggins asked, and Levi saw Tex suppress a smile. Anthony was less restrained.

"Seriously?" he snorted. "You think there are still game wardens running around, worried about folks shooting rabbits?"

Wiggins' face reddened in the lamplight. "I guess not. Stupid comment. Sorry."

Levi shook his head. "No need to apologize, and I know I'm coming on strong, but you need to understand the AT's your lifeline and your 'Mega Plan B.' 'Cause I got a sneaking suspicion you both, but you especially, Bill, are so worried about your families that as soon as you roll out of that driveway, you're thinking about heading north by the most direct route possible, caution be damned."

No one spoke and the uncomfortable silence grew.

"All right, I'll admit it," Wiggins said. "Tex and I've been considering some other routes."

"Well, stop considering them," Levi said, "because they'll likely get you killed."

Tex sighed. "How long you figure, Levi?"

"Getting you to Jersey, four or five days, and that much longer for Bill to get to Maine, assuming you can drive the whole way."

"Ten days! That can't be right," Wiggins said. "Even at thirty miles an hour on this convoluted path, I should be able to make it to Maine in three or four days tops, driving straight through."

"But you're not going straight through, because we've got no night vision to give you, and driving at night lit up like a Christmas tree is an invitation to be ambushed," Levi said. "Any bad guys can see you coming a long, long way off, and way before you know they're even there. You're gonna plan each day's trip, including a stopping point, and get there in plenty of time to check out the site, hide the car, and make camp away from the road so, if you need a fire, neither it or what you're cooking can be seen or smelled." Levi paused for emphasis. "Now get this straight. If you're not moving, you're hiding. You're most vulnerable when you're stationary, and you need to act accordingly."

Both Wiggins and Tex nodded slowly, resigned rather than enthusiastic, and Levi walked over to Old Blue and returned with a small backpack. He fished in the pack and produced an automatic pistol in a holster as well as what looked like a plastic rifle stock and laid both on top of the road map spread over the hood of the SUV. Several boxes of ammunition followed.

"Either of you have any experience with handguns?" Levi asked.

"I've been to the range a few times," Wiggins said.

"Uhh… actually, I used to shoot competitively," Tex said.

Levi reached for the Glock. He ejected the magazine then racked the slide back and left the action open before handing the nine millimeter pistol to

Tex. "Winner, winner, chicken dinner," he said. "Tex will carry the main defensive armament when you're outside the vehicle. When you're moving, whoever isn't driving will have the pistol out and ready."

Tex nodded, and Levi and Anthony watched with approval as she examined the pistol expertly, closed the action, and then checked and inserted the magazine before checking out the holster. Wiggins was looking less sure, instinctively reacting to a perceived slight to his manhood.

"This is perfect, actually," Levi said. "Tex, that's a small-of-the-back holster. Do you have an overshirt you can wear with the tail out?" Tex nodded and Levi looked back and forth between Tex and Wiggins. "Good. If you're attacked by surprise, it will likely be when you're out of the car, and any attackers are unlikely to perceive Tex as a threat. They'll move on Bill first, and that may give you the edge."

Wiggins nodded, on board now, and then pointed toward the plastic rifle stock. "And what's that?"

Levi picked up the plastic stock and pried a rubber boot off the butt, revealing various items stored neatly inside. "This is a Henry survival rifle, which will bring home the bacon, or more likely the rabbit, if you need it."

Levi deftly assembled the little rifle in seconds, and then pointed out the two small magazines.

"It's a twenty-two-caliber semiautomatic and it comes with two eight-round magazines. I suggest you keep both fully loaded at all times. You'll notice there's a good supply of two different types of ammo. The stuff in the blue box is 'quiet' loads, reduced power for low noise, but it's fine for taking small game at any distance you'll likely be shooting. The advantage is if you DO have to hunt, the gunshots won't draw attention to you. The downside is these rounds don't have enough recoil to cycle the bolt, so when you're shooting them, the rifle isn't semiautomatic—you'll have to cycle the bolt manually between shots. The other ammo is regular twenty-two long rifle, and if you have to use the rifle for defense, that's what you need to use. A twenty-two doesn't have much stopping power, but in semiautomatic mode, it can at least make someone think twice about charging you. But like I said, it's mainly a hunting weapon."

"What's with the red dot?" Wiggins pointed to one of the magazines.

"I was getting to that," Levi said. "I put a dot of nail polish on one, so you could tell the mags apart in an emergency, and I loaded the one with the red dot with the regular rounds and the other one with the low-noise rounds. I suggest you maintain that so you can switch out quickly if needed."

"Sound's good," Wiggins said, "but to be honest, I hope I don't have to use either."

"I do too," Levi said, "and if everything goes well, you won't. The gas tank's full, and you've got fifty gallons in Jerry cans. I don't like to see you carrying all that gas inside the car, but there really isn't an option. You got food and water for twelve days, a bit longer if you need to stretch it. I've also packed both of you 'escape packs,' because if you do have to abandon the car and haul ass, you likely will be doing it under duress. Mostly it's food, gallon ziplock bags full of crushed noodles and pasta for carbs, nuts for fat, and jerky for protein, along with three liter camel packs of water and a small bottle of bleach for disinfecting water if need be. I also threw in some other odds and ends, which you'll figure out if you need it, lighters, space blankets, paracord, stuff like that. Don't mess with the bags, just keep them handy. And don't forget to take the AT guide, maps, and ammo—"

Wiggins smiled and held up his hand to stop Levi. "You know you told us all this before, Levi. I think we have it. Really."

Levi hesitated. "Well, okay. Let's get the stuff loaded, then."

There were nods all around, and the group began transferring the supplies from Old Blue to the Toyota. Fifteen minutes later, the task was complete, and everyone stood silently in the middle of the barn, reluctant to part ways.

Anthony broke the silence. "Well, good luck and God's speed."

Tex stepped over and wrapped him in a hug. "You take care of these folks, Anthony," she whispered into his ear, and Anthony squeezed her tight before he let him go and transferred her embrace to Levi. "Thank you, shipmate," she said softly, and Levi only nodded, unable to speak.

Tex let go of Levi and stepped back to let the men exchange handshakes.

"Oh yeah," Levi said, extracting a piece of paper from his pocket, "I almost forgot. These are the radio frequencies we worked out with the *Pecos Trader* and the Coasties in Wilmington, as well as the times we'll all be listening and some security codes. When you get home, try to let us know you got there safely and then keep in touch."

Wiggins and Tex nodded, and after another short awkward silence, Wiggins spoke. "I'll kill the lanterns."

"I'll get the barn door," Tex added, and Levi and Anthony got into the cab of Old Blue.

Ten minutes later, Levi was driving through the darkness, lost in thought, when he felt Anthony's hand on his shoulder.

"Don't you fret, Levi," the older man said. "You did all you could."

"Let's just hope it was enough," Levi said.

M/V *Pecos Trader*
FLORIDA STRAIT

DAY 13, 2:00 P.M.

Hughes pressed the binoculars to his eyes and strained to make out more detail of the line of white marking the ocean's surface to the east, where the gentle swell was breaking over a barely submerged reef.

He heaved a sigh of relief and lowered the glasses. "I think that's Elbow Cay behind us, so at least I can scratch running aground off my list of things to worry about today."

Beside him, Chief Matt Kinsey chuckled. "Which still makes the list pretty long, I imagine."

"You mean like staying as far away from the US coast as possible and hugging the Bahamian shallows, with absolutely no working navigational aids while simultaneously hoping to avoid detection by US radar and stay clear of Cuban waters?"

"Well, you're two for two, so far," Kinsey said. "You've managed to avoid grounding in Bahamian waters, despite lack of navaids, and my Coast Guard folks haven't hailed us yet, so I'm thinking that's a good indication the alert from the navy at Jacksonville got lost in the confusion."

"Yeah, I have to say I'm pleasantly surprised," Hughes said. "What do you make of that?"

Kinsey shrugged. "I'm thinking everybody's shorthanded. If they haven't hailed us by now, we might have a shot at sliding by unnoticed, as long as we stay as far south as possible."

"I'm thinking the same thing," Hughes said. "All in all, I'm starting to feel a lot better about this."

"Captain! I think you'll want to see this," called Georgia Howell from the radar.

"What is it?" Hughes asked as he and Kinsey crossed the bridge toward the radar.

"I've got a small, fast target approaching from the south," Howell said, "making better than forty knots and headed right for us. ETA approximately ten minutes." She moved aside to let Hughes take her place.

"What do you make of that, Matt?" Hughes asked.

"Smuggler maybe? Some well-heeled Cuban-American taking advantage of the chaos to reunite more of the family?"

"Maybe," Howell said, "but then why isn't he headed straight for the Florida coast?"

"Well, we'll find out soon enough," Hughes said, and walked to the port side of the bridge to stare south through his binoculars.

A few minutes later, he spotted a speck on the sea, growing in his binoculars as it raced toward the ship. It was a fast patrol boat, similar to the Coast Guard boat they carried as deck cargo, with several uniformed men aboard and a menacing-looking bow-mounted machine gun.

"Oh shit," Hughes said, "that's a Cuban patrol boat."

"What the hell do they want?" Georgia Howell said. "We're a good ten miles outside Cuban waters."

"Maybe they don't see it that way." Kinsey turned to Hughes. "What are you going to do, Captain?"

"Well, normally I'd call the Coast Guard, but now? Who the hell knows?"

"Ahh… I think I'd rather be on a FEMA storage tanker just about anywhere than in a Cuban prison," Georgia Howell said, "because given what's going on, I don't think anyone's going to be spending any resources trying to get us back."

"Good point," Hughes said, moving to the VHF. He keyed the mike and started to transmit. "US Coast Guard, US Coast Guard. This is—"

Everyone dropped to the deck instinctively as the port bridge windows shattered and spiderwebbed from a well-placed burst of machine-gun fire, followed immediately by an amplified voice with a thick Spanish accent.

"AMERICAN TANKER! AMERICAN TANKER! STOP TRANSMITTING IMMEDIATELY AND STOP YOUR VESSEL OR WE WILL OPEN FIRE!"

"I think you already did, asshole," Hughes muttered.

Kinsey and Howell crouched with him on the deck. A few feet away, Pete Sonnier, the AB on watch, squatted near the steering stand. "They seem pretty serious to me, Cap," he said.

Hughes nodded and looked back and forth between Kinsey and Howell. "Don't stand on ceremony," Hughes said, "'cause it's not like I have a clue what to do here." He nodded to where the VHF mike dangled on its cord a few inches off the deck. "I don't think they can hit us here, so I can probably continue to call the Coast Guard before they can get aboard. I'm sure the Coasties can have an armed chopper over us before they can force us into Cuban waters."

"Presuming anyone answers our call in a timely manner," Kinsey said. "Remember they're shorthanded as hell and low on resources. And if we do play that card and no one responds, I'm pretty sure our new amigos are going to be pretty pissed."

"AMERICAN TANKER! DO NOT TRANSMIT AND STOP YOUR VESSEL AT ONCE OR WE WILL OPEN FIRE! BE ADVISED WE ARE EQUIPPED WITH ROCKET-PROPELLED GRENADES AND WILL USE THEM! REPEAT, STOP YOUR VESSEL AT ONCE!"

"All right, that's it," Hughes said. "Georgia, ring the engine room and tell them to stop the engine. I'm going to have to talk to this asshole."

Howell nodded and duckwalked over to the control console and reached up for the phone. Within seconds, they felt the vibration change as the big diesel rumbled to a halt and the ship started to slow. When he was confident the patrol boat had seen the ship slowing, Hughes rose and walked toward the port bridge wing, motioning the others to stay back out of sight.

He approached the side of the bridge wing with his arms raised so they'd have no doubt he was surrendering. When he spotted the boat approximately a hundred feet off the port side, the first thing he saw were armed men, one at the stern with an RPG and another manning the machine gun in the bow. Both weapons were pointed directly at *Pecos Trader* 's bridge—and him. Midships in the boat near the small glass-windowed pilothouse stood another man, obviously in charge, with the bullhorn in his hand and a pistol on his hip. There was a fourth man in the pilothouse at the wheel. All four wore the uniforms of the Cuban Border Guards. The officer type raised the bullhorn to his mouth.

"AMERICAN TANKER! YOU HAVE ENTERED OUR WATERS WITHOUT PERMISSION AND HAVE VIOLATED OUR SOVEREIGNTY. COME TO A COMPLETE STOP AT ONCE AND DEPLOY YOUR PILOT LADDER. DO NOT, REPEAT, DO NOT ATTEMPT TO USE YOUR RADIO OR WE WILL OPEN FIRE. LOWER BOTH YOUR ARMS AND THEN RAISE YOUR RIGHT ARM IF YOU UNDERSTAND!"

Hughes considered shouting a protest in return, but suspected it would be useless. He dutifully lowered both arms, then raised his right arm as instructed.

"GOOD! NOW DEPLOY YOUR PILOT LADDER AND PREPARE TO BE BOARDED. YOU HAVE FIVE MINUTES TO COMPLY. LOWER AND RAISE YOUR RIGHT ARM AGAIN IF YOU UNDERSTAND."

Hughes did as instructed and waited a moment to see if there were further instructions. When there were none, he turned and went back into the wheelhouse.

"You heard?" he asked Kinsey and Howell as he approached their position back in the chart room, out of sight from the patrol boat.

They both nodded, and Hughes continued, "Anybody got any ideas, or should we all start brushing up on our Spanish?"

"Well, obviously we aren't in Cuban waters, and he doesn't want us to use the radio, or use it himself," Howell said, "which I'm figuring is why he's using the bullhorn; he doesn't want to attract anyone's attention."

"I agree," Kinsey said, "and as screwed up as things are in the States, I suspect it's ten times worse in Cuba. These guys, with or without Cuban government authorization, probably figured they can take advantage of US inattention to snag as many resources transiting near their island as possible. Kind of make sense, actually."

"Question is," Hughes said, "what are we going to do? They can't get on board easily until we lower the pilot ladder, but if we don't let them on, they'll just stand off and machine gun us or hit us with RPGs. The cargo is inerted, so they probably can't blow us up, but even if we evacuate the bridge and keep everyone locked down in the house, a couple of RPGs into the bridge would probably wipe out all our controls and we're toast anyway. But on the other hand, if they DO get on board, we're screwed too, because they'll force us into a Cuban port."

"Not necessarily," Kinsey said, "could you see how many they have aboard?"

"Four," Hughes said. "An officer type and three others, one at the helm and two handling weapons."

Kinsey considered a moment, then said, "Okay, I think we can handle that, but I need a bit of time. How long can you stall them?"

"AMERICAN TANKER! YOU HAVE TWO MINUTES TO DEPLOY YOUR PILOT LADDER OR WE WILL OPEN FIRE!" came the amplified voice.

"Obviously not long," Hughes said, turning to Howell. "Georgia, get some of the deck gang and start rigging the pilot ladder, be as visibly awkward and clumsy as possible. How long do you think you can drag it out without being too obvious?"

She shrugged. "Ten minutes anyway, maybe fifteen."

Hughes looked at Kinsey.

"That will have to do," Kinsey said. "Let me get my guys lined up."

Once again, the amplified voice rose from the ship's side.

"AMERICAN TANKER! YOU HAVE ONE MINUTE TO DEPLOY YOUR PILOT LADDER OR WE WILL OPEN FIRE!"

Howell nodded and started for the stairwell door as Hughes looked toward the port bridge wing. "I better show myself to keep this guy calmed down until he sees us working on the pilot ladder."

Kinsey nodded and started for the stairs behind Howell as Hughes moved out on the bridge wing again to motion to the Cubans that work was in progress.

Ten minutes later, Hughes stood at the ship's side on the main deck, watching Georgia Howell direct the final securing and deployment of the pilot ladder as the Cuban boat floated twenty feet away, the Cuban officer on the small boat visibly irritated by the delay. Finally the rope ladder unrolled down the ship's side, and the little boat nosed in toward it. The officer motioned a man to lead the way up the ladder while he and the second Cuban sailor hung back, waiting their turn. Hughes stepped away from the side of the ship and moved toward the open watertight door of the deckhouse, where Matt Kinsey waited just out of sight.

"Looks like three out of the four in the boarding party," Hughes said softly, "the officer and two sailors. The officer has a sidearm, and the other two have what look like AKs."

"Good," Kinsey replied. "I figure the officer type will place himself on the bridge and send at least one guy to the engine control room. They don't have enough people to completely contain and control the crew, so I'm thinking he's just going to control the bridge and engine room and get us into actual Cuban waters ASAP. He'll probably call help from there. Now we just need to figure out where he decides to put the third guy, and we can take them down fast. If we can achieve complete surprise, this might be painless for all concerned."

"What about the boat? If he gets away or calls for help, there's no way we're outrunning any reinforcements at our blinding top speed of fifteen knots."

"Well, the officer used the bull horn, so I'm counting on the fact they're probably under orders to maintain radio silence outside of Cuban waters," Kinsey said, "and as far as the boat getting away, I've got that covered. Trust me on that."

"I sure as hell hope so," Hughes said. "Now I gotta go greet our visitors. When I figure out what's up, I'll pass the word."

"Okay, but remember, if any shooting starts—"

"I know, hit the deck. Everybody knows." Hughes moved back to the ship's side near the top of the pilot ladder.

He reached it just as the first Cuban stepped on the deck, his head on a swivel as he unslung his assault rifle and motioned the Americans away from the ladder. The officer was next, and after a quick glance at the assembled Americans—that lingered on Georgia Howell a bit too long—he stepped over in front of Hughes.

"You are the *capitan* ?" he asked.

Hughes extended his hand. "Yes, I'm Captain Jordan Hughes."

The Cuban ignored the outstretched hand. "I am Lieutenant Hector Ramos of the *Tropas Guarda Fronteras* or, as I believe you *yanquis* refer to us, the Cuban Border Guard. You have entered the waters of the sovereign Republic of Cuba without authorization, *Capitan* , so I regret to inform you I must place your vessel under arrest. We will proceed at once to the nearest Cuban port, which is in this case Matanzas, where you will stand trial. If it is found your trespass was unintentional, you and your crew may be returned to the United States, but unfortunately your vessel and your cargo will be forfeited." He smiled for the first time. "And you appear to be fully loaded, so exactly what is your cargo?"

"There must be some mistake," Hughes said. "We're at least ten miles from Cuban—"

The Cuban's face clouded. "There is indeed a mistake, *Capitan* , and you have made—"

"*Teniente, mira el barco alli!* " said the last Cuban to board.

Ramos's gaze followed the pointing finger of his subordinate to the bright orange hull of the Coast Guard boat stowed on deck some distance away. Unconsciously he rested his hand on his sidearm.

"You are a military vessel? You have US Coast Guard aboard?" They were accusations rather than questions.

"No, no," Hughes said. "We are only carrying the boat as cargo. We're supposed to deliver it to the Coast Guard station near our destination in Texas."

Ramos studied the boat for a moment, then smiled. "It is a fine boat, *Capitan.* Unfortunately you will not be able to make delivery as intended, but I can assure you it will make a welcome addition to our little fleet and we will make good use of it, after an appropriate change of color, of course. Now, I repeat, what is your cargo? It is unusual to see a loaded tanker southbound in these waters."

Hughes shrugged. "These are unusual times. We are carrying diesel and gasoline. We were unable to enter port at Wilmington due to lack of a pilot, so we decided to return to Texas, as most of the crew lives near there."

"A most fortunate decision for the people of Cuba," the Cuban said, pleased by the unexpected bonus of the patrol boat and somewhat more relaxed. He turned and spit out some rapid-fire Spanish.

"Now, *Capitan* ," he said, "please have an officer escort one of my men to the engine room and instruct the crew there not to make any trouble. Then I will go with you to the bridge and we will be on our way. Understand?"

Hughes nodded and motioned Howell over. When she arrived, he said, "Please take one of these guys to the engine room and tell Dan not to try anything funny."

She nodded and Hughes looked at the Cuban, who nodded in turn and directed one of his men to follow Howell.

"Now, *Capitan* , the bridge, if you please," the Cuban said, and Hughes led the way across the main deck to the deckhouse entrance to start the long climb up to the bridge. He noted with satisfaction both the remaining Cubans were following him.

On the bridge they found an anxious Pete Sonnier peering out the port bridge window to where the Cuban patrol boat had moved out a few hundred feet from the ship. The AB turned when he heard the door open and blanched when he saw the two armed Cubans with the captain.

"Everything's cool, Pete," Hughes said. "We'll get through this."

Sonnier nodded and moved to the steering stand.

"Is she still on the mike?" Hughes asked.

"Oh… yeah, I guess so," Sonnier said. "When the mate called down and stopped the engine, I didn't even think about the autopilot."

"Yeah, me neither," Hughes said. "I guess we were a bit distracted."

He turned to Ramos. "With your permission, I will have the helmsman take the ship off autopilot, as I presume you intend to give us a new course."

"Exactly so, *Capitan* , and after you do that, please call the engine room, as I wish to speak to my man there."

Hughes nodded. "Take her off the mike, Pete," he said, then walked over to the console and called the engine room.

"Engine room, Chief speaking," Dan Gowan answered.

"Is the Cuban down there with you, Dan? The guy up here wants to speak to him."

"I'll put him on," Gowan said, and Hughes handed the phone to the Cuban officer.

There was a short exchange in Spanish, which seemed to satisfy Ramos, and he hung up the phone.

"Very well, *Capitan* ," he said, "please order the engine back up to sea speed and come to a new course of two hundred ten degrees true."

Hughes nodded and did as instructed. Vibrations throbbed through the hull as the massive ship slowly built speed back up. They rode in silence, Sonnier behind the wheel, staring ahead except for occasional glances at the gyro repeater, and Hughes studying the Cubans as they, in turn, studied the bridge console and instrumentation. After ten minutes Hughes broke the silence.

"You said if we were found not guilty, we would be returned to the US. How?"

Ramos shrugged. "That is not my concern."

Prick, thought Hughes, but rather than punching the guy, he returned the shrug and smiled. "It will work out, I suppose. Would you like something to eat? We have plenty and my cook makes very good sandwiches. Roast beef? Ham and cheese?"

The look on the Cuban's face was a combination of greed and suspicion.

"Don't worry," Hughes said. "I'm not trying to poison you. How about I have a variety sent up and you choose which one you would like me to eat first? Would that be satisfactory?"

Ramos considered it for a moment, his hunger obvious. "Yes. That would be acceptable… and thank you."

"No problem." Hughes walked to the phone to call the galley.

"Yeah, Polak," he said into the phone. "Send up an assortment of sandwiches to the bridge. Yeah, mix 'em up. Enough for Sonnier and I and our two guests. Oh, and while you're at it, send some down to the engine room for the chief and our guest down there."

"Got it. Two on the bridge, one in the engine room," said Kinsey in Hughes' ear, "which side is the patrol boat on?"

"I'm not sure when we'll make port, Polak. Several hours at least," Hughes said into the phone.

"I copy, the boat is on the PORT side of the ship," Kinsey said, "glance at the bridge clock NOW and in exactly five minutes, create some diversion to get the Cubans to the STARBOARD side of the bridge and well out of sight of the boat. Do you copy?"

"Copy that Polak, and send some spicy brown mustard up with the sandwiches, okay? Great, we'll be waiting." Hughes hung up.

Ramos raised his eyebrows. "I must say, *Capitan* , you are taking your arrest remarkably well."

Hughes shrugged. "I learned long ago life is less stressful when you don't worry about what you can't control."

"A very intelligent philosophy," the Cuban said.

They lapsed back into silence as Hughes kept watch on the bridge clock in his peripheral vision. At approximately the four-minute mark, he strolled over and studied the radar screen, then screwed up his face in a look of puzzled concern.

"What is it?" Ramos asked, moving toward the radar.

Hughes shook his head as Ramos joined him at the radar. "I don't know. Some sort of radar contact, but it's intermittent. There!" He pointed to a nonexistent blip. "Did you see it?"

"I saw nothing," Ramos said as Hughes moved from behind the radar to retrieve his binoculars from the storage box by the bridge window, then turned and started out the door to the starboard bridge wing.

"Where are you going?" Ramos demanded.

"There's something to starboard. I'm going to check it out." Hughes hurried out the door before the Cuban could object.

He rushed to the far side of the bridge wing, binoculars pressed to his eyes as he scanned the open ocean for the nonexistent radar contact. He heard Ramos approach behind him, and he lowered the binoculars and shot a quick glance back at the Cuban. Ramos was scowling as he approached, and behind him, Hughes could see the second Cuban was also interested and was standing in the wheelhouse door, watching the confrontation about to unfold between his superior and the *yanqui capitan* .

Hughes turned and pressed the binoculars back to his eyes.

"There is nothing! Come back inside at once, or I will—"

"There!" Hughes lowered the glasses and pointed into the distance. "See for yourself." He offered the binoculars to Ramos.

Ramos put the glasses to his eyes and looked out over the open ocean.

"And what exactly am I looking for?"

Matt Kinsey stood with the door from the stairwell to the chartroom slightly cracked, straining to hear the conversation on the bridge. When he heard Hughes exit the wheelhouse over the Cuban's objection, he waited a few seconds and then eased the door open quietly to enter the chartroom, crouched low behind the large chart table, two of his men close behind. They were all armed with pistols.

He peeked around the chartroom curtain and cursed. Both Cubans were on the starboard side, but one was in the wheelhouse door, blocking access to the second. They had to take the first man swiftly and silently to subdue the second before he could react. And there was no time; Hughes couldn't distract the Cuban officer forever.

Kinsey flashed a signal, and one of his men holstered his sidearm and drew a stun gun. Kinsey and his backup charged, widely separated so they both had clear shots at the Cuban in the doorway with his back to them, while the Coastie with the stun gun circled far left, approaching the Cuban swiftly while staying out of the other two men's fields of fire.

The man with the stun gun leaped on the Cuban, placing his left arm around the man, pinning the AK tight against the man's body by hugging him close. He jammed the stun gun electrodes into the Cuban's neck, intent on incapacitating him and dragging him from the doorway without alerting the Cuban officer.

It almost worked.

Unfortunately, the young Cuban was a very recent conscript, pressed into service only after the blackout. Long on enthusiasm if short on training, not only was the young Cuban holding his finger inside the trigger guard, he'd inadvertently moved the fire selector switch to 'full auto' mode. Electricity coursing through his nervous system contracted the muscles in his trigger finger, sending a loud burst of automatic fire ricocheting off the bridge wing deck. The surprised young Cuban, and his equally surprised assailant, collapsed in a tangled heap in the wheelhouse door, foiling Kinsey's plan to rush the bridge wing.

Hughes flinched and ducked instinctively as something stung his left ear and all hell broke loose behind him. His ears rang from the unexpected gunfire, and things seemed to move in slow motion. He spun to see Kinsey just inside the wheelhouse door, staring in horror at a tangle of arms and legs blocking the doorway. Then Kinsey pointed a gun at Ramos, who dropped the binoculars and began to claw his sidearm from its holster. Hughes rose from his crouch, partially spinning as he put all his weight and strength into the right elbow he hammered into the Cuban's face. Something gave under his elbow, and Ramos collapsed, his pistol still in the holster.

Hughes steadied himself on the bridge rail and watched as Kinsey and his men cleared the young Cuban from the door and then rushed out to subdue Ramos. The Coasties fell on the two Cubans with duct tape, and as they were trussing them up, Hughes heard Pete Sonnier call from the wheelhouse, his voice cracking from stress.

"The boat heard, Captain. She's circling our stern!" Sonnier yelled.

"Shit!" Hughes said, looking at Kinsey. "What now?"

Kinsey looked up at the top of the wheelhouse. "TORRES!" he shouted. "THE BOAT'S CIRCLING ASTERN. YOU GOT THIS?"

"I'M ON IT, CHIEF!" came the reply, and Hughes looked up to see a face peeking over the edge of the deck on top of the wheelhouse, obviously one of the Coasties lying prone to keep from being spotted by the boat.

"LIKE WE TALKED ABOUT, TAKE OUT ANY COMMS FIRST."

"PIECE OF CAKE, CHIEF. I ALREADY CHECKED IT OUT WHEN THE BOAT WAS ON THE OTHER SIDE. TWO ANTENNAS."

"ROGER THAT! YOU ARE WEAPONS FREE!"

Hughes saw the man nod, then the head disappeared to be replaced by a thin pipe. It took him a moment to realize it was a rifle barrel.

"What happens if he runs?" Hughes asked. "You gonna shoot the boat driver?"

"Only if he makes us," Kinsey said. "Now let's get inside. The less he can see, the closer he may come to try to figure out what's going on, and that will make it easier for Torres. He's good, but he's not a magician."

Hughes nodded and followed Kinsey back into the wheelhouse.

"That's got to be a pretty tough shot," Hughes said, when they were back out of sight.

Kinsey shook his head. "Not a problem. Torres is cross-trained as a chopper gunner. He used to fly with the HITRON squadron out of Jacksonville and his job was to incapacitate the 'go fast' smuggling boats. And among the equipment we're 'transferring' to MSU Port Arthur, there just happens to be two fifty-caliber Barrett sniper rifles. He'll get the job done."

Just as he finished speaking, the boat pulled into view, steering a parallel course two hundred yards to starboard. The boat held station for several minutes, and it was apparent it would come no closer.

"Doesn't look like he's gonna take the bait," Kinsey said. "Torres will have to take his shot—"

A shot rang out and the top of the wheelhouse on the boat erupted as the shot took out one of the antennas. In less than two seconds, a second shot wiped out the remaining antenna.

A rooster tail shot up behind the boat as the driver rammed both throttles to full speed and turned to race directly away from *Pecos Trader* . No shots followed.

Hughes tensed, waiting for another shot, and the boat opened the distance at almost fifty knots.

"He's getting away—"

The shot shattered the silence as the big slug tore into the starboard outboard, shutting it down forever as the boat suddenly swung to starboard and slowed abruptly. The driver struggled to compensate for the now uneven thrust, wrestling the wheel as the boat continued on an erratic corkscrew track. A final shot sounded and the port outboard coughed smoke and died, the boat drifting powerless several hundred yards from this ship.

"I take it back," Kinsey said, "maybe he is a magician."

WARDEN'S OFFICE
FEDERAL CORRECTIONAL COMPLEX
BEAUMONT, TEXAS

DAY 13, 5:00 P.M.

Spike McComb leaned back in the chair, put his feet up on the warden's desk, and smiled. He had on a relatively clean correctional officer's uniform and his hair was neatly trimmed. Across from him sat Owen Fairchild, aka 'Snaggle' for his dental issues, similarly dressed and barbered.

"Some of the boys are pissed, Spike," Snaggle said. "You said we was goin' on jackrabbit parole and we're still here."

"'Cause I ain't a dumb ass," Spike said. "It didn't come to me right off, but I finally figured out this is the best place we could be."

Snaggle shook his head. "Don't seem right, breakin' out of the joint and then hangin' around. There ain't much law around, and lots of easy pickings."

"And after we take what we want, where we gonna keep it? And when all these dumb asses get all boozed up and are lyin' around drunk, what's to keep a bunch of other assholes from sneaking up and blowing 'em 'way? Answer me that, genius."

Snaggle shrugged and said nothing. McComb pointed in the direction of the maximum-security unit. "Over there at max security, we got about the closest thing to a castle we're likely to find. Razor-wire-topped fence AND big thick walls with guard towers all around and one way in and out. All those things designed to keep us in is just as good to keep people out. Not only that, but we got all the cells we need to keep people to work for us and we got plenty of guns, for now anyway."

McComb smiled. "And the beautiful part is, until we're strong enough, no one's the wiser. Where else would you expect cons to be but in a prison? We both been out to have a look, and you know I'm right. The law's spread pretty thin, but there's still a few around. We just stay low profile until we're strong enough to take over."

Snaggle nodded as realization dawned. "Okay," he said, "but what about the mud people in max security? It's gonna start stinkin' even worse if they die and are lying around in all the heat. Nobody's likely to want to hole up anywhere near there."

"Move 'em over to medium security and leave them to rot," McComb said. "Do it now while they can still move on their own."

"Why don't we make them clean the place up before we move them out?"

McComb shook his head. "Most of them are too far gone, plus they know we ain't gonna let 'em go, so no telling what they might try. We'll get more work out of fresh civilians. Besides, they'll be easier to keep in line."

Snaggle nodded. "I gotta hand it to you, Spike, that's pretty smart."

McComb smirked. "That's why I'm the captain. Now what's the final head count?"

"We got almost a hundred soldiers, and all of them are getting cleaned up like you said. Lucky one of the guys used to work in the barbershop, so the haircuts don't look too bad. We pieced together about a dozen uniforms off the dead COs—the rest of the stuff was too bloody. We can also dress a few guys in civvies we took off bodies here in the admin complex—oh yeah, that reminds me, since we're staying, what do you want to do with all the bodies? They're gonna start stinking too."

"Pile them up over in the admin area of medium security. We'll bury them after we 'recruit' our workforce," McComb said. "Then put together patrols to go out tonight and scavenge for food and supplies. Use the prison vans we found over in the motor pool. Is there enough gas?"

Snaggle nodded. "A couple of hundred gallons and most of the vehicles have some gas in the tanks. It won't last long. And where they gonna find supplies? I figure most of the stores have been stripped by now, and the law is probably all over what's left."

"That's why they're going at night. Put two 'COs' per van, and the story if they're stopped is they're looking for an escaped prisoner. Have 'em cruise residential areas, looking for lights or the sound of generators. Anybody with a generator like as not has both food and fuel. This is hurricane country, so I expect they'll find more than a few. Bring anybody they find so there ain't any witnesses left. We can use 'em to start our workforce. Oh yeah, have them bring the generators too."

Snaggle rose from his chair. "Anything else?"

"Yeah, remind the boys I get first shot at any women they bring back. It's been a long season without rain."

CHAPTER THIRTEEN

Hughes stood on the starboard bridge wing, staring down in the early morning light at Georgia Howell as she supervised the offloading of the Cuban patrol boat. He watched her raise her hand to signal Nunez in the cab of the hose-handling crane, and the boat descended further and settled gently on the calm blue sea. Hughes glanced to the lightening sky in the east and willed the mate to hurry.

"Second-guessing yourself?"

Hughes turned to see Matt Kinsey walking out the wheelhouse door.

"Not really," Hughes said. "We couldn't leave them floating around that close to Cuba. If they got picked up before we got out of range, we were screwed, and we sure as hell can't take them with us. Short of shooting them, marooning them somewhere with a chance of making their way back to civilization seemed the only choice."

"If there's any civilization left," Kinsey said.

"You know what I meant."

"I know, just jerking your chain a bit, Cap," Kinsey said and looked east toward Dry Tortugas. "Though I doubt our passengers will be excited about your choice of disembarkation ports."

"Well, I'm pushing the envelope as it is, and this is as close to Key West as I'm willing to get," Hughes said. "We're leaving them food and water, and Dan broke up some old pallets and made them multiple paddles. They can land on Dry Tortugas and make their plan and then all they have to do is follow the rising sun to the Marquesas Keys and then island-hop up the keys until they get to Key West. They should be able to make it in three or four days, a week max."

Kinsey nodded. "I'm sure dumping the useless outboards made the boat considerably lighter and easier to paddle."

"That was the idea." Hughes looked distracted. "My only real concern is if they make it to Key West and start raving to your Coastie buddies about the *Pecos Trader* . We've been lucky enough to slip past, and I'd just as soon our name didn't come up again."

"I don't think you need to worry," Kinsey said. "In normal times, four Cubans paddling into port in a disabled patrol craft with a tall tale would likely be front-page news, but today there's so many things going down, I doubt it would even register."

"That's probably true," Hughes said, "but all things considered, I could have really done without this whole experience."

Kinsey grinned. "Look at the bright side, we got another machine gun, an RPG launcher and four grenades, three AKs and a pistol out of the deal, along with a lot of ammunition. The Cubans might be short on food, but they seem to have plenty of hardware."

"There is that." Hughes turned to look down at the deck. "Seems it's time to wish our guests 'bon voyage.' Care to join me?"

"Wouldn't miss it for the world," Kinsey said.

When Hughes and Kinsey arrived on the main deck, they found the Cubans lined up, hands still bound with duct tape. Georgia Howell was instructing Lieutenant Ramos as to his location and the easterly route necessary to reach the inhabited area of the Keys. The three enlisted Cubans were standing docilely, unsure what to expect and obviously frightened, but Ramos's face was red with rage, in stark contrast to the white of the tape the second mate had used to stabilize his broken nose. When the Cuban saw Hughes approach, he turned and vented.

"This is an act of piracy, an outrage!" he hissed. "You cannot abandon us here. How do you expect us to return to Cuba?"

Hughes shrugged. "As someone said to me very recently, that is not my concern."

"You will pay for this *Yanqui* !"

"I already have, Ramos," Hughes said, "by taking the time to drop your sorry ass here instead of just casting you adrift. However, that's still an option, so if you'd like to be dropped off in the middle of the Gulf of Mexico instead of spitting distance from land, just keep talking."

The Cuban glared at Hughes but held his tongue, and Hughes motioned to the armed Coasties to escort the Cubans to the pilot ladder. At the top of the ladder, Georgia Howell produced a pocketknife and cut the duct tape from each man's hands to allow him to descend to the waiting boat. Ramos was the last down, and as soon as he was aboard the small boat, Howell motioned for Kenny Nunez to cast the boat off and begin hauling the pilot ladder back on board.

Hughes walked to the ship's side and stood beside Howell, staring down at the boat as it paddled away.

"Good riddance," Howell said.

"I'll second that," Hughes said. "Did you give them plenty of stores?"

"Twenty gallons of water and two cases of Spam," she replied.

Hughes burst out laughing. "Seriou—seriously?" he asked.

"Serves the bastard right for checking out my ass when he thought I wasn't looking," Howell said. "Now let's get this ship to Texas."

"I'm with you, Mate," Hughes said, and they started for the bridge.

MAYPORT NAVAL STATION
JACKSONVILLE, FLORIDA

DAY 14, 6:00 A.M.

"How are the new guys?" Luke asked. "Jarheads, right?"

Washington nodded. "From Lejeune. Corley and Abrams are their names. Gibson knows them both and says they're good troops."

Luke grinned. "Corley and Abrams? Sounds like a friggin' law firm."

A smile flitted across Washington's face, disappearing as quickly to be replaced by what was becoming a perpetual worried frown.

"So what's the drill, LT," he asked, "another 'recon patrol? What are we supposed to steal today?"

"It's a tough one," Luke said. "Evidently my efforts to restrict our 'acquisitions' to things abandoned hasn't gone unnoticed. Rorke came to me last night and 'reminded' me we're to concentrate on food. He pointed out his other 'recon teams' were producing much more and he expected today's mission into a new area to 'yield significant results.' All of which means we can no longer just go through the motions."

Washington shook his head. "I… I don't think I can steal food out of folks' mouths."

Luke sighed. "I don't like it any better than you do, Sergeant, but if we don't do it, someone else will, likely someone more aggressive about it than us. Besides, we both took an oath, and as screwed up as this is, we're still following the orders of our lawfully appointed superiors. We don't get to choose which orders we follow." He relented a bit. "It's not like we have a lot of options here, Washington."

Washington looked unconvinced, but nodded. "Who you want to take?"

Luke considered a moment. "Long, Gibson, and the two new jarheads. And I suppose we need to take at least a couple of the others. I guess Grogan and one more. Which one do you want?"

Washington shrugged. "Six of one, they're all assholes. Morton, I guess."

"All right. We'll roll out at oh eight hundred," Luke said.

***

Luke stared out the window as the Humvee moved along US 17 North, aka Main Street North. There were cars stopped in the middle of the road where they ran out of gas, but the drivers of most had coasted to the right shoulder, no doubt sure they would come back 'when things got back to normal' to retrieve their vehicles. The two Humvees were traveling at a steady clip of thirty to thirty-five miles per hour, with two commandeered civilian pickups sandwiched between them, all maintaining their safety intervals to allow them reaction time if the driver ahead had to swerve around obstacles in the road.

He'd chosen US 17 in preference to I-95 a bit further to the west, because intelligence from chopper flyovers indicated I-95 was a parking lot, with refugees straggling its entire length, heading north. Luke wondered briefly what would happen when the northbound refugees met the no doubt equally desperate southbound horde from Savannah. By all accounts, the situation was dire, with bodies beside the interstate, bloating in the Florida sun. Impromptu refugee camps had sprung up around both abutments of the Nassau River bridge, where people too exhausted or discouraged to move on were fighting for the limited shade of scrubby trees and drinking the near brackish river water. It wasn't something he was eager to see—each foray 'outside the wire' brought fresh scenes of horror.

Nor was this route free of horrors. His driver swerved around a late model BMW with both front doors open, blocking the view ahead, then swerved again to avoid the bodies of an elderly couple lying in the road, their mangled skulls leaving no doubt they'd met a violent end.

"Jesus!" Long said, instinctively slowing the vehicle. "Should I stop, LT?"

Luke shook his head. "They're beyond help, and unfortunately I suspect that's a sight we'll be seeing a lot more of. But call back and advise the others to watch it when they pass the BMW."

Long complied and Luke studied the passing landscape, mostly pine forest on the left with scattered residential neighborhoods on the right. His orders were to bypass them all and go straight north to the town of Yulee, turning east there on A1A toward Amelia Island and Fernandina Beach. Rorke seemed to think the A1A corridor was far enough from Jacksonville proper to hold 'greater promise,' and Luke was instructed to find and work the most promising subdivisions while identifying others for attention by additional 'recon teams.' It hadn't escaped his notice the area was also far enough away from any FEMA command presence for Rorke's 'off the book' operations to go largely unnoticed. FEMA would likely turn a blind eye in any event, but Luke sensed Rorke was being careful to avoid anything that might create a conflict with his benefactors.

**

Thirty minutes later they were headed east on A1A when they reached a commercial retail area on the left, a long row of fast-food outlets and chain restaurants lining the road in front of expansive parking lots serving big-box stores of various types. Luke spotted the sign for a Publix supermarket and directed Long to pull into the parking lot. It was a long shot at this point, but if they could scrape together a reasonable yield from the supermarket, they might minimize the civilian contact he was dreading. The rest of the little convoy followed his vehicle into the deserted parking lot and came to rest in front of the supermarket.

"Long, get up on the Ma Deuce and keep your eyes open," Luke said. "I don't think we should have any problems, but let's be careful."

"Roger that, LT," Long said, as Luke dismounted.

Washington walked up as Luke was getting out of the Humvee, a look of doubt on his face.

"I know, I know," Luke said. "It's probably stripped, but it doesn't hurt to look. Take two guys and do a quick recon. If the shelves are bare, check to see if there's anything left in back."

"Roger that," Washington said, then yelled, "Gibson, Abrams, you're with me. Move your asses."

The three men disappeared into the building and came out a few minutes later. Washington emerged last and gave Luke a shake of his head as he approached.

"Damn, it stinks in there," Washington said.

"Rotten meat and fish?" Luke asked.

"Among other things. It's bad in there, LT—three bodies, two women and a man. Looks like the women were shot and the man's head was beat in with a can of creamed corn. The can busted and it's lying there in his blood."

Luke suppressed a shudder. "I don't suppose there was any food?"

"Not a crumb anywhere—unless you count the creamed corn," Washington said.

"All right, I guess we have to do this. Leave Long on the Ma Deuce and get everyone else down here so we can go over the op."

Washington nodded and began shouting orders and the men gathered around Luke.

"All right, given all the commercial development, I'm thinking there are plenty of subdivisions nearby. We're going to head south at the last intersection we went through and find the first one. I'll drive one Humvee with Long up top and Sergeant Washington will drive the second one with Gibson on the Ma Deuce there. We'll stay in reserve to respond with overwhelming force if need be. I doubt we need it, but better safe than sorry."

There were nods of agreement as Luke continued. "Grogan, I want you and Morton in one pickup and Corley and Abrams in the other. You guys will be going door-to-door in pairs to collect, one street at a time. Washington's Humvee will take a position at the entrance to the street being worked by Grogan and Morton, and Long and I will support Corley and Abrams. If either group runs into a big problem, specifically armed resistance, I want BOTH Humvees to respond, and the collection team that's temporarily unsupported is just to hold in place. Is that clear?"

Again there were nods before Luke continued, "Now get this straight, we're not going in and stripping these people of all their food. I want you to go door-to-door, identify yourselves as members of the FEMA Special Reaction Force and politely but firmly inform residents there is a mandatory food collection operation in process. Tell them though we are authorized to seize all food and fuel, we will only requisition fifty percent of their stores at this time, assuming they cooperate. Tell them they have ten minutes to collect their contribution and bring it curbside to load into the pickup, then move on to the next house. Inform them if we believe they're holding back, we will enter their homes to verify the amounts. Further inform them if verification shows they failed to deliver fifty percent of their stores, we will take it all. You are to stay together and you are NOT to threaten them, harm them in any way beyond the warning I have indicated, or enter their houses. Is that clear?"

"That's bullshit," Grogan said. "This ain't a food drive. They'll just give as little as they think they can get away with and it'll all be crappy stuff. This ain't what Colonel Rorke wants and you know it, Kinsey."

Washington moved towards Grogan, but Luke waved him off. "We may get less than half of what they have," Luke said, "but I'm betting there are plenty of houses and we'll get enough to fill these two pickups before the day is out, and without harming anyone or leaving them completely without food. Since that's all we can carry anyway, that seems like a win for all concerned or, at least, less of a loss." Luke's voice hardened, "And that PRIVATE Grogan, is the first and last time I ever intend to explain an order to you. And you will address me as sir or lieutenant, or Lieutenant Kinsey, or even LT, but if you ever disrespect me again, it will be the last time you disrespect anyone. Is that clear?"

Grogan glared and, after a long moment, bobbed his head once.

"I didn't hear you, Private. I asked you if that was clear?"

"Yes, SIR," hissed Grogan between clenched teeth.

"Good, now are there any other questions?" Luke asked.

Corley, one of the new men, raised his hand and Luke nodded.

"Ahh… what if no one answers the door, LT?"

Luke considered a moment. "In that case," he said, "pound on the door with the butt of your weapon and announce loudly you assume the house is abandoned and you're going to break in. Give anyone inside a couple of minutes to respond. If no one responds, notify us you have a potential breach situation and then breach the door. That is the ONLY circumstance under which you will enter a home without a specific direct order from either myself or Sergeant Washington. Is that clear?"

There was a muted chorus of 'yes, sirs,' and Luke nodded at Washington.

"All right," Washington yelled, "let's mount up and get to it."

***

They found the first residential area a half mile south of the intersection on the left side of the road, where what had been a carefully landscaped side road marked the entrance to an upscale subdivision of large new homes on spacious lots between the main thoroughfare and a man-made lake. Homes backing on to the busier main street were protected by a handsome brick privacy wall at least twelve feet high.

The little convoy turned into the subdivision entrance and immediately encountered conditions requiring a plan modification. The entrance yielded on to a small traffic circle with streets branching off to the left and right. After a hurried consultation between Luke and Washington, they decided both Humvees would maintain station at the traffic circle, with Grogan and Morton working the street to the south while Corley and Abrams took the street to the north.

The two collection teams parked their pickups a half-dozen houses down their respective streets and started canvassing. The civilian responses varied from tentative to argumentative, but politely meeting resistance with a few minutes of interaction before dropping the not-so-veiled threat of total confiscation and then moving on was working well. After reflection, all of the residents decided giving up something under their control was much preferable to having these intruders in their homes. In a few minutes, sullen residents emerged from their homes with plastic grocery bags and cardboard boxes, usually small, to cast resentful looks at the Humvees as they deposited their meager offerings into the bed of the waiting pickups. The process was slow, but it was undoubtedly faster and less stressful than having a confrontation at every house. The threat of entering nonresponsive houses was also effective, as several homeowners answered their doors just before Luke authorized breaches.

"So far, so good," said Luke, as he stood with Washington in the little traffic circle next to the two Humvees.

Washington grunted, "True, but that asshole Grogan was right about one thing. I suspect we're getting a ton of creamed spinach and pickled beets."

Luke shrugged. "Rorke said food, he wasn't specific."

Washington chuckled. Every fifteen or twenty minutes, the collection teams moved the slowly filling pickups a few houses down the street, diverging in opposite directions from the Humvees. At the ninety-minute mark, the Corley and Abrams team still had a long stretch of straight street visible ahead, but the pickup assigned to Grogan and Morton was moving abreast of an intersection. Washington climbed into the driver's seat of the Humvee and keyed the mike on the radio.

"Shopping Cart Four, this is Shopping Cart Two, do you copy? Over," Washington said.

"Shopping Cart Two, this is Shopping Cart Four, go ahead. Over," came Grogan's voice over the speaker.

"Four, what is the status of the side street? Is it a through street? Over."

"Negative Two, I say again negative. It's a cul-de-sac. Over."

"We copy, Four, intersection is a cul-de-sac. Leave your vehicle parked on this street where we can keep it under observation and have residents carry their... their..." Washington was momentarily stumped as to what to call the food they were collecting. Donations? Contributions? Tribute? After a moment he punted, "Their stuff out to the truck."

"Shopping Cart Two this is Shopping Cart Four. We copy. Anything else? Over."

"Yes, Four, please say estimated time to clear the cul-de-sac. Over," Washington said.

"About a dozen houses. At five minutes a house, I estimate one hour minimum. Over," Grogan said.

"Two, I copy. We will not have a visual on you, so if you run into problems, get on the horn ASAP. Over."

"Affirmative Two. Shopping Cart Four out," Grogan said.

Washington racked the mike and crawled out of the Humvee to stand beside Luke.

"You heard?" Washington asked.

Luke nodded.

"You think I should move down and cover them in the cul-de-sac?" Washington asked.

Luke looked down the road in both directions and then back at the entrance to the subdivision.

"No," he said, "because it's just dawning on me this might not be the best place to be. We got a lake on one side and a pretty stout brick wall on the other, and this entrance is the only way through the wall we know of. We could probably bust through if need be, but I don't see any place to get a running start. So no, Sergeant, I'm fine with both the Humvees here watching our six unless we actually need to provide close support. Better safe than sorry."

Washington nodded. "I agree. Hopefully we'll have the trucks full in another couple of hours and we can get the hell out of here."

***

"This blows," Morton said as he and Grogan trudged across the lawn of the first house on the left in the neat cul-de-sac. "We'll be dicking around for hours doing this touchy-feely shit, and we could have already filled both trucks up a couple of times over if we just cleaned out the first six or eight houses we hit. Publix and those other stores aren't far away, and if these assholes are still all hunkered down in these houses, I'm thinking they got at least some of the loot. I'm betting they got plenty stashed."

"Tell me about it," Grogan said. "Kinsey's a prick. Him and his crap rules... hey, I just thought of something!"

"What?"

"Since they can't see us, let's speed things up. Washington's expecting us to be here an hour at least, so we can ditch all that nicey-nice crap and work all these houses and then take a break."

"Sounds good to me, bro," Morton replied just as they reached the front door of the house.

Grogan grinned and pulled open the storm door to hammer on the inner door with the butt of his weapon, leaving dents in the beautifully stained wooden door.

"OPEN UP! FEMA! OFFICIAL BUSINESS!" he yelled. Beside him, Morton smirked.

The door opened tentatively to the full width allowed by the security chain and an elderly woman's face appeared in the crack at waist level. "Y-yes? What is it?" she asked, fear in her voice.

"You got five minutes to get half your food and any fuel to the pickup truck at the entrance to the cul-de-sac," Grogan snarled. "If it's not out there in time, we're coming back and taking everything you got. Any questions?"

"B-but I don't have much—"

"Not my problem," Grogan said, "comply or we'll come back and take it all."

"I-I'm in a wheelchair. I can't get it out to the stree—"

"Again, not my problem, grandma," Grogan said. "But if it ain't out to the truck in five, we'll be back to help you, and I guarantee you won't like it. You have a nice fucking day!"

Morton burst out laughing as the two turned to cut across the yard to the next house.

"Outstanding," Morton said.

Grogan smirked, pleased with himself. "Did you time me?"

"A minute, more or less."

"I'm gonna try to do the next one in forty-five," Grogan said.

"Shit no, man! Let's take turns," Morton said. "I bet I make the next one in under thirty."

"All right, that'll make it interesting. What's the bet?"

Morton thought for a minute. "I got two six packs of brew stashed. How about you?"

"You're on. I got half a bottle of Jack Black squirreled away. Fastest time takes it all."

The two raced from house to house down the same side of the street, circling the cul-de-sac as they delivered their ever briefer ultimatums with cheerful brutality, until they arrived back at the entrance to the cul-de-sac across the street from the old woman's house.

"I still think you cheated," Grogan grumbled.

"Seventeen seconds, bro," Morton chortled, "that Jack is gonna go down so smooth—"

"Watch it, man! You want Washington to see us?" Grogan said, grabbing Morton's arm and pulling him back as he neared the main road.

Morton grinned. "Sorry, bro, just thinking about that Jack. How much time we got?"

Grogan looked at his watch as Morton eyed the steady stream of residents carrying parcels to the pickup, noting with satisfaction the 'contributions' seemed much more substantial.

"That only took us fifteen minutes," Grogan said. "We got at least forty-five left, easy."

"This is gonna finish filling the truck," Morton said. "Maybe we should blow off the break and just report back. Besides, I do want to get me a taste of that Jack."

"Don't be a dumb ass. If we show back up in fifteen or twenty minutes, Kinsey's gonna know we didn't follow his stupid rules, and give us a ration of shit. We just gotta chill till he's expecting us. I'm gonna sit my ass down right over there under that big shade tree."

Morton nodded and the two started across the yard, until Morton grabbed Grogan's arm and dragged him down behind a hedge.

"Whoa! Dude, check it out!" Morton said, and nodded across the street to the old lady's house as he peeked up over the hedge.

Grogan followed suit and saw a slim young woman in a sundress carrying two plastic grocery bags and walking down the old lady's sidewalk, headed for the pickup at the entrance to the cul-de-sac.

"I guess Granny's 'I'm all alone in my wheelchair' story was bullshit," Morton said.

Grogan nodded as he eyed the woman hungrily. She was in her late teens or early twenties, and the simple sundress did nothing to hide the curves of her slim body. She had long blond hair pulled back in a ponytail.

"Now that is one fine piece of ass," Grogan said as he watched the woman deposit the bags in the pickup and start back toward her house, hurrying now, as she looked in all directions. "You reckon it's just her and the old lady?"

"That's my guess," Morton said, "'cause I'm thinking if there was a husband or father or brother, he'd have hauled the stuff to the truck."

"You thinking what I'm thinking?" Grogan asked.

"If you're thinking you know how to spend the rest of our little break, I believe I am," Morton said, then added, "First dibs."

"Screw you, Morton! You already got my whiskey, so I got first dibs on the woman. Besides, you probably only need about seventeen seconds anyway, seeing as how you're so fast and all."

"Screw you back, Grogan," Morton said, but he was laughing as the two men rose and moved toward the old lady's house.

"What's up, Sergeant?" Luke asked as Washington lowered the binoculars.

"I don't know," Washington said, "but it doesn't seem right. A bunch of people started dropping off food in the pickup not long after Grogan and Morton started canvassing. That's way faster than I expected, and now there hasn't been anyone there for the last fifteen minutes."

"You think you should—"

Gunfire sounded down the street from the direction of the cul-de-sac, a few individual shots, possibly a handgun, followed after a brief pause by semiautomatic rifle fire.

"Shit!" Washington said as he swung into the driver's seat on the Humvee and grabbed the mike.

"Shopping Cart Four this is Shopping Cart two. Sitrep, NOW. Over," Washington said.

"We're taking fire, repeat, we're taking fire. Grogan is down, repeat, Grogan is down. I am withdrawing to the pickup. Over," came Morton's voice.

"We copy, Four. Support is on the way. Over."

Washington looked at Luke, who was already in the driver's seat of his own Humvee, picking up the mike. "Shopping Cart Three, this is Shopping

Cart Actual. Suspend your current operation and move pickup to our current position to assume control of the subdivision entrance. Shopping Cart Actual and Shopping Cart Two are moving in support of Shopping Cart Four. Confirm. Over."

"This is Shopping Cart Three, we copy. On the way, LT," Abrams said.

Luke cranked up the Humvee and started after Washington, who was already racing toward Grogan and Morton's pickup. They arrived within seconds of each other, bracketing the pickup, just as Morton ran across a lawn and ducked behind the truck, rising to shoot toward the house, then moving into the more secure area behind Washington's Humvee. Gibson and Long manned the M2s, searching for threats, as Luke and Washington exited their vehicles on the sides away from the house and moved beside Morton.

"What the hell happened, Morton?" Washington demanded.

"Me and Grogan heard screaming coming from that house. We got there and found the door kicked in and stumbled upon a bunch of gangbangers, must be a dozen of them, maybe more. Anyway, we got in a firefight and Grogan got hit. They almost got me too. I had to leave him; there was too many of them," Morton said.

"Is Grogan dead?" Luke asked.

Morton nodded. "Absolutely, LT. He took a round in the head. I hated to leave him, but it was just too hot. I think there may be more of them. We need to get out of here 'cause this place will be crawling with bangers in a few minutes."

"We're not leaving anyone." Luke moved to peer around the Humvee at the house. "Damn! The place is on fire. There's smoke coming out the windows."

"The dude is DEAD," Morton said, "and we shouldn't risk anyone just to recover a body."

Luke kept his face impassive. "All right, Morton, settle down. Take cover behind the pickup and keep an eye on the front door. I have to think about this."

"The dude is DEAD," Morton repeated, but assumed the position behind the truck as ordered.

Luke nodded at Washington and stepped away as far as possible. "What do you think of that story?" he asked softly.

"It's a fairy tale. The gunfire we heard wasn't nearly sustained enough to be a firefight, and if there were bangers in there, they'd be opening up on us. They're all trigger-happy assholes with no fire discipline at all, and the only one shooting when we got here was Morton." Washington looked toward the house. "And if we want to find out what went down, we don't have much time before it goes up in smoke."

Luke nodded and drew his sidearm. "Get Long down here, but leave Gibson on the Ma Deuce just in case there's a miracle and this asshole is telling the truth."

Washington nodded and hurried to carry out those orders as Luke walked back over to Morton. Morton stiffened when he saw the handgun and Luke saw the man's weapon move a bit.

"Don't even think about it, Morton. Set your weapon down gently against the truck, face away from me and put both hands on the back of your head."

"What the fuc—"

Luke leveled the gun at Morton's head. "I'm not going to ask twice, and it's well within my authority to shoot you for disobeying a direct order while in contact with the enemy."

"All right, all right," Morton said as Long climbed out of the Humvee.

"Long, zip-tie Private Morton's hands and sit him down behind the pickup. If he makes an aggressive move, shoot him. Got it?" Luke asked.

"Absolutely," Long replied.

Luke looked at Washington. "Okay, Sergeant, let's go take out these gangbangers."

Washington nodded and they approached the house on opposite zigzag paths, taking advantage of available cover to stack up on opposite sides of the splintered front door.

Washington pulled out a flash bang and looked a question at Luke, who nodded, and the big man activated it and tossed it into the house. Both men rushed in on the heels of the explosion and found the house—empty—or at least not occupied by the living. The smoke was emanating from smoldering curtains in the family room, evidently set on fire by Morton before his hasty retreat. Washington pulled them down and dragged them through a patio door to toss them into an inground pool with green scummy water, then returned, leaving the patio door open to help clear the room.

Luke stared at the scene, rage rising within him. Grogan was dead, sure enough, lying face up with his pants and underwear around his ankles, his face disfigured by the exit wound of a gunshot. There was also an old woman on the floor beside a wheelchair, dead of multiple gunshot wounds, and a young girl near the woman, dead of the same cause. The girl was naked and there were angry red marks on her body from where her underwear had been ripped from her body. There was a Colt 1911 on the floor beside the girl.

Luke looked at Washington, who only shook his head, as if incapable of speech, and both men turned and left the house. At the Humvees, Luke stood staring down at Morton.

"Let's hear it, Morton," he said.

"It was an accident, LT. We didn't mean to kill 'em. We just wanted to have a little fun, you know."

"Go on," Luke said, his face a mask.

"Well, I taped the old lady's trap to shut her up and taped her hands to the wheelchair and then rolled her out of the way into a bedroom, but the old bitch got loose somehow. The next thing I know, I'm watching Grogan do his business and she rolls out with a Colt and shoots Grogan in the head. Right there in front of me, for Christ's sake. Then she starts shooting at me, but I've stripped off most of my gear and I have to dive behind the couch, and by the time I can get to my gun and shoot the old bitch, the girl got out from under Grogan. Then when I cap the old lady, the girl picks up the gun and starts shooting at me, so I have to shoot her too. I mean, I didn't have a choice, it was self-defense."

"So you figure you'll just make up this fairy tale and burn down the house, and we're all cool, huh?" Luke asked.

Morton shrugged. "It seemed like a good idea at the time." Then he continued, "Look, LT, I know we screwed up and I'm sorry I didn't come clean. I'm willing to take any punishment you want. Why, when Grogan and I screwed up in Uganda, Rorke had us on all the shit details for six months and—"

"So you've done this before?"

"No, not exactly like this, but some chick's kid brother got pissed off and tried to kill us, so we had to defend ourselves, and Rorke had to smooth it over with the head dude in the village. I think he bought him a bunch of goats or something—"

"Shut your mouth, you sick bastard," Washington said. "I heard enough."

Washington stalked away, jerking his head for Luke to follow. He stopped some distance from the Humvees and turned to Luke.

"What are we gonna do, LT? If we take that piece of shit back, you know Rorke's gonna let him off with a slap on the wrist. Five will get you ten, he'll pay lip service to 'severe punishment' and a few weeks from now Morton will just be in another unit. This is messed up."

Luke said nothing as Washington articulated his own worst fears. He looked over at Morton on his knees and the truck full of looted food. Beyond the truck he could see people starting to emerge from houses along the cul-de-sac, their body language telegraphing their fear, even at a distance. And here and there, he saw angry gestures and an occasional pistol or hunting rifle. None of the residents understood what had happened just yet, but when they did, a conflict was inevitable.

What had Rorke called it, 'medieval Genghis Khan shit'? A lawless time with no rules, except those made by men with power for their own benefit. Was that a system he could live under, even under duress? He turned back to Washington and looked him in the eye.

"WE aren't going to do anything, Sergeant. This is entirely MY responsibility and if it goes sideways, no blame will be on you or any other member of this unit. Is that clear?"

"But, LT—"

"Sergeant Washington, please confirm your understanding of the difference between your responsibilities and mine by saying yes, sir."

Washington came almost to attention. "Yes, sir!"

"Very good, Sergeant." Luke turned and marched back to Morton.

"Private Morton, you have confirmed you killed the two women in the house across the street, is that correct?"

Morton looked confused. "Yeah, like I said, I shot them in self-defense —"

"Private Morton, you stand convicted by your own testimony of two criminal acts against the civilian population, specifically violations of Article 118 of the Uniform Code of Military Justice, or murder. Furthermore, and also by your own testimony, both such criminal acts occurred during the commission of a violation of Article 120 of the Uniform Code of Military Justice, specifically rape, making these crimes especially vile in nature. The penalty for these crimes is death. Accordingly, by the legal precedent which allows for the summary execution of soldiers in emergency situations with no recourse to legal process, and in light of your own confession, I hereby inform you of my intention to carry out that execution."

Luke drew his sidearm. "Do you have any last words?"

"Wh-what do you mean?"

"I mean I'm about to blow your sorry ass away, but you get to say something first."

"You can't do this!"

Luke shot Morton between the eyes.

"Yes, I can," he whispered as he looked down at Morton's lifeless body, "and I wish I'd done it a lot sooner." He straightened.

"Sergeant Washington!"

"Yes, sir?"

"Sergeant, throw Morton's remains on the pickup truck and then take Private Long and go collect Grogan. We've done enough to these people without leaving them our garbage to deal with. Then I want Long to drive the pickup and we'll all withdraw to the traffic circle and pick up Shopping Cart Three as we exit the subdivision. We need to get out of here ASAP before anyone else is hurt. We'll rally in the Publix parking lot. Clear?"

"Yes, sir," Washington said, and nodded to Long as he stooped to pick up Morton's body.

Thirty minutes later, Luke directed the four vehicles to form a hollow square in the center of the Publix parking lot. Everyone dismounted in the center except for Gibson, who stayed on the Ma Deuce, scanning for threats.

"Can you hear me okay up there, Gibson?" asked Luke from the center of the square.

"Yes, sir."

"Good. Okay, people, listen up. As you know, this is a confused situation, and we're all doing the best we can. We all volunteered for the SRF on the understanding we'd be helping in the recovery, and no one told us at the time the transfer was permanent, or we'd be 'discharged' if we attempted to resign from the SRF. I can no longer in good conscience follow the orders I'm being given, but I sure as hell am not going to let them disarm me and dump me God knows where. I'm taking one of the Humvees and a share of the stores and leaving. Anyone who wants to come with me is welcome, and anyone who wants to return to base can do so in the other vehicles. Your call."

"But where you gonna go, LT?" Long asked. "I heard standing orders are anybody who bugs out is classed a deserter."

"I can't answer that question because I don't have a plan, but I do know I'd rather be a deserter than associated with this mercenary scum they're pairing us with, following orders I believe are criminal. My dad's in the Coast Guard up in Wilmington, so I guess I'll head that way." He paused. "But I want all of you to think VERY hard before you decide to come with

175

me or just strike off on your own. I have no hard feelings either way, and after you commit, there's no turning back."

There was murmuring and head nods, but after the briefest of pauses, Washington spoke.

"I'm with you, LT."

"Make it three," Long said.

"Four," Gibson called down from the Ma Deuce. "My folks' place is just northeast of Wilmington anyway, so that works for me. I'll stay with you at least that far, LT."

Gibson's agreement was followed quickly by nods from the other two Marines.

Luke nodded. "All right then, gentlemen, I guess we're all officially rogues and outlaws."

There was a long silence as they all reflected on his words, but slowly Washington's face split into a grin.

"Hell, LT, this is the best I felt since the friggin' lights went out!"

FORT BOX
WILMINGTON CONTAINER TERMINAL
WILMINGTON, NORTH CAROLINA

DAY 14, 9:00 A.M.

Chief Boatswain's Mate Mike Butler watched from his raised vantage point on the deck of the container ship as across the terminal, large forklifts stacked empty containers into a makeshift wall a hundred feet inside the chain-link fence surrounding the terminal.

"Fort Box, huh? Accurate, but not real original."

Beside him, Sergeant Josh Wright grunted. "I'm more interested in defensible than original. We couldn't defend the entire terminal perimeter now anyway, even with the crew-served weapons. This way, we limit the wall to what we can defend and expand it as the need arises and we have more manpower. And we can set up inside the fence, leaving good fields of fire between the new wall and the original fence. We just concentrate the ships on one section of the dock and just build out from there. The added bonus is there aren't any nearby buildings high enough to let the gangbangers, or anyone else, snipe at us inside the new walls."

Butler nodded and followed Wright's gaze down the length of the dock. Three other fully loaded container ships were tied up bow to stern, just forward of the ship he was on, and two grain carriers, with full cargoes of corn and wheat respectively, rested forward of the farthest container ship. The container ships were tied up with their starboard sides directly to the dock, so they could all be worked by the terminal cranes, but the grain carriers were rafted side by side with one tied off abreast of the other to reduce the length of dock the ships occupied and thus minimize the length of defensive wall to be constructed. Two loaded product tankers were similarly rafted together side by side, sharing the single berth in the product terminal just downriver, previously occupied by *Pecos Trader* . Given the importance of fuel, 'Fort Box' was being extended downstream to include the product terminal within its protective walls. The few ships carrying cement, paper, and other bulk cargoes of no immediate use had been moored at various docks downstream, outside the defensive perimeter of the fledgling fort. Food, water, and defense of same were priorities now. Anything else was a distant second.

Butler turned his gaze to the substantial but increasingly crowded patch of asphalt being enclosed by the growing wall of containers.

"Well, expansion can't be too soon for me, since our 'defensible' area is already chockablock with RVs, travel trailers, your swimming pool waterworks, and God knows what all," Butler said. "You know we still need room to get the stuff OFF the ships and some place to put it, and the transporters need room to move around—"

Wright held up his hand. "And we're leaving you plenty of room next to each ship and a lane to get the containers out of the defended area. You'll just have to store them out beyond the wall until the stuff is needed. They'll be behind the fence and in sight and within coverage of the M2s on the wall. It's not like the bangers can steal a whole container. They got no clue what's in which box anyway. Hell, we got the manifests, and it's still tough to find stuff among all these boxes. It's getting easier, though, now that we got a few folks assigned full time." Wright nodded. "We're in a hell of a lot better shape than I ever thought possible."

"That we are," Butler said. "It's an embarrassment of riches, really. We need to start distributing some of this stuff."

"Just as soon as we have a defensible perimeter and the ability to safeguard what we have. I agree with Major Hunnicutt on this one—if we try to start helping people before we're prepared, everything could go tits up in a hurry. I'm thinking another three or four days max, then we can start on a relief/feeding station. "

"Where?" Butler asked.

"We're leaning toward Pine Valley Country Club. It's a straight shot up Shipyard Boulevard on a wide open road with no pinch points or likely places for the bangers to ambush us. We can set up another small container fort there in the middle of one of the golf courses and maintain open fields of fire. Then we can install a field kitchen and forward supply dump for food and water with enough guys to defend it. We won't need many because we're only a radio call and a ten- or twelve-minute ride away. We set up mess tents outside the secure area of the new fort and have the people file through to be fed. It's inevitable a refugee population is going to gravitate there, but there's a lot of open land on the golf courses. Also it's far enough away that we don't have to worry about attracting a shanty town around us here at Fort Box. We have to maintain clear fields of fire if we have any chance of holding this place against an attack, by the bangers or anyone else."

"Sounds like you got it worked out," Butler said.

"Mostly, but sanitation and water issues are gonna be a problem. But hell, we haven't even solved those here, at least in the long run."

"I think our water problems may be solved. Our snipes were talking to the engineers on the *Maersk Tangier* . They figure they can run the ships' evaporators. There may be health concerns using the river for feed water, but beggars can't be choosers. They're working on a way to convert some of the ship's heat exchangers to raise and hold the outlet water at a high enough temperature to kill any remaining bacteria, just to be on the safe side. If it works, I think you can count on your little swimming pool waterworks staying full no matter how hard you pump it. Sanitation is a different issue. We can't just be dumping our sewage in the river, especially right by where we're gonna be taking in our drinking water feedstock, but they're working on it."

"How're the ships' crews taking their new forced residence?"

Butler shrugged. "The Americans seem to be okay with it. I mean, no one's forcing them to stay, and if they want to head overland back to their homes, we offered to supply them and wish them Godspeed. The foreign crews are a different story, since they're pretty much stuck here. We'll just have to see how that plays out."

Wright nodded and they lapsed into silence until Butler spotted Singletary moving along the docks, looking up at the ships.

"Damn!" Butler said, pulling back from where he'd been leaning with his forearms resting on the ship's rail.

"BUTLER! WAIT UP!" came the cry from below.

Butler backed away from the rail to ensure he wasn't visible from the dock below.

"NO NEED TRYING TO DODGE ME AGAIN, BUTLER," Singletary yelled up. "I KNOW YOU'RE UP THERE AND AIN'T BUT ONE WAY OFF THAT SHIP. SO I'M JUST GONNA SIT MY ASS DOWN HERE AT THE BOTTOM OF THE GANGWAY 'TIL YOU DECIDE TO COME ON DOWN."

Wright grinned. "Looks like you're busted. What's all that about?"

Butler sighed. "In a moment of weakness I promised Levi I'd help this asshole find a boat to get back to Baltimore. Like I didn't have enough to do already. Anyway, he's been bugging me for two days straight now, so I guess I'd better take care of it and get him out of my hair."

"He probably just wants to get home to his family, like everyone else."

"Yeah, maybe, but that's not the vibe he gives off. It's not like he's worried, but more like he's—I don't know, afraid he's missing out on something, I guess is the best way to describe it. Kind of 'entitled' somehow. Anyway, it just doesn't feel right," Butler said.

"All the more reason to get rid of the bastard," Wright said. "If he's trouble, we don't want him around. Besides, how long can it take to find a boat, load him up with fuel and supplies and wish him bon voyage?"

"I don't know, something tells me it's not going to be that easy," Butler said, moving toward the gangway.

***

Butler stood outside the small cabin of the patrol boat and looked upstream at the Cape Fear Memorial Bridge looming over the river. He spotted movement and raised his binoculars. Sure enough there were two figures on the bridge, one pointing at the patrol boat. The second figure nodded and jumped on a motorcycle to speed off in the direction of Wilmington. Butler keyed his throat mike so he could be heard over the roar of the outboards by both the helmsman and the machine gunner in the bow.

"We may have a welcoming committee, so punch it up to full speed, and zigzag so they can't be sure where we're going to cross under the bridge. These are probably the same assholes who tried to bombard Levi and Anthony."

"Roger that," the helmsman replied.

"Guns, possible threat on the bridge. Do you see him?" Butler asked.

"I got him, Chief," the gunner replied.

"Roger that, Guns. Track him, but only fire on my order."

"Roger that, Chief."

The boat began to zigzag and Singletary stuck his head out the cabin door.

"What's going on? Why we zigzagging?"

"Possible threat on the bridge. Don't worry about it, Singletary. Just stay in the cabin."

Singletary muttered under his breath and pulled his head back in. Butler resumed his watch of the solitary figure on the bridge, surprised to see the man now had binoculars trained on the boat. The man let the glasses fall to his chest on the neck strap and raised an assault rifle.

"Shooter! Weapons free!" Butler said into the throat mike, and the M240 machine gun on the bow spoke at once, silencing the threat before the man got off a single round.

Butler heard movement beside him and turned to see Singletary in the cabin door.

"GET BACK IN THE CABIN, SINGLETARY!"

Then they were under the bridge, zigzagging up the river.

"Helm, maintain full speed and secure zigzagging. Keep us on the west side of the river as far away from Wilmington as possible."

"Roger that," came the reply, and Butler heard the distant sound of motorcycles from the Wilmington side of the bridge. No doubt their reception on the return trip would be a bit warmer.

Five minutes later they passed the battleship *USS North Carolina* in her permanent berth, and a few minutes later, they stayed right when the river split, now hugging the west bank of the Northeast Cape Fear River. They continued upstream until the lift bridge serving US 74 came into view, and in its shadow, the marinas lining the eastern bank of the river. Butler raised his binoculars and glassed the length of the bridge, but it seemed clear.

"Helm, cut your speed. We need to go boat shopping. Guns, stay alert. I don't know who those guys on the bridge were, but they know we're on the river, so they might come looking for us."

Butler got affirmative replies and stuck his head into the cabin.

"Get on out here, Mr. Singletary, and let's find you a boat. I don't want to hang around here too long."

Singletary grunted an acknowledgment and exited the cabin to stand at Butler's side as the boat slowed to a crawl along a long stretch of floating docks jammed with boats.

"We should be able to find something here," Butler said. "I'd like to avoid transiting under the bridge."

Singletary grunted again, looking down the long line of boats.

"Most of 'em look to be sailboats."

"True, but there are quite a few powerboats. There's a nice little Boston Whaler over there—"

"Ain't got no cabin, in fact, none of these powerboats have a cabin. I'm probably gonna have to live in this thing when I get to Baltimore, you know," Singletary said.

I guess the asshole's got a point, thought Butler.

"All right, Mr. Singletary, let's have a look upstream on the other side of the bridge," Butler said, and keyed his throat mike.

"Haul ass under the bridge at full power and go on by the docks nearest to the bridge. Guns, get the sniper rifle and come back to the stern. Any threat's likely to come from the bridge and you can't cover that with the M2 on the bow when we're headed upstream. I want you scanning for threats, but especially the bridge. Do you copy?"

"Roger that," said the gunner, moving aft as the helmsman accelerated to blast under the bridge.

Two hundred yards past the bridge, Butler ordered the boat to slow again and began cruising along another extensive stretch of floating docks. Butler spotted something and motioned the helmsman to pull alongside a moored vessel.

"Here we go, Mr. Singletary," Butler said, "this looks like just what the doctor ordered. About twenty-five feet, I'd say, a nice little cuddy cabin, twin outboards so you'll have a backup if one breaks down, and I'm pretty sure we'll find a berth as well as a galley and a head. Looks perfect."

Singletary was looking further up the dock. "What about that one?"

Butler followed Singletary's pointing finger to a power yacht occupying a long length of the dock several berths away. It was sixty or seventy feet long and obviously a custom-built luxury vessel. He looked back at Singletary. "You're not serious?"

"Damn right I'm serious. Why wouldn't I be serious?"

"That's a lot of boat for one man to handle, and I expect it burns through fuel pretty fast," Butler said.

"Let me worry about handling it," Singletary said, "and you said I could have all the fuel I needed. It ain't like you don't have tanks of it sitting around."

"I'm talking about AFTER you get to Baltimore," Butler said. "You won't have access to fuel. Besides, that's way more boat than you need to get to Baltimore or to even live on after you get there. This cuddy boat is a better choice, anyway."

"Oh, I see, y'all don't have any problem taking RVs and trailers and such, but if I want to pick out my own boat, then you decide it's too good for me. What's your problem, Butler, it ain't like it's your boat."

Butler's face hardened. "There's a big difference between taking a twenty- or thirty-thousand-dollar trailer to house a family or a group of single guys and stealing a half-million-dollar yacht. You want to take the yacht? Hop out now and be my guest, but just keep on trucking when you pass our docks because I'm not giving you jack. I agreed to help you get home, not outfit you like a friggin' Saudi prince."

"That ain't fair!"

"Tough. You want the cuddy boat or not? Make up your mind, because in two minutes, we're headed back downriver, with you or without you."

Singletary glared at Butler. "Fine. I'll take the friggin' cuddy boat."

"Then hop out and check it out. I suspect you'll have to break into the cabin and I doubt there's a key around. You got any problem hot-wiring the ignition?"

"I think I can handle it," Singletary said.

"I figured you probably could," Butler said, earning him another glare from Singletary.

A few minutes later, Singletary had the engines running on the boat, and Butler nodded approval.

"You got enough fuel to get back? I want to go the long way around and avoid trouble at the bridge," Butler yelled across to Singletary.

"Easy," Singletary replied, and Butler nodded and motioned for the helmsman to move the Coast Guard boat back into the river. As he did so, the gunner resumed his place at the bow machine gun, and Singletary cast off and fell in behind the Coasties.

The Coast Guard boat roared downstream at full power, dropping speed a bit only when Singletary was falling behind. At Peter Point, they turned hard to starboard, continuing up the Cape Fear River and bypassing downtown Wilmington and whatever reception committee might be awaiting them atop the Cape Fear Memorial Bridge. They continued up the

Cape Fear River until its juncture with the Brunswick, and then turned south downstream on the Brunswick until it once again intersected the Cape Fear River, some distance downstream from the container terminal. It tripled the length of the trip, but given the speed of both of the boats, it wasn't a real issue. It was early afternoon when they turned into the Cape Fear River and headed upstream to the newly christened Fort Box.

SAME DAY, 4:00 P.M.

"I don't know, Singletary," Mike Butler said, "I think I'd wait and leave in the morning. You can't really travel at night with all the navigational aids out, so you're not going to get very far tonight. If you leave at first light, that would give you time to get in a good day's run and plenty of time to find a good anchorage for the night."

"Why don't you let me worry about that? I got the fuel topped up and plenty of extra, and all the food and water is loaded, so I'm ready to go. And I'm tired of all your crap anyway."

"Yeah, you're welcome," Butler said, and turned his back to walk away from the dock.

Singletary shot the finger at the retreating Coastie's back, moved down the vertical ladder to where his boat rested beneath the high container dock, and cast off, happy to finally be on his own. The boat was laboring a bit, loaded down as it was with all he could possibly get aboard. However, even at that he figured he'd reach his destination with a couple of hours of daylight left; plenty of time to get his stores shifted over and prepare for an early departure tomorrow morning. He smiled. Maybe he should have thanked Butler for showing him a way not only around the bridge, but also around 'Fort Box' and its collection of assholes.

As he approached the mouth of the Brunswick River, he began a long sweeping turn to starboard and started upstream. He knew where he was spending the night, all right, and it wasn't anchored in the weeds on some Godforsaken mosquito-infested stretch of the Intracoastal Waterway. He figured his new yacht would have a pretty nice master bedroom.

Singletary looked around the main salon, not believing his good fortune. He'd been over the yacht from stem to stern, and been even more delighted to discover the tanks were topped up with diesel. That had been a worry, since all the extra fuel he'd taken from Fort Box was gasoline. He'd figured he might have to scavenge fuel from the other diesel-powered boats in the marina, but that would take time. Without that worry, he was free to depart at first light.

All of his stores were aboard, and he cursed once again at a lost opportunity. If Butler hadn't been such a prick about the yacht, he'd have been able to take a lot more stores. He'd also loaded the extra gasoline from the cuddy boat aboard the yacht. Even though he couldn't use it directly, he figured it would be useful to barter.

Nothing to do now but relax, and he walked over and examined the fully stocked bar—an unexpected bonus. The former owner of the boat had exceptional—and expensive—tastes. Singletary reached up and slipped a brandy snifter from the rack and lifted a bottle of Courvoisier from the recessed hole that secured it against movement of the boat. He poured himself an ample measure and held the snifter to his nose, savoring the aroma, then took a tiny sip, allowing the taste to spread through his mouth before it slipped down his throat. He reached over to set the bottle back in the recess, thought better of it, and carried both the bottle and the snifter to the table beside a leather-upholstered easy chair. He knew he was going to have more than one, and there was no need to strain himself by getting up and down, now was there?

***

He was the captain at last, and not of some crappy tanker stinking of gasoline and diesel, but a luxury yacht, crewed by all those fools and stuck-up bitches from his old neighborhood. He called the shots and they did exactly like he said or they didn't eat. How did they like that shit? Everything was going along just fine until... until some fool was poking him in the forehead with something hard. What the hell...

Singletary opened his eyes to stare at a huge gun held perhaps two inches away from the bridge of his nose, the hole in the barrel looking as big as a half dollar. He followed the gun to the hand that held it, and then up a long arm to stare into the face of the meanest looking black dude he'd ever seen.

"Wh-who are you?"

"I'm Kwintell Banks, nigga, but the question is who are YOU, and what you doin' on MY boat, drinkin' MY booze."

"I… I'm Jerome Singletary, and I didn't know it was your boat… I mean, I didn't know it was anyone's… I was just looking for a place to sleep…"

"That so? Looks like to me you was getting ready to steal my boat. That right? Best tell the truth, or it'll go hard on you," Banks said.

"Yes, but I didn't know it was yours. I'm very sorry. I'll pick another boat."

"You see, that's the thing. They're ALL my boats, including the one you and those crackers stole earlier. Though I do thank you for bringing it back, all filled up with nice things. Just for that, I'm gonna kill you fast so you don't suffer too much."

Banks backed away, and Singletary became fully aware of his surroundings for the first time. Lights were on in the cabin, and he saw four men with Banks, all heavily armed. He saw Banks holster his pistol and then point at him with his free hand.

"Take this fool into the middle of the river and then shoot him in the head. We got enough dead people stinking things up around here without adding another one."

Two of the men nodded and dragged Singletary out of the chair and toward the door, deflecting his efforts to resist as if he were a child.

"Wait, wait! I have information. I can help you."

Banks held up his hand and his underlings stopped but retained their grip on the squirming Singletary.

"So what you gonna tell me, Singletary? You gonna tell me about those crazy crackers and their tame Toms, building their little fort down on the docks? We watching 'em all the time, and I know how many they got and what they doing. It don't matter because they got those machine guns and grenades, so we ain't dumb enough to start a fight with them. No need anyhow. If they want to stay inside their little fort, that's fine by me. We got everything else and we're already spreading out into the country, figuring ways to put people to work growing food. We might even let them keep a little. Not too much, mind you, but just enough to make sure they stay alive so they can keep working for us. So you see, you don't really know nothing."

Banks nodded at his two underlings, and they started for the door once again.

"Wait, I know other things. There's… there's this guy named Levi with a hideout near here with a lot of food. Guns and ammunition too, and a generator, I think. And a lot of other stuff, gold and silver too. I… I know where it is. He tries to keep it quiet, but I heard him talking. I'll tell you, just let me go."

Banks stopped his henchmen again and rubbed his chin, deliberating. After a moment he nodded and his men returned Singletary and dumped him down on the couch.

"All right," Banks said, "start talking. And it better be good or your death ain't gonna be near as easy as the one you just avoided."

SKYLINE DRIVE—NORTHBOUND
APPROACHING FRONT ROYAL, VA

DAY 14, 1:00 P.M.

Bill Wiggins gripped the wheel, white-knuckled as he negotiated the twisting switchback, tires squealing on the asphalt. Tex looked up from the map.

"You're not going to do your family any good piled up at the bottom of a cliff in the back of beyond."

"Sorry," Wiggins said as he came out of the turn and focused on the next one. "I guess that thirty-five mile an hour speed limit might be pushing the envelope on some of these turns. I thought the Blue Ridge Parkway was winding, but this damn thing's a corkscrew. I bet there's not a hundred yards of straight level pavement on the whole drive."

Tex smiled. "Yeah, it might even be enjoyable if we weren't trying to get home in the middle of the apocalypse.

"That would be if you're not driving."

"Hey, I offered," Tex said.

"You did, sorry for bitching. But anyway, you're the mate. That naturally makes you the navigator."

Tex nodded, and they lapsed into silence as Bill's mind wandered back over the last thirty-six hours. As Levi predicted, the run to the Blue Ridge Parkway had been the most harrowing leg of the journey thus far. Two weeks into the power outage, gasoline was scarce and the roadside littered with stalled cars, making a moving vehicle all the more conspicuous. Even on secondary roads they encountered haggard pedestrians, undoubtedly refugees leaking into the countryside from the nearby interstates and major highways. They were a mixed bag, both individuals and family groups, many with haunted looks as if they no longer had a destination, but continued in the forlorn expectation wherever they were going was better than where they'd been. The children were the worst, crying from hunger or thirst, or both. It was all Bill and Tex could do to resist stopping and sharing their food.

At stream crossings, camps had sprung up—odd collections of tents and shelters improvised of plastic or blankets, as if some had concluded there really wasn't any better place, and they could best cheat death a bit longer by conserving their energy. Mostly they flew by these places, transiting before the residents knew they were there. Mostly. At one small bridge they'd been confronted by a human chain, four dirty desperate men spread across the road, armed with a collection of hunting rifles and pistols. Bill floored it as Tex leaned out the window, firing the Glock over their heads to scatter them as the Highlander roared over the bridge. They rode on in silence for some time, each aware it could easily have been them on the roadside were it not for Levi's generosity.

They reached the Blue Ridge Parkway with three hours of daylight left on the first day, and again as Levi predicted, found the route empty. The popularity of a twisting, scenic road-to-nowhere wasn't great during a disaster. Their next major concern had been near Roanoke, where the parkway skirted the more congested urban area. They pressed on the first day and stopped for the night fifty miles south of Roanoke, pulling well off the road into the trees. Feeling a bit foolish, they'd strung fishing line knee high between trees and attached bells as a crude 'early warning system.' They ate a cold supper to avoid a fire, then sacked out in the hammocks Levi provided. They both slept fitfully and were on the road north at first light, transiting the Roanoke area without incident.

Bill brought himself back to the present as they passed a mileage sign for Front Royal, Virginia. Tex still had her nose buried in the map.

"Front Royal in five miles. That's the northern terminus for Skyline Drive. Where to, navigator?"

Tex looked up. "It's complicated. Find an overlook to stop and I'll show you."

Bill snorted. "Shouldn't be a problem. There's one about every ten feet on this damn road."

Sure enough, they rounded a sharp curve and he pulled into a scenic overlook. He put the car in park and leaned over to study the map Tex spread out on the seat between them.

She traced a route on the map with her finger. "We're about eight miles west of the AT at Front Royal, but it starts running northeast at this point, through a couple of state parks to where it crosses US 50 near Paris, then continues northeast to cross Virginia State Route 7 just west of Bluemont. Our best bet is to go through Front Royal and take Happy Creek Road out of town. That'll get us under I-66 at a place where the road passes under the interstate with no interchange and gets us to the Shenandoah River. There are a series of interconnecting rural roads paralleling the river, which also parallels the AT. Our access point to the AT will be everywhere a substantial road intersects both the river and the AT. At those points, we can jump on the road, go a mile or two east, and have access to the AT as a backup, just like Levi said. That works as far as Bluemont. After that, we'll take another look."

"You think we'll have any problem getting through Front Royal?"

She shrugged. "Who knows? It's not real big, maybe fifteen thousand. I'm actually more concerned about I-66 because we're only about sixty or seventy miles out of DC. Given what we've seen on the secondary roads, I gotta think the I-66 corridor is a horror show. What I like about this route is this Happy Creek Road approaches and leaves the interstate at a right angle and transits under it with no interchange. If we're lucky, maybe we can blow right under the interstate in a hurry, with minimal contact."

"Sounds like a plan." Bill started the car.

Five minutes later, he exited Skyline Drive to turn north on the broad expanse of Stonewall Jackson Highway. There was the usual collection of convenience stores, fast-food restaurants, and motels increasing in density as they neared Front Royal, all closed, of course. There were hollow-eyed pedestrians as well, some registering surprise at the moving car, but most moving mindlessly to some undetermined destination.

"Notice anything strange about the pedestrians?" Bill asked.

Tex nodded. "They're all walking away from town. That can't be good."

Two miles up the highway, just past the intersection with State Route 55 East, two police cars were drawn across the road. A police officer got out of one of the cars and raised his hand as Bill approached and stopped fifty feet from the roadblock. The cop approached, well to the side, his hand on the butt of his holstered sidearm. A cop got out of the other car and approached from Tex's side. Both men's uniforms were rumpled and dirty, and neither looked as if they'd shaved in several days.

"This doesn't look promising," Bill said, as he rolled down his window. "Is there a problem, officer?"

The officer grunted. "Yeah, there's a lot of problems. You interested in one in particular, or would you like a list?"

Bill smiled. "Sorry, I guess I meant is there any problem with us coming through?"

The officer shook his head. "No refugees. I'm gonna have to ask you folks to turn around and go back the way you came."

"We're not refugees," Bill said. "We're headed north. We just want to go as far as Happy Creek Road and take it out of town. If you'll let us by, we won't even slow down in Front Royal."

"Yeah, that's what they all say."

"No, really. How about you escort us? That way you can make sure."

"And does it look to you as if we have enough manpower to be providing 'private escorts' through town? Walt and I've been here over twenty-four hours without relief. So again, I ask you to turn around."

"I understand, but we really don't want to stay. If you'll just let us—"

"Sir, you DON'T understand. Nobody's getting into Front Royal who doesn't belong here. We tried to help at first, what with all those folks fleeing DC and running out of gas, coming down from the interstate on foot. They were grateful for a day or two, and then more people kept showing up and they stopped asking and started demanding, and it got real ugly. A lot of good folks got killed before we sorted it out, and there's plenty of hard feelings. So even if I was to LET you past, driving a car full of who knows what, I reckon you wouldn't make it out of town alive, so you might say I'm doing you a favor. Now TURN AROUND."

Tex leaned across the seat and looked up at the cop. "Is there any other way north, officer?"

"None I'd recommend," he said. "You can take State Route 55 East to US 17, but 55 parallels the interstate for five or six miles at least, and it's like the Wild West out there. The gangs started coming out from DC, hitting the outlying communities as long as the gas held out, and we didn't have enough manpower to do anything but establish control here in town. Even now, they're still coming out on motorbikes and hitting farms and homes near the interstate. A moving car at this point might as well have a sign saying 'Good Stuff—Take Me.'"

Bill looked at Tex. She shrugged. "I guess we take 55 East and hope for the best."

"Your funeral," the cop said, and Bill backed the car around and turned east at the intersection as Tex stuck her head back in the map. In the distance, Bill saw another police cruiser on the side of the road, positioned to observe all of the cross streets leading off of State Route 55. He had no doubt if he attempted to turn north into town, the police would be on him in short order.

Bill passed the cop and watched in his mirror until he was out of sight. They were just passing Remount Road.

"I assume you're working on plan B?"

"Absolutely. If they're spread as thin as he says, the cops can't be everywhere. I see one last shot at getting up to Happy Creek Road. The third street ahead on the left should be Jamestown Road. It connects to a lot of surface streets winding through subdivisions on the east side of town. It's convoluted, but it should get us where we need to go."

Bill nodded and began to study the left side of the road. He saw Jamestown Road about half a mile later and made the left. They hadn't gone a hundred yards when the center of the windshield shattered with a heart-stopping crack. He slammed on the brakes, throwing them forward against their seat belts, staring at the hole in the middle of the shattered glass.

"Crap!" Bill said as he jammed the gear shift into reverse and stomped the gas, looking over his shoulder as they raced backwards and another round struck the front of the car.

He slammed on the brakes again when he hit the highway, barely managing to avoid crashing into the opposite ditch as the tires squealed and the car shuddered to a halt. He slammed the transmission into drive and raced east on 55, not stopping until they were a mile out of town with nothing on either side but trees. He sat there, afraid to let go of the wheel because he knew his hands would be shaking.

"Are you all right, Tex?" he asked.

"I… I think so, but what the hell was that? No 'turn around' or 'halt' or anything."

"I guess the cop was right," Bill said. "That's a town full of pissed-off people. One thing for sure, we're not going through any part of Front Royal. Is there any other way to get over to the river?"

She shook her head and reached for the map. "I don't think so, but I'll have another look."

"Okay. I'll see if that second shot hit anything vital."

Bill got out and was relieved to find the second round buried in the composite bumper. Had he been just a bit slower, the bullet would have likely gone through the radiator and then done more damage in the engine compartment. As it was, they got off light with a hole in the windshield and a bullet in the bumper. A few inches either way and one of them would be dead or the vehicle disabled. He was beginning to appreciate Levi's caution. It was amazing how being shot at clarified the mind.

He got back in the car. Tex was frowning.

"We're screwed," she said. "Like the cop said, in a couple of miles this road veers north and converges with I-66, running right beside the interstate for almost six miles, in places no more than a hundred yards away. Whatever bad guys came out of DC likely used the interstate, and a lot of them might still be there. If we run that gauntlet successfully, then we head back north on US 17 to Paris, where we can take US 50 a few miles west and get back on our 'parallel the Shenandoah' plan. The problem is, US 17 is also a major road, so I'm thinking it may have attracted its share of desperate people leaking off from the interstate. That's the bad news."

"There's good news?"

"The whole distance back up to Paris is like eighteen miles on good straight roads. If you wind this baby up to seventy or eighty and bob and weave around any obstacles, and I get ready to hang out the window and pop some warning shots off at anybody who looks like they might even be thinking about stopping us, we could be back on track in half an hour."

Even under the circumstances, Bill couldn't suppress a smile. "Wow, you're getting into the postapocalyptic stuff. That's like Mad Max in a Toyota Highlander."

Tex bristled a moment, then chuckled. "Eat your heart out, Tina Turner."

"How about access points to the AT? Given what's happened in the last hour, I'm a bit less skeptical about Levi's paranoia."

"The next one's actually on this road, about four miles east and smack in the middle of the area where this road parallels I-66. The AT emerges from the woods and crosses under the interstate, running due north on Turner's Lane, then branches off back into the woods about a quarter mile north. Then it runs through two state parks. The next access is where it crosses US 50, west of Paris and after we run the gauntlet."

"How about behind us?"

"All the way back by Front Royal and back up Skyline Drive about five miles, which would mean we'd have to hike at least a half day to get back to the I-66 crossing just ahead of us, and still have to cross under the interstate in the open and on foot," Tex said.

"Well, that's not happening," Bill said. "I guess it's Mad Max. You ready, Tina?"

"Ready as I'll ever be, I guess."

Bill nodded and pulled back on the road, accelerating eastbound. The road was empty and he was doing eighty a few minutes later when Tex pointed out the AT crossing at Turner Lane. Almost immediately thereafter they began to encounter stalled cars, a few in the middle of the road, mixed with scattered pedestrians, forcing him to slow. However, he was able to maintain a steady fifty miles an hour as he slalomed around the obstacles, hoping no pedestrian wandered out from between the stationary cars. Not that they seemed so inclined. In fact, their heads rose sharply at the sound of the approaching engine, and the refugees hurried away from the roadway.

"Not exactly Mad Max," Tex said as they wound through the obstacle course, "but I guess it'll work."

Just as she finished speaking, the woods on the right opened up on a vast expanse of pasture jammed with refugees and a mass of crudely constructed shelters.

"What the hell—"

Tex glanced down at the map. "Water," she said. "Looks like a pretty substantial creek parallels the road. I guess all these poor bastards gravitated here for the water."

A sickening smell wafted through the open windows, redolent of too many humans living together without benefit of basic services or hygiene. They shuddered as hundreds of refugees turned toward the sound of the car, their body language telegraphing anxiety, even at a distance.

"I'm not liking this at all," Bill said as he swerved around another car. "What's ahead?"

Tex glanced down at the map. "There's an interchange just ahead at a wide spot in the road called Markham. There's not much there but a vineyard. Then we've got three or four miles of this before we head north on US 17. No guarantee what we're gonna find there either."

Bill nodded and kept driving, pushing the speed up to sixty as he wound down the highway.

They saw a sign announcing their approach to State Route 688, then passed a large attractive building on the right, with a sign identifying it as the vineyard sales office. There were multiple vehicles in the parking lot. They whizzed by and then heard engines cough to life behind them.

"Motorcycles?" Tex asked.

Bill glanced in his mirror as two motorcycles rocketed out of the parking lot, engines snarling.

"Motorcycles," he confirmed, and accelerated.

Tex turned in her seat. "Maybe they just want to talk—"

They both cringed as the back window of the SUV shattered.

"Or maybe not," she finished, unbuckling her seat belt and crawling between the seats into the back. "I guess this really is Mad Max shit."

The back of the SUV was piled high with stores, and Tex crawled across on elbows and knees, pitching with the car as Bill swerved around stationary vehicles. She steadied herself with her right hand and balled her left fist to hammer at the shattered safety glass, managing to dislodge a large sheet, which hit the pavement behind the car in a dazzling display of flying glass shards flashing in the sunlight. Only then did she reach behind and draw the Glock from its holster and assess the situation.

Which sucked.

She was on a swaying, bouncing platform, shooting a handgun at equally (and unpredictably) mobile targets. The only upside was the targets were getting closer, but since they were armed, that was a somewhat dubious benefit. But their attackers had challenges as well. Steering a motorcycle one-handed while negotiating obstacles and shooting with the other hand wasn't easy. When they shot, they had to slow a bit, negating the added agility of their vehicles and allowing Bill to draw ahead. After their initial (and lucky) fusillade with no return fire, they'd apparently decided to concentrate on closing the distance. That would change as soon as they started taking fire. She had to take them out quickly.

Tex watched a moment. They were mobile, but the obstacles they were negotiating were not. If she concentrated her fire on the front corner of a stalled car just as one of the motorcycles swerved around it, they'd move into her field of fire. She steadied herself as she felt Bill swerve around a car, and as it came into view behind her, she targeted the right front headlight. When the lead cyclist was almost abreast of the front of the car, she fired a half-dozen shots in rapid succession just as the man swerved back toward the middle of the road—directly into her field of fire.

She'd been hoping for center-mass hits, but she was a bit high. A single round penetrated her attacker's face shield, driving him backwards off the bike directly in the path of the remaining cyclist. The front wheel of the second man's bike struck the body of his fallen comrade and the driver fought to maintain control—and lost. He slammed into a stalled car straight on at over fifty miles an hour and rocketed through the air to land some distance away, unmoving.

Tex holstered the Glock and clawed her way back to the front, squeezing between the seats just as they flew past the highway interchange. She glanced forward to see the road was suddenly free of stalled cars, and felt the SUV accelerate as Bill split his attention between the road ahead and quick glances in the rearview mirror.

"Damn! Remind me never to piss you off."

"Lucky shot," Tex said.

"Uh-oh! Let's hope your luck holds."

Tex turned back to the road, to see a big tractor trailer rig moving across the road from a side street a quarter mile ahead of them. Two cars pulling across the road in front of the big rig left no doubt it was a roadblock.

"Looks like they have radios!" Tex said as she felt the SUV decelerate rapidly, and another round punctured the windshield and several more struck the front of the car.

"And assault rifles! Get down!" Bill yelled as he stomped the brakes even harder and twisted the wheel, causing the SUV to swap ends, skidding backwards toward their attackers as Bill once again stomped the gas and smoke billowed off the screaming tires before they finally grabbed and the car shot back the way they'd come.

"Where the hell did you learn that?"

"Empty parking lots when I was a teenager," Bill said. "There's not a hell of a lot to do in small towns in the middle of the Maine woods."

Tex twisted in her seat and stared back at the roadblock.

"More cycles?" Bill asked.

"Negative. Looks like a jacked-up four-wheel-drive pickup with a bed full of shooters," Tex said.

Just then, steam or smoke billowed from under the hood, and Bill glanced down at the dash.

"The engine temp's going straight up! They must have hit the radiator," he said.

"What are we gonna do?"

"What can we do but ride and hope? How far ahead is that AT access we passed?"

"Three miles at least. Can we make it?"

"Who the hell knows. I should be able to stay ahead of these assholes through the obstacle course as long as we can keep moving. I've had a little experience now and that jacked-up truck has a high center of gravity. He can't bob and weave too quickly."

A round shattered the passenger-side mirror, and they both flinched.

"Should I return fire?"

Bill shook his head. "Not much point now. We don't really have a fighting chance to escape unless we make the AT. If they do end up catching us, it might be better if we haven't killed quite as many of them."

Tex watched as Bill hurtled down the road, all caution gone now as the SUV caromed along the congested path, missing some cars by inches and glancing off others. She twisted in her seat and stared back.

"You're opening up a lead, a pretty good one."

Bill nodded, then frowned as horrible sounds started coming from under the hood. He glanced down at the instrument panel again.

"We're red-lined on the engine temp and the oil pressure isn't looking too great either. Say a little prayer this'll all hold together long enough to make Turner Lane. Maybe if we can build up a big enough lead, we can be out of sight when we make the turn. What's the road look like there, you remember?"

Tex jerked out the map and pulled it open. "Mostly straight and open, but there is a slight curve. It's not much, but we might be out of their sight a couple of minutes. The only problem is when they round that curve, the road runs straight for a long way. If they don't see us, it'll be obvious we turned off somewhere and Turner Lane is the only option."

"Let's just hope they aren't as smart as you," Bill said.

Tex twisted back to watch their pursuers, shutting out the ever-increasing din of the dying engine and willing their lead to increase. Finally she watched the truck fade out of sight as the angle between the vehicles changed. She snapped her head to the front. Turner Lane was in the near distance.

"There it is," Bill said. "Can they see us?"

"No. We just lost visual contact."

"I make it a quarter of a mile to the turn. Were they further back than that?"

"I don't know. Maybe," Tex said.

"Just keep looking. Hopefully we'll be under the interstate before they spot us."

Tex kept her eyes fixed behind them and felt Bill braking hard as he ran up to the intersection at almost full speed, the engine shrieking, accompanied now by a burning smell. She gripped the seat back as he cornered on two wheels, then whipped her head to the right to look out the passenger window back the way they'd come. They roared north on Turner Lane, and were almost past a farmhouse when she glimpsed the nose of the truck rounding the curve.

"Did they see us?" Bill demanded.

"I don't know, but I saw them for a second, so we have to assume they did. Besides, if they get much closer, they'll be able to track us by sound. We're not exactly inconspicuous."

Bill nodded as they sped under I-66, engine shrieking and smoking. "How far is the AT access?"

Tex was fumbling with the AT guidebook. "Should be just after Walker Ridge Road forks off to the right. I don't know how well it's marked. It might be just a blaze on a tree or something."

"Guess we'll find out. We're going to go off road whether we find it or not. If they see the abandoned car, they'll just run us down—"

"There!" Tex pointed to white blazes on a tree, barely visible across a small open meadow.

Bill veered off the road without slowing and they bounced through a shallow drainage ditch to rumble across the meadow, trailing smoke. In seconds they plunged into the trees, following a narrow walking path through thick foliage, branches slapping against the side of the car.

"What's ahead!"

Tex fumbled with the guidebook. "It says a small footbridge over a stream—"

The foliage opened somewhat, revealing the bridge not more than thirty feet away, a neat little structure perhaps three feet wide with handrails, the depth of the stream it crossed unknown.

"Hold on!" Bill shouted and floored the accelerator as he jerked the wheel to the right. They bounced through the shallow stream and up the other bank, back on the narrow hiking trail winding its way up a steep hillside. A hundred yards up the hill, the Toyota shuddered and died.

They sat in the sudden calm, the smells of the dying engine thick in their nostrils, the silence broken only by the tick of the overheated engine cooling for the final time.

The sound of the pickup grew behind them, then faded away to the north.

"They went past," Bill said, relief in his voice. "Where does Tucker's Lane go and how soon before they figure out we're not still ahead of them?" Tex was already studying the map.

"It dead-ends about five miles up. That's the bad news. The good news is it has at least a dozen side roads that dead-end off of it. It should take them quite some time to figure out where we gave them the slip."

"All right, I guess we ought to grab Levi's escape packs and get the hell out of here. Let's do a quick check and take some extra food if we have room. But we ought to be out of here in ten minutes tops."

"Agreed," Tex said.

They climbed out of the SUV and did a quick inventory, adding things to the packs as they could fit them, and eight minutes later they shouldered their packs and started north.

"Just out of curiosity," Bill said as they labored up the steep hill under the unfamiliar weight of the packs, "did you happen to notice how far it is to Maine on this friggin' goat track?"

"Twelve hundred and one miles to Mount Katahdin," Tex said, "but I think probably only around eleven hundred to where you're headed."

"Wonderful. Just friggin' wonderful!"

CHAPTER FOURTEEN

UNITED BLOOD NATION HQ
(FORMERLY NEW HANOVER COUNTY
DEPARTMENT OF SOCIAL SERVICES)
1650 GREENFIELD STREET
WILMINGTON, NC

DAY 15, 10:00 A.M.

Jerome Singletary fought back the pain and lifted his face from the blood-spattered road map spread in front of him.

"I CAN'T show you on the map! I've never been there that way, so I don't know the way by the road."

Kwintell Banks glared. "Then show me on the river. The river shows on the map."

Singletary shook his head, causing more blood to escape his flattened nose and drop on the map. "It's not the same. This here's a road map. Where it shows the river isn't accurate."

Singletary had no idea if that was true, but it made no difference since he had only the vaguest idea where that asshole Levi's camp was anyway. He did know if Banks concluded he didn't know, or figured he could get there without help, Singletary was a dead man.

"So what you saying? We need some sort of special map?"

Singletary nodded. "A river chart. Maybe we can find one on one of the boats. I'll help, if you let me go."

Banks scoffed. "You know that ain't happening."

"Then put me with some of your men to look, or you might as well shoot me now, 'cause you can't beat something out of me I don't know."

Banks dropped his hand to his holstered pistol and glared. Singletary began to shake, fearful he'd overplayed it.

Then Banks relaxed a bit. "All right. I'll put two soldiers on your ass, and you go look for this map. But you try to run, you gonna wish you were already dead. Understand?"

"Absolutely," Singletary said, "but one other thing—"

Banks' hand went back to his side. "What 'other' thing would that be?"

"Even when we find the chart, you need a guide. I mean, the chart will get you close, but all that riverbank looks alike. You need someone who's been there before. And you can't just roar up in some big-ass noisy boats, he'll hear and maybe ambush you. You need fishing boats with electric motors so you can sneak up on him quiet like. I can help with all that stuff."

Banks cocked an eye. "How you know so much about this? I thought you was a city boy?"

In truth, all Singletary knew was what he gleaned from eavesdropping, but that fact seemed unlikely to keep him alive.

"I learned from Levi. He wanted me to stay with 'em on the river, but I need to get back to Baltimore. Before I left his place, he showed me everything. I know the whole setup," Singletary lied.

"I don't know. Special maps. Special boats. Might all be more trouble than it's worth. Maybe I'll just cap yo' ass and be done with it."

"It's worth it, man! Levi's got all sorts of shit! He's real tight with them soldiers and Coast Guard guys. They was even talking about giving him some grenades."

"Grenades? Why the hell didn't you say something before?"

"'Cause I'm not sure," Singletary said, "but I am sure it's worth your while, grenades or not. He's got a lot of stuff there."

Banks hesitated, then nodded to two men standing nearby. They moved to each side of Singletary, hooking him under the arms and dragging him to his feet.

"Okay," Banks said, "you go find the stuff you need. And I hope you ain't bullshittin' me, 'cause if you are…"

Relief surged through Singletary. "Don't you worry a bit. I won't let you down…"

But Banks had already turned his back as the two thugs dragged Singletary into the hall and started toward the door to the street, unaware their captive was already plotting his next move. He might not know where to find Levi, but he did know his chances of escape were much better on the river.

FEMA
EMERGENCY OPERATIONS CENTER
MOUNT WEATHER
NEAR BLUEMONT, VA

DAY 15, 10:00 A.M.

The Honorable Theodore M. Gleason, President of the United States, sipped his coffee then set the bone-china cup back into its saucer on the walnut table. He was the only occupant of the well-appointed conference room. He wore khaki trousers and an open collar golf shirt, but for all its informality, the look he cultivated was studied and deliberate. He sat not at the head of the huge table but midway down its length and closest to the door into the room. He would greet his guest personally and as equals, without the barrier of the table or by subtle implication any other barriers between them. A part of an artful lie, of course, but he hoped a convincing one.

It was what he did. He was a politician, and a good one. Some might consider that a pejorative, but he cared not at all, for he was a student of history. Statesmen might be venerated in the history books, but it was politicians who made things work. To his mind, his was the noblest of professions, and he was a proud practitioner of the political arts.

He looked up as the door opened. Representative Simon Tremble looked rumpled and sleep-deprived. He was badly in need of a haircut and sported a two-day growth of beard. Gleason rose with a practiced smile and outstretched hand.

"Simon, thank you for coming."

Tremble ignored Gleason's hand and looked him in the eye. "I had a choice?"

Gleason's smile flickered only slightly as he dropped his hand. "Oh, there's always a choice, Simon. But have a seat." He gestured to a chair beside his own. "Coffee?"

Tremble shook his head and dropped into the offered seat as Gleason took his own chair.

"Simon, I just wanted to let you know how much I regret the necessity —"

Tremble arched his eyebrows. "Necessity? Arresting the Speaker of the House and the President Pro Tem of the Senate was a 'necessity'? For God's sake, Ted, we're from your own party! It's not like we were wild-eyed anarchists!"

Gleason's face hardened. "I gave you an opportunity—"

"Opportunity? Is that what you call it? Sorry, but from where we were sitting, it looked a whole lot like an ultimatum."

Gleason tried another tack. "I understand, Simon, I really do, but this is a disaster of unprecedented scope. I had to be decisive and must continue to be. There's just no time for business as usual."

Tremble shook his head. "I might buy the argument we need to streamline things and take immediate action, even to the point of stretching constitutional safeguards to near breaking. But what you and Crawford are implementing, totally without oversight or regard for dissenting opinion, is an absolute outrage."

Gleason spoke through clenched teeth. "I had to do it."

"That would be a hell of a lot easier for me to believe if you hadn't been quite so eager to declare yourself king, Mr. President. Or should I say Your Majesty?"

Gleason's face reddened, but he recovered his composure quickly. "I guess we'll just have to agree to disagree on the necessity, Simon, but I didn't ask you here to debate. What's done is done, and I hope we CAN agree it's in the nation's best interest to get power restored as soon as possible. So I'm asking for your public support. It will go a long ways towards reassuring folks out there if you join me in some of the emergency broadcasts."

"Un-frigging-believable! You lock me and my son up without access to a soul, and now expect me to endorse your coup? But why talk to me one on one? I figured you'd want Senator Leddy in on the deal too, along with anyone else you've had under house arrest. What's the problem, did Jim turn you down?"

Gleason hesitated. "I'm sorry to say Jim Leddy died five days ago."

Tremble sat shocked. "H-how did he die?"

"Very suddenly. A brain aneurysm. But he didn't suffer, thank God."

"Is there… was there a service? I'd like to pay my respects."

"We thought it best not to upset the public with news of yet another loss. There's been so much bad news as it is. There was a cremation and a small family service."

Tremble glared. "How thoughtful of you. What about Linda? How is she holding up?"

Gleason shrugged. "She was upset, as you would expect."

"Was?"

"I haven't seen her since the memorial service," Gleason said.

"And why is that?"

"As you know, Mount Weather shelters the national leadership and their dependents. With Jim's unfortunate passing, Linda no longer qualifies. It's tragic, but these are difficult times. Linda was provided air transport to her and Jim's last home of record," Gleason said.

"YOU DROPPED A DEFENSELESS WOMAN IN THE MIDDLE OF SAINT LOUIS?"

"She was disembarked with her luggage at the St. Louis airport. It was all according to established policy, of course," Gleason said. "I'd think you would be all for established policies. After all, my deviation from policies to take 'unilateral action' seems to have upset you no end."

Tremble's face clouded and he clenched his fists as he half-rose from his chair.

Gleason continued quickly. "But let's talk about something more pleasant. How's Keith, by the way? What is he, eighteen now?" Gleason paused. "Oh, to be eighteen again, even in these troubled times. I do hope we can avoid mandatory conscription, but then again, we all have to do our part. I'm sure a patriotic young man like Keith would make a valuable addition to the new Special Reaction Force. Of course, a young man with a father in the national leadership always has options, assuming you decide to stay, of course."

Tremble sank back into his chair and glared at Gleason.

"Food for thought, Simon," said Gleason as he reached over and patted Tremble's knee, "just food for thought."

Gleason flashed his perfect white teeth in another million-dollar smile and rose.

"I'll give you some time to think. Help yourself to the coffee on the sideboard, and let the fellow at the door know if you'd like anything to snack on. We try to keep things civilized, even in the midst of disaster. I'll be back in an hour or so for your decision."

Day 15, 1:00 p.m.

McComb leaned back in the warden's chair, his feet on the desk.

"So how'd it work?"

Snaggle flashed his gap-toothed grin. "Slicker 'n snot on a doorknob. I gotta hand it to ya Spike, bustin' the guys outta Stiles was genius. We drove right up in the federal CO uniforms and prison vans in broad daylight and those dumb-ass state assholes let us in easy as you please. Weren't many of 'em left anyway, so it didn't take long to take care of 'em. We had a lot more brothers in the state lockup too."

"How many we free?"

"Just over two hundred Aryan Brotherhood of Texas, and maybe that many more new recruits. Like you said, we only took recruits who seemed hardcore, and left the others locked up with the jigs and beaners." Snaggle smirked. "I expect the rest of the whites will be a mite more enthusiastic after a day or so without any food or water. They wasn't gettin' much anyway, but the state assholes seemed to be doing a bit better about feeding 'em than they was doing by us."

McComb shook his head. "We're tight on food and such anyway, and better off to have committed ABT soldiers we know we can trust, so we'll look at recruits hard from here on. Any of the whites that don't measure up we'll use in the labor gang unless they look to be trouble, then we just leave 'em to rot with the mud people. Everything set up now at Stiles?"

Snaggle nodded. "We left guys in the Texas state CO uniforms running the place, so it looks normal if anyone checks, or at least normal considerin' what's going on. The brothers we freed are setting up quarters in the admin buildings, and I left a few of our guys in charge to run things. Nobody at Stiles outranked you in the Brotherhood, but I brought the three or four top guys over here to our group so we can keep an eye on 'em, just in case. We don't want nobody gettin' no wrong ideas on who's in charge."

"Good man. How's the scavenging going?"

"Could be better, but we're building up the stores a little at a time. It would go a lot faster if we could just blow through and take stuff, but we're keepin' it low key, like you want."

"Any problems?"

"Not with the scavenging, the boys are getting pretty good at it. They just drive up in uniform and one of 'em knocks at the door politely. When folks answer the door, they give 'em the old 'be on the lookout for escaped prisoners' and then check out the situation while the other guys circle around the house. Then they either bust in and take everything or pull back and figure out the best way to take 'em. They ain't leavin' no witnesses behind, and so far it's all been smooth along those lines, but..." Snaggle hesitated.

"Out with it. What's the problem?"

"Well, we're still short of women. I mean, me and you and the rest of the top guys have our pick. And I ain't caught up by a damn sight, but I'm feelin' a lot better in that department. But the problem is, we ain't got enough women to go around yet, especially good-lookin' ones, and it's causing some problems. I mean, some of the junior guys go out and grab some good-lookin' bitch, and the next thing he knows, he brings her back here and he goes to the end of the line. Some of 'em are starting to grumble, and to be honest, I don't think it's good for morale."

"All right, I get it. We'll have to cool it with the rank thing and make sure everybody gets a fair shot at the women." McComb smiled. "In a few weeks when we control everything, women will be crawling up the road begging us to take 'em, so I guess we can be patient. I mean, now that we've had a little taste to hold us awhile."

"Good call, I think," Snaggle said. "Just one more thing. One of the scavenging teams ran into a deputy sheriff patrol last night—"

"Goddammit, I told you to avoid—"

Snaggle held up his hands. "It's cool, Spike, we got it handled. They took 'em out before they got on the radio, and they brought the cruiser back here. We got it hid in the motor pool."

McComb struggled to contain himself, but slowly calmed. "I suppose it was gonna happen sooner or later. What about the bodies?"

"Body," Snaggle said, "we stripped the uniform and dumped him with the others in the medium-security administration building. They took the second deputy alive, and one of the guys recognized him. Seems like the asshole busted him some time back, and he wanted payback. They got him over in max security, having a little fun with him. I made 'em strip him to his skivvies first. I figure we might be able to use the uniform."

"All right," McComb said, "just as long as nobody saw..." He trailed off.

"What's up, Spike? What're you thinking?"

But McComb was already on his feet, moving toward the door, and Snaggle fell in behind, hurrying to keep up as McComb raced out of the building. Five minutes later they rushed through the entrance to the max-security unit, where an ABT soldier in a CO uniform manned the security checkpoint.

"Where's the cop?" McComb demanded.

The soldier smirked. "In the dining hall so everybody could watch."

McComb raced for the dining hall, with Snaggle trailing, and burst in to find the deputy tied to a chair, blood covering his battered face as he slumped forward with his chin on his chest, and convicts lined up before him, each apparently waiting their turn to beat the man. Others cheered them on, and a few enterprising souls were taking bets on which blow would finish the cop off.

"All right, all right, knock it off!" McComb yelled as he walked into the room. His order was met with jeers and catcalls. But he leveled a stony gaze at the audience and the jeering stopped as abruptly as it began.

"I got better use for this asshole," McComb said, "supposing you morons ain't killed him." He walked over and raised a bloody eyelid with his thumb and poked a finger in the cop's eye, and the cop's head jerked back at this latest and unexpected assault.

McComb nodded and turned to Snaggle. "All right, he's alive, or alive enough, anyway. Get him in one of the private offices and send somebody over to the motor pool for a car battery and a pair of jumper cables, and make sure the battery has a good hot charge. Matter of fact, better have 'em bring a couple of extra batteries as backups."

***

Two hours later, McComb straightened, handed the jumper cable leads to Snaggle, and wiped the sweat from his forehead with the back of his hand.

"That's all he knows. Shoot him in the head and throw him with the others."

"He's still alive, maybe we should give him back to the boys," Snaggle said. "You know, just for morale."

"I don't give a damn, do what you want. I doubt he lasts another ten minutes anyway, and he served my purpose."

"You think he was tellin' the truth about FEMA? And what about the National Guard? Don't sound right they ain't together. I mean, I thought they would be actin' more like after one of the hurricanes."

McComb shrugged. "It kinda makes sense in a way. The FEMA assholes are all concentrating on that nuke plant over by Bay City, probably trying to get the power back. That's fine by me, it's over a hundred and fifty miles from here with Houston in between. And with almost all the National Guard units in East Texas detailed to help out in Houston and Dallas, that mostly leaves the local yokels and a few state troopers minding the store here." He smiled. "Which is gonna make this a lot easier."

JACK BROOKS REGIONAL AIRPORT
US HIGHWAY 69
NEDERLAND, TEXAS

DAY 15, 5:00 P.M.

Snaggle looked around nervously, checking the setup for the tenth time. The Bureau of Prisons' transport bus was a hundred yards down the entrance road to the airport, pitched forward into the shallow ditch, not quite at a right angle to the road. A dozen ABT soldiers still dressed as prisoners and carrying guns of various types stood around, talking and smoking, ready to play their parts.

Spike McComb stood next to him, both men uniformed as federal corrections officers, as were six of their fellow prisoners. To complete the ruse, two prisoners wore the uniforms of the most recently deceased Jefferson County sheriff's deputies. All ten men stood behind the deputies' captured cruiser and two of the Bureau of Prison's sedans, the three vehicles drawn across the road to form a roadblock to prevent the escape of the prison bus—or so it seemed.

"I don't know, Spike, this seems a bit risky," Snaggle said. "I mean, what if too many of 'em show up at once?"

"Relax, you heard what the guy said. There ain't that many of 'em left to patrol at any one time. Hell, I'm worried we won't draw up enough of 'em. I figure where we are, we'll most likely get a few Port Arthur cops and county deputies. I hope it'll be enough to go to the next part of the plan, 'cause I don't think we can pull this off twice. Even cops ain't that friggin' dumb."

Snaggle nodded, and McComb turned, cupping his hands to yell over the fake roadblock. "Okay, boys, get ready and make it look good. Start shootin' when you see the cop cars arrive, and make damn sure you're shootin' high because if any one of us gets hit, whoever fired the shot is a dead man."

There were waves and sarcastic comments as the men followed orders and crawled under the bus, and McComb gathered the other men around for final instructions.

"Okay, minimum blood. I don't want the uniforms messed up. We take 'em down from behind with the stun guns and then cap 'em with the little twenty-two to the head at close range. Everybody got that?"

There were nods of understanding.

"Okay, boys, showtime!" McComb said. He walked to the deputies' car and reached in for the radio mike.

"OFFICER DOWN! SHOTS FIRED! OFFICER DOWN ON US 69 IN NEDERLAND AT THE ENTRANCE TO THE AIRPORT. REQUEST IMMEDIATE ASSISTANCE FROM ALL UNITS IN THE VICINITY. REPEAT. OFFICER DOWN! SHOTS FIRED! OFFICER DOWN ON US 69 IN NEDERLAND AT THE ENTRANCE TO THE AIRPORT. REQUEST IMMEDIATE ASSISTANCE FROM ALL UNITS IN THE VICINITY."

He replaced the mike and listened, but didn't respond to the flood of requests for more information. He knew those units that could respond would, because nothing had a greater priority than 'officer down,' and the less they knew, the more confused they'd be when they arrived. He listened for units responding along with their ETAs, and held up fingers for each separate response he heard so his men would know as well. In moments he'd registered five responding units, with arrivals spread over the next fifteen minutes, and he heard the first siren in the distance.

It went like clockwork as the cons under the bus kept up a steady fire and their fake police colleagues crouched behind the roadblock, rising sporadically to return fire. The officers in each responding unit interpreted the scene exactly as intended and parked their cruisers to rush to McComb's side, peering over the roadblock at the prison bus as McComb's men took a step back and jammed stun guns into their necks. The helpless would-be rescuers were then dragged out of sight on the opposite side of the roadblock and dispatched with a single small-caliber round to the head, as all the while the radio shrieked requests for status updates.

It was over in twenty minutes and McComb counted the dead and inventoried his spoils—four Port Arthur cops, three Jefferson County deputy sheriffs, and two Beaumont cops, along with five captured police cars. All the radios were active now as dispatchers sought more information, and McComb knew they had to move quickly.

"All right, Snag, just like we planned, get the guys out of the bus and into these dead cop's uniforms now—no, wait—have six of 'em dress out, but leave one dead cop from each service in uniform and throw 'em in the cruisers. They'll respond better if they think one of their own is down. We have to hit the Port Arthur Police Department and the sheriff's department office in Port Arthur together, 'cause they're closest and only a block apart. We'll split the guys into two teams; you take the sheriff's office and I'll take the police department. You know the story, the only change is you carry the dead deputy in with the first guys, so it looks like he's hurt and you're helping him in. No lights and sirens until we're half a block away, then light 'em up and raise holy hell. Be fast, don't give 'em a chance to figure things out, and take out the dispatcher first thing. Got it?"

Snaggle nodded and set about his tasks. Ten minutes later a convoy of police cars was streaming towards downtown Port Arthur, packed with fake cops and correction officers. The Bureau of Prisons' sedans with the remainder of the cons followed a half mile back. When the convoy reached the corner of Procter Street and Beaumont Avenue, McComb lit up the lights and siren, signaling all units to do the same, and the convoy split to complete their separate missions.

McComb led his three-car force to a skidding halt in the police department parking lot, disgorging his men. McComb and one of his cons grabbed the dead policeman and hurried into the building in front of the group, blood trailing down the dead man's shirt from the head wound. They burst into the lightly manned police station, with McComb screaming an alarm.

"THERE'S BEEN A MASS ESCAPE FROM THE FEDERAL PRISON! THERE MUST BE TWO HUNDRED OF THEM AND THEY'RE ARMED AND HEADED THIS WAY. GET EVERYBODY OUT HERE RIGHT NOW AND START LOCKING DOWN THE BUILDING! THEY'RE RIGHT BEHIND US!"

The cops would have figured it out, given half a chance, but McComb didn't give them one. In the two minutes of confusion generated by his arrival, his men swarmed through the lightly manned police station, killing without warning or mercy. The dispatcher was the first to go, and by the five-minute mark, the cons were in total control. McComb dispatched an underling to bring the rest of the force in the prison sedans in to help with the cleanup, and another to check on Snaggle's progress at the sheriff's department.

Five minutes later, Snaggle showed up in person, grinning from ear to ear.

"Fish in a barrel, Spike," Snaggle said, "we got 'em all."

"The dispatcher?"

"Got her myself first thing. Nothing went out."

"All right, we still gotta move fast. We leave uniformed guys at each place to deal with any who straggle in from patrol or shift change or whatever. We got guys standing by at the prison to reinforce here, so when we go back by there, we send a dozen more down for each office. Right now, we gotta get up to Beaumont. We still got the sheriff's office there, as well as the Beaumont PD and the highway patrol office out on Eastex Freeway." McComb looked at his watch. "We should be done in two hours."

"I don't know, Spike, we done real good here. I think maybe we just ought to wait—"

McComb glared at his underling. "Thinking's my department. Yours is doing what you're told. That 'officer down' call likely went everywhere and they're all tense and nervous now, probably not thinkin' too good. We give 'em time, they're gonna figure things out, so we strike fast before that happens. Now I want everybody ready to roll in ten minutes. Got it?"

TEXAS DEPARTMENT OF PUBLIC SAFETY
REGION II, DISTRICT B
7200 EASTEX FREEWAY
BEAUMONT, TEXAS

DAY 15, 7:00 P.M.

The Texas Highway Patrol troopers had been the last to fall and the hardest to take down, even though they had the least manpower. They'd been the most suspicious, and McComb's men ended up fighting a pitched battle with the holdouts, losing four men in the process. Fortunately, they had managed to take out the dispatcher quickly. That was especially important to McComb, as the highway patrol would be the most likely to transmit a distress call to authorities at the state level.

Nonetheless, he was pleased. They'd managed to take down all remaining law enforcement in the entire county in an afternoon, and if their luck held, no one would be the wiser for a while. For sure the state authorities, assuming there actually were any state authorities left, would have their plate full, and it looked like FEMA only cared about the nuclear plant over in Bay City. The National Guard was up to their asses in alligators in Houston and Dallas, so that pretty much left Jefferson County, Texas, as his new kingdom.

He nodded as Snaggle walked up. "Good work, Snag, and pass that on to the boys. We need to get these three locations in Beaumont fully manned. We can surprise any stragglers and take care of them as they drift in, but I had another idea too. We got all the personnel records, so I want to put someone on checking out where every cop of any kind lives. I reckon some of them haven't come in to work for one reason or another, but we gotta take 'em out, just to be on the safe side. Send guys in state trooper uniforms to each local cop's house and check it out. That way, the local cops won't necessarily pick up on it if they don't recognize the state troopers. Then you send guys in local cops' uniforms to the state troopers' homes for the same reason. If they find the cop, take 'em out and don't leave no witnesses. Then search and bring back all their guns, spare uniforms, and what have you. In a few days, we can make sure every uniformed cop in these parts is one of our guys. Then we don't have to lay low and can pretty much do what we please. We make the two prisons our strongholds and consolidate our loot and prisoners there, so we always have a place to fall back to and defend if things go sideways. Other than that, we take what we want and live like we want."

McComb's grin widened. "I think I'm gonna like being chief of PO-lice."

M/V *PECOS TRADER*
GULF OF MEXICO—WESTBOUND
EAST OF SABINE PASS, TEXAS

DAY 15, 7:00 P.M.

Hughes leaned on the wind dodger in the fading light, staring at the western horizon.

"They'll be all right," said Dan Gowan, standing beside him.

Hughes turned, a sheepish smile on his face. "Was it that obvious?"

Gowan shrugged. "It doesn't take a mind reader to figure out a man would be worried about his family with all the craziness going on. But Laura's a smart lady, and y'all are pretty well supplied for emergencies. Like I said, they're all right." The chief engineer shook his head. "But Trixie's a different story. I do believe that woman wakes up in a new world every day, bless her heart. I am a bit anxious about her."

"Well, we'll find out soon enough, I guess. I figure we'll be hitting Sabine bar right at daybreak."

"You figured out what you gonna do when we get there?" Gowan asked.

"Yeah, I'd kinda like to know that myself, Captain," said Matt Kinsey as he stepped out the wheelhouse door onto the bridge wing.

Hughes sighed. "A day ago I'd say it depended on what we find when we get there, but the more I've been thinking about it, I've come to the conclusion it doesn't matter. For sure there'll be some ships anchored out, and I'm presuming there won't be a pilot. I mean, why would there be? Most of the traffic is tankers, and with no power to the refineries, there's no need for crude inbound, and no petroleum products outbound. So I'm thinking there'll be ships stacked up, not knowing what to do. I'm not gonna join that circus. I've timed our arrival for first light and we'll just head between the jetties and go upriver."

"No pilot? You seemed pretty worried about that at Wilmington," Kinsey said.

"I still am," Hughes said, "but this is a lot different. There's not that much current to contend with and we'll be heading into what little there is, which is a hell of a lot different than Wilmington. And while I've been to Wilmington maybe a dozen times, I've made the Sabine-Neches transit many times, probably pushing a hundred. I know all the waypoints and landmarks cold. I'll be nervous as hell, but it's not nearly as scary as coming down the Cape Fear River with a four- or five-knot current behind you. My biggest worry is what to do when we get where we're going."

Kinsey looked confused. "What do you mean? I figured you'd just tie up at your refinery dock."

"I have a couple of concerns. When we put the gangway down, it runs both ways. With resources in short supply, being a tanker loaded with fuel with containers full of food aboard makes us a pretty tempting target. My second concern is the crew."

Kinsey shrugged. "What about them?"

"They're all civilians, with families nearby they want to check on. I put that gangway down and we're liable to have an immediate exodus, and there isn't anything I can do about it. For that matter, I'm pretty sure you and your guys are thinking the same thing. But if everyone hauls ass with the ship tied to the dock, we can neither move it nor defend it," Hughes said. "I can't blame them, really. I certainly intend to go look for my family."

"Then don't tie up," Gowan said.

Hughes stroked his chin and nodded. "I guess we could anchor, not many places with enough water, though, since we're loaded. I'm thinking the Sun Lower Anchorage is probably the best. We've poked our bow in there to turn around often enough when fully loaded."

"Sounds like the best choice," Gowan agreed. "Then nobody can get to us except by boat, and it's plus twenty feet from the water to the main deck. We use the fast rescue boat or the Coasties' patrol boat to get back and forth to shore, and we can land pretty much where we want, out of sight of the ship. If anyone sees us, they can't really tell where we came from. And we can set up some sort of structured rotation for going ashore to look for families. The guys might not like it, but if you're controlling the boats to and from shore, they can't just say screw you and run down the gangway."

"That's it, then," Hughes said, turning to Kinsey. "Now we just have to worry about the Coasties and the navy. You think they're just gonna let us do what we please?"

Kinsey shrugged. "I guess we'll find out at daybreak tomorrow, won't we?"

CHAPTER FIFTEEN

Hughes studied the radar as *Pecos Trader* moved toward the sea buoy at reduced speed. Two dozen ships crowded the anchorage ahead, their Automatic Identification System transmissions broadcasting many familiar names—other tankers, all in ballast. Their presence was both expected and disappointing. Someone cleared their throat behind him, and Kinsey moved up beside him at the radar screen.

"Looks like Wilmington, Act 2," Kinsey said. "Any luck with a pilot?"

Hughes shook his head as he stepped to the VHF and picked up the mike. "I tried twice. Let's see if anyone is home at the Coasties' house."

He spoke into the mike. "Port Arthur Traffic, Port Arthur Traffic, this is the tanker *Pecos Trader* . My ETA at Sabine Bank Buoy is zero five thirty and I require a pilot. Repeat, this is the tanker *Pecos Trader* . My ETA at Sabine Bank Buoy is zero five thirty and I require a pilot. Over."

There was no answer and Hughes repeated the call, with the same response. He shook his head. "With all the ships at anchor, even if Port Arthur VTS doesn't respond, I'd think someone at anchor would be butting in to let us know what's going on—"

"Tanker *Pecos Trader* , repeat, tanker *Pecos Trader* , this is the tanker *Ambrose Channel* . Do you copy? Over."

"Now that's more like what I expected," Hughes said, and keyed the mike.

"*Ambrose Channel* , this is *Pecos Trader.* We copy. Over."

"*Pecos Trader* , be advised there is no pilot service and Port Arthur VTS is nonoperational. At least they haven't responded to any calls from anchorage in the ten days we've been here. Over."

"We copy, *Ambrose Channel* . What's going on? Over."

"Who knows? Most of us have no loading orders. A navy ship came by five days ago and instructed us to wait here at anchor. I guess they're trying to figure out where they might need us. So here we sit, at least as long as we have fuel and stores, which might not be very long. Welcome to the club. Over."

"Thank you, *Ambrose Channel* , but I don't think I want to join. This is *Pecos Trader* , out."

Hughes reracked the mike and looked over at Chief Mate Georgia Howell.

"You ready to do this, Mate?"

"Do I have a choice?"

Hughes sighed. "Not really."

***

Hughes was sweating, despite the early hour, as he kept *Pecos Trader* in the middle of the channel and crawled upstream at a fraction of the speed an experienced pilot might employ. Periodically he moved from one bridge wing to the other, looking down the side of the ship to gauge his position relative to the shore from different perspectives. If he put her aground, there'd be no tugs to pull her off. He had Pete Sonnier, his best helmsman, on the wheel, and Georgia Howell was handling engine orders, but despite the presence of his 'A Team,' the stress was palpable. Kinsey was on the bridge in case they encountered the Coast Guard, but Kinsey seemed to sense the tension and was keeping to the chartroom, available if needed, but out of the way.

For all Hughes' anxiety, things were going well. He'd timed their arrival and transit at high slack water to avoid the strong westerly set of the current, and successfully negotiated the known shallow spot on the inside of the turn some distance from the entrance to the jetties. They were in protected waters now, less subject to the vagaries of wind and current, and he let himself relax a bit as he walked to the port bridge wing. They passed the Sabine Pilot Docks on the west bank, the pilot boats all tied up and the small parking lot completely empty.

"CHIEF KINSEY," he shouted back towards the wheelhouse, "COAST GUARD STATION COMING UP. YOU MIGHT WANT TO HAVE A LOOK."

Kinsey was at his side in seconds, and they watched as the ship drew abreast of the Coast Guard station, a neatly kept jewel in the otherwise scruffy industrial blight of the shoreline. The building was a sparkling white in the Spanish style with a red tile roof, and set in a broad expanse of verdant green lawn. But even at a distance, the beginnings of decay were obvious; the St. Augustine grass was overgrown and encroaching on the sidewalks, and there were no cars in the parking lot or boats at the dock. The place looked abandoned.

"Looks like nobody's home," Hughes said.

Kinsey nodded. "They must've been re-tasked somewhere, especially since the boats are gone. If they'd just taken off on their own, I doubt it would have been by boat, so I'm thinking they probably got reassigned to the Houston-Galveston area. There's a lot more marine traffic there, especially if the refineries here in Beaumont and Port Arthur are shut down." He shrugged. "But that's just a guess."

"Good a guess as any," Hughes said, "and at least we don't have to worry about having to finesse our way around another obstacle."

Kinsey looked relieved, and Hughes moved back into the wheelhouse, leaving Kinsey alone on the bridge wing.

Things continued smoothly, and apart from some anxiety when transiting the highway bridge just north of Texas Island, Hughes was growing confident he might actually reach the anchorage without going aground. They'd seen zero activity ashore, but given both the circumstances and the early hour, he wasn't surprised. That changed as they drew abreast of downtown Port Arthur and Hughes caught movement ashore out of the corner of his eye. He took a quick look at the arrow-straight section of the channel ahead, then moved out to the port bridge wing, grabbing the binoculars from their storage box on the way out the wheelhouse door.

"What we got, Chief?" he asked Kinsey.

"Looks like cops, so maybe things haven't gone completely to hell here."

Hughes nodded and raised the glasses. A police cruiser was stopped on the road paralleling the channel, with two officers standing at the open doors and staring at the ship.

"Sheriff's deputies based on the car and the uniforms," Hughes said.

He watched the men jump back in the car and race along the road, lights flashing and siren wailing, to a small waterfront park in the far distance well ahead of the ship. The cops exited the car and left the lights flashing to race out on to a small dock projecting slightly into the channel.

"What the hell…"

"Well, this is a first," Kinsey said. "I think they want you to pull over."

"Those friggin' idiots! Don't they realize I can't…" He trailed off and shot Kinsey an exasperated look.

"Probably not." Kinsey shrugged. "Your call, Cap, but stupid though they may be, they might represent the only authority around here. It might not be wise to piss 'em off at this point."

Hughes looked at the channel again. He had plenty of water depth and no traffic in a straight channel, and he was only creeping along. He could probably accommodate them without too much risk. He nodded and handed Kinsey the binoculars before stomping back into the wheelhouse.

"STOP!" he called out to Georgia Howell.

She looked startled, but after a moment's hesitation confirmed the order and passed it to the engine room while Hughes gave the helm orders to edge the *Pecos Trader* a bit closer to the west bank of the channel.

"HALF ASTERN!" Hughes ordered, and the ship began to slow from its already snail-like pace. Moments later he ordered 'STOP' again and nodded with satisfaction as the big ship drifted to a halt about fifty feet off the dock where the two cops stood. He turned to Georgia Howell.

"Mate, keep an eye on things while I talk to these knuckleheads. If it looks like we're drifting into trouble, let me know."

"Yes, sir," she replied, and Hughes hurried back out on the bridge wing.

"Y'ALL COME ON IN AND TIE UP," shouted one of the cops.

Hughes suppressed a curse. "I CAN'T TIE UP TO THAT, IT'S A FISHING DOCK," he called. "IF I PUT THIS SHIP ALONGSIDE, I'LL CRUSH IT LIKE AN EGG. BESIDES, WHY DO YOU WANT US TO TIE UP?"

There was a discussion between the cops, as if they were unsure. The spokesman turned and yelled back to the ship, "WE NEED TO SEARCH Y'ALL FOR CONTRABAND AND HOARDED GOODS. ALL SUPPLIES ARE BEING CENTRALIZED BY THE COUNTY GOVERNMENT FOR THE RELIEF EFFORT."

Beside Hughes, Kinsey studied the cops through the binoculars. "Unless the cops are okay with swastika neck tattoos," he said under his breath, "I suspect those guys aren't really cops."

Hughes nodded slightly and improvised.

"WELL, I CAN'T TIE UP HERE," he yelled back down, "SO WHAT DO YOU SUGGEST?"

Another conversation between the fake cops.

"TIE UP AT THE FIRST DOCK THAT WILL TAKE YOU. WE'LL FOLLOW YOU THERE," the spokesman said.

"THAT WOULD BE WHERE WE'RE GOING ANYWAY," Hughes yelled back. "WE NEED REPAIRS. DO YOU KNOW THE BLUDWORTH MARINE SHIPYARD IN ORANGE?"

"NO, BUT WE'LL JUST FOLLOW YOU."

"WELL, GOOD LUCK WITH THAT UNLESS YOUR CRUISER'S A MARSH BUGGY BECAUSE THE ROAD DOESN'T RUN BESIDE THE CHANNEL. BESIDES, IT'S NOT EXACTLY LIKE WE CAN RUN AWAY FROM YOU."

More conversation ashore.

"ALL RIGHT, WE'LL MEET YOU AT THIS SHIPYARD, BUT DON'T TRY NO TRICKS," the spokesman said.

"FINE, WE'LL SEE YOU THERE IN THREE HOURS," Hughes yelled back.

The pair moved to their car, and Hughes flashed Kinsey a smile. "I guess those boys aren't from around here."

"I'm not from around here either, but I know there's no way a ship this size is getting anywhere near Orange. That's a tug and barge yard anyway. Why'd you pick that?"

"Because it's the farthest place away I could think of that might sound reasonable to someone without a clue. Right now they're probably rushing to look it up in the phone book or someplace. It'll be listed as a shipyard, and they don't exactly strike me as the sharpest tacks in the box, so I'm hoping they'll haul ass for Orange. If they're as dumb as I think they are, they probably won't figure it out even after they get there, so they'll sit around and wait for us to show up, for a while at least. By that time, we ought to be safe in our anchorage."

***

"What kind of ship? A navy ship. A cargo ship? What?"

"Hell, I don't know, Spike! A big one."

Spike McComb looked at the pair before him and suppressed an urge to kill them.

"So lemme get this straight. You two spot a big-ass ship comin' up the channel and lose it? How do you lose a friggin' ship, for Christ's sake?"

"There was one of them orange Coast Guard boats on the deck and one of the guys on board had on a uniform of some kind," the second of the pair volunteered.

"Shit!" McComb said. "That ain't good. We don't need the Coast Guard around here messin' things up."

"Maybe they stole the Coast Guard boat," Snaggle said, joining the conversation. "WE got uniforms, so that don't necessarily mean nothing."

McComb rubbed his chin. "Could be you're right, but I still don't like it. We need tight control of our territory and I don't like the idea of no Coast Guard pukes running around. Hell, they're as bad as cops, worse maybe 'cause they got better guns. And for all we know, this ship's full of prime cargo of some kind."

He thought about it a moment longer and then turned to Snaggle.

"Snag, get on top of this. It ain't like there are a lot of places to hide a big ship. Figure out where it might be and start lookin' for it."

"Okay, Spike, whatever you say. But things are goin' pretty smooth and we're really bringin' in the loot now that we got 'police backup,'" Snaggle said. "You want me to pull some boys off scavengin' and put 'em looking for this ship?"

"Maybe we should do both. We got anybody lookin' at the river? You know, houseboats, marinas, places like that? A lot of them boats have generators, so there's likely people living aboard. Might be a whole new source of loot and labor."

"I never thought of that," Snaggle said. "The sheriff's department has a boat somewhere, maybe we'll start up the Marine Patrol again."

"Get it done," McComb said.

STATE HIGHWAY 11
WEST OF CURRIE, NC

DAY 16, 10:00 A.M.

Luke studied the thick woods on either side of the road ahead, alert for an ambush. They'd looped far inland, avoiding interstate corridors and population centers, keeping to local roads and the occasional small town, stretching the four-hundred-mile trip to twice that, and lengthening it farther by traveling only during daylight. They'd consolidated all their stores into a single pickup to save fuel and abandoned the second truck in the Publix parking lot along with the two bodies. Plenty of good people were going unburied, and none of the now ex-SRF troopers had the slightest remorse about dumping the remains of the dead mercenaries like the trash they were.

Two nights running, they set up the vehicles in a triangular laager well off the road, with trip wires and noise makers all around and someone keeping watch on one of the Ma Deuces. Keeping to the hinterland had been a wise choice—one they'd debated at some length given their Humvees' thirst for diesel. They'd maintained a constant watch for abandoned gas stations along their route, and possible sources of residual fuel in underground storage tanks. As it turned out, stations farther off the beaten path weren't yet scavenged as thoroughly as those in more populated areas.

Fuel wasn't plentiful, but it was adequate, helped no doubt by scavengers concentrating on gasoline rather than the diesel their Humvees guzzled. Luke smiled at the memory of their only 'armed confrontation' at a dilapidated country store as they hand-pumped diesel into their Jerry cans. An older gentleman had appeared, brandishing a shotgun and less than happy over the theft of fuel. Some placating discussion and allowing him his choice of the contents of the stores truck ended the affair without bloodshed.

"Won't be long now," Gibson said from behind the wheel. "My folks' place is just past this intersection with fifty-three."

"Anxious to get home?" Luke asked.

Gibson gave a solemn nod. "And kind of afraid of what I might find. My folks' farm is back here in the sticks, though, so I ain't too worried. I joined the Corps 'cause I never much wanted to be a farmer, but I gotta admit, when times get tough, at least country folks have something to eat."

"That's a fact," Luke said, just as they passed the intersection, another paved rural road leading off to the left at an angle. Ahead he could just make out the guardrails of a fairly substantial bridge of some sort, but Gibson slowed and made a right turn onto a gravel track before they reached the bridge.

"This leads to my folks' place. My family owns a pretty fair strip of land between this road and the river beyond the trees to our left. Almost four hundred acres all told. Been in the family since before the war," Gibson said. Despite his professed aversion to farming, Luke could hear pride of ownership in the young man's voice.

"World War Two?"

Gibson laughed. "The War Between the States."

"There have been a few since then, you know," Luke said.

"Yeah, but none of 'em happened in North Carolina," Gibson replied, still smiling. Then his smile faded. "Leastwise, not until now."

Luke nodded and they rode in silence for a couple of minutes until Gibson took his foot off the gas and let the vehicle roll to a stop.

"What's up?" Luke asked.

"Our driveway's about a hundred yards ahead on the left. Might be better if I went ahead on foot. My dad's a veteran, but he ain't a real big fan of the government in the best of times. No tellin' how he might take it if two armed Humvees roll in, especially with these uniforms. If there are SRF units up here, and they got 'em doing what we was doing in Florida, I think we got about a fifty-fifty chance of a warm reception."

"How's that going to be any different if you go in alone? You're still wearing the uniform," Luke said.

"Because I'm walking up the driveway with my helmet off and my hands up, yelling 'Dad, don't shoot,' that's why."

"And what happens if someone other than your folks are there and they're not friendly?" Luke shook his head. "I don't like it, Gibson. You do it your way, but I'm trailing behind out of sight to lay down some covering fire in case you gotta turn around and beat feet out of there."

"Look, LT, I know you mean well, but—"

"No buts, Gibson. I can't stop you from going in like you want, but you can't stop me from providing backup. That's just the way it is."

Gibson sighed. "Okay, LT, I'll give you the layout, but be careful. Even with me there, Dad's not gonna take kindly to anyone pointing a gun at him."

The feeling's mutual, thought Luke, but he only nodded.

They exited their vehicle and Gibson described the entrance to his family's farm and briefed the others before he set off for the house with only his sidearm. His helmet was off and suspended from his web gear. Luke let him get fifty yards ahead and started through the tall grass in the field to his left, heading for the sunken creek Gibson told him ran roughly parallel to the road. He hit it and jogged upstream, hidden by the creek banks. He rounded a bend to see a large culvert ahead where the driveway crossed the creek. He redoubled his efforts, splashing through the shallow creek to the culvert and then crawling up the left bank, to peek over and see Gibson's back as he walked, hands above his head, toward an ancient, but well-maintained farmhouse with a large barn nearby. Luke sighted his assault rifle on the house in the distance beyond Gibson.

"HELLO IN THE HOUSE! DON'T SHOOT! IT'S ME, DONNY!"

For a long minute, nothing happened, then the door of the house opened, followed by the squeak of the wooden screen door. A man appeared holding a rifle. His body language was tentative as he peered into the distance.

"DONNY? PRAISE GOD! IS THAT REALLY YOU, BOY?"

"IT'S ME, DAD—"

Luke heard the squawk of a radio and he watched in his scope as the man raised a walkie-talkie to his face, but he was too far away to hear what was said. The man on the porch looked up, his body language changing from tentative to tense.

"DONNY! GET DOWN!" the man shouted, and the dirt immediately in front of Luke exploded in his face from the impact of a three-round burst. He jerked his head back below the bank just as another burst shredded the earth where his head had been. In the near distance behind him, he heard the Humvees firing up, no doubt intent on bringing their Ma Deuces to bear if the Gibson homestead was occupied by bad guys. This was going to hell in a hurry, thought Luke as he chanced another quick 'peek and duck,' rewarded by another three-round burst.

"DAD! RICHARD! STOP SHOOTING! THEY'RE FRIENDS!"

Luke heard footsteps pounding toward him and ducked into the metal culvert under the driveway, just to be on the safe side.

"LT? LT? Are you hit?" came Gibson's voice above him.

"Not yet," Luke said as he moved out of the culvert and looked up, "but I'm not sure I like my odds. Are they done shooting at me yet?"

Gibson moved to the side of the stream and reached down a hand. "Yeah, and you're lucky. My brother, Richard, don't miss too often."

Luke took Gibson's offered hand and pulled himself up the steep creek bank just as the little convoy roared around the turn into the driveway. Luke signaled them to hold in place and turned to follow Gibson back toward the farmhouse and Gibson's father, who was now off the porch and halfway down the long driveway, running to meet them. In the distance over the approaching man's shoulder, Luke saw another figure exit the barn and rush toward them, a rifle slung across his back.

Gibson's dad reached them and wrapped his son in a hug. "Donny! Thank God you're home, boy. Your mom's been worried sick ever since the lights went out." The man straightened and released his son. "I'm sure glad to see you, but what are y'all doing here?"

"It's a long story, Dad. But first meet Lieutenant Kinsey. LT, this is my dad," Gibson said.

The older man extended his hand to Luke. "Vern Gibson, Lieutenant, and sorry about before. We thought you was holding a gun on Donny."

"Understandable, Mr. Gibson and no harm done. And call me Luke. I expect I'm not a lieutenant anymore anyway."

Vern Gibson eyed their uniforms. "I was wonderin' about that, but I expect we'll get to—"

"Damn, Donny! If it weren't bad enough you was a jarhead, it looks like you done changed sides again," Richard Gibson said as he approached, the fierce hug he gave his brother giving lie to his taunt.

Luke assessed the newcomer quickly. He was an inch or so taller and perhaps a decade older than Donny Gibson, but there could be no mistaking they were brothers. Richard Gibson moved with the quiet confidence of a soldier, or at least a former soldier, but there was something a bit awkward in the hug. It took a moment to realize Richard's gloved left hand was actually a prosthetic.

Donny Gibson returned his brother's hug and then pushed him back and grinned. "Well, you ought to get along well with the LT here, aside from almost killin' him, I mean. He's one of you idiots who jumps out of perfectly good aircraft."

Richard looked at Luke and smiled. "Sorry about that, but I have to say this is about the only time I've been happy I'm not quite as accurate as I was before I lost the hand." He held up the prosthetic left hand and then extended his real right hand to Luke. "Richard Gibson, formerly of the 82nd Airborne."

"Luke Kinsey, 101st… formerly of the 101st Airborne."

"Dopes on ropes?" Richard asked, his wide grin taking the sting out of his words.

Luke laughed. "Can't say I haven't felt like it at times." Then he grew serious as he nodded at the other man's prosthetic. "Sandbox?"

Richard nodded. "IED in Anbar Province. I got off lucky compared to—"

"DONNY!" a small woman screamed, and then launched herself at Donny Gibson, hugging him fiercely and laughing and crying simultaneously. "Oh, thank you, Jesus! You've brought my baby home to me safe and sound."

Luke watched as the woman continued to hang on to Donny Gibson for all she was worth, rocking on her feet and overcome with emotion, unable to speak. Young Gibson returned her fierce hug then gradually tried to release her as his face colored in embarrassment, but his mother was clamped tight. After a long moment he whispered something in her ear and gently but firmly pushed her back. Anger flashed across her face.

"Well, you may not be a baby, young man, but you're MY baby and don't you forget it…"

She turned and saw the men all grinning at her, joined now by an attractive younger woman, joining the group in the first woman's wake.

"What are you grinning at, Vernon Gibson? And just when did you plan on coming to tell me Donny was home? Or were you just planning on leaving me and Evie down in that hidey-hole until it dawned on you I might be a little interested my youngest son was home?"

"I'm sorry, Virginia. I was just—"

"You were just out here having a 'man talk' without concern as to what it was like for Evie and me stuck down in the dark, listening to gunfire and not knowin' if you two were alive or dead. THAT's what you were doing."

"I'm sorry, Virginia, but—"

"Don't you 'I'm sorry' me, Mr. Vernon Gibson. And I'll tell you another thing! That is the LAST time I'm goin' in that hole. I can shoot near as good as you and Richard, and if there's a threat, I'm gonna be right beside you defendin' this place. Is that clear?"

Vern Gibson sighed. "Yes, ma'am."

Virginia Gibson sniffed and turned to Luke.

"And who might you be, young man?"

"Luke Kinsey, ma'am. I'm—"

"Anyone who can bring my son home safe and sound in these troubled times is welcome in my home," she said, looking over his shoulder and down the driveway. "And I suppose those men and trucks belong with you. How many of y'all are there?"

"Six counting Gibs… six counting Donny," Luke said.

"Well, I suspect y'all are hungry, seems like everybody is these days. Come on in and I'll fix y'all a home-cooked meal. Have to be breakfast this late in the morning and on short notice, but I'll feed y'all enough to hold you until supper time and then do something special to celebrate Donny's homecoming." She turned back to her husband without waiting for a reply.

"Vernon, best git them army trucks out of sight in the barn before somebody comes by and gets nosy, then show these fellas where to wash up. Richard, bring in some more wood and stir the fire up in the cookstove, then bring in all the extra eggs and some more of that bacon. Eva and I are going to start making biscuits."

She motioned to the other woman and they both started for the house, heads together as they planned the impromptu meal. Luke watched them go, a bit shell-shocked at the sudden turn of events.

"We best git movin', Lieutenant," Vern Gibson said. "Virginia can get real mean when she's riled up."

"She's not riled up yet?"

Vern Gibson laughed. "Oh, hell no. Not by a long shot."

***

The meal was simple and bountiful—huge platters of scrambled eggs and bacon, accompanied by heaped plates of biscuits with small crocks of fresh butter and homemade preserves, all of which the two women kept constantly refilled, and washed down with cold milk from heavy stoneware pitchers. Except for Donny Gibson, the men ate tentatively at first, feeling guilty about depleting the family's stores. However, repeated assurances there was 'plenty more' and the temptation of the best food they'd seen in weeks soon ate through their restraint. They began shoveling it down while Virginia Gibson looked on with approval, ready to refill the platters.

Finally Sergeant Joel Washington had his fill and leaned back in his chair.

"Ma'am, I do believe that was the best meal I've ever eaten in my entire life."

There was a chorus of agreement around the table as Virginia Gibson blushed. "It's nothing special, just eggs and such," she said. "I expect y'all were just hungry is all."

"We were that," Luke said, "but the meal was outstanding nonetheless. However, I'm still concerned we're depleting your stores. We didn't mean to come in and eat you out of house and home."

"Not a problem," Vern Gibson said. "We always had extra milk and eggs we sold, but we been keeping close to home what with things the way they are. Most folks around here been doing likewise, so y'all just ate up what was likely to go bad anyway."

"How do you keep the milk cold?" Neal Long asked. "You got a generator?"

Vern Gibson nodded. "We got a little generator in the barn, but we only use it when we have to. But folks was keepin' milk cold a long time before we got electricity in these parts. We got a springhouse that's been here almost two hundred years. It's the same spring where we get our drinking water."

"Looks like you've got a pretty good setup," Luke said.

Vern nodded again. "Too good maybe. This ain't been goin' on all that long, but I'm worried as it gets worse we're going to see more folks comin' around trying to take what don't belong to 'em. As a matter of fact, there's only two other farms on this road and yesterday we all agreed to plow up the gravel road from the state highway until our driveway and let it go back natural, just to keep strangers from poking their noses down the road. Ain't no point in invitin' trouble. Most of the farms here border the river, and we figure we can use it for transportation and tradin' among ourselves, just like folks did in the old days."

"Sounds like a plan," Luke said, smiling as he nodded toward Donny Gibson, "and you've got another good man to help with defense."

Donny Gibson flushed as his father nodded. "And we're obliged for you helping him get home. Y'all can stay here as long as you like. There ain't room in the house for everybody, but we can make the barn pretty comfortable this time of the year, and I'm sure we can find another woodstove before winter sets in. I figure farming's gonna get a lot more labor intensive, and Lord knows we can use the extra firepower if things get bad." He smiled. "And it ain't a bad place for outlaws to hang out. I reckon nobody's gonna be lookin' for you here."

Luke nodded. "That's a generous offer and we, or at least some of us, might take you up on it. But I really want to try to connect with my dad first. He's at the Coast Guard station down at Oak Island."

"Family's important," Vern agreed. "How you figure to get there?"

"That's a problem," Luke said. "I think we've been pushing our luck a bit, riding around in the Humvees and these uniforms. We haven't had any problems in the countryside, but I don't know exactly what to expect closer to a population center. For sure, we'll attract more notice, and if it's of the 'official' variety, we'll either get in a shootout or have to surrender. Even if we run into troops who don't know we're AWOL, they're likely gonna want to conscript us and our vehicles into their operation—not too many military commanders would warm to the idea of a lieutenant running around doing whatever he pleases. Do you have any idea what's going on in the city?"

"Not a real good idea, but we do have kind of a grapevine," Vern said. "I hear it's pretty bad with no law left to speak of. The gangs are runnin' things and they're starting to spread out from the city. One of our neighbors took his boat down quiet like one night and said there's some soldiers around the docks and a Coast Guard patrol boat in the river, but he didn't contact 'em. He just looked around a bit and came home."

Luke sat up straighter at the mention of the boat. "If we can contact the Coast Guard boat, I might be able to get word to my dad."

Vern nodded. "We got a couple of boats and I can take you downriver. Between me, Richard, and Donny, I reckon we can get you all into civvies. If we get stopped by the wrong folks, you're just farmers from upriver, comin' in to check out the situation."

"Sounds like a plan," Luke said.

APPALACHIAN TRAIL
MILE MARKER 998.6 NORTHBOUND
EAST OF BLUEMONT, VIRGINIA

DAY 16, 3:00 P.M.

Bill Wiggins stopped to catch his breath, trying to ignore the pack straps cutting into his shoulders and his aching back and feet. Tex stepped up beside him and looked up the hill.

She flashed a weary smile. "Only another half mile."

Wiggins snorted. "It's not the half mile I mind. It's the three-hundred-foot vertical part."

She nodded and took the lead. He fell in behind her to trudge up the incline.

It was their second full day afoot and they'd covered barely twenty-five miles total. The afternoon they'd fled, the first three miles were a steep climb, and he immediately doubted the wisdom of overloading their packs. They reached the ridgetop and only two miles further when by mutual agreement, they moved off the trail and made cold camp. They'd used the remaining daylight to empty and reload their packs, abandoning heavier items they'd grabbed in their hasty flight. The only consolation was eating their fill of food they would have otherwise left behind. They started the next day on full stomachs.

They made twelve miles the second day, crossing US 50 at Ashby Gap and continuing four miles to the Rod Hollow shelter, arriving with two hours of daylight remaining. They were limping by the time they made camp in the woods, well away from the shelter, Wiggins more than Tex.

They boiled pasta in the little pot of the ultralight camp stove Levi had included in the pack. They wolfed it down plain, carbs to balance the nuts and jerky they'd eaten through the day. The little AT guidebook was already proving invaluable, for its list of water sources alone. They topped their camel packs at the shelter before retreating to their hidden campsite and stringing their bell-studded fishing line through the trees.

When Wiggins removed his boots to massage his aching feet, he'd found the nails of both big toes purplish and tender to the touch. Roomy, steel-toed work boots were fine for standing on the engine-room deck plates for long hours, but far from ideal for hiking. Tex was having similar problems, though her toenails weren't yet discolored. But exhaustion proved an effective anesthetic and they'd crawled into their hammocks with the setting sun and slept like the dead to rise, stiff and sore, at first light.

They breakfasted on leftover cold pasta, jerky, and a handful of nuts, then donned extra pairs of socks to pad their aching feet. They laced their boots extra tight across the insteps, seeking to protect their battered toes, and started north with the rising sun—to find even more challenging terrain. Yesterday was long grueling climbs followed by equally long descents, but the past hours had been a roller coaster in comparison: a seemingly endless series of steep climbs with equally steep downhill grades, jamming their toes despite the tightness of the laces.

Wiggins was close to hobbling, and despite having made only ten miles for the day and with several hours of daylight remaining, he'd readily agreed to Tex's suggestion they start looking for a place to camp. He limped up the hill behind her now, trying not to fixate on their poor progress—two and a half days to make twenty-five miles—at this rate it would take him over four months to reach his family, provided his feet held out. He shook off the gloom and spoke to Tex's back.

"So what does the guidebook say about this Bear's Den place?"

"It looks to be a fairly substantial facility," she said. "It's a state park and listed as 'the premier hiker's hostel on the AT.' Looks like they have showers and food service, though I doubt if there's anyone there at this point. I'm just hoping we can liberate some toilet paper and… other things. Levi was a bit stingy with paper goods. We can hunt food, but we can't make toilet paper and I'm not a big fan of leaves."

"You think we'll run into anyone?" he asked.

"I'm thinking no," she said back over her shoulder, "but it's probably more likely there than other places. It is a park off a paved road."

"Wait up," Wiggins said, and Tex complied, her eyebrows raised in a question as Wiggins caught up with her.

"Let's leave our packs hidden back here off the trail and approach this place cautiously. If we have to run, we're not doing it with packs on our back. We can loop back later and get them. For that matter, maybe we ought to just keep to the woods and bypass this place."

Tex shook her head. "My camel pack ran dry a mile back and the next water source beyond Bear's Den is at least two hours, given our rate of travel. And what if it's dry? How's your water?"

"I'm almost dry too," he admitted. "All right, then I guess it's the 'cautious approach' scenario. Let's get a little closer to the top, then ditch our packs. I'm thinking we don't walk into the place from the trail but circle around and give it a good look from cover first."

Tex grinned. "You're getting so damned paranoid; Levi would be proud."

"I became a convert as soon as people started shooting at us."

Tex nodded and started back up the hill. When the trees began to thin, they moved off the trail and took off their packs. Wiggins opened his and pulled out the little survival rifle, quickly assembling it and slapping in a magazine.

"Going squirrel hunting?" Tex asked.

"Hey, it's better than nothing. You got the Glock?"

Tex reached around and patted the small of her back. "It hasn't been out of reach since the first shots were fired."

Wiggins nodded and they moved through the woods to the edge of a clearing. There in the center stood an impressive stone lodge built into the side of a low hill with a door to a daylight or 'walk out' basement in the rear. They kept to the woods and crept all the way around the building, alert for any signs of habitation.

"No activity, no cars," Wiggins whispered. "I'd say no one's home."

"I agree," Tex said. "Let's go back around. That basement door is supposed to be the hikers' entrance, accessible twenty-four hours a day."

Wiggins nodded and they emerged from the clearing and walked to the rear of the lodge. Sure enough, the door had a keypad.

"What's up with that?" Wiggins asked.

"According to the guidebook, you're supposed to enter the 'mileage code' for access. Not that it matters, since there's no power."

Wiggins was looking around. He spotted what he was looking for and returned with a large rock and smashed a window.

"I don't think that's what they had in mind for 'hiker access,'" Tex said.

"Hey, we got our share of the payoff money from the ship, I'll leave a couple of hundred bucks."

"Works for me," Tex said as Wiggins tapped glass shards from the window frame with the rock and reached inside to unlock the window.

"I'm smaller," Tex said. "Boost me in and I'll unlock the door."

Moments later they were inside, examining a row of bunk beds and a lounge with basic amenities. Wiggins followed Tex down a hall to a bathroom, and heard her emit a relieved sigh. He followed her gaze to a tampon dispenser on the wall and suppressed a smile. Couldn't really fault Levi for not putting that essential in his 'getting home' bag, he thought.

He walked to the sink and turned the faucet, surprised when water gushed out. Pressure was low, but adequate and he let it run a long moment to make sure it wasn't just residual water in the line.

"Damn! Running water. I'm thinking that must mean gravity flow from a tank—"

"And I'm thinking SHOWERS! Try the hot water," Tex said.

"Fat chance," Wiggins said as he twisted the knob. Warm water gushed across his hand.

"Well, I'll be damned. Must be solar."

"Hallelujah!" Tex said, and Wiggins laughed and nodded to a shelf piled with towels and personal-sized soap and shampoo.

"Ladies first," he said. "I'll have a look around and stand watch out here just to make sure no one catches us by surprise. After you've showered, you can return the favor. But first, let's go back and grab our packs."

An hour later, they had both finished their showers and were sitting in the lounge area of the hiker hostel.

"We still have daylight left, and I'm feeling much better," Wiggins said. "Should we try to put a few more miles behind us?"

Tex shook her head. "I think both our feet could use the rest. I also think we have to face facts. We can't continue like this. We've been hiking less than three days and we're both near crippled. We HAVE to get better footwear, or we're unlikely to make it at all."

"And how we gonna do that? It's not like there's an REI or a Cabela's on the trail."

Tex flipped through the guidebook. "There's a general store in Bluemont, and this is hiking country. They might have something. Even sneakers or running shoes would be better than these work boots."

"Okay, how far to Bluemont?"

"A mile and a half as the crow flies, but about three times that overland. We can take the AT down to Snicker's Gap, but then we'd have to get on the road. From the switchbacks, I'm guessing it will be a hell of a climb up the road to Bluemont."

"I don't know, Tex. An eight- or nine-mile round trip that doesn't get us any closer to home, to check out a store that's surely not open and probably doesn't have what we need if it is? That doesn't sound promising."

"We can use your patented 'rock method' to open it, and we just leave money if we find what we need." She sighed. "But you're right, anyway you hack it, it's the better part of a day's trip and doesn't get us any closer to home."

"What's the next possibility?"

"Harpers Ferry. A bit over twenty miles, but that's a fairly populous area, and I'm a bit worried about straying off the trail there. In fact, I was already worried about Harpers Ferry anyway."

"Why?"

"Because we cross both the Shenandoah and the Potomac rivers there, and given what we saw at Front Royal, I'm guessing there'll be roadblocks on the bridges. And a boat's pretty much a nonstarter, even if we could find one, because both rivers are full of rapids at that point. It's bridges or nothing."

"So is there any good news?"

Tex looked over at the rows of bunks. "Well, if we stay here tonight we don't have to sack out in those damned hammocks. I mean, they're better than sleeping on the ground with the creepy crawlies and they are light to carry, but they're getting old real quick. I could use a good night's sleep on a mattress."

Wiggins looked skeptical. "I'd love to sack out in a real bed too, but we're sitting ducks if anyone stumbles in here when we're sleeping."

"If anyone shows up, it will likely be from the road, and they'll break in the front and we'll hear them. And just to be on the safe side, we'll barricade the door from the upstairs down here to the basement to buy some more time, and keep our packs by our bunks and ready to go. At the first sign of trouble, we'll wake up, grab our gear, and be back in the woods before anyone even knows we were here."

"It's tempting," said Wiggins, "but I think it would be a mistake."

Tex looked crestfallen, but she nodded. "Yeah, you're right."

Then Wiggins smiled. "But the mattresses aren't nailed to the bunks. There's nothing says we can't carry a couple of them out into the woods a ways and set up our camp there. We can always drag 'em back in the morning if we want to be stand-up citizens. We'll need to come in and top up our water anyway."

Tex grinned. "And use a real toilet as long as it's available."

"Sounds like a plan," Wiggins said.

"This stinks, Mom. And it's hot! How much more do we have to do?"

Laura Hughes wiped the sweat from her forehead with the back of a gloved hand. She looked across the large garden to where her daughter Jana rested on her knees, her fifteen-year-old face contorted in anguish at the latest perceived injustice. Laura sighed.

"All right, just finish those two rows and we'll call it a day. We've made a good dent and it's not like the weeds won't be here tomorrow."

"TWO ROWS? REALLY? That's not fair! I've done TWICE as much as Julie. Why does SHE get to stay inside just because she's sunburned? You TOLD her to use sunblock. Now she gets to stay inside while I work like a SLAVE. And I did what you told me to. It's not fair."

Laura suppressed her anger, something she was having to do more frequently as the days dragged. She took a calming breath.

"You're right, Jana, it's not fair, but neither is life, so you'd best learn to deal with it. Regardless of how Julie got sunburned, she IS burned and that can't be undone. If she gets back out in this sun too soon, she could get seriously ill and we have no way to handle that. That leaves just the two of us. To keep eating, we need to keep the garden in good shape and I can't do it by myself, so fair or not, you have to help me. And it's not like Julie isn't working. She's washing all the clothes by hand and I've given her ALL of your inside chores." She paused and her voice softened, sounding weary to the bone. "I'm doing the best I can, honey, and it's not fair to me either, but help me out here a little, please."

Jana stared at her mother for a long moment and then a single tear rolled down her cheek. Her shoulders began to shake in silent sobs. Laura was on her feet in an instant, stepping over the rows separating them, to kneel at her daughter's side and fold her into an embrace.

"It's okay, honey, it's okay," she said, patting Jana's back. "I didn't mean to upset you."

"N-no, Mom," Jana stuttered between sobs, "it... it's ME who... who should be sorry. You... you're working so hard... and Dad's gone and we don't know... we don't know whe... when he's coming home... or even if he's okay. And the power's out and we don't even know if it's coming back... and we haven't seen any of our friends... and people are getting really mean and it just SUCKS so bad." Jana took a ragged breath, tears flowing freely now. "Mom, I'm just so scared, and Julie is too." She sniffed loudly, and Laura released her to peel off her own gloves and dig a crumpled handkerchief from the pocket of her jeans.

"Blow," she said as she held the handkerchief to Jana's nose.

Her daughter complied and Laura smiled. "You haven't done that since you were a little girl."

Jana smiled back through the tears. "I remember."

Laura pulled her close in a fierce hug. "Then remember I took care of you then, and I'll take care of you now."

Laura released her daughter and stood, then reached down to grab a hand and pull Jana up after her. "And on second thought, I think we've done enough today. What say we go in and have a big glass of iced tea?"

Jana nodded emphatically. "Thank God for the generator. I don't think I could stand this without ice. And since making tea is an INSIDE job, I do believe the sunburn queen can SERVE me my tea."

Laura burst out laughing. "You just talked me out of an hour of weeding, so don't push your luck. I am NOT going to spend my OWN goof off time refereeing another fight between you two. I get to play hooky a bit too, you know."

***

Day 16, 5:00 p.m.

"There ain't nothin' out here, Willard," said Kyle Morgan. "We ain't seen jack since we went through that shitty little town a while back. We need to go back and check that out. There's likely some loot to be had there."

"Would you just shut the hell up and do what I tell you," said Willard Jukes. "Who's in charge here, anyway?"

"I'm just sayin'—"

"And I'm just sayin' shut the hell up! We been over it. We find an isolated place nobody's likely to find; otherwise it's too risky," Jukes said.

"I know, Willard, but I been thinking. Maybe we should just loot like usual. If Snag or Spike find out—"

"Don't you go gettin' chickenshit on me now. You're just as pissed as I am about bringin' in all the good stuff and having it dripped back to us like we're some sort of pimply-faced jerk-off kids on an allowance. And I'm doubly pissed off about the pussy. We brought in eight or ten of them bitches our own selves, so we should at least get one apiece for our very own, and the pick of the lot too, leastwise of the ones we brung in."

"I know, Willard, but if we get caught..."

"For the umpteenth time, we AIN'T gonna get caught. We just find us an isolated place on one of these crappy country roads and take it. Then when we find some good stuff or really smokin' hot bitches, we bring 'em here along with our share of the loot and take the rest of the stuff back to Spike. We'll lock the women up first until we got 'em broke in good, then we have 'em run the place. We visit when we want. And here's the beauty part, if anyone gets suspicious, we just close down and 'find' the location and bring all the loot back to the prison. The women won't say nothin' 'cause they know we'll kill 'em if they do. Matter of fact, we can kill one of 'em ahead of time, just to show the others we mean business."

Jukes paused and looked at Morgan. "It's just like skimmin' in the old days except now there ain't no cash involved. I used to do it all the time and I never got caught, for that anyway."

Morgan said nothing, but gave an unconvincing nod.

They rode in silence a few minutes until they approached a minor intersection.

"Take that road to the left," Jukes said, and Morgan complied.

"This don't look like it goes nowhere," Morgan said.

"Every road goes somewhere, it's just a question of what's at the end of it," Jukes said, "and in this case, I'm thinking this one will take us to that buncha trees way over yonder."

Morgan followed Jukes' pointing finger to a dark green blot far across the flat pastureland.

"Why there?" Morgan asked.

"'Cause if we can see 'em this far away, that means they're damn big trees. Trees like that don't just spring up in the middle of this flat pastureland. They gotta be planted and a long time ago at that. Like as not, there's a house there, and maybe a pretty big one. And you can't get a whole lot more isolated. Must be ten miles to the nearest neighbor, easy."

They rode in silence, broken only by the road noise outside the car, barely audible through the closed windows over the welcome hum of the air conditioner. The green blot grew in the windshield, and as they neared, they saw a large white farmhouse nestled in the edge of the trees and a barn and other outbuildings nearby. Jukes looked at Morgan and grinned as the car turned up the long drive.

"Now this might be just the ticket," Jukes said.

HUGHES' RESIDENCE
PECAN GROVE
OLEANDER, TEXAS

DAY 16, 6:15 P.M.

Laura was in the kitchen, putting together a salad for supper as the car turned up the drive. She'd decided to let the girls goof off a bit more, and they were in the air-conditioned guest room, playing video games. It wasn't the best use of generator fuel, but the social isolation was especially hard on the girls. She was learning allowances from time to time made their new lives tolerable.

She looked up at the sound of the tires on gravel and parted the curtains over the sink. Her heart almost stopped at the sight of the police car. A hundred scenarios played out in her mind since the power outage, and among those were half-formed and quickly dismissed visions of official notification of something bad happening to Jordan.

Panic set in as she watched the cop car roll to a stop, and she gripped the edge of the kitchen counter and squeezed her eyes shut to say a short but fervent prayer for her husband's safety. She opened her eyes to look out the window again, studying the car more closely—Jefferson County Sheriff's Department—now that was strange. Two deputies got out of the car and moved towards her front door. She hurried to meet them.

The front door was open in an attempt to catch a bit of a breeze. As she hurried across the living room, she studied the approaching deputies through the latched screen door. They were both large men, their uniforms stretched tightly across muscled shoulders, the short sleeves of their khaki uniform shirts straining around bulging biceps. Both had heavily tattooed forearms. She sensed something was wrong immediately, despite the disarming manner of the first deputy up on the porch. She didn't open the screen door.

"Afternoon, ma'am. How are you?" the deputy asked through the screen.

"I'm fine, officer. How can I help you?" she replied.

"Well, it's us who hope to do the helping," he said. "We're just visiting folks to make sure they got what they need and to see if there's anything we can do to assist."

"Quite commendable," Laura said, "but I'm a bit confused. Y'all crossed the county line about three miles back. This is Chambers County."

The man hesitated only a fraction of a second, then smiled and nodded. "Times like these, we all gotta help each other out, so county lines don't mean much. If folks need help, we'll do our best to give it. Protect and serve, that's what it's all about."

Laura nodded. "Again, quite commendable, but we're fine." She immediately regretted the 'we.'

The man didn't register the plural, he just nodded. "I'd say so. Looks like you have a nice setup here. Is that a generator I hear running?"

"Just a small one. We, that is my husband and I, run it a few hours a day to keep the fridge cool and the freezer in the barn from defrosting. We don't have enough fuel for more than that."

"Well, might be we can help you out with the fuel. I'll check it out when we get back to the office and see if there's some allotment to spare. In the meantime, I guess we'll be going." He turned as if to leave, but the second deputy looked confused. Then the first deputy turned back.

"Actually, there is one thing you could do for us if it ain't too much trouble," he said.

"Yes?"

The man flashed a sheepish grin. "I hate to ask, but bein' as how y'all got a working fridge and all, do you think we could have a couple of glasses of ice water. Cold water's been pretty scarce since the power went out, and we're parched from riding around in that car all day. A cool drink would be welcome."

She hesitated. "Of course. Wait right here and I'll bring it out."

"Thank you kindly," the deputy said, and Laura nodded and turned to go back to the kitchen.

As soon as she was out of their sight, she raced to the kitchen pantry and retrieved the Glock 19, racking the slide to chamber a round before stuffing it into the back of her shorts. She'd considered closing and locking the front door on the pair, but knew they'd break through the latched screen door and the old wooden front door in seconds anyway, and decided not to alert them in order to buy a little time. She left the pantry and raced down the hall to the spare bedroom. The twins looked up in surprise.

"Okay," Laura whispered, "I don't have time to explain. There are some very bad men at the front door. I want you to slip out the back door and hide in the barn until I come get you. The gun safe in the garage is open, so stop on the way and get Dad's shotgun and the .30-.30. Be quiet and be careful not to be seen. Do NOT come back to the house until I come to get you, no matter what happens. Do you understand?"

They both started to speak at once, but Julie got her protest out first. "But, Mom—"

"QUIET!" Laura hissed. "No buts. Just do it and do it now!"

"Wh-what if you don't come?" Jana asked. "Wh-what if the men come?"

Laura's face hardened. "Then shoot them. They're dressed like deputies, but they're fakes, so don't hesitate or believe anything they might say to lure you out of hiding. When they... go away... or you shoot them, take the truck and get to the Smiths' house as soon as possible."

"What... what about you?" Julie asked, almost sobbing now.

"Don't worry about me," Laura said, struggling to keep the emotion from her voice. "Now GO!"

Both girls nodded and then wrapped Laura in a fierce group hug. She hugged them back and then broke away, pushing them towards the door, emotion robbing her of the power of speech. In the hall, she watched them move quietly toward the back door, then turned back toward the kitchen, the Glock at the small of her back a cold comfort.

***

Jukes licked his lips as he watched the woman's ass through the screen door as she disappeared around a corner. He tried the screen door and found it latched.

"What we gonna do?" asked Morgan.

"Nothing," Jukes said, "she ain't gotta clue. When she comes back, she'll open the screen door. We'll grab her and have a little party. Easy as pie."

"Why don't we just bust in and grab her now?"

Jukes shook his head. "'Cause this is our new place, dumb ass. There ain't no need to be destructive."

Morgan looked around nervously. "What about her husband?"

"I swear, Morgan, sometimes I think you're dumber than a day-old turd! There ain't no husband, leastwise not close, or he'd of answered the door, now wouldn't he? And if he drives up, we'll hear his tires on the gravel and we give him a nice warm welcome. Maybe we can even let him watch us do his old lady before we kill him. Now you got any other stupid questions?"

Morgan glared at Jukes and fell silent, nursing his resentment.

"How long does it take to pour two glasses of water?" Morgan said.

Jukes looked pissed. "Not this long," he said, and pulled a switchblade from his pocket to pop the blade and slice the screen adjacent to the hook. He pocketed the knife and stuck his hand through the opening. The screen door opened with the shriek of dry hinges.

***

Laura heard the plaintive squeak of the screen door followed by hurried footsteps, and was reaching for the Glock just as the men entered the kitchen, guns drawn. Outmatched, she moved her hand away from the concealed weapon and decided to play for time.

"What is it? What's wrong? I was just getting your water, but I wanted to check the pantry. I think we have a little coffee left, and I thought you might like some."

The lead deputy holstered his sidearm, motioning his partner to do the same.

"Well, that's right nice of you, ma'am," he said, "and sorry to bust in, but we were concerned something might be wrong. Can't be too careful these days, ya know."

Laura nodded and moved toward the fridge. "I'll get that water now."

The big man moved closer—already too close, she realized. He closed the distance between them and pinned her arms to her side in a tight hug.

Laura felt the hard bulk of his body pressing against her, along with evidence of his aroused state. He stank of stale sweat, and his breath confirmed dental hygiene was not a priority. She felt rough stubble scratching her face as he bent and nuzzled her neck. She fought down revulsion and willed herself not to resist. She pressed her body back against him.

He lifted his lips from her neck and drew back to look at her, smiling.

"Well, well, well. Now ain't this a nice little surprise," he said.

Laura managed a smile of her own and shrugged in his grasp. "I'm not stupid. I know you're going to take what you want, so I don't see any need to get hurt in the process."

The man relaxed his grip. "Now that there is a good attitude, and I think we're gonna get along just fine." He spoke back over his shoulder. "What'd I tell you, Morgan. This is gonna work out perfect—"

Laura had worked her right hand to the small of her back, and though still in the loose embrace of her attacker, she whipped the Glock between them and pressed it to the man's crotch.

He looked back at her, anger clouding his face as he squeezed her tighter, which only managed to dig the Glock more forcefully into his crotch.

"That's a nine millimeter with hollow points. I've already used about half the trigger pull, and it's only going to take a twitch to discharge it," Laura said, "so unless you want to start singing soprano, I suggest you let me go and tell your friend over there to put his gun on the kitchen island and lay down on his stomach."

Her attacker dropped his hands to his sides and spoke over his shoulder again, to where his partner had his pistol out, pointed at Laura in a two-handed grip.

"You heard her, Morgan. Do what she says."

"Screw that," said the second man. "I got her dead to rights. I can drop her right now."

"And she twitches and blows my junk away, you idiot. NOW PUT THE GUN DOWN!"

Laura watched the one called Morgan's face as indecision warred with the need to comply. He started to lower his gun to the kitchen island when the sound of a floorboard squeaking came through the door to the hallway. He whirled towards the hallway door, gun still in hand.

"There's somebody else here," he said.

The girls, thought Laura, and as Morgan moved toward the hall doorway with his gun raised, her only instinct was protecting her children. She whipped the Glock from her attacker's crotch toward Morgan.

But freed from the imminent threat of emasculation, her attacker was too fast for her. As she brought the gun up, he hammered her wrist with his left hand before she got a shot off, and the Glock clattered on the floor. Simultaneously, a powerful right fist to her gut doubled her over. She dropped like a rock and lay gasping, her own attacker all but forgotten as she focused on Morgan framed in the hallway door with his gun drawn. Then there was a deafening blast and the back of Morgan's shirt erupted in a red mist as he sailed backwards to land on the kitchen floor, a lifeless lump.

"MOM?" she heard, followed by running footsteps, and her blood ran cold as she whipped her head toward the remaining attacker. He had his own gun out, ignoring her to focus on the immediate threat. He dropped behind the cover of the kitchen island, only his right knee visible to her as he crouched, waiting for his target to appear in the hallway door.

The footsteps were coming closer, but her attempts to call out a warning yielded a barely audible croak. She spotted her Glock halfway to the fridge and clawed her way toward it, forcing her oxygen-starved body to move, reaching the gun a scant second before her daughters burst into the kitchen. She flopped over on her back and sent a round into her attacker's exposed knee.

The man screamed in pain as he collapsed on the floor, his body in full sight now as he brought his own gun to bear. But Laura was faster and put shot after shot center mass, not stopping until the slide locked open and her hand started shaking so badly the gun fell from her hand and clattered on the floor beside her.

And then her daughters were beside her, and she hugged them tight with trembling arms and sobbed great racking sobs, and vowed come what may in this strange new world, no one would harm her children while there was life in her body.

***

They were big men, with the heavy musculature of bodybuilders, and it took improvisation to get the bodies into the trunk of the police car. Laura backed the cruiser up to the front porch and she and her daughters dragged the bodies most of the way on a plastic shower curtain before spanning the distance between the open trunk and the elevated porch with planks from the barn. Even at that, it was over an hour after they started when they rolled the second body in and closed the trunk.

"Okay," Laura said, "I'm going to park this out of sight in the barn until we're ready to leave. Y'all get cleaned up and make sure you get all the blood off. I'll do the same when I get back, but I don't want to take too long. I want to be rid of them before anyone comes looking."

The girls gave subdued nods, and Laura's heart went out to them. She'd have done anything to spare them the grisly task, but it was simply beyond her physical capability to do it alone.

"What are we going to do with them?" Julie asked quietly.

"I'm gonna drive their car to the Boyd's Bayou crossing down the road. You girls will follow me in the truck, and when we get there, we'll push their car into the bayou. We've had a lot of rain, so the water should be deep enough to cover it."

"But we can't drive," Jana said. "We don't even have our learner permits yet."

Laura shook her head. "But you both know HOW to drive. Dad's been letting you drive the truck around the pasture for two years."

"But what if the police… oh yeah. I guess that's not really a big deal," Jana said.

Laura nodded, longing for a time when a ticket for driving without a license was the worst thing they had to worry about.

"All right, go get cleaned up. I'll be right back," she said.

Half an hour later, Laura was behind the wheel of the cruiser as she turned on to the county road, hoping against hope they didn't encounter any other traffic. She looked in the rearview mirror and confirmed the girls were following at a safe distance, then looked back to the road ahead, second-guessing her hastily devised plan. The bayou was about fifty feet wide and varied from four to eight feet in depth, depending on the season. They'd had a fair amount of rain over the last few weeks, but the bottom of the canal was irregular. What if there wasn't enough water near the bridge to cover the car? She willed herself to stop worrying and focus on the task at hand. She didn't have a better plan. This one had to work.

After the longest four miles she'd ever driven, she spotted the bridge, a low, unimposing concrete span raised a few feet higher than the road to accommodate the bayou at full flood, approached by a gradual ramp on either end and fitted with steel guardrails on each side. She slowed, coasting to a stop near the top of the slight incline just before entering the bridge proper. She put the cruiser in park and rolled down all four windows, then cut the wheels to the right and left them there. She got out just as the girls stopped behind her, and motioned them out of the truck.

"Okay, I'm gonna get in the truck and pull it up against the back bumper of the cop car so it doesn't roll backward. I want one of you to get in the cop car and put it in neutral, then get out and shut the door and get well out of the way. Got it?"

Both girls nodded. "I'll do it," Julie said, moving to the cop car as Laura climbed behind the wheel of the truck.

When Julie completed the task and both girls were safely on the other side of the narrow road, Laura pressed the accelerator. As soon as the cop car started to move, she mashed down hard, sending both vehicles surging forward twenty feet before she stomped the brakes, stopping the truck as the police car shot off the road and bounced down the slight embankment toward the bayou. It hit the water with a grand splash and plowed forward, sending a bow wave to bounce off the opposite bank. It sank steadily, the weight of the engine pulling the front end deeper, until water began to pour into the open windows and the car plunged under the water.

Almost.

The car came to rest with a narrow strip of the trunk lid showing, reading SHERIFF in bright green letters against a white background. Laura watched it with a lump in her stomach and willed it to sink. It didn't.

"What are we going to do, Mom?"

She turned to find Jana and Julie beside her, looking down at the still-visible evidence of their deed.

"Not much we can do, except maybe pray for rain. Get in, girls, we need to get out of here before anyone sees us."

CHAPTER SIXTEEN

DAY 17, 5:00 A.M.

Congressman Simon Tremble sipped the coffee, his appreciation of the improvement in rations since he'd 'joined the team' tempered by the knowledge of widespread privation outside the privileged bubble of Mount Weather. He set the mug on the coffee table and picked up the bound notes for the 'briefing' he was scheduled to deliver over the FEMA National Radio System. He shook his head and tossed the offensive document across the room.

It was little more than a scripted cheerleading session, full of lies about 'help being on the way,' and assurances 'things will be improving soon.' He had difficulty reading it without flying into a rage, and he knew he could never speak those words into a microphone without betraying all he held dear. He stood and paced the living area of the small apartment he shared with his son, then stopped to look out the window at the lush foliage just becoming visible in the growing light of predawn. Sunlight and scenery was one advantage at least, of being 'special guests' of the President.

The massive underground complex at Weather Mountain teemed with bureaucrats and their lackeys, and it would be all but impossible to sequester anyone there confidentially. But spread over more than four hundred acres of mountaintop, the sprawling surface facility over the underground complex was impressive in its own right, and separate buildings lined roads winding through strips of untouched woodland. Tremble and his son were on the third floor of just such a building, at the far end of an access road with no internal traffic.

The whereabouts and involuntary nature of the residence of the former Speaker of the House of Representatives was on a need-to-know basis. The windows were sealed and there was a twenty-four-hour guard, always one of the same three men on rotating eight-hour shifts, with the guard who came on at six a.m. every morning providing their daily rations.

The guards were stone-faced, communicating by gestures and curt commands, obviously instructed to limit interaction. Tremble gently chided them at every opportunity, carrying on unfailingly pleasant, if one-sided conversations, telling jokes and doing anything he could to provoke a reaction. None wore name tags, but he'd named them all, and called them by their fictitious names. Come what may, it wouldn't hurt if their keepers viewed him and Keith as people, rather than assignments. He had no doubt these same guards might one day be given other, harsher orders, and if he built some rapport, no matter how tenuous, the guards' actions or facial expressions might telegraph the change.

He'd made most headway with the guard he'd named Sam, the morning man who brought the daily food ration. In recent days Tremble had even seen a suppressed smile tugging at the corners of Sam's mouth from time to time as he delivered the punchline of a particularly funny joke. Not much, but it was there. Sam, or whatever his real name was, acted a bit less guarded when he came into the apartment with the rations or when he stuck his head in for the head count every two hours.

Tremble picked up on other things as well. The guards did periodic visual checks during the day and entered the apartment to check on their sleeping forms at night, which told him electronic surveillance was unlikely. That made sense given the 'ad hoc' nature of their confinement in a totally isolated and secure facility like Mount Weather. Apparently neither the President nor the Secretary of Homeland Security felt there were any conversations between Tremble and his teenage son that warranted eavesdropping. If only the bastards knew.

His thoughts returned to Keith, the center of his universe for the ten years since cancer had taken Jane. He'd do anything to keep his son safe, but he knew Keith would never be safe under Gleason and Crawford's control. Tremble had no doubt as soon as he'd served his purpose, both he and Keith were loose ends. His worry was tempered with pride at Keith's response when he'd explained the situation to him yesterday, just laying out the facts without attempting to influence his son's opinion. Keith had fallen silent while he weighed the options.

"Do you really think President Gleason is setting himself up to be some sort of dictator?" Keith asked.

"A month ago, I'd have laughed at the suggestion," Tremble replied, "but after meeting him face to face, I have no doubt. As the saying goes, power corrupts and absolute power corrupts absolutely. If he has his way, we may get limited electrical power restored to serve the needs of those he's deemed worthy of saving, but we'll have paid for it with the complete loss of democracy."

"Then there are no options, Dad. You can't do what they want, and I'm sure not becoming one of their thugs. They might as well kill us both now. We know they're probably going to sooner or later anyway. On the other hand, as soon as you resist, they may separate us to increase the leverage, so I'd say pretend to go along and then we take a shot at getting out of here. Right now they need you, so they'll be hesitant to kill you, and if they kill me, they know you won't cooperate. That means if we try and fail, we're not any worse off than we are now."

From the mouths of babes, Tremble recalled thinking, then revised the thought—at eighteen, his son was a powerfully built young man and mature beyond his years. When did that happen? he wondered, a wistful smile on his face. Keith's bedroom door opened and his son walked into the living area, fully clothed.

"Fresh coffee in the pot," Tremble said, nodding toward the small kitchenette.

Keith returned his nod. "Might as well enjoy it while we can." He moved toward the kitchen, returning a moment later with cup in hand to sprawl on one end of the small sofa.

"You been up all night?"

"Since about two," Tremble replied, "I woke up and couldn't go back to sleep. I was just about to come in and wake you."

Keith shook his head. "I've been awake an hour or so myself. Nerves, I guess."

Tremble nodded. "Same here. You sure you're okay with this, son? Maybe I can play them a little while longer and form a better plan?"

"But what if they separate us? Then we're screwed. We're on borrowed time as it is, Dad."

Tremble nodded again and fished something out of the back pocket of his slacks before sitting down on the couch beside Keith and handing him the flattened ziplock bag. Inside was a document, folded small.

"What's this?"

"You've read it," Tremble said. "It's my official copy of Secretary Crawford's memo to the President detailing the 'recovery plan.' I got a copy because I was Speaker, and since we were already 'sequestered,' no one bothered to take it back. I put it in one of the ziplock bags from our food ration to protect it. I want you to take it."

"But why? You should keep it to prove—"

Tremble cut him off. "We have to get word out about what's going on. If we both make it, I'll take it back and get copies spread around. But if… if I don't make it, nobody is likely to take the word of an eighteen-year-old kid. I'm sorry, that's a fact. However, some documentation gives you at least a fighting chance to be heard. And if… if…"

"If I don't make it," Keith finished for him. "You're Speaker of the House, so people are much more likely to take your word without any backup documentation. Okay, Dad, I got it. Makes sense."

Tremble nodded and glanced at his watch. "Sam should be bringing the food soon. Let's go over the plan again.

'Sam' was right on time, and forty-five minutes later Tremble and his son were sitting on the sofa when they heard the low murmur of conversation outside the door, signaling the change of shift. Tremble nodded to Keith and pretended to turn his attention to the briefing script while his son quickly retreated to the small bathroom. There was a tap on the door before it opened to reveal the more genial of their keepers, who closed the door behind himself and moved toward the kitchenette with a plastic grocery bag, looking around as he did so, as was his routine.

"Good morning, Sam," Tremble said, "and what wonderful treats did you bring us today?"

The man scowled as he set the bag on the small counter separating the living area and kitchenette. "Where's the kid? I gotta see you both for shift change. You know that."

Tremble inclined his head toward the bathroom door. "Answering the call of nature, I'm afraid. I'm sure he'll be out any time." Tremble rose and walked toward the kitchenette. "There's fresh coffee, want a cup?"

The man shook his head as Tremble moved past him into the kitchen to refill his empty cup and returned to lean with his butt against the counter. He held the coffee in his left hand and studied the guard standing a few feet away, glaring at the bathroom door.

"KEITH! HURRY UP AND GET OUT HERE. SAM'S WAITING," Tremble yelled. The door to the bathroom opened, right on cue.

Keith came out muttering apologies, then stumbled and went down on one knee, drawing Sam's full attention. Tremble threw scalding coffee into the guard's face, and the man closed his eyes reflexively and stepped back, groping blindly for his sidearm. Tremble connected with a rising punch starting from his waist and landing on the point of the guard's chin, snapping the man's mouth shut and dropping him like a rock. Tremble was on top of the unconscious man immediately, stripping him of sidearm and stun gun, and handing Keith the man's handcuffs as his son reached his side.

"Hurry. Turn him on his stomach and cuff his hands behind his back in case he comes to," Tremble whispered. "Pete will be outside waiting for Sam to take over the shift so he can leave."

No sooner had Tremble spoken than the doorknob began to turn, and he crossed the small living area in four long strides and stepped behind the opening door. 'Pete' rounded the door to find a nine millimeter an inch away from his forehead.

"Just come on in, Pete. Lock your fingers behind your head, and don't make any sudden moves. I don't want to kill you, but I will if you make me." Tremble's tone left no doubt he meant it.

'Pete' nodded, his eyes wide, and did as instructed as Tremble closed the door with his foot, then pressed his back against it until the latch clicked, never once losing focus on the man in front of him. He instructed his captive to face the wall, then used his free hand to remove the guard's sidearm.

"Now keep looking at the wall and strip, very slowly," Tremble said. "One wrong move and you're dead."

The guard complied, and as soon as he was down to his underwear, Tremble instructed him to lay on this stomach and held the gun on him while Keith cuffed the man with his own handcuffs, bound his feet, and gagged him with strips torn from a bed sheet. Together, they then uncuffed and undressed 'Sam,' who was regaining consciousness but showing no signs of fight. When they finished, they put the cuffs back on and bound his feet and gagged him before stripping their own clothes to don the uniforms.

Keith finished first and sat down on the couch with one of the pairs of boots. He looked inside the shoe and quickly pulled his face back. "Whew! Sam here could use some odor-eaters, that's one rank pair of boots. Anyway, they're elevens. That'll work for me. How are yours."

Tremble sat down beside his son and checked the other guard's boots. "They're twelves, I'm good."

Moments later they stood side by side at a wall mirror.

"What do you think, Dad?"

"Close enough," Tremble said. "If we pull the caps low, we can definitely pass at a distance, at least until they raise the alarm."

"What now?" Keith asked.

Tremble held up the keys he'd fished out of 'Pete's' pocket. "I didn't see any security cameras on the buildings here. My guess is the bulk of the security effort is concentrated on the perimeter fences. So we get in their car and just try to drive out. Best I can tell from listening through the door, they report in randomly, but Pete here was due off shift, so we don't know if his failure to show up or log out someplace might set off an alarm. We'll keep his radio, so maybe we'll know if anyone starts getting suspicious."

"All right. Let's do it," Keith said, but his father hesitated, casting a pointed look at Keith's sidearm.

"You okay with that?"

"I've used it at the range, I'm good," Keith said.

"Trust me, shooting at another human being who's shooting back at you is quite a bit different. Don't hesitate to use it if you have to, but understand up front it's not nearly as easy as you think. You need to get your mind around that, because it could save your life."

Keith swallowed and nodded, and Tremble pulled him into an embrace. "I love you, son."

"I love you too, Dad."

Tremble fought down his own emotion and patted his son on the back.

Two minutes later, caps pulled low, they were in a black SUV moving at the posted speed limit along a well-paved road winding uphill through the western half of the complex. There were only a few people moving around the many buildings they passed, and Tremble heaved a relieved sigh. The early hour was working in their favor.

"How much further?" Keith asked.

"A mile or so on this road because of all the switchbacks," Tremble said, "then we'll pass over Blue Ridge Mountain Road. That's a state highway that cuts the camp in two. They couldn't close it, so they put high fences on either side and then built an overpass on this road to connect the east and west halves of the surface facility. The overpass is just around the next bend. After the overpass, we pass the back side of the main gate security building one street over and go down about two hundred yards to make a one-eighty back toward the gate. Then it might get hairy."

"So we just drive through the gate? No one's gonna stop us?"

"Not hardly, that's why it gets hairy, but the security is set up to keep people out and we've got that going for us. That and human nature."

"I don't follow," Keith said.

"There are steel barrier posts at the gate which hydraulically retract into the pavement to let vehicles pass. They're kept deployed on the entrance side of the gate and have to be lowered every time to admit a vehicle. The same thing is SUPPOSED to be true on the exit side, but it takes a minute or so to raise and lower the posts and is a bit of a pain in the ass. The bigger concern has always been people coming in rather than going out, and I noticed the few times I've been here the barrier posts on the exit gate were kept down in favor of using the secondary, and fairly flimsy, bar gate. We're pretty remote here, without much in the way of external threats, so I'm hoping they haven't changed their ways. We can crash the lift bar."

"What happens if the posts are up on the exit gate?"

Tremble's jaw tightened. "Then we're screwed."

They made the sweeping turn in silence and were moving across the overpass when the radio sprang to life.

"Unit Twelve, this is Control. Do you copy? Over."

Keith looked at Tremble. "So are we Unit Twelve?"

"Not a clue, but I'm guessing yes," Tremble said.

"Should we answer?"

"No. We don't know their communications protocol and risk alerting them if we say the wrong thing. If we're silent, they might get antsy, but they'll still be unsure. We're only a couple of minutes from the gate, and that's his first call. He'll probably try at least a couple of times before sounding an alarm. The cat's out of the bag when we crash the gate anyway, but maybe we can get there before anyone picks up the problem."

Keith nodded. They rode in silence, the back of the main gate security building visible one road over on the left. The radio squawked again.

"Unit Twelve, what is your status? Respond immediately. Over."

"Sounds like he's at the antsy stage," Keith said as his father slowed to make the U-turn back toward the main gate.

"All we need is a bit more time, and then it won't make any difference," Tremble said as he turned the SUV. As the exit lane became visible, he let out a relieved sigh. "Thank God, the posts are down!"

He increased speed, the gate now only a hundred yards away. The next transmission dampened his elation.

"All stations, repeat, all stations. This is Control. We have a non-responding unit. Initiate Protocol Alpha. Repeat, initiate Protocol Alpha."

"Hang on!" Tremble said as he saw the guard in the glass booth look down and press something on the console in front of him. He stomped the accelerator and held it there as the tops of the barrier posts began to peek from the pavement ahead.

"Air bags!" thought Tremble, much too late, as the SUV blew by the startled guard and hit the bar gate, smashing both front headlights. The heavy vehicle brushed the lift bar out of the way without slowing or bumper contact and the air bags didn't deploy. A fraction of a second later, the front tires contacted the rising barrier posts, now ten inches above the ground, and the vehicle leaped airborne, throwing both occupants forward against their straining shoulder belts, inducing a brief feeling of weightlessness before the vehicle crashed down. Again their luck held as the posts were below bumper level and the deceleration alone was insufficient to trigger the air bags.

The SUV careened down the road, tires shrieking, as Tremble fought for control. For three long, heart-stopping seconds, the issue was in doubt. Then he regained control and once again floored it, rushing toward the intersection ahead. Barely slowing, he turned north on Blue Ridge Mountain Road, roaring onto the two-lane blacktop in a controlled skid, then stomping the accelerator once again. He glanced to his right to see his son ashen-faced, knuckles white as he gripped the grab rail. Slowly Keith's face split into a wide grin.

"You did it, Dad! Where we going now?"

"Away from here," Tremble said, "but we won't have long. They'll be after us in a heartbeat and we have to—"

There was a loud bang and the SUV lurched to the right, once again testing Tremble as he fought the car to a stop on the shoulder. They both jumped out and looked down at the shredded right front tire.

"Damn it!" Tremble said. "I guess the damn posts got us after all. Must have weakened the tire."

"Let's change it," Keith said, starting for the rear.

"No time. Get back in. Driving on a flat's still faster than we can move on foot. We'll drive as fast and as far as we can, and abandon it on some side road out of sight. We were going to have to ditch it anyway, but if we can delay them finding it, the more time we'll have to get away."

DAY 17, 6:25 A.M.

Gleason opened his eyes at the low buzz, groggy as he peered through the gloom at the glowing face of the alarm clock. Why the hell was the alarm going off? He groped for the button to kill the noise, then cursed as he overturned a glass of water on the bedside table. Fully awake now, he sat up as he realized the low trilling was not the alarm but the phone.

"What?" he barked into the receiver.

"Mr. President, I'm sorry to disturb you—"

"Then why the hell did you? What was so important it couldn't wait an hour or so?"

"Mr. President, I have Secretary Crawford on the secure link from Weather Mountain. I tried to take a message, but he insisted—"

"All right, all right. Just put him through."

"Yes sir," the operator said, and Crawford's voice came on the line.

"Good morning, Mr. President—"

"No, Ollie, it's not good morning. It will be a good morning in an hour or so when I've had my coffee. Now what's so damned important it couldn't wait until then?"

"It's Tremble, Mr. President. I'm afraid there's been a problem."

"Look, we've been over this. If he's not cooperating, squeeze the kid. He'll come around."

"I'm afraid Tremble... Tremble isn't here any longer."

"What the hell are you talking about? What do you mean 'not here'? Where the hell else would he be? Did you move him someplace?"

"I'm afraid he's... he's escaped, Mr. President."

Gleason struggled to contain himself. When he spoke, his voice was full of quiet menace. "And how did that happen, Ollie?"

"He and his son overpowered their guards, stole their uniforms, and escaped in their vehicle."

"So you're telling me a paunchy fifty-year-old politician and his pimply-faced teenage son overpowered two of your overpaid FEMA troopers and escaped from what is supposed to be one of the most secure facilities in North America. Is that what you're telling me?"

"Tremble is far from a sedentary politician and you know it. He was an airborne officer and served in both Iraq and Afghanistan. In fact, he still holds a commission in the North Carolina—"

"OF COURSE I KNOW THAT, YOU FRIGGIN' IDIOT! AND SO DO YOU! SO WHY THE HELL WEREN'T YOU WATCHING HIM MORE CLOSELY?"

Silence grew on the line in the wake of Gleason's outburst, broken by a sigh.

"All right, when did they escape and what are you doing to recapture them?"

"Less than ten minutes ago. A two-man chase team is leaving now and we're mobilizing a larger effort and preflighting the chopper in case we need it. The good news is there aren't many roads they can take, and the better news is all the facility vehicles have trackers. We know right where they are. Right now, they're headed north on Blue Mountain Road, at about thirty miles an hour, so we figure their car must be damaged. I'm confident we'll have them surrounded in less than an hour, but that's really not the reason I awakened you, Mr. President."

"Then what?"

"They're armed, and I doubt they'll surrender willingly so…"

"So you want permission to take them out, is that it?"

"I don't see any reason to risk good men—"

"Well, let me give you one. You screwed things up with Senator Leddy completely. First you killed his wife in front of him—"

"With respect, Mr. President, how was I to know she had a heart condition? It wasn't in the medical record."

"All right, all right. It's a damned waste, but the PR broadcasts will likely only buy us a few more weeks of calm compliance in limited areas anyway. So the preference is to take Tremble and his son alive, but take them out if you must. However, make those knuckleheads of yours understand that's not plan A. In fact, I don't want them taken out unless you PERSONALLY determine it's necessary. Is that clear?"

"Yes, Mr. President," Crawford said.

"And Ollie?"

"Yes, Mr. President?"

"It goes without saying anyone our fugitives make contact with may learn more than is good for them—or us. You take my meaning?"

"Absolutely, Mr. President. There will be no witnesses."

VIRGINIA STATE ROAD 601
AKA BLUE RIDGE MOUNTAIN ROAD
NEAR BLUEMONT, VIRGINIA

DAY 17, 6:39 A.M.

The SUV leaned right. Tremble nursed it along at thirty-five miles an hour, right side tires in the grassy verge. Of course 'tires' was a bit of a stretch, because the remains of the right front tire left them some miles back, its remnants spread all over the pavement behind them. The bare rim on pavement had been deafening, but worse than the noise was the incriminating evidence. Tremble had glanced in the mirror to see a line chewed in the pavement by the battered steel rim, leaving a trail a blind man could follow.

His attempts to compensate were only partially successful. Running with the right wheels off the pavement lessened the noise and left a much less obvious track, but they were still leaving a visible trail. And the steel rim digging into the dirt of the verge made the vehicle increasingly difficult to steer. Even with power steering, he was fighting the wheel constantly, his forearms aching from the effort.

"This is no good, Keith," he said. "We need to ditch the car. We're going too slow and our tracks will lead them right to us."

"There's a turnoff just up ahead on the left, you think it's a through road?"

Tremble shook his head. "I doubt there are any before we get to Highway 7, but we'll take it as far as it goes. We knew we'd have to take our chances on foot anyway. These woods are thick and we'll find a place to hide."

Keith nodded and Tremble horsed the wheel to the left, grimacing as the bare rim clanked and chewed its way across the pavement, leaving the equivalent of a flashing neon sign pointing in the direction of their flight.

BEAR'S DEN HOSTEL
18393 BLUE RIDGE MOUNTAIN ROAD
NEAR BLUEMONT, VIRGINIA

DAY 17, 6:40 A.M.

"That feels a LOT better," Bill Wiggins said as he walked around the lounge area, alternating between walking and raising himself on tiptoe. "It still hurts, but not nearly as bad."

Tex shook her head. "Better than nothing, that's for sure."

Necessity was the mother of invention, and they'd cut up the ample supply of washcloths in the hostel bathroom to pad the overly spacious toes of their work boots. It wasn't perfect, but it would cushion their toes somewhat going downhill.

Bill laughed. "Now if we could just figure out a way to get a couple of these mattresses in our packs, we'd have it made. That was the best sleep I ever had last night, bugs and all."

Tex nodded. "Me too. You ready to head out?"

"Ready as I'll ever be, I guess…" He stopped. "Hear that?"

She cocked an ear. "Something heading this way, but making too much racket to be a car. What do you think it is?"

"I don't know," Wiggins said, hefting his pack, "but no one we've met so far has been friendly, so I don't think we should be here when whoever it is arrives. Let's get into the woods. We can watch from there and just haul ass after we check it out."

Tex shouldered her pack to follow Wiggins out the door.

They jogged the well-worn path across the clearing to the AT access point, then darted off the path at the tree line, hiding behind adjacent tree trunks. As they waited, the sound of a laboring engine grew louder, accompanied by another sound neither could identify. The vehicle lurched into view, leaning to the right, and the mystery was solved. The tireless rim of the right front wheel slung gravel into the wheel well, producing a roar that almost drowned out the engine noise. The car stopped abruptly and disgorged two uniformed men, sidearms visible even at a distance.

"What do you make of that?" Tex asked quietly.

"Nothing good. Let's get the hell out of here," Wiggins said. They melted back into the woods and started downhill toward the AT, aching toes momentarily forgotten in the adrenaline rush to put this latest threat behind them.

***

Tremble got out of the car and looked around as Keith moved by his side. Their heads jerked in unison at the sound of an engine heard faintly through the dense woods.

"Damn! Already? I figured we'd have more time."

Keith pointed to the path worn through the clearing and they both started down it at a run.

"We'll follow this and get as deep in the woods as we can. If we hear them following, then we find a place to ambush them. We have to break contact or we don't stand a chance," shouted Tremble as they ran. Keith nodded his understanding.

***

Bill Wiggins turned back on to the AT and continued down the steep incline at a breakneck pace, his heavy pack adding to his downward momentum as he struggled to keep his feet on the rock-strewn path. His heart was pounding and he could hear Tex's labored breathing. Well behind them, he heard the faint sound of others crashing down the same path. They'd never outrun anyone, encumbered as they were with the heavy packs. He spotted a row of saplings lining the trail, and changed course slightly to grab the trunk of the first as he passed, clutching it momentarily to check his speed before releasing it to grab the next, bringing himself to a halt while remaining upright. Behind him, Tex followed suit, stumbling to a halt beside him. The sound of pursuit was unmistakable now.

"Why the hell are they chasing us?"

"I don't think they are," Wiggins said between labored breaths. "They can't even know we're here, and I'd like to keep it that way. I say we go off the trail and hide. After they get well ahead, we'll get back on the trail. If they double back, we should hear them before they see us, and we'll just reverse the process."

Wiggins nodded and they moved off the trail into the woods to once again hide behind tree trunks. Less than two minutes later the men flashed by, unencumbered by backpacks and racing downhill as if the devil were on their heels. They looked to be policemen of some sort, but why they were here was a total mystery. Not my problem, thought Wiggins, just stay the hell away from us.

The sound faded quickly, and Wiggins waited a couple of minutes before he turned to Tex.

"What do you think?"

"The guidebook shows it as steep downhill for another mile or so, through Snicker's Gap and across State Route 7. At the rate they're moving, I'd say we can maintain a good walking pace without too much fear of running into them."

Wiggins nodded and they moved back toward the trail. They were almost there when he felt something wrong. "Damn!" he said, staring down at his foot. "My lace broke."

"Can you tie it back together?"

"It'll probably just break again. Levi put some paracord in our packs, I'll just use some of that." Wiggins shucked off his pack and sat on a fallen log.

"I'll wait for you on the trail," Tex said. "I've given the ticks enough opportunity to crawl aboard, brushing through all this foliage."

Wiggins nodded absently, digging through the pack in search of the paracord, as Tex moved back on to the trail. He was pulling his improvised lace tight when a sharp command pierced the foliage.

"Freeze! And keep your hands where I can see them."

He dropped off the log onto his knees and crawled toward the trail, slowly separating foliage with his hand. Tex was facing one of the uniformed men and staring into the muzzle of an M4. Where the hell did that assault rifle come from and how'd they get back up the hill without us hearing? he wondered.

"Very slowly, turn and then drop the pack, put your hands on the back of your head, and get down on your knees," the man said.

Tex moved to comply. As the pack slid down her back and to the side, it tugged her shirttail over, exposing the Glock.

"Gun!" screamed the man, rushing forward with his M4 trained on Tex to kick her hard in the back, driving her face down on the path. He squatted and thrust his gun to the side of her head. Rage boiled up in Wiggins as another man rushed into sight, his own rifle slung, and quickly tossed Tex's Glock to the side. Wiggins heard Tex gasping for breath as the second man patted her down none too gently.

"Clean," said the second uniform, and the first man nodded. They dragged Tex to her feet.

"We're looking for two men dressed like us. Have you seen them?" the first uniform asked.

Tex nodded, unable to speak.

"When?"

"A... a few minutes... they ran by..."

"What did they say to you?"

Tex shook her head. "No... nothing... I... I hid in the woods."

"Why are you armed?"

"Pr... protection," Tex gasped.

The first uniform ran out of questions.

"What the hell we gonna do with her?" the second man asked. The man's face was heavily bruised, as if he'd been beaten.

"She saw them, you know the orders."

"Yeah, I know the orders, but I'm not doing it on the strength of a verbal."

The first man seemed ready to explode. "Look, asshole, it's your fault we're on the shit list for letting Tremble and the kid escape, so don't get us in even deeper by questioning orders! I had to do some fast talking to get them to let us head out first, and if we don't get 'em back, we'll probably both be in a 'fugee camp this time tomorrow."

"All right, then call it in for confirmation, and we can update Control at the same time. If they stay on the AT, they have to cross Highway 7. They can chopper a team there and we'll drive them right into their arms."

The first uniform shook his head. "You just don't get it, do you, Anderson? We do it that way and we'll get no credit at all. If we make the collar ourselves, it'll wipe out our screwup and we have a chance of redeeming ourselves and maybe hanging around a while—"

"But—"

"STOW IT! Cuff her arms around that tree over there and let's get on with it. We'll deal with her later."

Wiggins crept backwards and eased the little survival rifle out of his pack, moving soundlessly as he assembled it. He didn't like his chances, but he sure as hell wasn't letting them harm Tex without a fight. He slipped a magazine into the rifle and crept back through the foliage just as the two uniforms set off down the trail. He let them get out of sight then crossed the trail.

"Are you okay?" he whispered.

"Just peachy, except for being kicked in the middle of the back by a two-hundred-pound asshole. How are you at picking handcuff locks?"

"Not in my skill set, I'm afraid. But we'll figure out something. Did they take your gun?"

She shook her head. "I think they threw it over there where they put my pack."

Wiggins walked over and found the Glock. He shoved it in his waistband, then came back and studied the handcuffs.

"There's a wire saw in the pack, maybe I could cut through the tree," he said.

"This damn tree is almost a foot thick, Bill. It'll take you forever, and besides, even if you do my hands are still cuffed together."

"But we can find a place to hide and figure out a way to get them off. Besides, from what I overheard, it didn't sound like having seen those mystery guys was very healthy. You can't be here when those assholes get back."

Tex nodded, but Wiggins was already in the woods fishing in his pack for the wire saw. He shook it out of the little Altoids tin Levi stored it in and uncoiled it to cut a length of a one-inch-diameter branch from a nearby tree, then bent the branch and used paracord to secure the wire saw to both ends, improvising a bow saw.

"Sit on the ground and straddle the trunk," he said. "If I can cut it low, maybe when I weaken it enough I can push against it and snap it off."

Tex did as instructed, and Wiggins began sawing about six inches above the top of her head. The little saw ripped into the bark and the first inch of the tree as sawdust drifted down on Tex. Each stroke widened the cut and friction increased. Progress slowed exponentially.

Sweat dripped from Wiggins' forehead and his arm was already burning, but he gritted his teeth and pressed on.

"This might take a while," he said between labored breaths.

"It's not like I'm going anywhere," Tex replied.

***

In the end, their ambush site was chosen for them. Keith hurtled down the trail and landed on a loose rock, twisting his ankle to tumble head over heels down the steep slope. His father was several yards back, hard-pressed to keep up with Keith's youthful athleticism. He pulled up, trying to halt his own headlong rush, and managed a controlled fall back on his ass in preference to a face-plant down the hill. His forward progress stopped, he scrambled over to where his son sprawled on the trail, shaken and moaning.

"Keith, are you all right?"

"I twisted my right ankle. It hurts like hell."

Tremble raised the boy's pant leg and pulled down his sock, eliciting a soft moan. The ankle was starting to discolor and swell, but everything looked to be lined up correctly.

"I don't think it's broken, but you won't be running on that," Tremble said.

"I'm sorry, Dad. I screwed up big time."

Tremble forced a smile and patted his son's good leg. "No problem. We needed to set up an ambush anyway, and I guess this is as good a site as any." He pointed to large boulders on either side of the trail. "We've got good cover. If we take them down fast, we can still get away."

Keith shook his head. "You know even if we do, there'll be others, and we can't move fast enough to lose them now. It's better if I hold them off so you can build up a lead and get away. You have to let people know what's going on."

"Not happening, son. If I escape, you're just a liability. I doubt they'd even bother to take you back to Mount Weather."

"But, Dad—"

"No buts. Give me your hand and I'll get you set up behind one of these boulders. I don't know how many of them there are, but I'll take the left side and you take the right. Don't fire until I do, okay?"

"Yes, sir," Keith said and gave his father his hand.

***

Tremble was beginning to hope their pursuers had somehow missed the trail, when he heard muffled grunts of exertion uphill through the foliage. Keith nodded—he'd heard it as well. Tremble's heart sank when he caught glimpses of their adversaries through the foliage; both were wearing body armor and carrying long guns. That meant head shots, hard enough with a rifle, much less a handgun. He took in a deep breath and exhaled, then steadied himself, his pistol in a two-handed grip, arms resting on the flat top of the boulder—and waited.

Both men came into view and Tremble aimed at the man in the lead, firing as soon as he had a shot. He was gratified to see the man fall as Keith opened up beside him, sending a fusillade uphill and driving the second man to cover.

"Easy, son," Tremble called softly. "Conserve your ammo."

"You got one!" Keith whispered back, an elation in his voice Tremble didn't feel, knowing the fight was far from over.

***

'Sam' crawled through the foliage to where 'Pete' was kneeling behind a large rock, blood dripping from his right ear.

"You're hit!"

"The asshole took off a piece of my earlobe. I'll live."

258

"What are we gonna do?"

"I'm gonna stay here and keep their attention. You go into the woods on the right and work your way downhill off the trail. When you get in position below them with a good field of fire, fire a warning shot to let them know you can take them out at any time. If they don't surrender, shoot them both in the legs. Got it?"

Sam nodded and slipped quietly away through the foliage as his partner yelled downhill.

"IT'S ALL OVER, TREMBLE. YOU AND THE BOY LAY DOWN YOUR GUNS AND COME OUT WITH YOUR HANDS WHERE I CAN SEE THEM."

"THAT YOU, PETE? HOW'S SAM? SORRY I HAD TO HIT HIM."

"YEAH, IT'S ME. AND YOU CAN ASK HIM YOURSELF AS SOON AS YOU SURRENDER, BUT HE'S NOT TALKING TOO GOOD NOW ON ACCOUNT OF HOW YOU ALMOST BROKE HIS JAW. NOW DO AS I SAY AND NO ONE WILL GET HURT."

"WHY WOULD I DO THAT?"

"OH, I DON'T KNOW. MAYBE BECAUSE YOU'RE CUT OFF AND ANOTHER TEAM IS COMING UP THE TRAIL ON YOUR SIX EVEN AS WE SPEAK. ALSO BECAUSE OUR ORDERS ARE TO TAKE YOU ALIVE IF POSSIBLE BUT NOT TO RISK CASUALTIES DOING IT, BUT SINCE YOU'VE ALREADY SHOT AT US, WE CAN KILL YOU RIGHT NOW, NO QUESTIONS ASKED. YOU'RE NOT GETTING AWAY, SO THE ONLY QUESTION IS WHETHER YOU AND SONNY BOY LEAVE THESE WOODS ON YOUR OWN TWO FEET OR IN BODY BAGS. YOUR CALL, TREMBLE. I'M GOOD EITHER WAY."

"WELL, LET ME JUST THINK ABOUT THAT, PETE."

"SURE, TAKE YOUR TIME, ANYTIME WITHIN THE NEXT TEN SECONDS WILL BE FINE."

There was no response for several minutes and the man's impatience grew. Then there was the crack of a gunshot followed by the whine of a ricocheting round. The man smiled.

"AND THAT WOULD BE THE FIRE TEAM I TOLD YOU ABOUT, TREMBLE. THAT WAS A WARNING SHOT. YOU HAVE THREE SECONDS TO THROW OUT YOUR WEAPONS AND SURRENDER OR THEIR ORDERS ARE SHOOT TO KILL. ONE... TWO..."

The man's smile widened as he saw two pistols fly over the boulders and clatter on the rocks of the trail, followed by Tremble rising with his hands in the air.

"DON'T SHOOT! WE SURRENDER! KEITH CAN'T STAND BECAUSE HE HAS A SPRAINED ANKLE."

***

Tremble stood motionless, hands in the air as the two men converged on him from opposite directions. He nodded at Sam and got a glare in return. He wasn't surprised the 'fire team' turned out to be only Sam—it was the obvious maneuver and what he'd have done in a similar situation. He'd known their position was untenable from the moment Keith went down, but harbored the slim hope they might take down their pursuers on first contact. The outcome of the fight was a forgone conclusion when their first rounds failed to take out their opponents.

Pete held them at gunpoint while Sam frisked them. He also examined Keith, and Tremble clinched his teeth at his son's stifled moans.

"It's sprained all right, maybe even broken," Sam said. "He's definitely not making it back uphill without help."

"Then the friggin' hero here can carry him," Pete said.

"He's a big boy," Tremble said. "I'll need help."

"Not happening," Pete said. "You carry him, or we leave him here with a bullet in the head."

"I can make it, Dad," Keith said, "and you don't have to carry me. Just let me lean on you."

Tremble nodded and began to help his son to his feet under Sam's watchful gaze as Pete reached for his radio and raised it to his lips.

"Central, this is Unit Twelve, do you copy? Over."

He repeated the call with no response. "Crappy reception down in this holler. I'll try again closer to the top," he said to Sam.

His partner nodded, and they began the uphill trek, prodding their struggling captives before them.

***

Wiggins redoubled his efforts at the sound of the distant gunfire, his arm numb. He was a third of the way through the tree, and Tex sat below him, a pile of sawdust covering her head and shoulders. She stared at the ground to keep the sawdust out of her eyes.

"How much longer?"

"We're getting close," Wiggins said.

"You friggin' liar, how close really?"

Wiggins sighed. "A little over a third of the way. When I get halfway, I'll try to push it over."

"What do you make of the gunfire?"

"I'm worried it stopped. As long as they're shooting at each other, they can't be headed back. Now, who knows?"

"I agree… wait! Stop sawing a second!"

Wiggins did; then he heard it too. Sounds from downhill. He pulled the saw from the notch and set it down. Tex looked up and gave him a frightened nod, the action dislodging sawdust from her hair and causing her to squeeze her eyes shut again. He moved downhill and squatted behind a thick tree trunk to study the trail.

A minute passed and the sounds grew louder, low conversation punctuated by muffled groans. Then the tops of heads came into view followed by torsos. It was the two fugitives they'd seen earlier. He could see now one was considerably older and there was no mistaking the family resemblance. The older man was half carrying a man who could only be his son. The older guy looked familiar, and the memory of the earlier overheard exchange came flooding back. '… let Tremble and his son escape…'

Wiggins' blood ran cold. He had no idea what was going on, but knew without a doubt any witnesses had a very limited lifespan. He crouched, immobilized by fear as Tex's captors came into view behind their prisoners. Tremble stumbled and almost fell, and Wiggins could see he was struggling with the weight of his son.

"All right, take a break," called one of the captors, the one with a bloody ear. The captives moved to sit on a nearby boulder while their captors moved up even with them to stand in the middle of the trail.

Bloody Ear turned to his partner. "We're closer to the ridge now. I'll try Central."

The man turned his head to speak into a mike clipped to his shoulder.

"Central, this is Unit Twelve, do you copy? Over."

"Twelve, this is Central. We copy and request immediate sitrep. Over."

Bloody Ear grinned at his partner.

"Central, this is Unit Twelve. We have the subjects in custody. Repeat. We have the subjects in custody. Over."

"Copy that, Unit Twelve. We confirm you have subjects in custody. We have units about to deploy. What is your location and we will send assistance. Over."

"Central, we are on foot near Bear's Den but do not require assistance. We are returning to base ETA thirty minutes. Repeat. We are RTB in thirty mikes. Stand down assistance. Over."

"Negative, Twelve. We are sending assistance to your vehicle location. Over."

"Central, I say again we do not require assistance and believe presence of additional assets will attract unnecessary attention to the operation. Your call. Over."

There was no response for a moment and the other cop spoke to Bloody Ear.

"Maybe we should let them send—"

"Screw that. We need all the credit we can get on this to make up for your screwup. I'm not sharing this collar with anyone."

"Unit Twelve, this is Central. Very well, we confirm you are RTB in thirty mikes and we are standing down assistance. Please confirm you completed mission without complications. Over."

"Central, we have one loose end. Repeat. We have one loose end. Please advise preferred action. Over."

Again there was a long pause before the response.

"Unit Twelve, be advised loose end is best handled on site if local conditions permit. Please advise. Over."

"Central, we copy. We will tie up loose end on site. See you in thirty minutes. Unit Twelve out."

Any hesitation Wiggins harbored was laid to rest by the radio exchange. He pulled out the Glock and looked at it. The men wore body armor, and by the time they got close enough for him to get off a head shot, they'd be too close for comfort. That left the little rifle. They were well within range, and since he had to take head shots anyway, he liked his chances with the popgun a lot better. He stuffed the Glock in his waistband and raised the little Henry.

"All right," Bloody Ear said, "the break is over. Let's get a move—"

Wiggins pulled the trigger. He heard a muffled pop without even the slight recoil he expected from the little rifle. Bloody Ear stood unmoving and then slowly collapsed, but Wiggins was already targeting the second man. He aimed and tried to fire again, but the trigger wouldn't pull. Realization hit him between the eyes like a sledgehammer. He'd loaded the friggin' quiet rounds, without even enough recoil to cycle the bolt. In a panic he jerked at the bolt to chamber another round, his hands slipping on the small knob.

The second man seemed confused, unsure of the source of the attack until Wiggins' frantic movement caught his eye. He crouched to present a smaller target, and Wiggins' second round went high. Wiggins was attempting to chamber a third round when his target lifted the M4. The older man launched himself off the rock and struck the shooter hard in the side, sending his shot wild as the two men collapsed in a heap. Wiggins dropped the Henry and pulled the Glock to race downhill to where the men struggled for the M4. He jammed the Glock between the second man's eyes.

"Drop it!"

The man tensed for a moment; then the fight left him. He released the M4 to slump back on the ground, defeated. The older man struggled up and pointed the rifle at his recent captor, nodding to Wiggins as he did so.

"Keep him covered," Wiggins said. "I'm gonna check the other one."

The other man was dead, Wiggins' shot having taken out his left eye. There was no exit wound, indicating the low-powered round had ricocheted inside the man's skull, making multiple passes through his brain. He searched the man then took off uphill with the handcuff key.

***

Two minutes later the surviving FEMA man was cuffed to a tree some distance away, hasty introductions had been made, and Tremble gave Wiggins and Tex the short version of the State of the Union.

"We're screwed," Wiggins said to Tremble. "Even if we separate, they'll scoop up anyone in the vicinity who might have seen anything." He nodded toward their captive. "And then there's our friend here. Unless we dispose of him, he'll link us together anyway."

"I'm sorry," Tremble said, "we had no intention of endangering anyone else. I think you know that."

"Of course we do, Congressman," Tex said, "but—"

Tremble flashed a wan smile. "Considering the likely end of our short acquaintance, I think we're all on a first-name basis. Call me Simon."

Tex nodded. "All right, Simon. I was saying it doesn't matter how it happened, we have to deal with it. And given the fact you've been dealing with it a bit longer than we have, do you have any ideas?"

"We can't get far," Tremble said. "We're due back at Mount Weather in a bit more than twenty-five minutes. When we don't show up, they'll come looking. They already have a fair idea where we are, so they'll move to contain us. We need to get across State Highway 7 before that happens."

Tex and Wiggins nodded. "That makes sense," Tex said. "The highway is less than half a mile down this hill and there is a lot more woodland to search and fewer roads to access it north of the highway." She looked at Keith. "But we can't move very fast."

"Bill and I can probably carry Keith and still make pretty good time," Tremble said, "but you'll have to ditch some of your gear. After we cross the highway, we'll leave the trail and find a hiding place."

"What about him?" Wiggins nodded again toward their prisoner.

"I haven't figured that out yet," Tremble said. "Why don't y'all check what you can jettison and I'll go talk to our friend."

Tex and Wiggins nodded again, and Tremble got up off his rock and moved towards the captive.

* * *

"You present quite a dilemma, Sam," Tremble said. "I don't want to kill you in cold blood, but that seems the only logical choice."

The man surprised Tremble by shrugging. "It's George, not Sam. George Anderson. I reckon if you're gonna kill me, you might as well know my name."

"Very well, George. I have to say you seem remarkably calm about it."

George shrugged again. "You kill me or they kill me, so what's the difference? I've screwed up twice big time, and I've been around these people long enough to know that's not gonna go over well. I was thinking it would get me exiled to a 'fugee camp, but then I realized I know too damn much. They're not gonna just demote me or kick me out. They'll kill me, same as they'll kill you. So like I say, what's the difference? Y'all aren't gonna make it out alive and I'm never makin' it home to the Georgia backwoods. That's for sure. I wish now I'd never left."

Something clicked in Tremble's mind and a plan began to form.

"Why are you so sure we won't make it? These woods are pretty thick."

"And when we don't show up at Mount Weather, the search teams will be just as thick. They had four teams outfitting with more on the way when we left, along with a chopper with IR search gear. We stood them down, but they'll come back on line and be deployed in an hour, two at most. You can't get very far in that time, especially with the gimpy kid, and you can't hide your body heat from the IR, no matter how thick the cover is. You don't stand a chance."

"Assuming we do get past the infrared and the search teams, is there anything else we have to worry about. Tracking dogs maybe?"

George thought a moment, then shook his head. "Probably not. Mostly FEMA called on local sources when they needed tracking dogs, and you may have noticed things are a bit strained with the local folks these days."

Tremble rubbed his chin. "How'd you like a fighting chance at making it home to the Georgia backwoods?"

"I'm listening," George said.

***

Tremble walked back to the group with George in tow, without cuffs. Wiggins looked up and began clawing the Glock from his waistband.

"Easy, Bill," Tremble said. "There's been a change of plan. Our new friend George here has agreed to buy us some time."

"You gotta be nuts! You can't trust him. Why would you—"

"Because if we don't, we're toast. Don't trust him, trust me. Now are you with me?"

Wiggins hesitated. "Yes," Tex said; then Wiggins nodded.

"All right, pick a spot a bit off the trail to hide everything you're leaving and show George here where it is."

Wiggins looked skeptical and stalked off into the woods. He returned a moment later and motioned George and Tremble over, but Tremble noted he left his hand resting on the Glock in his waistband. He pointed through the foliage.

"See that big fallen tree, about seventy feet downhill?"

George squatted and peered through the trees. "Just barely," he said.

"We'll cache everything we leave behind it and cover it with leaves. We don't have time to bury it, but it'll be out of sight," Wiggins said.

George nodded, and Tremble motioned them back to where Tex was sorting out the contents of both backpacks. They looked down at the items spread out on the ground, and picked up a few things.

"These look like duplicates," Tremble said.

"Yeah, but two is one and one is none," Wiggins said. "We'll need—"

"We won't need anything if we're dead," Tremble said, ignoring Wiggins' glare as he slipped the items in his pocket. He looked at his watch.

"All right, we have twelve minutes before we'll be MIA. George, pick up your former colleague and start back south. Bill, you and Tex get everything repacked and see if you can maybe cut a couple of saplings and rig up a stretcher for Keith. We'll be able to move faster if you and I carry him that way, and maybe we can take more of the other stuff if we put your pack on the stretcher with him. Tex can carry what's left in her pack and scout ahead to make sure we're not ambushed. I'll be back as soon as I can. Y'all be ready to move."

"But where are you going?" Tex asked.

"To buy us some time, but I don't have time to explain," Tremble said as he scooped up the radio from where it rested on a rock and fell in behind George, who had his dead colleague in a fireman's carry.

"Wait a minute," Wiggins said, and ran over to George. "I might be able to use these." He unlaced the dead man's boots and tugged them off his feet, then stepped aside.

Tremble nodded and took the lead, his exhaustion forgotten as he set a grueling pace back uphill to the access cutoff to Bear's Den, then continued past it down the steep slope back toward a stream at the bottom of the hill as George labored behind him. He stopped at the stream.

"Okay, put him down," Tremble said, and George dumped his former partner on the trail.

"We'll make better time in the streambed," Tremble said, glancing at his watch as he splashed into the stream and away from the trail, George on his heels. They moved down the winding stream as quickly as conditions allowed, ever mindful of the time. The AT disappeared behind them in the foliage.

"Okay, this should be far enough off the trail," Tremble said, just as the radio crackled.

"Unit Twelve, this is Central. We request immediate sitrep. Do you copy? Over."

"Showtime," Tremble said, pulling the radio from his belt and handing it to George as he simultaneously drew his pistol. "And just on the off chance you haven't been straight up with me, if I sense the slightest hint of a double cross, you'll be the first to die. Got it?"

George nodded and took the radio.

"Central, this is Unit Twelve. We copy. Repeat your last. Over."

"Unit Twelve, our telemetry indicates your vehicle has not moved. What is your situation? Over."

"Central be advised the housekeeping task required more time than estimated, but it is now complete. However, we just arrived at our vehicle location to find a flat tire. We are changing now and will RTB in due course and will keep you advised of our progress. Over."

"Unit Twelve, we copy. Advise estimated departure from your current position. Over."

"Central, we estimate twenty to thirty mikes. Over."

"Unit Twelve, we copy. Advise when you begin RTB. Central out."

Tremble held out his free hand for the radio, keeping George covered with the pistol. George looked confused, but he handed the radio over, and Tremble slipped it on his uniform belt and then extracted the handcuffs he'd taken from the dead guard's belt. He tossed them to George.

"Now cuff your hands around that tree over there," Tremble said.

"Hey! What the hell are you talking about? That wasn't the deal!"

"I'll honor the deal, but I'm not quite that trusting, so move it. I don't have all day."

George glared and cuffed his arms around the tree trunk. Tremble holstered the pistol before unbuckling the gun belt and placing it out of reach. He moved toward George, pulling a length of paracord from his pocket as he did so.

"I'm going to tie your wrists with paracord, and when I'm sure they're secure, I'll take the cuffs off. Then I'm gagging you so you can't call out. I'll leave the gun and extra ammo hidden over there under some rocks. I'll also leave a wire saw and a lighter there." He held up a large folding pocketknife. "This I'm leaving on the ground under some leaves just beyond your reach. I figure a smart guy like you can get untied or think of a way to drag the knife close enough to use. You know where the others are discarding the extra gear, and you might or might not be able to get back to it."

"That's not the deal," George repeated. "I got no time to find a cave or other hiding place. When they put the chopper up, they'll spot me with the IR, sure as hell."

"Which means you better start working on getting loose as soon as I leave," Tremble said, "and heading south down the AT toward your Georgia backwoods. Just to be clear, I never promised you anything but a chance, and this is a chance. Or you can just stay here tied up, and when they find you, tell them I held a gun at your head to make you file the false report. I'm hiding the stuff I'm leaving so that won't give you away if you decide to just wait it out. Your call."

"Thanks for nothing, asshole."

"You're welcome," Tremble said, then pulled George's uniform shirt out of his belt and cut a piece off the tail to gag him before tying his hands with the paracord and removing the cuffs. He hid the other items as promised and dropped the knife just out of George's reach before starting back up the stream to the AT. The mostly uphill jog back to the others was grueling, but he had no time to spare. He reached them, gasping for breath, and bent over at the waist, hands on his knees as he sucked in long ragged breaths.

"I... I put the dead guard on the southbound trail... so... so maybe they'll look that way first... we got maybe fifteen minutes before we're expected back at Mount Weather, and that might stretch a bit. I think we got an hour or two at most to get across Highway 7 and find a hiding place. Are... are you ready?"

"What'd you do with the other one?" Wiggins asked.

"No time. Tell you later," Tremble gasped.

Wiggins nodded and walked to where Keith lay on a crude stretcher, holding Wiggins' pack and looking uncomfortable and embarrassed at his own helplessness. Tex grunted and shouldered her pack and Tremble moved to the other end of the stretcher.

"Let's lift on three," he said, and counted down. The load was well balanced and not as bad as he'd anticipated, but he knew negotiating the steep downhill path would likely make him rethink that soon.

"Take the lead and let's get the hell out of here, Tex," he said.

DOWNTOWN RIVERWALK
WILMINGTON, NORTH CAROLINA

DAY 17, 7:25 A.M.

Jerome Singletary stood on the dock, watching Jermain Ware loading extra ammunition aboard and feeling perverse pride in his little two-boat armada, thankful it hadn't been nearly as difficult to put together as he'd anticipated. Flat-bottom aluminum fishing boats were apparently not high on the 'things to be looted' list. He'd found several stacked in the back at the local outlet of a major chain store, with electric trolling motors and batteries at the same source. Charging the batteries had been a bit more of a challenge, but with Kwintell Banks' grudging approval, he'd used the generator at the "UBN Provisional HQ."

Best of all, he'd managed to pull it off without revealing he didn't have a clue what he was doing. He'd been equally fortunate to find a booklet of river charts in the third boat searched. He'd pored over it, hoping for a clue as to the whereabouts of Levi's hideout. He knew from eavesdropping it was on the Black River, a tributary of the Cape Fear, and two to four hours from the Wilmington terminal. His major problem was he didn't know the speed upon which that travel time was based. He did know it couldn't be too fast, because Levi's boat had only the small outboard and the electric trolling motor. He'd also heard them talk about weeping willow trees, which he hoped could help identify it if he could just get close.

Though truth be known, the location of Levi's camp was a matter of monumental indifference to him. He had no intention of leading Banks' men to it if he could at all avoid it. He doubted Levi would surrender easily. Bullets would be flying and Jerome Singletary had no desire to be in the middle of a gunfight. Rather, he planned to guide their boats ashore somewhere along the river with the stated intention of scouting Levi's camp from the landward side, then slipping away from his captors in the woods. It was a long shot, but pretty much the only shot he had.

He felt vibration through his feet and looked up to see Kwintell Banks striding down the dock from the riverwalk, his entourage in tow.

"You ready, Singletary?" Banks asked.

Singletary bobbed his head. "Just about. We're waitin' for the powerboat to come around. We'll put one man to drive the powerboat and tow the electric boats up the Cape Fear to the Black, that way we save the batteries. Then he'll anchor the powerboat in the river and get in with us. That'll give us three men in each boat and we go the rest of the way quiet like." Singletary paused. "Should be more than enough, seeing as how we're sneaking up on 'em. There aren't any men there except Levi and the old man. The rest are just women and kids."

Banks looked over at his lieutenant for confirmation. "How 'bout it Jermain? Y'all ready?"

Jermain Ware nodded. "Like he said, everything is ready soon as the rest of the boys get here with the powerboat."

"All right," Banks said, "remember you in charge. This shithead's just the guide, so don't trust him none."

Jermain nodded again and Banks smiled and motioned one of his entourage forward. Singletary noted for the first time the man was carrying a bag. From the looks of it, a heavy bag.

"Matter of fact," Banks said, "I got a little present for you, Singletary."

Singletary watched, horror stricken, as the minion set the bag down and extracted what looked like a cannonball attached to a leg shackle via a thick steel chain.

Banks laughed, enjoying Singletary's reaction. "Found this in one of the local museums. All sorts of interesting stuff in museums. Practical too." His smile faded. "Lift your pants leg."

"Just a minute! That wasn't the deal—"

Banks drew his gun and pointed it at Singletary's head. "Lift your pants leg. One. Two…"

Singletary stooped to lift his right pants leg and Banks' grinning minion hurried over to shackle the steel ball to Singletary's leg.

"I'll drown if I fall overboard!"

Banks shrugged. "Then don't fall overboard. Did you actually think I was dumb enough to let you out on the river where you could escape? No, you gonna be on the front of the first boat in, just in case it's an ambush or something. And in case you feel stupid enough to maybe try to cap some of my boys and unlock yourself"—he held up a padlock key—"ain't but one key and it's in my pocket, and I'm stayin' right here."

Banks looked over at Jermain. "He give you any trouble, or if it looks like he's bullshittin' us, or you take this Levi's camp and it ain't got the gold and silver and grenades and everything he promised, you just throw his punk ass out of the boat in the middle of the river. Don't be bringing his sorry ass back. You understand?"

Jermain grinned. "Straight up, boss."

Levi Jenkins' Fishing Camp
Black River, North Carolina

Day 17, 8:30 a.m.

Anthony McCoy watched his grandchildren climb in the flat-bottom boat, almost vibrating with excitement at the prospect of 'going to town.' He suppressed his smile and addressed them in a stern voice.

"Y'all settle down now, and put them life jackets on. Bein' on the river is serious business and y'all can't be poppin' around like jumping beans, ya hear?"

"Yes, Grampa," said the children in unison, marginally curbing their exuberance as they donned life jackets.

Anthony heard footsteps on the small dock and looked up to see Levi approaching with Celia and Jo, the two women looking almost as excited as the children. He held the boat while the women climbed in and got the children settled, then stood and nodded at Levi.

"Y'all should be there in two hours, now that we feel comfortable running in daylight. When is the Coastie patrol boat gonna be here?"

Levi shook his head. "He's not coming up this far. I agreed with Chief Butler on the radio to just meet 'em at the Brunswick River intersection. Nothing much to worry about on the upper part of the river and that saves them some time. Besides, Butler can't make it, so I don't want anyone else knowing our exact location. And though he didn't say it, I also know taking the time to escort us is a strain on resources. Everybody's got enough on their plate as it is these days. I appreciate the escort service and I don't want to abuse it."

Anthony's face clouded. "Why am I just hearin' about this now?"

"'Cause I knew you'd get your bowels in an uproar, that's why. It's only an hour's run to the intersection with the outboard, and I'm well-armed. We'll be fine until we meet up with the Coasties."

Anthony looked unconvinced. "I don't know, Levi, maybe you should postpone the trip until dark and run with the NV goggles and electric motors, just to be safe. Or maybe not go at all until we can work something better out."

Levi cocked an eyebrow. "Maybe you'd like to explain that to Celia and Jo and the kids," he said softly. "They been here three weeks and they're pretty much starved for some socializing. I didn't really realize how bad it was impacting them until I saw how they perked up when Wiggins and Tex were here. They're really looking forward to this trip and I don't want to be the one to tell 'em it's not happening. Fort Box is all we got that passes for a town nowadays. So if you want 'em to stay here, you go right ahead and tell 'em."

Levi looked at Anthony, one eyebrow cocked in a silent question.

Anthony sighed and shook his head. "All right, all right. But you call me on the radio the first thing when you get to Fort Box."

"I will. But why don't you come with us? We can set out extra feed for the animals to tide them over a day or so. I'm more concerned with leaving you here alone than I am with our trip."

Anthony shook his head again. "I'll be fine, and somebody needs to stay here just in case. You never know if you'll get delayed for some reason, and we can't risk the livestock. Besides, you'll need the room if you can talk Jimmy into coming back with you."

Levi nodded, but didn't move, reluctant to leave on a note of discord. Anthony sensed his hesitation and smiled. "Y'all go on now. Don't keep the Coasties waiting, else they might not be so accommodating next time."

Levi hugged Anthony and got in the boat.

GIBSON FARM
ON THE BLACK RIVER
WEST OF CURRIE, NC

DAY 17, 8:00 A.M.

Luke sat in the bow, watching as Vern Gibson deftly maneuvered the boat away from the riverbank. He had Long and Washington with him, and they were all clad in work clothes provided by the Gibson men. They were all long overdue haircuts and had several days' beard growth, so the only thing marking them as military was their M4s and the casual competence with which they handled them.

They'd decided one boat could be passed off as a scouting trip while two might look like an assault, and left the remainder of the group at the Gibson farm. Over Donny Gibson's strong objection, his father had exercised parental prerogative and assumed the role of local guide. The older Gibson had pointed out, leave periods aside, Donny had been away for several years and was no longer a familiar face to the neighbors along the river. Given the times, a boatload of armed strangers was apt to draw fire first and questions later, but having a neighbor at the helm should at least result in discussion before hostilities commenced.

Luke smiled at the recollection of the discussion. Donny had been inclined to debate the point until his mother had entered the fray, forbidding his participation on pain of unspecified but apparently feared consequences for both Donny and his father. Donny had flushed with embarrassment at the dressing-down, but grudgingly accepted his father's argument as correct. He stood on the bank as the boat pulled away, his hand raised in a wave of farewell, returned by his three colleagues.

"Gibson don't look too happy, LT," Washington said, "but I reckon he'd be a lot more unhappy if he crossed his momma. That is one tough lady." He looked back, suddenly self-conscious. He saw Vern Gibson smile.

"No offense, sir," Washington added lamely.

"None taken," Vern said. "Virginia's the toughest woman I know. It's one of the reasons I love her. And she's had her share of heartache. When

Richard lost his arm, it was nip and tuck for a while, and we almost lost him too. Then Donny up and enlisted. She didn't say nothing and she was proud, but it damn near drove her crazy with worry. Since the power went out and things started gettin' crazy, she's been praying for his safe return at least three times a day. We all have, truth be known. So she's gonna keep him close a while, and he just has to live with it. She's earned a little peace of mind, and then some."

The other men just nodded, unsure what to say, the silence broken only by the growl of the outboard.

"How long to Wilmington?" Luke asked at last.

"Hard to say, three or four hours, give or take," Vern replied. "The main channel is the Black River until we get down to the junction with the Cape Fear River around Roan Island, then the combined stream is designated the Cape Fear. Then we'll keep going a ways to the junction with the Brunswick, and we'll take that south and keep Eagle Island between us and Wilmington. The Brunswick rejoins the Cape Fear less than a mile south of the container terminal. My neighbor said the Coast Guard boat was docked at the terminal."

Luke nodded and turned his attention back to the river. The banks were heavily wooded, but occasionally an opening through the trees revealed an expanse of open field or a farmhouse set well back from the river. At one point they rounded a bend and saw a row of large homes along the shore, set on expansive lots and served by floating docks in the river. Most were deserted, but figures stood exposed on one or two of the docks, their postures telegraphing unease at being caught in the open, even at a distance. As the boat passed them and Vern raised his hand in greeting, Luke saw the people relax. He wondered how many rifle scopes had been pointed at them thus far in their journey and considered for the first time whether foregoing their body armor to look 'less military' had been such a good idea.

M/V PECOS TRADER
SUN LOWER ANCHORAGE
NECHES RIVER
NEAR NEDERLAND, TEXAS

DAY 17, 8:00 A.M.

Hughes stood at the rail with Kinsey and Dan Gowan, watching Georgia Howell's deck gang lowering the Coast Guard boat over the side.

"Any sign of our fake deputies?" Gowan asked.

Hughes shook his head. "No, and we're fairly well out of sight here. There's nothing much but marsh and mosquitoes on this riverbank, and we're far enough up in the inlet we can't be seen from the opposite bank except by someone actually standing on the dock at the Sun Terminal. Same from the river; I had enough water depth to get well out of the main channel. A boat needs to get dead even with the mouth of the inlet to see us." He paused. "Besides, it's not like we have a choice; this is the only place we'll fit."

Gowan nodded. "Let's just hope those dipshit deputies don't figure that out."

Matt Kinsey laughed. "I'd say we're safe. Those boys didn't look like the sharpest tacks in the box. But we'll keep a good watch anyway. I suspect a few well-placed bursts with the fifty will discourage them pretty quickly."

Hughes smiled. "*Semper Paratus.*"

"Absolutely," Kinsey said. They turned back to the ongoing operation just as the Coast Guard boat gently kissed the surface of the water.

"Looks like you're about ready to go, Cap" Gowan said.

Hughes nodded. "Any hard feelings from the crew?"

Gowan shrugged. "Not that I've heard. I guess they all pretty much feel like I do. Everyone knows we can't all leave the ship at the same time. Someone's got to be first and you've got as much right as anyone. More, actually. None of us would even be here if you hadn't decided to move the ship. Go get Laura and the girls and bring 'em back, then send someone else." The engineer shook his head. "Besides, going first might not be such a benefit, since you don't know what's out there. Personally, I'm thinking second or third looks pretty good."

"Yeah, that hadn't escaped me either," Hughes said.

"How many you think we should take?" Kinsey asked.

"Take? I figured y'all would just drop me off with some gas. I can't ask anyone else to do this; it's my family."

"You're not asking, I'm volunteering, as have all the others. You don't know what you'll find, and my guys are the only ones with any weapons training. I figure I'll take two guys and leave four here for security. Your folks can supplement them with the extra weapons if need be."

"That's very generous, Chief Kinsey," Hughes said. "I don't know what to say. I just sort of figured when we got here... well, actually, I don't know what the hell I thought was going to happen. I don't even know what we're going to do with folks when we bring them on board. We sure don't have room for everyone."

"We'll play it by ear, Captain. And I want to get over to Louisiana as soon as I can, and I'll definitely be bringing my family back if I can get them to come. My guys all feel the same way, but their folks are scattered up and down the coast from here to Corpus Christi. As far as what's gonna happen, all I know is *Pecos Trader* is the lifeboat with all the provisions and we're in a shit storm. None of us really want to stray too far. Now what do you say? Is four enough?"

Hughes shrugged. "I'd say it has to be. We have to get wheels, and we have to have room to bring Laura and the girls back."

"You're the local, so where do we get a ride?"

"Anything we find abandoned is unlikely to have keys, so unless we have someone who can hot-wire a car, that's a nonstarter. I figure a car dealership or auto repair shop is our best bet; some place we're likely to find both vehicles and keys. The closest are along the main drag in Nederland. Maybe three or four miles from the river through mostly good residential neighborhoods. The boat can drop us off across the river at the refinery dock, just downstream."

"So we grab a couple of cans of gas and hump it to the main drag on foot and go car shopping?" Kinsey nodded. "Sounds doable."

"We might not have to hoof it," Hughes said. "They keep bikes for the dock workers to use when they're working a ship. When the lights went out, everybody probably just went home, just like Wilmington. I can't see anyone coming back down to the river to scavenge a bunch of old bicycles. I'm betting they're still there, and they all have big deep carrying baskets for tools, so we can each carry a gas can."

Kinsey grinned. "Sounds good to me. If I was fond of walking, I'd have joined the infantry."

***

Fifteen minutes later, Hughes and his little shore party were headed downriver in the patrol boat, a Coastie at the helm and another manning the bow machine gun. Nothing moved on the river and the refinery dock came into view as soon as the boat cleared the inlet. Kinsey directed the helmsman to the middle of the river, and they were running abreast of the dock five minutes later, checking it out. There was an empty tank barge riding high at the extreme downstream end of the dock, but no signs of activity. Hughes pointed out a vertical ladder midway down the tall dock, and they moved toward it.

Kinsey motioned to one of his men, who scampered up the ladder, his M4 slung beside him. The man disappeared and moments later he returned to sound an all clear. The other three men scurried up after him. Hughes brought up the rear, a coil of rope over his shoulder, which he shrugged off when he gained the solid footing of the dock. He tossed one end of the rope back down to the waiting boat, where one of the remaining Coasties tied it to the first of the red plastic gas containers so Hughes could haul it up. They repeated the process and all four gas cans were lined up on the dock when Kinsey returned, a grin on his face.

"Bunch of bikes parked next to the dock office, just like you said. Ready?"

"Almost," Hughes said as he tossed the end of the rope back over the side. Minutes later he dragged it up, and a crow bar and a large pair of bolt cutters hit the concrete dock with metallic clangs.

"Can't forget the precision instruments," Hughes said.

Kinsey nodded, then leaned over the side and ordered the boat back to the ship.

"Think we should do a comms check?" Kinsey asked.

"Negative," Hughes replied. "We don't know who's listening. The ship's walkie-talkies have limited range anyway, so I think we should limit transmissions to calling the boat back when we get within range inbound."

"Agreed," Kinsey said, just as the other two Coasties appeared, each guiding a bike with either hand.

"Let's get loaded up and find us a ride," Kinsey said.

The bolt cutters made short work of the lock on the dock gate, and they pedaled two abreast down the cracked asphalt of the long road between the refinery and the tank farm. The Texas heat and humidity was already oppressive despite the early hour. The total lack of traffic combined with the eerie silence of the abandoned industrial area created a pervasive air of unreality.

"This is friggin' spooky," said one of the Coasties. "Not a soul in sight."

"Count your blessings, Jones," Kinsey said over his shoulder. "There are a lot worse things than spooky."

"Yeah, like friggin' hot! I'll be glad to get in a vehicle and crank up the AC!"

They emerged from the tank farm to cross Twin City Highway and took Canal Avenue south, running through residential areas showing the beginnings of decay, with what were once obviously manicured lawns now overgrown. Far from opposition, the people they saw on the streets took one look at their guns and uniforms and disappeared behind locked doors.

"Something's not right," Kinsey said. "I mean, I expected things to be screwed up, but these people act terrified."

Hughes nodded and picked up the pace, thinking of his family.

They had their pick of places on US 69, and Hughes turned directly off Canal Avenue into the lot of a Ford dealership. They rolled to a stop in a lot half full of new cars, with gaps in the rows indicating someone might have had the same idea. There was an equally large stretch of 'pre-owned' vehicles beyond that, with fewer vacant spaces.

"Looks like someone got here first," Kinsey said.

Hughes nodded. "I suspect anything left has had the gas siphoned out. Pickings are probably better over in the used-car section. Y'all go pick out a likely vehicle, maybe a big SUV," Hughes said. "I'll bust in to the building and see if I can find keys, providing previous shoppers left the keys for what they didn't take."

"How far is your place?" Kinsey asked.

"About twenty-five miles. Say sixty or eighty miles round trip by the time we get back to the refinery dock, depending on detours. Why?"

"We have twenty gallons of gas, so I'm for taking a car and a backup. Two is one, and one is none, as they say. If we somehow get disabled or break down near your place, it's a long hike back to the river. "

"Good point. Pick 'em out and get the VIN numbers while I try to rustle up the keys." He started for the dealership showroom, the crowbar over his shoulder.

He found the double glass doors ajar, and the showroom itself looked like a storm had hit it. The tile floor was carpeted with slick four-color sales brochures and all the drawers in the desk in the reception area were standing open. Hughes started down a long hallway, open doors on either side revealing Spartan cubicles where salesmen haggled with customers in better times. The further he got from the glass-windowed showroom, the darker it became, until finally he fished a small flashlight from his pocket.

At the end of the hallway in a larger office he found what he was looking for, a large key cabinet, the door torn off and hanging by one hinge. A glance inside and his hopes plummeted at the sight of empty hooks. He sighed and turned away but something crunched underfoot, and he smiled as his light illuminated a litter of discarded keys. Moving quickly, he dumped the contents of a nearby wastebasket and began scooping the keys into it. Five minutes later, he and Kinsey stood at the reception desk, searching for VIN numbers on the key tags in the better light of the glass-walled showroom.

"Here's the SUV," Kinsey said.

"Go get it gassed up while I keep looking for the pickup keys," Hughes said.

"All right," Kinsey headed for the door. "When you find it, throw the rest of those keys back in the trash can and let's take them with us. No telling when we might have to come car shopping again."

Hughes nodded absently and kept looking.

Ten minutes later, Hughes was at the wheel of a big Ford Expedition with Kinsey riding shotgun as they turned south on the access road for US 69. The two other Coasties trailed them in a full-size Ford pickup. There were scattered cars on the road, mostly on the shoulder, and Hughes passed them without slowing. He braked as they approached a deserted mall and swung right on Highway 365 as it passed under US 69.

"It's all rural roads from here," Hughes said as he accelerated, "and this wouldn't have been a road to attract refugees. We should make good time." He pushed the Expedition up to eighty-five and glanced in his mirror. The Coasties were right with him, eight or ten car lengths back. He accelerated to ninety-five and stared at the road ahead, running flat and straight through the coastal pastureland. His mind wandered as the SUV ate up the miles. With his myriad responsibilities, he'd compartmentalized worry about his family, because to do otherwise would have rendered him unable to function. But scant miles from home with an open road in front of him, all of his worries and fears came crashing down as he blasted down the blacktop, both eager and terrified of what might await him.

"You won't do your family any good if you hit a pothole at a hundred and ten and wrap us around a telephone pole. Besides, you're losing the pickup."

A quick glance in the mirror revealed the pickup some distance back. Hughes eased off the gas.

"Sorry," he said.

Kinsey shrugged. "Understandable. Are we making better time than you figured?"

"Yeah, but we're about to lose some. If I stay on this road, we'll pick up Texas 124 in Fannett, but that more or less parallels I-10 and I'd like to avoid it. I also want to miss Fannett and Hamshire, so we'll be taking to the back roads in a few miles."

"This isn't a back road?"

Hughes laughed. "Not by a long shot."

True to his word, a few minutes later he pulled off the highway on to a narrow path that ran due south through pastureland along a barbed-wire fence, little more than two graveled wheel tracks with weeds a foot tall growing between them.

"Doesn't look like anyone has used this lately, which is a good thing. We have maybe fifteen miles of this, and I'll have to do a lot of zigzagging and backtracking, but it will keep us off the public roads. We'll come up to the house from the back side, across the pastures. We should be pulling up behind our barn in half an hour. Be ready with those bolt cutters, we might have to 'unlock' a few gates along the way."

✳✳✳

Laura Hughes stood partially concealed behind the white wood fence and studied the approaching dust plume.

"They're in a hell of a hurry, whoever they are," she said softly, then louder, "What do you see, Jana?"

Jana Hughes stood beside her twin sister, wrists braced on the top rail of the fence to steady the binoculars.

"There are four of them, Mom, and they're wearing some sort of uniforms. Not like the deputies, these are blue, but it looks like they've all got on that black army stuff. You know, like vests. And there aren't any markings on either the car or the truck."

Laura considered the possibilities. Given their recent encounter, the fact the approaching men wore uniforms was alarming, and the lack of any markings on the vehicles further supported the idea they were some sort of rogue element. Only by chance had they been working in the garden and spotted the approaching dust cloud across the wide expanse of the mostly treeless pasture. An armed group approaching across private property was obviously intent on avoiding detection. Nothing about the situation spelled anything but trouble, and if she waited to find out what they were about, Laura had no doubt she and the girls would be easily overpowered. That wasn't happening.

"Well, whoever they are, they shouldn't be on our property. And there's no way I'm letting 'em get close enough to hurt us."

She looked over at her daughters. "We've only got the .30-.30 and the .308 that are effective at this range. I'll take the .30-.30. Julie, you're the best shot of the three of us, so I want you to take the .308. I'm going to try to stop them and I want you to take them after they've stopped, either through the windows or as they get out of their cars." She paused. "Can you do this, honey?"

Julie swallowed hard and bobbed her head once in response.

Laura fought down an urge to sweep both her daughters into her arms and run to the house and hide, but hiding and waiting for the authorities was no longer an option. She brought the .30-.30 up and steadied it on the fence rail, wishing for the hundredth time Jordan had gotten around to fitting the scopes still in their boxes in the gun safe. She crouched a bit and took aim through the iron sights. The SUV turned slightly and she couldn't see in for the glare, but she focused on the windshield where she knew the driver's body would be.

"Okay, Julie," Laura said, her rifle still on the approaching target. "Take a deep breath and calm down. Take your time and let me know when you're ready."

She heard what sounded like a deep sigh, then, "Okay, Mom, I'm ready."

"All right, I'm going to take out the driver of the SUV. Don't fire until you hear me shoot, but when I do, the pickup may slow or stop. You try to get that driver first. After that, we both just fire at whatever targets we've got. Clear?"

"Yes, ma'am."

Laura refocused, then took a deep breath and exhaled as her target made a slight change of direction and the glare off the windshield dissipated. She took another breath and held it as she slowly squeezed the trigger.

Beside her, Jana screamed, "MOM! DON'T—"

She felt the recoil of the unpadded stock into her shoulder as the gunshot echoed across the pasture.

"IT'S DAD!"

Even at a distance, she heard the crack as her bullet shattered the windshield, and watched horror-stricken as the SUV veered off the dirt track to come to rest in the field. Then tears flooded her eyes and nearly blinded her as she dropped the rifle and fought back great racking sobs, to rush across the pasture, screaming her husband's name.

DAY 17, 9:00 A.M.

"Missing? What the hell do you mean missing?" Spike McComb glared at Snaggle as the smaller man squirmed in the chair.

"Missing, that's all. They went out in their cruiser yesterday and they didn't come back, and they ain't answering the radio," Snaggle said.

"Who was it again?"

"Willard Jukes and Kyle Morgan."

"Wait a minute? Ain't those the two assholes doing all the bitching?"

Snaggle nodded. "The same."

"You don't think they did a jackrabbit, or maybe decided to go into business for themselves?"

"Well, maybe, but it don't seem likely. They'd have to know we'd find out, and then they'd be dead either way. Besides, I think they're both from around here somewhere, so I can't see no place for 'em to jackrabbit to. I think it's more likely they ran into trouble," Snaggle said.

McComb shook his head. "It don't matter. Only two things could have happened. Either somebody took 'em out, or they took off on their own, and we gotta deal with it either way. If someone took 'em out, we gotta find 'em and deal with it publicly so everyone knows not to mess with my PO-lice. And if they really did jackrabbit, especially after running their motormouths, we DEFINITELY have to bring 'em back and make an example of 'em. We can't have the rest of these assholes gettin' ideas." McComb paused. "Where was they working?"

"Last radio transmission said they was headed west toward the county line."

"All right, knock half the boys off whatever they're doin' and cover that area like a blanket. Find those assholes! And if they turn up dead, make sure people nearby know it ain't nice to piss off the PO-lice, but leave enough alive to spread the word."

"What if someone took 'em out and we can't figure out who did it?"

McComb released an exasperated sigh and shook his head.

"Jesus H. Christ, Snaggle! Do I have to do all the thinkin' around here? It don't MATTER who did it. You think we're gonna have a trial or something. Besides, why should I care who iced those ungrateful shitheads.

This is damage control. Just pick a few people nearby, SAY they did it, and kill 'em as an example. Got it?"

Snaggle nodded and rose from his chair.

"Wait a minute. You found that ship yet?"

"Not yet. The boys been having trouble getting the boat started, but last report I had said they should be on the river this morning. They'll find it. It's kind of hard to hide a ship."

CHAPTER SEVENTEEN

Singletary studied the chart intently, anxious to mask the fact he didn't have a clue where they were going. It backfired.

"For a guide, you sure got your nose buried in that map. You know where you going?" Jermain Ware asked.

"It's a chart, not a map, and around this next bend is the intersection with the Brunswick. We pass it by and stay right in this channel and go under the railroad bridge," Singletary said, hoping he was reading the damn chart right. He was on pins and needles as the boat turned left and it was all he could do to contain a relieved sigh as the railroad bridge and intersection came into view. Instead, he fixed Jermain with a superior look.

"What was that you was sayin'?"

Jermain grunted and guided the powerboat toward the railroad bridge, towing the other two boats, each with two men aboard. Once they were under the railroad bridge and around a bend, Singletary pointed ahead to the right.

"See that break in the bank over there?"

"Yeah, what about it?" Jermain asked.

"That's a little channel that runs alongside the river. We'll hide the powerboat there and go the rest of the way on the electrics."

"They damn slow! How far we got to go?"

"As far as I say, and they may be slow, but they're quiet. So unless you want to let everyone on the river know we're comin', why don't you do like I say?"

Jermain glared and turned toward the cut. Ten minutes later they had the powerboat anchored out of sight in the side channel and were shifting personnel between boats. Jermain took control of one of the electric-powered boats and indicated Singletary should join him. Singletary nodded and stood, his balance precarious as he held the iron ball.

"Look here," he said to Jermain and the other gangbanger in his boat. "One of y'all hold this damn steel ball for me so I can get over there."

Jermain smirked. "Hold it yourself, Mister High and Mighty River Guide."

"If I drown before y'all even get where y'all going because you gotta play the fool, just how pissed off you reckon Kwintell's gonna be?"

Jermain stared at Singletary for a long moment, then motioned the other man to take the steel ball. Unencumbered, Singletary transferred vessels easily and took his place at the front of the boat. He motioned Jermain to take off then immediately stopped him with a low cry.

"Hear that?" Singletary asked softly.

Jermain cocked an ear. "Sounds like another outboard coming downriver."

Singletary nodded. "Move the boat near the mouth, but keep it back out of sight. We'll be able to see 'em from behind after they pass. They won't see us unless they look back, so y'all stay quiet. We don't need no trouble now."

Jermain did as instructed, and the sound of the outboard increased. It was relatively quiet as outboards go, but still quite audible on the still river. The boat passed and Singletary could hardly believe his eyes. Levi was driving the boat with two women and two kids aboard, looking ahead and to both sides, but not back the way the boat had passed.

"Well, my, my, my," Singletary said softly, "don't that beat all. There goes Levi and his whole damn family. That only leaves the old man."

"Let's git 'em," Jermain said and turned the boat downstream.

"NO, FOOL!" Singletary hissed, terrified at the thought of getting into a running gunfight on the river with thirty pounds of iron shackled to his leg. He immediately regretted his choice of words as Jermain's hand flew to his sidearm.

"I mean that's not a good idea," Singletary said. "We can't catch 'em on the electrics, and if we switch over to the powerboat, we can't sneak up on 'em 'cause they'll hear the motor. It will take a while to catch 'em, and all that time, Levi can be layin' into us with that rifle, and it ain't like we'll have any cover."

Jermain seemed to be unsure, and Singletary pressed the point.

"Besides, they likely got a radio and they might call the Coasties or alert the old man back at their camp, and that would screw everything up. But this is perfect. Let 'em go about their business, and we just sashay on up the river quiet like and take the old man by surprise and clean out their camp. Then we leave a couple of boys there to wait for them to get back and surprise them and take whatever they bring back from Wilmington. I say we stay right here and let 'em get well out of sight around the bend, then head upriver just like we planned."

Jermain scowled and reached for their own radio. "I'm gonna call Kwintell and see what we should do."

Singletary shook his head. "That's exactly the wrong thing to do. You'd have to spell it all out in plain English for him to understand, and what do you want to bet them Coasties don't have a scanner, listenin' to radio traffic? They hear, they'll call Levi or the old man at his camp for sure, then we lost the surprise."

Jermain hesitated, obviously resistant to taking direction from Singletary but unable to deny the logic of his observations. Finally he nodded.

"All right," he said, and they sat there watching and waiting as Levi's boat disappeared around the bend. They waited a few minutes longer for the sound of the outboard to fade, then turned upriver, the powerful little trolling motors pushing the boats at a moderate but steady pace.

Singletary's mind raced. He'd racked his brain for a plan B ever since the ball was clamped on his leg, but now he saw a light at the end of the tunnel. Finding Levi's camp now offered his very best chance to survive, come what may. He had no doubt Jermain and the rest of the bangers would make short work of the old man, and then pitch in to loot the camp. At that point, he'd be on dry land and out of immediate danger, but the ball would preclude his participation in the looting. He might be able to slip away when they were focused on their task, or failing that, talk Jermain into leaving him as part of the crew to await Levi's return.

He liked his chances if left alone with only one of the others, who would now be more inclined to trust him, and there would likely be tools about the place he might use to free himself and escape. And even supposing none of those opportunities presented themselves, his success in delivering on his promise would prove his worth to Kwintell. He'd petition to join the gang and look for opportunities to escape when he wasn't being watched so closely. One way or another, he'd survive.

He bent his head to the chart. From what he'd overheard, he knew the camp was on the Black River, which joined the Cape Fear River some distance upstream. From the chart, the Black would be the larger right branch of the fork, some distance ahead. It didn't look like he could miss it, but after the fork things got tricky. All he could do was start looking for a stand of willow trees on the bank and hope he could spot it. His task was complicated by his urban roots—he had only a vague idea what a willow tree looked like, though he was pretty sure from the description it was droopy looking. He hoped like hell there weren't a lot of droopy-looking trees.

"How much farther?" Jermaine asked.

"It's a ways. We'll go right at the fork of the Cape Fear and the Black," Singletary said, with a confidence he didn't feel.

Time dragged as the little trolling motors powered them upstream at a steady clip, and Singletary began to worry they might run out of battery before they reached their destination. Then he relaxed as they swept around a long bend to the right and came upon the fork in the rivers.

"This is it. Keep to the right," he said.

"How far after that?" Jermain asked.

"A ways," Singletary said. "I only been there once, but I'll recognize it when I see it."

"Which side of the river?"

Fear shot through Singletary at the unanticipated but obvious question.

"The east bank," he said, glancing back at Jermain.

He suppressed a smile at the look of confusion on Jermain's face, and hoped pride would preclude any follow-up questions. Sure enough, the man's fear of appearing ignorant overcame his curiosity as to which side of the river they were searching, and he just nodded, as if satisfied with the answer. Singletary went back to scanning both sides of the river for droopy-looking trees.

Only belatedly did he realize Jermain's question presented another problem—he had to pick the right spot, or at least the correct side of the river—the first time. If they inspected an area on the right bank and it wasn't the entrance, he might be able to pass it off as a mistake and keep on looking. However, he couldn't then inspect a place on the left bank without revealing he was clueless. Jermain was ignorant, not stupid.

Tension built as they glided upstream, and a likely looking stand of trees grew close to the left bank, but they didn't quite fit Singletary's mental image. His forbearance was rewarded moments later as they rounded a bend and he spotted a much more likely prospect on the right bank—a stand of trees right on the water's edge, long limbs drooping over the river and trailing whiplike tendrils down to brush the water, shrouding the riverbank like a curtain. He hedged his bets with Jermain a bit.

"I believe this is it," he said quietly to Jermain. "Just nose the boat through them limbs hangin' down and let's make sure there's an inlet. A lot of these places look alike on the river, but it's either this one or the next."

Jermain reduced speed, barely moving as he nosed the boat up to the willow curtain at a right angle to the bank. The second gangbanger joined Singletary in the bow and they parted the thick willow curtain with their arms as the boat nudged through it. Sure enough, after working their way through a ten-foot thickness of trailing willow tendrils, the bow of the boat broke into a clear area, and they found themselves floating in a twenty-foot-wide channel, running inland at a right angle to the river between the trunks of two massive willow trees. It was dark and cool beneath the trees and Singletary could see the channel was obscured further on by a similar willow curtain.

He nodded up the little inlet. "You go through that and Levi's camp is just beyond."

"How far?"

Singletary had anticipated the question and dropped the last bit of info he'd gleaned from overheard conversation.

"A ways. There's a little dock, but you can't see it from the house."

Jermain nodded and moved to start the trolling motor.

"Wait a minute!" Singletary hissed. "What's the plan?"

Jermain shrugged. "One old man? I figure we just tie up at this dock and go up quiet like and surprise him. He gives us any trouble, we cap his ass. Why we need a plan?"

"What about me?"

"You stay in the boat. We'll come back and take care... we'll come back and get you later."

Jermain nudged the boat forward to make room for the second boat to move into the clearing near the tree trunks, and it suddenly occurred to Singletary he hadn't been the only one with a plan. Jermain wasn't likely to share credit with anyone for a successful raid.

After a hushed exchange with his men in the other boat, Jermain started through the second willow curtain as Singletary began to rapidly recalculate his own odds for survival. His mental exercise was interrupted by an event that changed those odds significantly, and not for the better.

The thick, heavy snake landed across Singletary's shoulders with a dull thud, surprising the snake perhaps almost as much as Singletary. As Singletary's terrified scream pierced the air, the equally frightened snake responded in kind, striking Singletary's right bicep. Singletary leaped to his feet, fighting the willow limbs and shaking his arm in an attempt to sling the snake off. He managed to break free of the snake's bite, but success was overshadowed as he lost his balance and plunged backward out of the boat, dragging his steel ball with him as five feet of pissed-off snake flew around the bottom of the boat.

Jermain and the other banger were on their feet now, screaming as well as they tried to avoid the snake. Then terror overcame common sense and their response was as dumb as it was inevitable. They drew their weapons and five seconds and twenty rounds later, the bottom of the aluminum boat was like Swiss cheese. As the boat sank, the snake swam away unharmed, perhaps the only participant satisfied with the results of the encounter.

The water was only six feet deep, and Singletary bobbed up and down off the bottom, dragging his leg ball through the mud until he could grab a protruding tree root and pull himself to the bank.

"HE BIT ME!" Singletary wailed. "I NEED A DOCTOR."

"If you don't shut up, I'm gonna cap you right here," Jermain said, hanging onto the side of the second boat.

"What we gonna do, Jermain?" the driver of the second boat asked.

"Pull us aboard and let's get to that dock. We need to take care of the old man, but it ain't gonna be no surprise now."

"What about him," the driver asked, nodding toward Singletary.

"Leave the fool here. We'll worry about him later."

**

Anthony McCoy's head jerked at the sound of the screams. He dumped the chicken feed on the ground and tossed the bowl aside to wade through the flocking chickens to his shotgun leaning against the house. The sound of rapid gunfire removed any thoughts of rescuing someone in distress. That much firepower this close to the camp could only mean trouble.

The disturbance came from the river, and he headed down the now well-worn path, but quickly thought better of it. He moved into the woods, paralleling the path and out of sight until he understood the situation. Staking out a position in the woods near the dock, he'd hardly settled in to his hideout when a boat pushed through the willow curtain with five heavily armed men aboard.

His first thought was of his family. Had they been caught on the river and attacked? Unlikely. Even if they'd been attacked and succumbed, Levi would have had time to get off a warning, and besides, sound travels far over water and he'd heard no gunfire. No, the camp was clearly the target, and he was both outnumbered and outgunned, and if they spread out, it would be difficult to defend against them. It was best to even the odds a bit while they were all together in the boat, but the shotgun presented problems of range and accuracy. The dock was at least fifty yards away and they were some distance farther.

He cursed himself for a stubborn old fool and wished he'd followed Levi's advice and started to carry the AR, or better yet, one of the M4s they'd gotten from the Coasties. Then he willed himself calm. His daddy had given him the Winchester Model 12 when he was ten years old, and the old twelve gauge had put a lot of meat on the table over the years—and even 'discouraged' a bunch of wannabee Klansmen one dark night years ago. He reckoned he could handle a bunch of bangers. Besides, his vision was none too good anymore, and it was comforting to know he just had to get in the vicinity.

He let the boat draw close and opened fire just before it reached the dock. His first load spread to punch into the boat driver's chest in a half-dozen places, and the man slumped as the boat veered away from the dock to push bow first into the opposite bank of the narrow inlet. Anthony ejected the shell before the man had even toppled over, and pumped four more loads of double-ought buckshot at the boat in quick succession. At least one more of the attackers was down, and all were showing signs of being hit, but two recovered quickly and began firing in his direction, wildly and without focus. He melted back into the woods to contemplate his next move.

***

Jermain rolled the dead driver out of the boat and took his place at the tiller of the trolling motor. Buckshot from one of the shotgun blasts had hit right at the waterline, and water leaked through the aluminum hull in half a dozen places to slosh around his feet. He cursed as he backed off the bank and swung the boat back over to the little dock. He'd lost one man killed outright and another seemed to be seriously wounded, and the rest of them suffered multiple non-life-threatening wounds in arms or legs. He was pissed.

He looked over to his least injured men leaning over a figure slumped in the bottom of the boat.

"How's Tyrone?" he asked.

"Gut shot—it's bad, man. He ain't gonna make it."

He cursed as he struggled out of the boat, nursing a leg wound, and tied off to the little dock.

"Leave him," he said to the man caring for Tyrone. "Y'all come on, but get the radio off Tyrone. I need to call Kwintell behind this shit."

The man shook his head and held up the radio. "Radio's busted. Looks like it took a bullet."

"Shit! All right, y'all come on. We gotta get that old fart."

One of the survivors shook his head. "I took one in the shoulder and can't move my right arm. I can't handle the AK."

Jermain removed his sidearm and held it out. "Then use this and shoot left-handed."

The man shook his head again. "But I can't hit nothin' with no pistol in my left—"

"TAKE THE GUN, GET YOUR SORRY ASS OUTA THAT BOAT, AND DO WHAT I TELL YOU OR I'LL CAP YOUR ASS RIGHT HERE! YOU UNDERSTAND?"

Cowed, the man nodded, and Jermain turned to his other soldier. "How 'bout you?"

"I took one in the leg, but I'm okay," the man said.

"All right. We goin' after him, but he's likely layin' up somewhere to ambush us again. We need to spread out so he can't target us all at one time. I'll go into the woods fifty feet or so, you"—he pointed to the man with the shoulder wound—"stay in the edge of the woods near the path, and you"—he nodded at the last man—"stay halfway between us. Then we all move together toward the house. He'll likely try to take one of you two, and when he does, I want the other one to open up on him, full auto. Force him down and keep his head down, to give me a chance to close on him fast. He likely won't hear me over the gunfire, and we can take him out fast. Any questions?"

The pair nodded, their expressions leaving no doubt about their lack of enthusiasm for the plan, but neither was willing to trade the 'possibility' of death for the certainty of it if they crossed Jermaine. They took their assigned positions and began moving through the trees.

***

Anthony knew one was down for sure, and possibly a second, and he wanted to take out at least one or maybe two more on his 'fighting retreat.'

They'd undoubtedly split up now to hit him from different angles, but if he struck again quickly, they wouldn't have a chance to get too spread out. The more he evened the odds now, the easier it would be later. He picked a likely spot twenty yards or so off the path and crouched behind the thick trunk of a white oak and waited for his next target. He didn't have to wait long.

The man was approaching from his left, just off the path in the tree line, and Anthony heard him long before he began to catch brief glimpses through the relatively thin cover near the path. The banger was obviously injured; his right arm hung useless at his side and blood ran off his fingertips, staining the ground. He held an automatic pistol awkwardly in a left-handed grip. Anthony could tell by looking the man wasn't a lefty. The shotgun would win that gunfight hands down, long before the man got close enough to hit him.

He heard another man approaching to his right, some distance away, but the cover was thicker there, and he couldn't see his attacker. He surmised they were coming in a line, with any others perhaps too far to his right to be heard, and began to worry about being flanked if he got pinned down. He definitely had to fall back, but needed to cut down the odds a bit first.

The injured man with the pistol was the logical target, but also the lesser threat, and taking down the still-invisible man to his right would definitely do more to even the odds. He decided to try for a double, figuring even if he missed the second man, he'd instill caution and buy time to get to his next hide.

He swung the shotgun toward the man with the pistol, waiting for him to step into a gap between the trees, then fired. A tight pattern of buckshot riddled his target's midsection, and Anthony ejected the shell and swung the gun before the man even hit the ground. He pumped four loads of buckshot through the foliage in the direction of his unseen stalker, and turned to run, moving as fast as his old legs allowed. He stuck to the path now, knowing he'd make better time, and confident the surviving attackers were in the thick woods to the west.

His breath was coming in gasps and he was halfway to the cabin when a man stepped from behind a big tree and slammed the butt of an assault rifle into his gut.

***

Jermain moved through the thick woods at a hobbling run, as fast as his injured leg would allow, his noisy passage masked by distance. He figured the old man would set up another ambush closer to the path; that was the logical thing to do. His reluctantly advancing underlings would trigger that trap, spurred on by the thought Jermain was at the far end of their short line of advance, ready to deal with them if they faltered. But unknown to them, he'd already rushed ahead, moving fast and circling wide in an attempt to take the old man from behind.

There were only two possible outcomes: his men would pin the old man down or the old man would win the fight and fall back looking for a new ambush site, and Jermain was prepared for either eventuality. If his men survived the ambush and pinned the old bastard down, he'd creep up from behind and back shoot him. But if the old man sprang his trap successfully and then retreated, Jermain would become the ambusher. Either way, the old man was going down.

He ran on, adrenaline masking the pain in his leg, and when he thought he'd gone far enough, angled right, moving to intersect the path. The woods began to thin a bit, and he was brought up short by the sound of gunfire—a single shotgun blast followed by four more in rapid succession—with no return fire. His men were either down or cowering, and either way he expected the old man to fall back in his direction. He took a position near the path behind a thick tree trunk and was rewarded moments later by the sound of boots pounding the packed earth and labored breathing. He steadied his AK against the tree, sighting up the path. The old man came into sight, running hell-bent for leather with his eyes on the path immediately ahead of him, oblivious to the threat farther down the path. Jermain aimed—and then thought better of it.

What if they had the good stuff hidden? The old man would be the only one who knew where it was. He couldn't call for reinforcements to search the place because the radio was shot up, and he sure as hell didn't want to be here by himself when that Levi asshole got back. And showing up empty-handed after losing his whole crew to one old man and then trying to explain to Kwintell didn't bear thinking about. He knew his odds of survival would be infinitely improved with a few cases of grenades or the gold and silver that fool Singletary was always babbling about. No way round it, he had to take the old man alive. Of course, he didn't have to be gentle.

He dodged back behind the tree and reversed his grip on the rifle, waiting for the old man to approach. He sprang from hiding to slam the rifle butt into his quarry's gut, sending the shotgun flying and dropping the old man flat on his back. Jermain flipped the old man onto his stomach and flex-cuffed his hands behind him with an electrical tie, then dragged him to his feet and pushed him down the trail toward the camp.

***

The thug heaved the rope a final time, and Anthony came almost off the ground, forced on tiptoe to relieve the racking pain in his arms and shoulders. He was suspended by his wrists from a crossbeam of the outdoor kitchen, and the sharp pain in his gut from the rifle butt was quickly palling compared to this latest abuse of his aging body. He stifled a moan and glared at the banger as the man tied the end of the rope to one of the support poles. He took satisfaction from the blood staining the leg of the man's jeans and his awkward movement, and regretted he'd failed to make every shotgun blast accurate. The man pulled the knot tight and limped back toward him.

"Now, old man, we gonna have us a little talk." The thug smiled. "You a pretty tough old bastard, I'll give you that. I looked around a little and y'all got a good setup here too. Thing is, I couldn't find the really good stuff, so you gonna tell me where you got it hid."

"What the hell are you talking about? We don't have anything hidden. It's ALL hidden here in the woods, so why would we need to hide anything from each other?"

"Don't play stupid! You know what I'm talkin' about. Where are the grenades, and the gold and silver?"

"Grenades? Gold? Silver? You been smokin' crack? Why would we have any of that stuff? We sure couldn't eat it."

"Don't act dumb. I know you got grenades from them soldiers at Wilmington, and Singletary told us about the gold and silver—"

Anthony scoffed. "SINGLETARY! So that's why you're here? Anybody stupid enough to listen to that fool is dumber than a box of—"

The blow was unexpected, driving into Anthony's midsection in the same place the rifle butt landed. The result was involuntary and equally unexpected, as the contents of his stomach erupted from his mouth, spraying into the thug's face. The man jumped back, then stood stock-still for a long moment, Anthony's vomit dripping from his chin. The rage seemed to build almost visibly until the thug trembled with rage, and he dipped a hand into his pocket to fish out a switchblade. The knife sprang open with an audible click.

"We still got some talkin' to do, old man, but you don't need your balls for that. Fact is, I figure an old man like you don't need 'em no way, so I'm gonna do you a favor and take 'em off."

Less belligerent now, Anthony closed his eyes and steeled himself as he felt the thug tugging at his belt, then something warm and wet splashed his face—followed a fraction of a second later by the unmistakable crack of a gunshot.

***

Anthony lay on the ground and braced himself as the big man probed his tender belly, looking over the man's broad back at the men standing behind him.

"I'm obliged, Vernon," Anthony said. "If y'all showed up a few minutes later, I reckon I'd have been changin' rows in the church choir."

Vern Gibson laughed. "Glad to help another river rat, Anthony, though I didn't know you were one. I figured you'd be at your place in Currie. When did y'all move here to the river?"

"Soon as the power went out. Levi figured it wasn't coming back anytime soon, and we were way too exposed on the county road."

Vern nodded. "That's a fact, though it looks like you're attracting a fair amount of trouble here too. Held your own right well too—taking down five out of six ain't bad."

"Five? I only got four that I know of."

"I was giving you credit for the snake-bit one we found in the willows," Vern said.

"Well, I'll be damned," Anthony said, "so THAT was the ruckus, then. Hadn't been for that snake, they'd have caught me flat-footed for sure. Guess they serve a purpose after all. Anyway, I'm obliged to you."

Vern nodded to the big man examining Anthony. "Then you ought to thank Sergeant Washington here. He took out the banger."

The big man finished his examination of Anthony and rocked back on his knees and flashed an embarrassed smile.

"And I do thank you, Sergeant," Anthony said.

"Not necessary, Mr. Jenkins," Washington said, "all in a day's work."

"How's it look, Washington?" said a young man who looked somehow familiar.

Washington shook his head. "I'm not a medic, Lieutenant Kinsey, but I think he's gonna be okay. He really needs to see a doctor, though."

"Kinsey," Anthony said. "I knew that face looked familiar. Your daddy in the Coast Guard?"

"Yes, sir," the man replied. "Is he here? I'm looking for him."

Anthony shook his head. "He took off a week ago on a ship headed to Texas. But I reckon they're checking in with the folks at Wilmington. We got a radio here, but their antenna is much taller. They can pass a message to him for sure."

The young man let out a relieved sigh. "Well, that's about the best news I've heard in a while. At least I know he's okay."

"Is there a doctor in Wilmington?" Vern Gibson asked.

"There was a medic with the National Guard unit," Anthony said, "and they were going to try to find medical personnel among the refugees, but I don't know if they did. But y'all don't worry about me. I'm fine right here."

"We're not leaving you," Vern said, "even if we got to tie you up. You need to get checked out."

"Somebody's got to stay here and feed the animals," Anthony protested.

"I reckon rabbits and chickens can get by on their own a few days," Vern Gibson said, "but even if they can't, we can cover it." He looked at Luke Kinsey. "You got 'em fed for today, and we'll likely overnight in Wilmington and head back up to our place tomorrow, so we'll stop in and check on them. Then we'll come down every day until y'all get back. How's that?"

"You don't have—"

"I know I don't HAVE to do it, but it's what neighbors do, and things bein' like they are, we're all gonna need good neighbors, Anthony."

Anthony grew quiet, then nodded. "I expect I can't argue with that. All right, have it your way. I'm all right, but I'll go get checked out if it makes you feel better. I gotta tell Levi and the others what happened anyway and I don't want to go into it over the radio. No tellin' what that puke Singletary told those bangers. I don't know how he found us to start with, but if they know we're here, I expect this isn't the end of our problems."

APPALACHIAN TRAIL
MILE 998.6 NORTHBOUND
JUST SOUTH OF BEAR'S DEN

DAY 17, 8:45 A.M.

George Anderson gasped as he sprinted up the hill, back toward Bear's Den, the gun belt on and the other items Tremble left in his pockets. He'd worked his way out of the paracord in less than ten minutes, but knew that was by design. He might be a country boy, but he knew a setup when he saw one, and he sure as hell didn't intend to be Tremble's diversion. Not that he didn't intend to bolt—he had no doubt he was on borrowed time as far as FEMA was concerned, and hauling ass was his last chance. However, he also knew his chances of outrunning pursuit were somewhere between slim and none, and the first thing they'd do when he didn't respond was deploy the chopper to check things out. They'd likely start with the known position of the car and work outward with IR scans. Ground teams were sure to follow, and quickly, but they'd take at least a half hour to get here, and the first priority was getting invisible to the chopper and fast.

He glanced at his watch as he broke into the clearing around Bear's Den and dashed toward the hostel. Their car sat right where they'd left it, and he changed course slightly, ripping open the door to grab the two half-full bottles of lukewarm water from the cup holders, stuffing one in each pocket before slamming the door and racing for the hikers' entrance at the back of the hostel. He moved inside, confident the thick stone walls of the building would mask his body heat, leaving only the task of finding a hiding place to wait out the ground search. Anderson liked his chances. The ground around the hostel and the various trails were now a confused welter of tracks, and four of the people making them were wearing standard-issue FEMA boots. With his partner's body likely to draw the search to the AT, the building itself was the last place they'd look, so he started a search for a hiding place.

He found it quickly—a deep narrow storage closet off the hikers' bunk area, almost empty. He grabbed a mattress off one of the bunks and maneuvered it through the closet door. Standing on end, it spanned the closet from side to side almost exactly. Perfect, he thought, and leaned the mattress out of the way against the long wall of the closet and went to the bathroom, hoping to drain a little water from the pipes to augment his meager supply. He was elated when water gushed from the faucet. Better and better, he thought, as he filled his bottles. He grabbed a small plastic trash can, in case nature called, and carried his amenities into the far end of the narrow closet and set them on the floor before returning for an armload of towels. The floor might get pretty hard over time and a little padding couldn't hurt.

In final preparation, he pulled three more mattresses off the bunks, standing them on end and leaning them in a row along the inside wall of the deep closet. He then maneuvered the mattress nearest the door across the width of the closet as he backed deeper inside the closet dragging it behind him. When he got to the next mattress, he let the top of the one he was dragging lean toward him a bit, then tossed it away from him and quickly flipped the next mattress across the closet in front of it before the first fell back against it. He repeated the process with the remaining two mattresses, dragging each back a foot or so each time. The top of the last one came to rest against the back wall of the closet, forming a nice little triangular cave near the floor of the closet, his shelter from prying eyes. All anyone looking in would see was a haphazard stack of mattresses in storage, filling the closet.

Anderson settled in to wait and thought about Tremble. Two can play this game, Congressman, and I'm not gonna be your damned decoy. In fact, maybe you'll be mine.

Tremble's arms and shoulders burned as he grasped his end of the stretcher and struggled up the steep hill behind Wiggins, straining to keep up with a man two decades his junior. Then he heard the distant thump of chopper blades to the south.

"TEX!" he called ahead. "I HEAR A CHOPPER. FIND US A SPOT OFF THE TRAIL AND GET THE SHELTER RIGGED FAST. WE DON'T HAVE MUCH TIME."

Tex raised her arm in acknowledgment and darted off the trail to her right. Without urging, Wiggins picked up the pace until he reached the point Tex left the trail and followed her path. They found her a hundred feet off the trail where the steep hillside shelved a bit, tightening a length of paracord between two trees. She finished as they set the stretcher down, and began throwing one of their two 'space blankets' over the taut cord.

She tossed some small plastic tent stakes in Wiggins' direction.

"We've only got enough stakes to do the corners. Find a rock and help me pound these in," she said, then turned to Simon. "It will probably be easier if you help Keith crawl under while we set it up. We're going to have to lay on top of each other to fit anyway."

Simon nodded and helped Keith hobble over to crawl under one side of the emerging pup tent before it was staked down.

"I'll stack all our other gear on the stretcher and spread the other blanket over it to shield any residual body heat," Tremble said, and the others only nodded as they worked feverishly, driven by the increasing volume of the approaching chopper.

Tremble finished and crawled into the end of the makeshift tent next to Keith as Tex and Wiggins finished pounding in the stakes.

"Remember to bring those rocks in with you. They may have residual heat from your hands," Tremble called and got grunts of affirmation moments before Tremble was grunting himself as Wiggins crawled through the opening to lie on top of him.

"Damn, Wiggins, you're a heavy bastard, and watch where you put your hands." Keith stifled a laugh in spite of the circumstances and then grunted himself as Tex crawled on top of him.

"I think I got the better deal, Dad," Keith said.

"Yeah, well, don't get excited, Romeo, or you'll find my knee in your balls," Tex said.

They lay sweating under the thermal blanket as the chopper drew nearer.

"You really think this is gonna work, Simon?" Tex asked.

"No clue," Tremble said, "but it was the only thing I could think of. The foliage is too thick for them to get a visual and it's pretty hot out, so there shouldn't be much of a temperature differential. With the blanket masking most of our thermal signature, I think we at least have a shot."

They fell silent as they willed the chopper to pass, and heaved a collective sigh as it continued north without slowing. They lay there another twenty minutes as the chopper reached the northernmost limit of its search pattern and flew back south, some distance away. Only when the thump of the blades had completely faded did they crawl from their improvised shelter.

"That bought us a little more time, at least," Tremble said as they folded their shelter. "But when they come back, they'll be searching on foot as well, and we can't hope to outrun them. We need to open up the lead and find a place well off the trail to hide a while."

"Why didn't we hear anything on the radio?" Tex asked.

Tremble shook his head. "We didn't hear anything on ours either after they realized we likely had one, so they must have changed frequencies. That's pretty much standard procedure if comms are compromised. And they probably suspected something after George's last transmission. At this point the radio's dead weight. I'll bury it here before we leave."

"You said hide 'a while.' How long is a while? I need to get home to my family," Wiggins said.

"Which won't happen if these guys find you," Tremble said. "We have to lay low several days at least."

"How long do you think we have to find a place to hole up?" Tex asked.

"I'd say that depends on whether our friend George is able to lead them on a merry chase in the opposite direction," Tremble said.

DAY 17, 9:40 A.M.

Gleason saw the number on the caller ID and snatched up the buzzing phone.

"It's about damn time, Crawford. You were supposed to call me hours ago, so you better have good news."

Crawford's hesitation told him all that needed saying.

"DON'T FRIGGIN' TELL ME HE GOT AWAY!"

"It... it's only a temporary setback, Mr. President. We have teams on them and—"

"You had a team on them at the butt crack of dawn! What the hell happened?"

"The first team did apprehend them and were bringing them in. With them in custody, we stood down the rest of the search, figuring it was best to try to keep the operation as low key as possible—"

"So how did we get from 'in custody' to 'we don't have them'?"

"I'm afraid the Trembles are proving more... resourceful than we'd anticipated. They managed to kill one of the team members and the other is missing—"

"Missing? What the hell do you mean missing? So Tremble is a friggin' magician now?"

"I mean neither he nor his body are anywhere to be found. We're beginning to suspect he may be in league with Tremble and—"

Gleason erupted, heaping obscenities and abuse on Crawford for a full minute, only stopping when he ran out of bile and began to repeat himself. The silence grew until Gleason himself broke it, calmer now.

"All right, what are you doing to recapture them?"

"We have a chopper up with infrared telemetry, searching likely areas, as well as search teams working both north and south on the Appalachian Trail. They don't have a vehicle—"

"That you know of," Gleason said.

"That's correct, Mr. President, but there are few roads in the area and less vehicle traffic due to the fuel shortage. I'm confident they're still afoot, and if they break the cover of the woods, we'll be on them in a heartbeat. We've already contained them by putting up roadblocks on the few roads into and out of the search area. It is a bit of a needle in a haystack, but they most assuredly are trapped in the haystack."

"All right, that's something anyway. Tremble can wander around the woods like Moses in the damned wilderness for all I care, as long as he doesn't get a chance to communicate what he knows. Thank God he hasn't been in contact with anyone else."

Silence.

"He HASN'T been in contact with anyone else HAS he?"

"There is... some evidence he may have been in contact with an unidentified hiker—"

"Christ on a crutch, Crawford—"

"But we're handling it, Mr. President. We're treating anyone we find in or exiting the search area as a potential witness."

Gleason sighed. "All right. That sounds like all we can do at the moment, but prioritize the search. Keep your roadblocks and containment efforts in place until we recapture or terminate them, but focus your search to the south. They'll be trying to get home to North Carolina, where Tremble has family and a network of personal contacts. And he may not be a spring chicken, but he has had all that snake-eater evasion and escape training, so his best shot is probably staying in the woods anyway. I want you covering the trails south like a blanket, is that understood?"

"Yes, Mr. President. I won't fail you."

"You've already failed me, Crawford, and if you do it again, you're going to get to enjoy the 'fugee camp experience, up close and personal. We might even let your new neighbors know you're the architect of their lavish lifestyle."

Gleason hung up before Crawford could respond.

HUGHES' RESIDENCE
PECAN GROVE
OLEANDER, TEXAS

DAY 17, 1:00 P.M.

Laura Hughes sat at the dining room table, struggling to deal with the flood of emotions washing over her as she clutched her husband's hand: relief, unbridled joy—and anger. He sat beside her, dealing with emotions of his own, as their twin daughters crowded round, standing at each shoulder with the whole family touching as if to assure themselves they were indeed, all together and safe once again.

"Jordan Hughes, whatever were you thinking, roaring up through the pasture like that? I almost killed you." She could hear the tremor in her own voice and knew she was near an emotional breakdown.

Jordan reached over and pulled her to him in a fierce hug. "But you didn't and that's all that matters. And I was thinking we needed to stay off the roads, but in hindsight we should have stopped well out and sounded the horn and gotten out. I'm sorry, sweetheart, but I was so concerned about getting home to you and the girls I never gave a thought to how roaring up unannounced and unexpected would look from your side." He flashed the lopsided grin she loved. "Besides, I'm still learning the finer points of this 'end of the world' stuff."

She hugged him back then pulled away and wiped her eyes with the back of her hand.

"Well, you're home now, so it's all good." She looked over to where Kinsey and his two men stood, staying politely out of the way while the family reconnected. "And where are my manners? Chief Kinsey, it's past lunchtime and I expect you and your men could do with something to eat. We normally just have a cold lunch in this heat, if that's okay. The girls and I will put together some sandwiches, and we've all the iced tea you can drink."

"That sounds great, ma'am," Kinsey said, "but don't go to any trouble."

"It's the least I can do for y'all helping Jordan get home. We have plenty of food AND room, so y'all are free to stay as long as you like. As a matter of fact, given how things are, having some more men about would be reassuring."

Kinsey said nothing but shot a knowing look at Hughes. Laura followed the silent exchange then focused on her husband.

"What was that look about?"

"Ah, Laura, I can't stay. I've got *Pecos Trader* anchored in the river with a lot of folk on board I'm responsible for—"

"What do you mean you can't stay, Jordan! You can't leave us—"

"I have absolutely no intention of leaving you, honey. We came to get you and the girls and take you back to the ship. We have plenty of stores there, and it will be a safe place to stay until we figure out what we're going to do."

"What do you mean, what we're going to do? We're going to stay here, of course. We have plenty here, and with the garden and the generator keeping the freezer going and the pantry, we can just stay here until they get the power restored and things get back to normal."

Hughes fell silent and exchanged another look with Kinsey.

"That's just it, Laura, the power's not coming back on, at least for a long, long time—years, not months. And things... things might never get back to normal, at least what we used to think of as normal."

Laura shook her head. "We've been without power longer than this after hurricanes. It's just going to take a while, that's all."

"No, babe," Hughes said gently, "it's not like that, because the power's down everywhere, and there are no spares to fix the problem. I don't fully understand it all myself, but I've seen enough to know we're not recovering from this anytime soon. Have you seen any linemen working anywhere or picked up any television signal at all when you have the power on?"

"No, but that doesn't mean—"

"Yes, I'm afraid it does. And it's only been three weeks, so things are going to get a whole lot worse. We probably can't imagine how bad it's going to get. I need to know you and the girls are safe, or at least as safe as I can make you."

Laura's face hardened. "Jordan Hughes, counting the girls, my family has lived at Pecan Grove for six generations, and I'll be damned if I'm abandoning it to let it be overrun by a bunch of looters! I'm staying right here!"

"Ah, Captain, I think me and the boys are going outside to do a security check on the perimeter while you folks discuss this," Kinsey said, then exited the room when Hughes nodded.

Hughes turned back to his wife and gave an exasperated sigh before running his hands through his hair. "Honey, even if I could justify abandoning the ship and the people on it—"

"It's a JOB, Jordan, it's not some holy mission. And your family should come first!"

"You DO come first, which is why y'all need to come back to the ship. It's safer there, and this place is practically impossible to defend, even if I stay—"

Laura glared at him. "We've done okay so far."

Both the twins nodded emphatically. "Mom's right, Dad," Jana said. "When the fake cops came—"

"What fake cops? What are you talking about?"

Laura suddenly looked less sure of herself. "We... we had some trouble yesterday. Some men came, dressed like sheriff's deputies, but I'm pretty sure they were convicts. They had a lot of tattoos."

Shaken, Hughes dragged the story out of her, including the less than successful attempt at sinking the car.

When she finished, he sat shaking his head, stunned at how close his family had come to tragedy.

"That clinches it, Laura, we HAVE to leave now. If those guys radioed in your location before they rolled in here, or if any of their buddies knew where they were headed and come looking for them, this is the first place they'll look. The pecan grove rising out of this flat pastureland draws in people like a magnet and you know it. If you won't think of yourself, at least think of the girls."

"Maybe that was just an isolated thing," she said, uncertainty in her voice.

"No way," Hughes responded. "We ran into fake cops in Port Arthur on our way in, also with skinhead tattoos—two times isn't a coincidence. If they're riding around unmolested in police uniforms and cruisers, I'm guessing it means there's no one left to challenge them. They'll be here sooner or later. You can count on it, and we can't be here when they come."

"But what about the food and supplies, and the garden, and the horses... someone has to feed the horses."

"We have plenty of food and supplies on the ship, at least for now. We'll gather up all the long-life supplies and make a hidden cache somewhere, just in case we ever have to leave the ship. We'll shut down the generator and hide it as well, and take anything frozen or refrigerated to the ship. And we can turn the horses out in the pasture, there's plenty of grazing here, and they can drink from the pond."

Laura looked around the room, no doubt grieving for over a century of pictures and family heirlooms she would have to abandon. Finally she seemed to steel herself and nod.

"You're right. Things can be replaced, but family can't. All we need to survive is each other, because if we don't have that, nothing else matters anyway. When do you want to leave?"

Hughes looked at his watch. "Sunset's around eight, and I'd like to be back on board before full dark. I figure to leave an hour and a half travel time, just in case we run into trouble. That gives us five hours to pack and get out of here. Can you make that?"

Laura stood. "We can do anything we have to do, but we won't be serving lunch. I'll throw some cold cuts and fresh baked bread on the kitchen counter and people can help themselves when they take a break. Come on, girls, I want to get up in the attic and start dumping out some of the plastic storage tubs we have up there. We can use them to cache the nonperishable stuff. And if we have time, I want to hide family pictures and other stuff up there in the attic. If we take the rope off the pull-down stairway and pin it closed with a dozen wood screws, it might discourage looters, the lazy ones, anyway."

"Good idea," Hughes said, "I'll go get the Coasties to help us."

***

Four hours later, Hughes stood in the barn, surveying the large circular hay bales stacked against one wall. There was a carefully constructed gap in the stack, a bit over three feet wide and bridged over by an inch-thick sheet of plywood resting on top of the first tier of hay bales, a quickly constructed hiding place for not only their generator, but stacks of plastic tubs containing all their nonperishable food.

"Whadda ya think?" he asked.

Laura examined the hastily improvised cache with a critical eye, then nodded.

"I think it will work, and it's a lot better than burying the stuff. Wet as the ground can get around here, I'd worry about the seal on the tubs anyway, and fresh dirt would probably be a dead giveaway. Those round bales weigh a thousand pounds each, and when you bury our cache under a couple of more rows of those, no one's getting at it."

"I agree, "Kinsey said, "though playing the devil's advocate, what if someone just cranks up the tractor and starts moving bales. I know it's unlikely, but still…"

Hughes stroked his chin, then nodded. "Good point. When I finish stacking the bales, I'll pull all the tractor spark plugs and fuses and hide them under the loose hay up in the hay loft. I'd just as soon not make it easy for someone to steal the tractor anyway. And since that's going to add a few minutes, I'd better get moving. Is everything else all ready, hon?"

"Just about," Laura said. "We have a few more things to load; then I'll feed the horses for the last time and turn them out to pasture. Maybe half an hour or forty-five minutes."

Hughes nodded and crawled on the tractor, to run the hay spear into a big circular hay bale to begin covering their cache.

BOYD'S BAYOU BRIDGE
NEAR PECAN GROVE
OLEANDER, TEXAS

6:00 P.M.

"It's their car all right, Snag," said the man into the radio.

"Did the idiots just run off the road, or does it look like they got hit? Over."

"Well, how the hell should I know? All we can see is the damned trunk lid. Over."

"Are there skid marks? Is the guardrail busted? Does it look like they tried to stop? USE YOUR GODDAMNED EYES! Over."

The man raised the radio again. "Ahh… none of that. Looks like it just rolled into the water. But like I said, we can't see nothin' but the trunk lid. If you want us to check it out better, we need a wrecker to pull the car out of the water. Over."

"I ain't wastin' time and gas to send a wrecker out there. We're losin' daylight, and if we don't get to the bottom of this quick, Spike's gonna be pissed. Now one of y'all strip down and drag the bodies out. And do it fast. Do you copy? Over."

The man cursed under his breath before responding. "We copy, Snag. This is Unit Seven, out," he said, then turned to his partner. "You heard him. Strip down and go check out the car."

"He was talkin' to you, not me. I ain't going in there, it's probably full of snakes and gators."

"He told me, and now I'm telling you, strip down!"

"You're not the boss just 'cause you're running the radio, Bolton. I say we flip for it, and if you don't like that, you can just kiss my ass and do it yourself."

Bolton considered for a moment, then reached for his door handle. "All right, let's get out and flip. I'd rather take my chances with a snake than get Spike and Snag pissed at us."

Five minutes later, Bolton's head broke the murky water of the bayou, and he moved toward the bank, sputtering and cursing. "Ain't a damn thing in the car, front or back."

"Well, they gotta be somewhere. They couldn't just fly off," his partner called down from the bridge.

"Yeah, smartass, well, unless they're in the trunk..." He paused as the logic of that possibility sank in. "Get the crowbar out of the back of the cruiser."

The man did as requested and then scurried down the bank to the edge of the bayou to pass Bolton the crowbar. Bolton waded back over to the car and stood in waist-deep water, trying unsuccessfully to pry the trunk open before moving away to point at the trunk.

"Blow the hell out of the lock and latch area—empty your magazine— that should weaken it."

His partner complied, and when the shooting stopped, Bolton waded back over with the crow bar and easily pried the trunk up to reveal the blood-soaked bodies of their former colleagues.

"Snag and Spike ain't gonna like this," Bolton said as he waded out of the water and started up the incline to their car, his partner close behind.

"'This is Unit Seven to Central Dispatch, do you copy? Over," he said into the mike.

"Seven, this is Dispatch. We copy. Over," came Snag's distinctive voice.

"Snag, we found Morgan's and Juke's bodies in the trunk of the cruiser. Somebody definitely took 'em out. Over," Bolton said.

A burst of obscenity came through the radio, followed by silence. Snag returned to the air a moment later.

"All right, we already got units working that way. We'll have 'em rally on you and start combing the area. I want to show them local yokels what happens when you mess with the law. Where are you exactly?"

Bolton looked at his partner and shrugged. "I don't know exactly. The last good-size road we turned off of was Texas 124, but we been wandering around the back roads and they ain't got no signs. I reckon we're a good three or four miles off 124 now."

"What's a landmark on 124 where we could rally?"

Bolton thought a minute. "There's some kind of old chemical plant or refinery. Looks like it was probably closed even before the blackout, but if you come down 124 from Beaumont, you can't miss it. It's on the right."

"All right, I'll have everyone rally there, work your way back there, but check out houses along the way. Somebody had to do them two in, and I'm bettin' they ain't far away. You turn anything up on the way to the rally point, sing out on the radio and we'll figure out how to get to you. Understood? Over."

"Understood. We'll git 'er done. This is Seven, out."

HUGHES' RESIDENCE
PECAN GROVE
OLEANDER, TEXAS

DAY 17, 6:15 P.M.

"That it?" Kinsey asked, and both Jordan and Laura Hughes nodded.

"How you want to do this, Chief Kinsey?" Hughes asked.

"I think it's best if you take your family in the SUV," Kinsey said. "Then me and the boys will ride in the pickup, me driving and two in the bed with M4s. There's still enough room to move around in the bed of the truck, and they can bring the M4s into play much more easily if we need 'em. I figure the pickup can either run interference in front and they can shoot over the top of the cab, or they can be a rearguard and shoot behind us, depending on the situation."

"Sounds good," Hughes said, turning to his wife. "Hon, let's get the girls in…"

Everyone looked up at the sound of an approaching car, and watched as a Beaumont PD cruiser cleared the edge of the pecan grove and started up the long drive. Then the driver apparently saw them and skidded to a stop, both occupants of the cop car staring at them in disbelief.

"More fake cops!" Hughes said. "Honey, get the girls and y'all get down behind the SUV, NOW!"

Laura moved to comply, and Kinsey turned to face the cop car, M4 raised. His men followed suit.

"How do you know for sure they're fakes," he asked over his shoulder. "These are city cops and the others were sheriff's deputies."

"'Cause they're at least twenty miles outside their jurisdiction," Hughes said, standing beside Kinsey with the .308 trained on the cop car. "A county sheriff's deputy MIGHT stray a bit, but no city cops are driving twenty miles outside the city limits by mistake."

***

"Shit, Bolton, whadda we gonna do? Those look like navy guys or somethin'! Look at those M4s."

Bolton grabbed the bullhorn and pulled open the door. "If they was gonna shoot us, they would have opened up as soon as they saw us. Let's see if I can bluff 'em," he said, stepping out of the car.

"THIS IS THE BEAUMONT PO-LICE! DROP YOUR WEAPONS AND LIE FACE DOWN ON THE GROUND! NOW!"

"I DON'T THINK SO. JUST GET BACK IN YOUR CAR AND DRIVE AWAY AND NO ONE HAS TO GET HURT."

Bolton got back in the car and reached for the radio.

"Central Dispatch, this is Unit Seven. Do you copy? Over."

"We copy, Seven. What is your ETA at rally point? Over."

"We have a problem. I think we found who offed our guys, but they look like navy or something and they all have assault rifles. We are outgunned. Over."

"What do you mean navy?"

"Some of 'em have on blue coveralls and caps and they all got on body armor. Definitely look like military. Over."

"How many is 'all'? Over."

"Four shooters and some women. Over."

"All right, hold 'em there if you can, but if you have to move back, stay in contact so we know where they are. I'll send everybody in the area your way. Can you give me any better directions? Over."

"South of Texas 124 a couple of miles. If you get in the area, look for a clump of tall trees—sticks out like a sore thumb. Ya can't miss it if you're close. Over."

"We copy. Central Dispatch out."

Bolton nodded. "I guess we just sit and watch and wait."

"How the hell we gonna 'hold 'em' here if they decide to leave?"

Bolton shrugged. "I reckon we just sit here and block the drive. They'll likely fire warning shots if they get ready to leave, and we'll just back out of the driveway and down the road a ways and follow 'em. Like as not they'll run right into the other boys comin' in. It ain't like there's a lot of roads to choose from."

***

"You think they're just gonna sit there?" Hughes asked.

"Looks like he was talking on the radio, so yeah, I think they're gonna sit there and wait for backup," Kinsey answered.

Hughes nodded. "That's my thinking too, and we need to break contact and be long gone when they arrive. I'll get the girls into the SUV and take off and y'all provide the rearguard like you planned. But if they try to follow, we have to leave them sitting right here; otherwise they'll keep bringing the others down on us."

"I'm way ahead of you, Cap," Kinsey said. "We'll keep 'em covered and then move out after you."

Hughes nodded and lowered his rifle as he backed away. Seconds later Kinsey heard car doors slamming and the SUV's engine cranking.

"All right," Kinsey called to his men, "I'll keep 'em covered while you two set up in the bed of the pickup. Let me know when you got 'em covered again and I'll get behind the wheel."

"Roger that, Chief," Jones said, and Kinsey heard the two men scrambling into the back of the truck.

"Ready, Chief. We got 'em covered," Jones said, and Kinsey lowered his M4 and jumped behind the wheel, giving a tap of the horn to let Hughes know he was ready. Hughes waved his arm out the window in acknowledgment and started past the barn and toward the pasture. Kinsey followed, glancing in his rearview mirror at the cop car in the driveway. Don't do it, he thought, then shook his head as the car started to move.

***

"Where the hell they goin'? That ain't nothin' but a cow pasture."

"Must come out on a road somewhere," Bolton said, starting the car, "and we gotta stay with 'em, else we'll be in deep shit."

The cop car had barely started moving when the M4s in the truck ahead of them spoke in unison, and two separate three-round bursts shredded both front tires, followed by half a dozen rounds in the radiator. Bolton braked and the car thumped and bucked to a stop on the ruined tires and steam began to billow out from under the hood. He beat the steering wheel with the palms of his hands.

"SHIT! SHIT! SHIT! We're gonna catch hell from Snag and Spike on this one."

He sighed and reached for the radio. "Better let 'em know quick, or it'll be worse."

Federal Correctional Complex
Beaumont, Texas

"GODDAMN IT!" yelled Spike McComb, flinging a chair across his newly established 'central dispatch' office for emphasis. Snaggle flinched as the metal chair smashed against the wall with loud bang, and the other cons fidgeted in their own chairs, glancing at the door as if they might take flight to avoid McComb's rage.

"We'll get 'em, Spike, don't worry," Snaggle said.

"I ain't worried, you moron, I'm PISSED! Those ain't navy guys, it's them damn Coast Guard pukes you dumb assholes let git away. You know, the ones you can't seem to find on a GIGANTIC GODDAMNED SHIP! And imagine that, here they are not even a day later causing trouble. Who would have guessed?"

"The boat's working now," Snaggle said, "and I got 'em on the river—"

"Never mind the damn boat, one problem at a time. And I'll start runnin' the show since you can't seem to find your ass with both hands. Bring me a damn map. NOW!"

Snaggle hurried to rummage through a desk drawer and produced a road map, which he spread on the desk in front of Spike.

"All right, where are those idiots who just got their car shot up?"

Snaggle pointed at an area on the map. "Round about here, best I can tell."

McComb rubbed his chin as he looked at the map. "If these assholes came from this ghost ship, then it stands to reason they're headed back to it, and it's got to be somewhere on the damn river, even if you assholes can't find it. That means they gotta be heading back east, toward the river—and us." He looked a little closer at the map and pointed to a blue line. "What's this creek here?"

Snaggle squinted. "Looks like Taylor's Bayou and then it branches off and becomes Hillebrandt Bayou…" He trailed off as the implications became obvious.

McComb nodded. "That's right, they gotta cross it and there ain't that many bridges. We just set up at each crossing and we'll pick 'em up at one of 'em for sure."

Snaggle ran his finger up the blue line. "Looks like bridges on 73, 365, 124, and I-10, but I doubt they'd use I-10, it's pretty much a parking lot."

"I agree," McComb said. "Get those other bridges covered right away."

"We'll have roadblocks up in—"

"Not roadblocks, you idiot! Cover 'em out of sight; then when we pick 'em up, we'll let 'em lead us back to the ship. When we know where they hit the river, we can take 'em out. The ship's gotta be somewhere nearby."

TEXAS HIGHWAY 365
DUE EAST OF FANNETT, TEXAS

Hughes pulled out of the pasture and through the shallow drainage ditch, stopping the SUV on the slight incline and motioning out the window with his left hand for Kinsey to pull abreast of him. The Coastie rolled up beside him as requested and powered down his passenger window to speak to Hughes across the empty cab of the pickup.

"We've made good time," Hughes said. "This is 365, the road we came out on. It's a straight shot due east back to Nederland."

Kinsey nodded and Hughes continued. "My only concern is the bridge. If they moved fast, it could be blocked, and if they blocked this one, chances are the other two are blocked as well and we're screwed. We have to hope they didn't and haul ass east as fast as we can."

"You want us to take point?"

"I figure that's probably best. If we encounter resistance, you might be able to brush them aside, or if the opposition is too strong, we can reverse course and you'll be in position to be the rearguard," Hughes said.

"Sounds good. I got no problem until we get back to Nederland, but once we get there, it would be better if you resume the lead if we have to bob and weave, because you know the local streets."

Hughes nodded and Kinsey powered up his window and swung on to the blacktop, leading the way east, and Hughes and the SUV brought up the rear. It was Hughes' turn to keep up now as Kinsey floored the pickup in an attempt to get across the bridge before they were cut off. He roared down the road after the pickup flat out for fifteen minutes, gratified when the bridge came into view with no sign of a roadblock.

He would have been less pleased had he noticed the police cruiser a hundred yards off the paved road along a gravel track, hidden from view by a small clump of squat Chinese tallow trees.

FEDERAL CORRECTIONAL COMPLEX
BEAUMONT, TEXAS

"We got 'em," chortled Snaggle as the radio transmission faded and he high-fived the con next to him.

"Don't be counting your chickens just yet," Spike growled. "You morons could still screw this up. Now, get back on the radio and tell the unit that spotted 'em to get on their tail, but stay back a ways so they can't be sure it's a cop car. Then tell the rest of the units to converge along their path but to stay at least a block or two away from 365. I'm thinking they'll head straight for the river, and most of those roads down to the river run through or between the refineries without many crossroads. After they turn down one of them, they're committed, and we'll know where they're headed. We just pile in behind them."

Snaggle nodded and raised the mike to issue the new orders.

TEXAS HIGHWAY 365
EASTBOUND
APPROACHING CENTRAL MALL

Hughes divided his attention between the pickup truck ahead of him and studying the faint dot in his rearview mirror. There was definitely a vehicle down the long straight road far behind them, but it was so far back he couldn't be sure what it was.

"Girls, put your young eyes to use and see if you can tell anything about that car back behind us," he said over his shoulder. He heard abrupt movement as the girls swiveled in their seats.

"I... I think it's a police car," Jana said, "at least there looks like there's something on top of it."

"She's right," Julie agreed, "definitely something on top."

Hughes blew out his cheeks. "Damn," he said, reaching for the handheld radio in the console between the seats.

"I thought you didn't want to use the radio in case they might intercept your transmissions," Laura said.

Hughes shook his head. "If they're following us, they already know where we are, and Kinsey needs to know."

Hughes keyed the mike. "Salty Dog One, this is Salty Dog Actual. Do you copy? Over."

"This is One. Go, Dog. Over."

"We have company on our six, so I will pass you and lead to the extraction point. Be aware it might get messy. Over."

"Dog, we copy. Take the lead and I will chat with the home folks. Over."

Hughes acknowledged and swung into the left lane, passing the pickup as it slowed almost imperceptibly. As he flashed by, he jerked his thumb behind him and the two Coasties in the truck bed nodded, and one turned his attention to the rear as the second shooter continued to look ahead. Kinsey gave him a short toot of the horn and a tight smile. As Hughes settled into the lead, he heard the radio crackle to life on the console beside him as Kinsey transmitted.

"This is Salty Dog One to Magician. Do you copy? Over."

Hughes heard Torres' slight Hispanic accent. "This is Magician. I copy. Over."

"Magician, be advised we may be coming in hot. ETA at extraction point in fifteen mikes. Over."

"One, we copy. Advise any change in ETA. Magician out."

They roared past Central Mall on their right, slowing only slightly to dodge the occasional car in the road, as Hughes considered the options. Best to stay on the wider main roads if possible, because there was always the possibility a smaller road might be somehow blocked. Decision made, he kept the pedal to the floor until the approach to Twin City Highway came into view, then flicked his right turn signal briefly to alert Kinsey before taking the turn entirely too fast. The SUV fishtailed and swung on to the access road to flash by a strip center and a huge HEB supermarket.

Seconds later he was turning left on to Twin City Highway, with Kinsey right on his tail. Time seemed to drag after that, despite his heavy foot, and they moved northwest up Twin City Highway, slaloming around many more abandoned cars than they'd encountered to date. Finally, he spotted the interchange with Texas 366 ahead, and exited left to take the long swooping curve that put him on 366, headed east now, with his landmark just ahead. He veered left onto a narrow paved road between a tank farm and the Nederland Little League complex and roared toward the river and the refinery docks, glancing in his rearview mirror to assure himself Kinsey was still with him—two miles to go.

FEDERAL CORRECTIONAL COMPLEX
BEAUMONT, TEXAS

"They made the turn toward the river by the Little League fields. I doubt there are any turnoffs that'll take 'em anyplace but the river. We got 'em, Spike!" Snaggle said.

McComb nodded. "All right, have the chase car plug the hole and close on them, then put as many units down that road after 'em as you can. How many units are close?"

"We got two units nearby and I'll have 'em running up the chase car's tailpipe, with three more behind them inside of two minutes and several more on the way. We can have at least six cars and twelve men on 'em by the time they hit the river. And the boat's just a ways downstream. Running flat out, I can probably have her up to that section of the river in maybe five minutes. They ain't gettin' away."

"About damn time something went right," McComb said. "Do it!"

Snaggle nodded and started issuing orders over the radio.

REFINERY DOCK ACCESS ROAD
NEDERLAND, TEXAS

Hughes sped down the access road, the high chain-link fence marking refinery property on his right and the tracks of the railroad spur serving the refining complex and tank farms on his left, confining him in the narrow corridor that ran straight to the river. The fence posts on the right flew by in a blur as he worked to avoid the frequent potholes in a road that saw more than of its fair share of heavy truck traffic. The SUV hit a particularly bad pothole and he fought the wheel to maintain control, then looked in his rearview mirror.

"Damn! That was a bad one. We're all buckled in, but I hope Kinsey doesn't bounce his guys out of the back of the truck," Hughes said.

"It seems longer than I remember. How much farther?" Laura asked.

"The main refinery gate's coming up," Hughes said, nodding ahead. "That's about the halfway spot. The road forks to the left just before the main gate and runs through a fenced corridor between the refinery and the Sun tank farm next door, straight down to the dock gate. Maybe a mile, give or take." He glanced over at her. "Don't worry, babe, we're almost there."

As if to emphasize his words, he began slowing the SUV and then veered left just before the main gate.

"Hang on," he cried, just before the SUV bumped violently over the railroad tracks and onto the road between the fences, down to the refinery docks.

He straightened and accelerated just as he heard the sound of gunfire and glanced in his rearview mirror to see the pickup come into view. It bounced across the tracks, its occupants hanging on for dear life as the pickup leaned to one side. The gunfire was steady now.

"Salty Dog One to Salty Dog Actual. Do you copy? Over."

Hughes snatched up the radio. "Go ahead, One."

"There's at least three cruisers behind us and closing fast. They got one of my rear tires with a lucky shot. We can't outrun them and we're bouncing around so bad my guys can't shoot. We'll make a stand here and hold 'em off while you get your family to the boat. Over."

"Negative One! Repeat. Negative your last! I'll slow and let you close on me; then I'll stop and let y'all hop in and we'll get to the river."

"That won't work. They're too close and they'll take us while we try to transfer. Get your family to the boat, Cap, then worry about us later. Salty Dog One out."

Hughes started to protest but could only watch in the mirror as Kinsey braked the truck and swung it across the road. The three Coasties leaped out and took defensive positions behind the pickup turned barricade just as three police cruisers bumped across the railroad tracks in rapid succession. Subject to the now accurate fire from the Coasties, the fake cops braked and moved their own cars across the road to form a barricade, and Hughes turned his full attention to the road ahead and accelerated.

A minute later he roared through the dock gate and slowed as he drove up the ramp onto the refinery dock, blowing out a relieved sigh when he saw the Coast Guard boat in the middle of the river. Both the helmsman and gunner were watching the dock and returned his wave as he rolled toward the nearest vertical ladder down to the water. He stopped by the ladder and opened his door, pausing to listen to the distant gunfire. Gunfire was good, because if it stopped, they were all in trouble.

"Okay, Laura, leave everything and let's get you and the girls safe on the ship," Hughes said, and his wife nodded and motioned the twins out of the car. They reached the top of the ladder just as the Coast Guard boat settled against it.

"We've got company, and a lot of it," Hughes called down. "Kinsey's holding them off, but you need to get my family to the ship and then get back here ASAP."

The helmsman nodded. "Torres is—"

He jerked his head up at the sound of powerful outboards approaching at full throttle, echoing around a bend in the river downstream.

"Christ! What now?" Hughes said.

"I doubt it's the cavalry. What do you think, Captain?" the helmsman asked.

"I think we don't have time for this crap, but it's coming whether we have time or not." He paused, thinking. "Okay, they haven't seen us yet and we can't be sure who it is. Y'all pull out of sight over behind that barge downstream until we find out. That way, you can surprise them if need be."

The helmsman considered a brief moment then nodded, easing the boat further downstream to shelter behind the barge, out of the sight of anyone approaching from downriver.

Hughes turned to Laura. "Honey, get the girls behind the car and lie flat on the dock. Anyone in a boat on the river won't be able to see up here on top of the dock."

"What are you going to do?" Laura asked.

"I'm gonna stand at the edge of the dock. That way they'll focus on me and likely won't even notice the patrol boat when they pass it."

"Jordan Hughes, you'll do no such thing! What if they just shoot you? You come with us, right now."

The gunfire increased in intensity, and Hughes shot a worried look back the way they'd come. "Honey, we HAVE to suck them in and deal with them quickly so I can get back and pick up Kinsey." The outboards were louder now and Hughes glanced downstream to see a boat rounding the bend. "They're coming. Now get down out of sight."

Laura wrapped him in a fierce hug and whispered in his ear, "If we survive this, I may very well kill you myself."

Hughes hugged her back, then smiled down at her.

"You may have to get in line. Now quick, you and the girls get down."

She moved to comply and Hughes looked downstream. He could see the boat clearly now. It was similar to the Coast Guard boat except the flotation collar was blue instead of orange and JEFFERSON COUNTY SHERIFF was written on the side. Hughes moved to the edge of the dock and waved his arms to attract attention, and the pitch of the outboards changed abruptly as the occupants of the boat saw Hughes and slowed, moving in his direction.

The boat had two occupants, both in sheriff's department uniforms. As hoped, both focused on him and didn't spare a backwards glance as they passed the barge where the Coasties were hiding. The boat stopped twenty feet from the dock and one of the men stepped out of the aluminum cabin with an AR-15 and pointed it up at Hughes.

"Put your hands up, then come down that ladder, nice and slow like."

Hughes raised his hands. "You do realize I can't do both of those things at once?"

"You know what I meant, smartass, so git your ass down that ladder or I'll drop you where you stand."

"Actually, maybe you should put YOUR hands up unless you'd like a fifty-caliber enema," Hughes said, inclining his head downstream.

The fake deputy glanced aft and found himself looking down the barrel of the machine gun in the Coast Guard boat, not fifty feet away. But rather than laying down his gun, he acted on instinct—a bad one, as it turned out. His attempt to raise the AR to his shoulder was answered by a short burst from the machine gun, shredding his chest and spraying blood through the open cabin door on the helmsman. The helmsman also acted on instinct, jamming the throttles forward in an attempt to escape upriver. The boat had traveled perhaps twenty-five feet when the fifty caliber spoke again, sending rounds through the thin aluminum walls of the cabin like they were tissue paper, three of them catching the helmsman in the back. He slid to the deck, never to rise again, as the boat roared upstream at an angle, to run aground on the opposite bank of the river, the outboards still straining in a futile attempt to push the boat through the riverbank.

Hughes was moving as soon as the boat was no longer a threat, waving the Coasties back to the ladder before turning back to the dock.

"Come on, ladies, your boat's waiting," he called as Laura and the twins appeared from behind the SUV.

Less than a minute later, his family was aboard the boat, moving upstream toward the *Pecos Trader* and safety, and Hughes jumped back in the driver's seat of the SUV and did a three-point turn to head back to Kinsey's side.

"There's too damn many of them, Chief," Jones said, from where he sheltered beside Kinsey behind the engine block. Kinsey nodded and looked down the length of the pickup to where Bollinger sheltered behind the rear wheel and axle, the left shoulder of his blue coveralls ripped and the cloth around the tear stained darker by blood.

"How's the shoulder, Bollinger?" Kinsey asked.

"It's just a graze," the man replied. "Hurts like hell, but it's stopped bleeding. I'm okay, Chief."

His statement was punctuated by gunfire as Jones lifted his M4 above the hood of the truck and fired a three-round burst in the general direction of their attackers, without exposing his head or shoulders. His burst was answered with a sustained fusillade and the body of the pickup rocked as it was hit with round after round.

Jones shook his head. "We must have taken out at least a half dozen of the bastards, but they just keep multiplying. None of 'em can shoot worth a damn, but if they keep throwing lead at us, they're bound to get lucky sooner or later. Just throwing three-round bursts in their general direction isn't likely to work much longer either."

"I know that, Jones," Kinsey said, "but what do you suggest? You may have noticed we're in a flat straight strip of ground between two tall fences. There isn't crap for cover here, so we can't fall back. The second we move out from behind this truck, we're dead meat—"

His response was broken by another sustained round of firing, impacting the entire length of the truck.

"What the hell…" Kinsey dropped flat on the ground and peered under the truck. He saw four men coming toward them at a run, only the lower halves of their bodies visible from under the truck.

"Damn, they're trying to keep our heads down while they charge. Shoot under the truck—take out their legs."

He started firing immediately and was joined on the ground by his teammates. They dropped their attackers in seconds, leaving them screaming on the asphalt.

"That should hold 'em for a—"

Kinsey flinched as a bullet ricocheted off the asphalt in front of him and whined by his right ear.

"Damn! Back behind your cover," he yelled, and the trio scrambled back behind the more substantial cover of the engine block and the rear suspension, just as the area under the truck erupted with ricochets, some bouncing up to strike the undercarriage of the truck while others whined off into the distance behind them.

"Well, I guess THAT defensive move isn't going to work again," Kinsey said.

"This ain't looking too good, Chief," Bollinger yelled, just as an even more furious round of firing began rocking the truck.

Much more of this, and the damn truck will just be shot apart, thought Kinsey, just as the smell hit him.

"Oh, great, just what we need, gasoline! They must have punctured the gas tank with one of those ricochets," Jones said. "Instead of being shot, we get to be barbecued."

Kinsey's mind raced, and he stuck his finger in his mouth then held the wet finger up. He dropped it and duckwalked back to the door of the truck to reach up and rip the door open. Keeping low, he grabbed one of their discarded plastic water bottles from the floorboard and then fished the roadside emergency kit from the pocket on the open door. He slammed the door just as the movement drew the attention of their attackers, who sent a hail of bullets ricocheting under the truck in his general vicinity. One clipped the heel of his boot and knocked him on his butt, but he got to his knees and scrambled behind the front wheel and engine block before any more connected.

"Bollinger, can you see where the gas is coming out?" Kinsey asked.

Bollinger leaned down and looked around the rear wheel and under the truck.

"Yeah, it's about a pencil-size stream. I'm gonna be in the puddle pretty soon, by the way," Bollinger said.

"Can you reach the leak?"

"I guess so, but why?"

Kinsey held up the plastic water bottle. "'Cause I want you to catch this, then fill it up with gas and toss it back to me. Got it?"

"Ahh… I don't think plastic bottles work for Molotov cocktails, Chief, and none of us has a good enough arm to hit those assholes anyway," Jones offered.

"SHUT UP!" Kinsey said. "And make yourself useful. Dig the flares out of that emergency kit."

Kinsey turned back to Bollinger, who nodded and held out his hand to receive the toss of the empty water bottle. A minute later he tossed it back to Kinsey, capped and three-quarters full.

"Sorry, Chief, the leak was slowing down, so I guess the tank level has dropped down even with the puncture. That's all I could get."

"Should be enough," Kinsey said.

"Enough for WHAT?" Jones asked.

"Enough to get the supplies burning in the bed of the truck and make a smoke screen. There isn't much wind, but it's blowing in their direction. Maybe it'll give us enough cover to haul ass."

"Will that stuff even burn?" Bollinger asked.

Kinsey shrugged. "Who the hell knows, but I don't have any better ideas." He looked at Jones. "How many flares do we have?"

"Four."

"All right. I'm gonna reach up through the busted-out window and sprinkle a little of this gas on the upholstery in the cab; then I'm gonna go back and slosh the rest of it on the supplies in the bed, and hope the bastards don't see me and take my hand off or shoot my feet out from under me. Jones, toss a couple of those flares back to Bollinger. When I'm done with the gas, I want you guys to strike the flares and toss them into the truck; Jones' go in the cab and, Bollinger, I want yours in the supplies. Then we wait a bit for the smoke screen and run like hell for the river."

"Sooo… what if there isn't a smoke screen?" Jones asked.

Kinsey sighed. "Then we have to run like hell anyway, because when things get to burning and heat up that half-full gas tank, this thing's gonna blow."

Jones and Bollinger both nodded and watched Kinsey duckwalk down the length of the vehicle between them, reaching up one-handed to splash gas through the shot-out passenger window and over the side of the truck into the bed. When the gas was gone, he tossed the empty plastic bottle into the truck bed and nodded, signaling them to strike and deploy their flares.

The synthetic fabric of the upholstery caught first and filled the air with the vile smell of gasoline and burning plastic as a satisfying plume of smoke billowed from the cab to float across the road, obscuring but not totally blocking the view of their attackers. The fire in the bed produced less smoke, but did contribute somewhat to the haze.

"I think that's about as good as it's going to get, boys," Kinsey said. "We gotta haul ass, but don't bunch up or run in a straight line. Got it?"

The two men nodded.

"We all raise up and unload on them through the haze to get their heads down, then you two take off while I stay back and lay down cover fire. Then I'll run past you and you return the favor, shooting over the truck and through the haze from some distance back. Then we'll leapfrog again. If we're lucky, we might be able to open up the distance before they figure out what we're doing—then we all run like hell."

The plan almost worked. The wind shifted to blow at right angles across the road just as Kinsey finished laying down covering fire, sweeping the road clear. Left with no smoke screen, Kinsey had no option but to drop back down behind the now blazing pickup while his men in the open survived solely due to the timely arrival of Hughes, who pulled the SUV across the road to form a defensive position. Forced back by the heat of the now blazing pickup, Kinsey bolted for the cover of the SUV as rounds ricocheted off the asphalt around him.

He ran for all he was worth, expecting a hammer blow between his shoulder blades at any moment. Then he heard the familiar and authoritative bark of a Barrett fifty-caliber sniper rifle, speaking three times in quick succession. By the time he'd reached the shelter of the SUV scant seconds later, incoming fire had all but ceased as the big gun continued to speak. Kinsey turned to watch in amazement as the huge rounds penetrated the cop cars like they were cardboard, and screams of maimed and dying adversaries filled the air. In moments, the few remaining ambulatory survivors leaped into a partially intact cop car behind the barricade and fled back the way they'd come.

Kinsey keyed his mike. "That you, Magician?"

Torres' distinctive voice came through the speaker. "Abra-fucking-cadabra, boss. Sorry I'm late. I had to find a good spot."

Kinsey looked around. "Where the hell are you?"

"Look up and to your right."

Kinsey did and spotted Torres waving at him from the catwalk high atop a massive storage tank three hundred yards away in the neighboring tank farm.

"Outstanding job. Now pack up and get down here. We need to get back to the ship."

CHAPTER EIGHTEEN

DAY 18, 9:00 A.M.

Hughes set his coffee cup down and leaned back on the sofa, reaching for Laura's hand as he did so. She gave his fingers a reassuring squeeze and settled back beside him as he looked at the group gathered around the coffee table in his office sitting area. His gaze rested on Kinsey.

"I can't thank you and your folks enough for helping me get my family here, Matt," Hughes said.

Kinsey shook his head. "You'd have done the same, and none of us would be here if it wasn't for you. My only regret is I didn't think to grab one of those bastards still breathing. We could sure use the intel. I know we're all frantic to bring the rest of the families in, but we have to know what we're up against before we leave *Pecos Trader* shorthanded defense-wise."

"Well, that sheriff's boat increases our mobility a bit, anyway," Gowan said, flashing a smile at Georgia Howell. "Fast thinking, Mate!"

Monitoring the radio traffic the previous evening and hearing of the disabled police boat, Howell set out with a few volunteers and retrieved the vessel from the bank. It would be a welcome addition to their boat fleet.

Howell flushed at the praise. "Have you had a chance to check it out?"

Gowan nodded. "The First and I went over it this morning. Other than busted windows and bullet holes in the aluminum superstructure, she's fine. None of the controls were hit at all."

"Definitely a plus," Kinsey said. "I planned on taking the patrol boat to Baton Rouge to look for my family anyway, but I was really worried about leaving you here without some cover. Now we can mount the second M240 on the police boat and leave a couple of my guys here to run it and train some of your folks. I'll feel a lot more secure knowing you have adequate protection."

Hughes was about to speak when the phone on his desk rang. He excused himself and walked over to his desk.

"Captain speaking."

"Captain," said the second mate, "I've got Wilmington on the radio and they have a message for Chief Kinsey."

"What is it? I'll pass it along," Hughes said.

"Ahh… they're still on. I think Chief Kinsey may want to take this one personally."

"Okay, we'll be right up."

Moments later, Hughes followed a puzzled Kinsey across the bridge and over to the radio station.

"Fort Box, this is *Pecos Trader* . I'm putting Chief Kinsey on. Over," the second mate said, handing Kinsey the mike.

"We copy, *Pecos Trader* . Wait one. Over."

Hughes raised his eyebrows. "Fort Box?"

The second mate shrugged. "Yeah, that's what they've started calling it because—"

"*Pecos Trader* , this is Fort Box for Chief Kinsey. Over."

"This is Kinsey. Go ahead Fort Box. Over," Kinsey said.

There was a pause and then, "Dad? This is Luke. Over."

Kinsey looked shocked; then his face split into a wide grin and his eyes glistened before he turned away from the others and wiped them with the back of his hand, momentarily speechless as emotion washed over him.

"Dad? Do you copy? Over."

Kinsey spoke into the mike. "Yes, Luke, I'm here. It's great to hear your voice, son. How did you get there? Over."

"It's a long story, Dad. I'll tell you when I see you. What about Kelly and Aunt Connie's family? Are they okay? Over."

"I don't know," Kinsey said, "but I'm going there as soon as I can. It may take a few days. We have a lot of issues here. Over."

"Yeah, here too, but I'll try to get to you all as quick as I can. Meanwhile they don't want us talking too long, so I need to sign off. Over."

"Okay. I'll let you know about the family as soon as I know myself. And work hard on getting here." Kinsey looked around, a bit embarrassed. "I love you, son. Over."

"I love you too, Dad. Be careful. This is Fort Box, out."

Kinsey handed the mike to the second mate and turned to Hughes, still smiling.

"That's the best news I've had in over three weeks," Kinsey said.

Hughes nodded, returning Kinsey's smile. "Maybe this will all work out after all, Chief."

SUN OIL DOCK
NECHES RIVER
NEAR NEDERLAND, TEXAS

DAY 18, 9:00 A.M.

Spike McComb stood behind the huge loading arms and looked straight across the river into the anchorage inlet. He glared at the massive ship floating in the distance, with the Coast Guard boat and HIS patrol boat moored to its side. The longer he watched, the madder he got. He exploded at the most convenient target. Snaggle saw it coming and steeled himself before McComb even opened his mouth.

"TWELVE MEN AND MY NEW PATROL BOAT! CAN'T YOU IDIOTS DO ANYTHING RIGHT?"

Snaggle hesitated, unsure of the proper response. He tried positive spin.

"But we know where they are now, right? And they likely can't get away. That ship ain't goin' nowhere fast."

McComb grabbed Snaggle by the shirt and threw him against a vertical pipe so hard his head bounced off it. "SO WHAT, YOU MORON? THEY GOT OUR BOAT! And did you see that machine gun? They obviously got radar too, so we're not likely to be able to sneak up on 'em, and they'll cut us to pieces crossing open water, even if we get another boat."

McComb released Snaggle so abruptly the small man banged his head on the pipe a second painful time. McComb turned to glare at the ship once again.

"But I'll figure out something. 'Cause this is MY county now, and nobody comes in here and messes with me. I'm gonna have that ship and everybody on it, and you can take that to the friggin' bank!"

324

FORT BOX
WILMINGTON CONTAINER TERMINAL
WILMINGTON, NORTH CAROLINA

DAY 18, 9:30 A.M.

Luke Kinsey stood in the radio room, smiling like an idiot in the wake of his conversation with his father. He'd put the various possibilities out of his mind over the last few stressful weeks, dreading the worst. Confirming his father was alive and safe impacted him more profoundly than he would have thought possible. Now if his sister and Aunt Connie's family could only be brought to safety, the family group would be complete.

He felt a hand on his shoulder and turned to see the smiling face of Major Hunnicutt.

"I imagine there's a happy man in Texas about now."

Luke nodded. "No happier than the one right here, Major."

"So you're planning on joining your father in Texas? How you gonna get there?"

Luke shrugged. "Not a clue at the moment. Everything happened so fast I haven't had time to give it any thought."

"Well, we can provide supplies. That's the least we can do since y'all rescued Anthony, but beyond that we can't do much for you." He hesitated. "Of course, if you change your mind, you're always welcome here. We can always use more good folks."

"I appreciate that, but—"

"But family comes first," Hunnicutt said. "I get that. However, while you ARE here, I'd like to include you in our daily progress meetings so you can get a feel for what we're trying to accomplish. I'm figuring your dad and Captain Hughes are gonna set something up in Texas, and the more we share info, the better chances we all have to get through this. We're a long ways apart, but we'll face similar challenges. And I'd also like you to share what you told me about this Special Reaction Force."

"Sure, I'd like that. But what's the setup? I mean, who's in charge? Is it military or civilian or what?"

Hunnicutt grinned. "We're sort of making it up as we go along. I'm senior military, but both Sergeant Wright and Chief Butler have a lot of experience and some damn good ideas. And Levi Jenkins isn't military at all, but he's got a better handle on this whole situation than all of us put together, so he's welcome to the meetings anytime he's here. Then together we pick other folks to attend the meetings if we have any need for their particular skill set. We actually kind of do things by consensus. I've never been a big fan of 'committees,' but damned if it doesn't seem to be working for the moment, mainly because we don't seem to have any dumb asses involved." He frowned. "I suspect that won't last, but we'll cross that bridge when we come to it."

"Okay. I'm in. Just let me know when," Luke said.

"That would be now," Hunnicutt said. He led Luke down a hallway.

The group was already gathered when they entered the small conference room. Sergeant Josh Wright and Chief Mike Butler were there as expected, along with both Levi and Anthony. The older man got a clean bill of health from the resident medic, though he was still moving a bit slowly after his beating. Despite his pain, Anthony smiled and nodded when Luke entered the room, obviously pleased to see him at the meeting. The last attendee was a bit of a surprise; Vern Gibson sat at the conference table beside Levi Jenkins.

Hunnicutt motioned Luke to an empty chair and took his own seat at the head of the table.

"Okay, folks, I know we're all busy, so let's get right to it. Josh, please give us a quick overview on the defensive wall and the aide station?"

Josh Wright nodded. "The perimeter wall around Fort Box is finished, at least until we decide to expand it. We have clear fields of fire between the new wall and the original razor-wire-topped fence around the original perimeter of the terminal, and protected firing positions for the M2s at regular intervals. We're good to go there. As far as the aide station, we've picked out a level spot in the middle of one of the golf courses at the Pine Valley Country Club. We'll start moving empty containers there today, and should have a basic defensive position built by sundown. I figure we're two to three days from having the defensive outpost, storage area, and field kitchen completed. I think we can get the mess tents up the next day and be able to start feeding folks the day after that." He paused. "Of course, we'll try to shorten that if possible."

There were nods around the table.

"Good work, and stay on it," Hunnicutt said. "There are a lot of hungry people out there so this is Job One. Any intel on the bangers?"

"Just the usual," Wright said. "Except for their ill-advised run at Levi's place, they're concentrating on low-hanging fruit. They've grabbed all available resources for themselves, and are using food and water to control the local population. They're definitely steering clear of us, but that's liable to change when we move out from the fort and start helping the general population."

Hunnicutt nodded. "We'll just have to deal with that when it happens. But speaking of threats, I'm getting a little nervous about our government friends. I'm sure you've all seen the choppers flying over these last few days and all know we've been in intermittent radio contact with FEMA. They seem very interested in our level of stores, supposedly so they can 'supplement' our local relief efforts. Like the rest of you, I'm skeptical."

He nodded toward Luke. "Luke here was 'recruited' for the FEMA Special Reaction Force, and he's provided the first hard intel regarding what FEMA is actually up to. I've asked him to share his experiences."

Luke acknowledged Hunnicutt's nod and then related everything he'd observed from his short service with FEMA. By the time he'd finished, there were clenched teeth and balled fists around the table.

"In light of what we now know," Hunnicutt said, "we have to decide how best to respond to FEMA—"

"Fuck 'em," Chief Mike Butler said, a sentiment met with cries of agreement.

"I'd say that's pretty much unanimous, then," Hunnicutt continued, "but I doubt that's going to go down well. We have to add them to our list of potential threats, probably near the top of the list. Again, something we'll have to address if and when the time comes.

"But moving on and on a more positive note," Hunnicutt said, "our list of allies has grown as well. You've all met Vern Gibson, who has a farm upriver. At Levi and Anthony's suggestion, I invited him here. Levi, would one of you gentlemen like to tell us what you have in mind."

The three looked back and forth, each waiting for the other to speak. When no one did, Levi sighed and broke the silence.

"Just this, Major. There's a lot of stuff in these containers and the grain ships, but when it's gone, it's gone. For a community to survive, you need farms, and farms along the river are the best bet. Vern here says he and his neighbors are already trading among themselves, but with a little more labor and fuel, they can produce much more than they need. Likewise, we probably got stuff in these containers they need, and if we can get a stable community going here, at least it will be a place to trade. However, that's gonna take a little help from Fort Box here."

"I'm listening."

"The bangers and other marauder types aren't stupid. Sooner or later they're gonna start raiding the countryside, just like they tried to hit us yesterday," Levi said. "Fact is, I suspect they may already be doing that along the main roads. But between the Guard and the Coasties, y'all have fast boats and generally outgun the marauder types, at least for now. We're thinking you can maintain the safety of the river and we can distribute radios to the river farms that don't have them, kind of like a 911 to call a quick reaction force on one of those fast boats. In time, as you recruit more people out of the refugee population, maybe we can set up manned security stations up and down the river—I'm sure the farmers will donate the land and the labor to build small stations and docks."

There were general murmurs of agreement as Levi finished.

Hunnicutt nodded. "Sounds like a damn good idea to me. I take it from the comments everyone else likes it too?"

Everyone voiced approval and Hunnicutt nodded again. "We'll do it, then, but I don't know about the stations. We're stretched on manpower at the moment, so I don't know how long before we'll be in a position to staff those."

"Only need one at the moment," Anthony offered, "at the junction of the Brunswick and the Cape Fear. That way you could bottle up any bangers coming up the Cape Fear from Wilmington, and keep the Brunswick open so we can all come and go safely to Fort Box. I'm thinkin' two or three guys with one of them machine guns would do nicely, hidden in that nice little wooded knoll by the railroad bridge. They could see anybody comin' round the bend from Wilmington at least three hundred yards away. Hell, we'll even donate a pair of night-vision goggles to the effort."

Hunnicutt smiled. "And that would also solve your immediate worries about a re-visitation from your banger friends?"

Anthony shrugged. "It's all about back scratchin', Major."

Hunnicutt laughed. "That it is." He turned to Josh Wright and Mike Butler. "How about it? Can we spare the manpower to support this?"

Both men nodded, without hesitation. "We're stretched, but we can make it work," Butler said, "because they're right. Those river farms are likely to be our lifeline, at least in the long run. We need to start bringing them into the fold as soon as possible."

Hunnicutt nodded. "Okay, folks. That's it for this morning unless anyone has any other business. And for what it's worth, I think we're making real progress here. Let's all hit the bricks and see if we can save some folks.

FEMA
EMERGENCY OPERATIONS CENTER
MOUNT WEATHER
NEAR BLUEMONT, VA

DAY 19, 8:00 A.M.

The Honorable J. Oliver Crawford, Secretary of the Department of Homeland Security, glared at the man standing across from his desk.

"What the hell you mean you've got nothing? There's at least three people out there. Maybe four since we don't know about this 'loose end' those morons reported before they screwed the pooch. They can't have just friggin' disappeared."

"Agreed, sir, but I don't know what more we can do. We've sealed off all roads that touch the trail within a hundred miles, and I've put men searching the trail on foot in both directions; fifteen miles in either direction from Bear's Den." The officer shook his head. "We found nothing. It's hard to believe, but they either got past us, or they're holing up somewhere."

"What about the choppers?"

"We've had two up in rotation constantly, covering the trail from Bear's Den south for two hundred miles, just as you ordered. Every inch of that section of the trail is being scanned at least every two hours, but the foliage is too thick to see anything this time of year, and the IR isn't infallible either. It's possible to screen your body heat if you know what you're doing, especially in summer, and it picks up deer, bears, wolves too, all with body temps very close to humans—"

"GODDAMN IT! I DON'T WANT A BUNCH OF MEALYMOUTHED EXCUSES! YOU BETTER START PRODUCING RESULTS OR YOU AND THIS BUNCH OF ASS CLOWNS ARE GETTING A ONE-WAY TICKET TO 'FUGEEVILLE, ALONG WITH YOUR FAMILIES! IS THAT CLEAR?"

"Ye-yes, sir."

Crawford took a deep breath and tried to regain his composure. "What about dogs? Why aren't you using them?"

"Ahh… that's a bit of a problem. We use contract handlers and… well, let's just say the local guy isn't being real cooperative. These are mountain folk and they're not real fond of the federal government, less so since the power went out. His place is pretty remote and he's forted up. Made us state our business standing in the middle of the road, then told us to leave. When we weren't doing it fast enough, he shot the side mirror off one of the cars."

Crawford started staring again, visibly struggling to control his rage. "And why did you let him get away with that, may I ask?"

"The rules of engagement say to bypass resistance, and I didn't think it was worth the distraction now that—"

"I DON'T GIVE TWO SHITS WHAT YOU THINK! YOU'RE NOT ALLOWED TO THINK, AND I'LL BE DAMNED IF I'M GOING TO STAND BY AND LET SOME TOOTHLESS HILLBILLY THUMB HIS NOSE AT THE UNITED STATES GOVERNMENT. NOW YOU TAKE WHATEVER RESOURCES YOU NEED AND GET THIS REDNECK AND HIS MUTTS WORKING THAT TRAIL! IS THAT CLEAR?"

The man nodded, fearful any other response might provoke another tirade.

"All right," Crawford said, "now get out. And you better not screw this up!"

BEAR'S DEN HOSTEL
APPALACHIAN TRAIL
MILE 999.1 NORTHBOUND
NEAR BLUEMONT, VIRGINIA

DAY 19, 8:00 A.M.

George Anderson stood in the kitchen of the hostel, gulping water in an attempt to fill an empty stomach and assuage his hunger. It had been two full days since his former FEMA colleagues descended on Bear's Den in force. From the sounds he overheard from his dark hiding place, he figured they'd used the grounds as a staging area for searching the closest section of the trail. That activity seemed to last forever, but he steeled himself to wait and didn't emerge from hiding, hungry and thirsty, until things had been quiet a full twenty-four hours.

He set the empty water bottle down on the counter and contemplated his next move as he heard the chopper blades thump by overhead and then move away to the south. The chopper was routine now, crossing over Bear's Den at intervals varying from ninety minutes to two hours, from sunrise to sunset. The repetition told him they were doing scans, and the fact Bear's Den seemed to now be the northern terminus of the search pattern told him his hope of Tremble becoming a decoy was a dead issue. For whatever reason, the search was to the south, and directly in his path. He'd just have to live with it.

No longer pressed for time, Anderson began a detailed search of the hostel. A kitchen drawer produced a double handful of condiment packets as well as small packets of salt and pepper and some plastic picnic cutlery. He tore open packet after packet of ketchup, mayonnaise, and mustard to suck them down greedily, then washed them down with yet another bottle of water. Enough to dull the ache in his gut for now at least, and he continued his search.

The kitchen trash yielded empty water bottles, and in a nearby storage closet he found a discarded nylon backpack with a broken strap. Another closet produced a small quilt like those used for padding furniture when moving. Frayed at the edges, it smelled of mold and mildew. Perhaps best of all, the guest laundry trash produced a discarded jug of chlorine bleach, with a bit left in the bottom—enough to purify several gallons of water. He drained the jug into one of the empty water bottles and capped it tight.

The shelves of the small hikers' store on the main floor were empty, but he hit pay dirt in one of the cabinets—a small paperback booklet titled "The AT Guide" and bearing a publication date of several years before—probably the reason it was still there—he smiled as he flipped through it. Far back in a dust-covered cabinet he found another treasure, a full carton of a dozen protein bars. The faded ink on the carton was a testament to its age, and a gnawed corner and liberal sprinkling of mouse droppings bore evidence as to why it had been abandoned.

Anderson shook the mouse turds off and opened the box, extracting a bar and ripping the wrapper off. The bar was dry and hard, the embedded chocolate chips grayish white with age. He bit off a piece with difficulty and chewed half a dozen times before swallowing and taking another bite. It was the best thing he'd ever tasted. He finished the bar and, dry-mouthed, hauled his booty downstairs to the kitchen, where he ate two more mice-gnawed bars, washing them down with more water.

Hunger appeased, he glanced at his watch. He had well over an hour before the chopper returned. He grabbed the damaged backpack and was out the door, heading for the spot Tremble's group had cached their surplus gear. The path was all downhill, and he made it to the cache in less than fifteen minutes. He was disappointed but not surprised to find it contained no food—or little else. It looked like they'd only dumped nonfood items for which they had duplicates: a large Victor rat trap, several heavy-duty black plastic contractor trash bags tightly rolled, another small hank of paracord, a half-roll of duct tape, and a ziplock bag full of fire starters. Slim pickings perhaps, but better than he expected.

Anderson had piled the stuff into his ragged backpack and slung it over his shoulder by the one good strap when he noticed another pile of leaves.

He brushed them away to find a pair of well-worn leather work boots, and he recalled the guy stripping the boots off his dead partner. After a moment's hesitation, he knotted the laces together and hung the boots around his neck, then took off for the hostel.

By the time the chopper thumped over again, he was ready. He'd used some of the paracord to repair the broken pack strap, then filled the pack with his meager supplies. He'd then cut the boots to pieces with the knife Tremble left him, bundling the soles and leather together, wrapped with one of the boot laces before it went into the pack. You never knew when leather might come in handy. He kept out one soft leather boot tongue and combined it with the other boot lace to fashion a sling, which he tested just outside the hostel door, using pebbles as projectiles. It was awkward, but with practice, he might take a rabbit or squirrel. The packing quilt was rolled tight and secured to the pack with more paracord, and four plastic water bottles were full and stowed in side pockets on the pack, where he could get to them. As an afterthought, he flushed the plastic bleach jug well and filled it with water. It just fit in the main compartment of the pack, adding eight pounds, but you could never have enough water.

He drank his fill from the kitchen faucet one last time, then rechecked the guidebook. He had an hour and a half to two hours before the chopper returned and almost four miles to cover over up-and-down terrain to reach a good-size stream. He could make that standing on his head.

An hour and twenty minutes later, struggling up a steep slope and still over a mile from his destination, Anderson heard the chopper approaching from the south and realized his error. He'd timed the chopper at the extreme northern end of its run, but once in the search area, it would fly over twice on each circuit, north and south bound, likely scanning on each run. Knowing he'd never reach the stream in time to soak the quilt as he'd intended, he slipped off his pack and fumbled with the knots holding the quilt, the sound of the chopper growing louder. Panicked at the unyielding knots, he slashed the paracord with his knife and threw the quilt on the ground in a heap before soaking it with the water from the bleach jug.

The chopper was almost on him now and he tossed the empty jug to one side and collapsed on the ground beside his backpack, pulling the sodden quilt over both himself and his gear. The chopper thumped overhead, hidden by foliage and without slowing. When it returned a few minutes later, he feared it had picked him up, but it passed again with no hesitation, now on the southbound leg. He gave a relieved sigh and rolled from under the quilt, then squeezed it as dry as possible before rerolling it. He tied it up with a carrying handle this time, so the wet quilt wasn't in constant contact with his pack.

It was a learning experience—the weight of the pack and steepness of the terrain slowed him more than he'd figured, and the extra water provided an unexpected benefit. He no longer had to adjust his speed to be near streams during flyovers as long as water sources afforded an opportunity to top up his big jug. The little AT guidebook showed multiple water sources along his route.

More confident now, he endured three more round-trip flyovers and made another eight miles before he started looking for a place to stop for the night. Three hundred yards off the trail he found a steep bluff and walked along the bottom of the near vertical rock face until he found what he was looking for. An undercut formed a shallow cave perhaps four feet tall and twenty feet deep, his bedroom for the night. He stowed his gear at the back and took the knife to cut some evergreen boughs to make a bed. He had two protein bars and a bottle of water for supper, then spent the remaining daylight hours practicing with his sling.

The final overflight of the day drove him into his hiding place, where the sun-heated rocks and substantial overhang masked all trace of his presence. With his pack as a pillow and exhausted by the unfamiliar exertion, sleep came with the fading sun.

***

George awoke stiff and sore at first light. He counted his dwindling supply of protein bars and restricted his breakfast to half a bar, washed down with a full bottle of water. He decided to try to make the highway crossing before the first chopper flight.

He was roughly two miles from crossing US 50 at Ashby Gap, a four-lane highway with a wide grassy median strip and a right of way cleared on either side. It was a logical place to intercept travelers on the Appalachian Trail, and his first major challenge. He'd driven the road countless times during his daily commute, back before everyone moved onto the base at Mount Weather. However, he'd never looked at it from the perspective of someone attempting to sneak across it in 'stealth' mode.

A half mile from the crossing, the first chopper flight of the day forced him under the wet quilt and he lay there until the return southbound flight a few minutes later. He was up and on his way again before the sound of the chopper faded. The trees thinned and he slowed, moving from trunk to trunk until he had a good view of the highway crossing in front of him left to right, fifty feet down a gradual slope. It looked clear, but he'd be totally exposed for a distance of at least two hundred feet. He was weighing the risk when a black SUV turned on to US 50 from Blue Ridge Mountain

Road. He watched the car move in front of him and go west a few hundred yards before pulling to the shoulder in the shadow of some trees, right next to another black SUV he'd missed. Anderson looked at his watch—six a.m. straight up—shift change.

Sure enough, the men in the two cars spoke through their open windows; then the car being relieved started up and drove down Highway 50 to turn on to Blue Ridge Mountain Road, no doubt headed back to Mount Weather. This was not good, and Anderson considered his alternatives. There were one or two places nearby where streams ran under the highway, but he couldn't recall exactly where they were. That had never been important when he drove the road, and distances at sixty miles an hour and on foot were two completely different things.

He sighed. It was what it was. He'd have to stay in the woods north of the highway and head west until he found a stream, then follow it south and wade through the culvert beneath the highway. Once across, he'd find his way back to the trail. More importantly, in getting to the culvert he'd have to stay well back from the farmhouses along the highway and hope he didn't have to cross too many open fields. He cursed under his breath and faded back into the trees before he shouldered his pack to pick his way west through the dense undergrowth.

That's when he heard the dogs in the far distance, baying wildly as they came down the Appalachian Trail.

CHAPTER NINETEEN

Day 20, 5:35 a.m.

Bill Wiggins and Simon Tremble made their way toward the plaintive squeals, moving carefully in the predawn light. Wiggins grimaced as they reached the source of the sound. The rabbit had almost escaped the snare; rather than breaking its neck as intended, the loop had caught a hind leg and the sapling jerked the animal skyward, to twist and squeal. Wiggins moved quickly, snapping the animal's neck before removing it from the snare and adding the now lifeless body to the plastic grocery bag they were using as a game sack.

"I hate when we don't get a clean kill," Wiggins said. "He could've been hanging here for hours. And it's not like it's always quiet. Shooting him might have made less commotion and been a lot more humane."

Tremble shook his head. "He'd have been squealing if he was being killed by a wolf or a fox, but a gunshot's an unnatural sound. Even that little popgun of yours has a sound signature that'll carry a ways. We all need some protein and we can't eat up what little jerky you and Tex have; you'll need it going north, and besides, it wouldn't last long anyway."

Wiggins sighed and inclined his head toward the snare. "Yeah, I know. Should I reset it?"

Tremble shook his head. "Between the rabbit and the squirrels we took out of the deadfalls, we have enough for today. We're not burning many calories hunkered down, and the meat won't keep anyway, so no point taking more than we can use. Let's step off into the woods a ways and skin and gut these. I want to keep the offal away from the cave; no point in drawing up predators."

They made short work of dressing their game, then started back through the woods toward their hideaway. They stepped over a small stream and set their guns and game on nearby rocks before turning back to the flowing water. Wiggins fished a small plastic bottle of soap from his pocket, another resource provided by Levi, and squeezed a dab into his palm before passing the bottle to Tremble. Both men lathered the blood off their hands, then squatted to rinse them.

"We haven't seen anybody since we dodged the chopper and search team the first day," Wiggins said. "You think they gave up? I mean, it's been three days, and I figured they'd be all over us like a blanket."

Tremble snorted. "They may not be looking here, but I can guarantee they're looking somewhere. Maybe Anderson drew them off, or they've just set up a perimeter and are waiting for us to cross it, but no, they haven't given up. Gleason won't want anyone to know his intentions, so Keith and I are probably now Public Enemies Number One and Two."

Wiggins stood up straight and slung water off his hands before patting them dry on his pants. He stood unmoving a moment and Tremble cocked an eye at him from where he still squatted at the stream. Then the older man rose and smiled, shaking the water from his own hands.

"You look like a man trying very hard to say something but unsure where to start, Bill," Tremble said. "Try the beginning."

"It's just… well, Tex and I've been talking, and we really appreciate the things you've taught us in the last couple of days, I mean the snares and deadfalls, and the Dakota fire hole and all that other survival stuff…" He trailed off.

Tremble smiled again. "Your tax dollars at work, and here I thought the army's attempt to kill me during SERE training was just an exercise. Now I'm using it to escape the government. Go figure."

"Well, that's kind of it. I mean, we wish you well, but I don't really know what we can do and…"

Tremble held up a hand. "And if y'all get caught with us, it won't go well for you, and your families need you. I understand. This is my problem, not yours and Tex's. I get that, and you have absolutely nothing to feel bad about. We're toxic, and in your position I'd stay as far away as possible. It's me that's sorry I dragged y'all into this and I'm grateful for your help. If you hadn't come along when you did, Keith and I would likely be dead by now. We owe you, not the other way around." He paused. "When you taking off?"

"We figure maybe tomorrow, if we don't see any more activity today."

"Are you up to it? How about your feet? We pushed pretty hard to get here, and you were in rough shape to start with," Tremble said.

Wiggins nodded. "It's a problem, and that's a fact, but mine are much better since I took that guy's boots, and Tex's feet weren't as bad as mine. She's had a couple of days off of them to rest up, but we still have to find her some better footwear—gotta be near some sort of population center to do that, though."

Tremble shook his head. "I don't know, maybe we should just separate and hide a while longer, just in different places. I can't help but think they'll be watching road crossings and such—"

"But not for a man and woman traveling together," Wiggins said.

"I think they'll be looking hard at ANYONE off this section of the trail that might have had contact with me or Keith. They might just take you out on the CHANCE you've come in contact with us."

Wiggins shook his head. "I know things are crazy, but for all that, I have difficulty believing the federal government has reached the point they're murdering people on the off chance they MIGHT have talked to you. And even if they are, we have our families to think about and we have to give it a shot. We can't just sit here forever."

"Your call," Tremble said as he walked over to pick up his gun and part of the game, "and I understand your urgency, because the most important member of my family is here with me, but I wish you'd wait a few more days."

Wiggins said nothing but fell in beside Tremble as they moved up the hill toward the cave.

***

Two hours later, Tremble sat on a rock under a tree thirty feet downhill from the cave, watching Tex grill the meat and listening for the sound of approaching choppers while keeping a sharp eye on the minimal smoke given off by the Dakota fire hole. It was a simple but effective arrangement, two holes about eight inches in diameter and a foot deep, dug a foot apart with the bottoms of each dug out so they connected underground.

A fire at the bottom of one hole drew oxygen from the second with the heat from the underground blaze in the 'fire hole' concentrated upward, where it cooked the meat on a grill of green sticks laid across the hole. The fire showed no light unless one peered directly into the hole, and burned hot and efficiently, so it could be fired with twigs and sticks broken by hand. Efficient combustion produced minimal smoke, and positioning the arrangement near a tall tree meant any smoke produced wafted upward along the tree trunk to be dissipated in the thick foliage overhead. An adjacent pile of excavated earth could be pushed in to smother the fire in less than two seconds and large flat rocks on the opposite side of the arrangement but far enough away from the fire to maintain their ambient temperature would cap both the holes a second after that.

The rocks would heat up in time, but it would take a while and look nothing like a human to the IR telemetry during a quick flyover. Detection was unlikely if they covered the fire and fled to the cave at the distant first sound of a chopper. Besides, not only did he not want to deplete Bill and Tex's stores, he got sick of jerky pretty quickly, and Bill and Tex's ultralight hiking stove was okay to boil water and pasta, but the fuel was limited, and it was a nonstarter for cooking much else. His mouth watered at the smell of the roasting meat.

"Damn! That smells good," he heard, and looked up to see Keith coming down the incline from the cave, picking his way carefully and supporting his weight on a crutch improvised from a tree limb.

"I made that crutch so you could get back and forth to do your business with a little privacy," Tremble said, "not so you could hobble around camp for the hell of it. You need to stay off that ankle if you expect it to heal."

"Hey, lighten up, Dad," Keith responded. "It sucks lying around in that cave all day, and I'm not helping at all. I thought I might come down and see if I could at least help with the cooking."

Tex looked up. "Got it covered, Romeo. All done. So sit your butt on that rock and give me your knife and I'll bring you some."

Tremble suppressed a smile as Keith flushed. Tex had nicknamed Keith 'Romeo' ever since the chopper scare and continued to tease him. Tremble sensed his son was more than a little smitten. Well, why not? Tex was likely only six or seven years older than his son, obviously smart and competent, and pretty in a very natural, no-makeup-required sort of way. He suspected she was also more than capable of taking care of herself.

"Uhh... thanks," Keith mumbled and unfolded the knife he'd found in the pocket of the uniform and handed it to Tex.

Tex accepted the knife and returned to the fire to spear a piece of meat and brought it to Keith. "Okay, you two," she said over her shoulder, "I'm only serving guys on crutches, so you're on your own. And that big piece of rabbit I put over to the side is mine."

Tremble laughed and took out his own knife to spear half of one of the squirrels. He saw Wiggins hesitate before doing the same. If you plan to make it all the way to Maine, my friend, you're probably going to have to eat things a lot worse than squirrel, he thought.

They ate in companionable silence, holding the hot meat on their knives to nibble while it cooled, then attacking in earnest when they could handle it, grease running down their chins. They ate until it was gone, leaving it to Tex to parcel the meat out fairly. When they'd dumped the bones in the fire hole and killed the fire, each was feeling pleasantly full. Tremble broke the silence.

"First light?"

Wiggins looked at Tex and nodded.

"Want to take one of the M4s?" Tremble asked.

"Negative," Tex said quickly. "Those are military-issue full auto. We could never explain them if we got caught, and they'd tie us right back to those FEMA guys. Besides, there's not much ammo anyway. Thanks for the offer, Simon, but it's not worth it."

Wiggins was nodding. "Tex is right, but we'll take one of those Sigs, though, and a little of the ammo. They're fairly common, so it shouldn't necessarily raise any questions if we're detained, and it's a nine millimeter like Tex's Glock so we can share ammo. That'll give us both a pistol along with the survival rifle. If we need more than that, we're probably screwed anyway. Our best defense is staying out of sight." He paused. "But what about you? We don't want to leave you with nothing. We'll split what we have."

It was Tremble's turn to decline. "You've got a long way to go, and y'all will need every bit of the food you've got and more. Dividing the food won't make much difference and there's plenty of game, so Keith and I can live off the land. But if you could spare a bit off that spool of wire I saw, some paracord for snares and such, and maybe a couple of those heavy garbage bags to carry stuff in, that would be great."

Wiggins looked at Tex, and she nodded. "Done," he said. "And I'll throw in a lighter. Levi gave us a half dozen and I didn't dump 'em 'cause they're light. But what about water? You got nothing to carry it in, nor anything to boil it in to sterilize it either."

Tremble shrugged. "There's a lot of water around, and as long as we can catch a spring where it surfaces and the water hasn't been contaminated with animal droppings, we should be all right. As far as carrying water goes, it is what it is, and we'll make do. I'm pretty sure if we hit one of the access points with a parking lot, we can slip down at night and raid a trash can for plastic water bottles."

Tex got a strange look on her face. "Just a minute," she said, and scrambled uphill toward the cave. She returned a moment later and handed two small packages to Keith and then stepped over and tossed two more in Tremble's lap. Keith was blushing, and Tex burst out laughing.

"Don't get any ideas, Romeo," she said, and Tremble looked down at the condoms in his hand.

"I found those in the side pocket of the pack and was starting to feel a bit negative toward Levi until I just figured out what they're for, besides the obvious, I mean. You can use 'em to carry water, and we can put a little of the bleach we're carrying in one of them as well, that way you can sterilize water if you have to," she said.

"So that's what those are for," Wiggins said. "I have some too, but we left Levi's place in a bit of a rush, and we didn't cover possible uses for those. When I found them, I was just a bit embarrassed to bring it up. We can let you have a few more, if you think you can use them." He laughed and shook his head. "That Levi's pretty resourceful."

Tremble looked at the condoms. "I think I'd like to meet this guy someday."

***

The four stood in the dim morning light, the leave-taking difficult despite their short friendship.

"Well, I guess this is it," Wiggins said, extending his hand.

Tremble nodded and grasped the outstretched hand, but didn't release it immediately. "You two take care of yourselves," he said, "and when you get home, if you have access to a radio, please spread the news about what's really going on to those folks in Wilmington and everywhere else you can. Whether we make it out or not, I feel better knowing that at least there's a chance Gleason's plans can be made public."

"You can count on it, Simon," Wiggins said, giving Simon's hand a firm squeeze before releasing it to offer his hand to Keith.

As Keith and Wiggins shook hands, Tremble turned to Tex and offered his hand. Even in the dim light he saw her eyes glisten with moisture, and she knocked his hand aside to wrap him in a hug.

"You take care, Simon," she whispered in his ear as he squeezed her back.

Tremble released her and she turned to hug Keith as well, quickly and fiercely before stepping back and wiping her eyes with the back of her hand and forcing a grin. "And you watch out for the old-timer, Romeo, and watch where you're stepping."

Keith merely bobbed his head in acknowledgment, as if not trusting his voice.

"I guess this is it," Wiggins said a second time, then shouldered his pack as Tex did the same.

They all stood for an awkward moment until Wiggins nodded a final time. "Take care," he said, and turned to walk into the woods. Tex stayed a moment longer then bobbed her head and turned to move after Wiggins. A moment later they were both out of sight, leaving Tremble and Keith staring at the spot where they'd disappeared into the thick woods.

"I hope they make it," Keith said quietly.

"Me too, son. Me too," Tremble replied.

They stood there quietly for a few minutes, each lost in their own thoughts. Finally Keith spoke.

"So what now?"

"We give them an hour to get on their way and then we pack up and move," Tremble said.

"What? Why?"

"Because as much as I hope they make it, their chances aren't good, and if they get caught, they know where we are."

"What do you mean! Tex and Bill would never rat us out—"

Tremble held up a calming hand. "No, not voluntarily," he said calmly, "but trust me. If they're caught, they'll be made to talk, because no one can resist forever."

Keith looked away, struggling to control his emotions. He swallowed several times before he could speak.

"So where are we going?"

"There's another cave about a mile south. I found it day before yesterday when I went out alone to set the snares. It's not quite as big as this one, but there's a little spring running out of it, so we'll have plenty of water."

"You planned on this? How did you know?" Keith asked.

"Family ties are strong motivators. Actually, I'm surprised they stayed as long as they did, and I really hope they make it back to their folks."

Keith nodded. "But what about us? We just hide in these woods for the rest of our lives? That means Gleason wins, doesn't it?"

"Nope, but we do hole up until that ankle of yours is a hundred percent, then we head south. It sounds like these folks in Wilmington are trying to put together a real recovery effort, and I'd like to be part of it."

EPILOGUE

OFFICE OF THE COMMANDER
U.S. FLEET FORCE COMMAND
U.S. NAVAL BASE NORFOLK
NORFOLK, VIRGINIA

DAY 25, 4:00 A.M.

Admiral Sam Wright reached for his coffee mug, wincing as the now stone cold and bitter brew shook him from his reverie. He shuddered and lifted his eyes from the memo to the large wall map on his office wall, festooned with colored pushpins representing the return of American military and diplomatic assets from across the globe. And they were all coming by ship—his ships, and already starting to clog the wharfs and anchorages of every naval waterfront facility, major and minor, from Kittery, Maine, to Bremerton, Washington, and all points in between.

And in the finest tradition of 'mission creep,' or perhaps 'mission gallop,' he was rapidly learning there was no coherent plan for dealing with the mass of humanity he'd been charged with 'bringing home to safety.' Ships arrived short on food, water, and fuel, and laden with people, to be shuttled to anchorages and ignored as the rapidly accruing liabilities overwhelmed the few remaining assets. He turned his eyes back to the memo.

25 April 2020
From: Chief - Naval Operations (CNO)
To: US Fleet Force Command (USFLTFORCOM)
Subject: Acquisition of Resources

As you are aware, recovery efforts are ongoing, focused on restoration of electrical-generating capacity at limited locations and the repair and build out of the electrical-transmission grid from those restored production facilities. Our national efforts must focus on this mission, if necessary to the exclusion of all else.

Pursuant to this goal, the President (POTUS), in consultation with the surviving members of congress now assembled at FEMA Command in Mount Weather, Virginia, has determined the most efficient course of action is a merger of the Department of Defense with the Department of Homeland Security, under the new title Department of Defense and Security (DEFSEC) to be led by Secretary Crawford, the present Secretary of Homeland Security (DHS). Secretary Tidwell will continue in a role similar to his current tasking as Secretary of Defense, but his new title will be Assistant Secretary of Defense and Security (ASECDEFSEC) and he will be reporting to Secretary Crawford (SECDEFSEC).

Secretary of the Navy (SECNAV) Murray has informed me, and I in turn inform you, that henceforth we will be taking direction from SECDEFSEC and cooperating more closely with FEMA forces, specifically the newly formed Special Reaction Force, the lead organization tasked with identifying areas where our acquisition efforts might best be focused.

The assets under your command will act primarily as support for Special Reaction Force (SRF) operations and be subordinate to them. While I understand there may be resistance to this change, I remind you of our obligation to conform to our oaths and responsibility to follow the orders of our lawfully elected leaders, regardless of any differing personal views, and know I can count on you to lead by example. Your full cooperation is both expected and appreciated.

SRF operations have already pacified areas around several nuclear power facilities, and recruitment efforts for both the nuclear infrastructure and farm labor programs are well under way. The biggest need at the moment is food, fuel, and other necessities, and the emphasis going forward is to concentrate on parts of the national logistical supply chain that were beyond the reach or technical ability of rioters and looters and that still hold a sufficient volume of resources. A preliminary list of those locations is appended, prioritized in order of probable execution. Please review it and stand ready to support SRF operations as and when needed.

Richard W. Whiteley
Chief of Naval Operations (CNO)

Wright flipped the page and stared at the long list of targets, focusing on the top name. He shook his head wearily and rose to cross to the chart table occupying a corner of his spacious office, then stared down at the chart of the Cape Fear River and the Port of Wilmington. Home sweet home, he thought, wondering for the hundredth time how he could keep the SRF thugs out of his hometown.

PUSHBACK

DISRUPTION - BOOK 2

Survivors of the Great Solar Storm struggle unassisted to rebuild a working society and save as many people as possible, as what remains of the federal government becomes increasingly corrupt and self-serving. FEMA's Special Reaction Force rises to become a power unto itself, and units of the regular military must decide whether to follow the orders of their chain of command—or their own consciences.

Available early 2016

Author's Notes

Apocalyptic tales have captivated the human imagination since the story of Noah and the great flood, and I'll admit to being a fan. Starting with classics like *The Earth Abides* and *Alas, Babylon*, I devoured these stories as a kid and have always enjoyed a good, convincing, post apocalyptic tale.

That said, I never figured I'd write one, because the key word is 'convincing,' and I doubted my own ability to convince readers to take that journey with me. My previous work is all in the 'thriller/action-adventure' category and set in the world of ships and the sea, environments I know well. I also suffer from an obsession for realism, and nothing happens in my Dugan thrillers that couldn't actually happen in real life.

But a post apocalyptic thriller? As much as I personally enjoyed reading them, I thought them well into the realm of fantasy. And if I couldn't convince myself to 'suspend disbelief,' I figured trying to convince others was a lost cause.

So what changed my mind? Strangely enough, it was a visit to the doctor about three years ago for a routine physical. I arrived ten minutes before my appointment time and settled in for what I assumed would be the normal half-hour or forty-five minute wait. Just as I turned on my Kindle, the battery died, so I had to resort to finding reading material from the meager selection of coughed-on/sneezed-on magazines.

(And for what it's worth, I'm convinced there exists a service dedicated to supplying medical offices three-year-old magazines on a range of topics of interest to no one.)

Imagine my delight when I found a recent issue of *National Geographic* with a cover story about solar storms. By the time the nurse called my name, I'd learned all about solar storms, their potential for damaging the power grid, and the Carrington Event of 1859. This seemed to be pretty serious stuff.

But surely it was overblown, right? If so, those pesky alarmists at *National Geographic* keep beating the drum. In April of this year, they released a long video documentary on solar storms. The whole thing is fascinating, but if you want to cut to the chase, start watching at about the fifty-minute mark.

(Internet links to all the stories cited in these Author's Notes are available at the end of these brief notes.)

After my doctor visit (I was pronounced healthy, by the way), I started doing a bit more research. Like every other subject one researches on the Internet, misinformation on solar storms abounds, but mixed with a lot of craziness was solid information from credible sources. For example:

Lloyd's – The venerable British insurer Lloyd's issued a twenty-one-page report in 2013 titled *Solar Storm Risk to North American Power Grid*. The entire report is fascinating reading, and the critical nature of high-voltage transformers and their vulnerability is covered in some detail. Of particular interest are these quotes from the very first page of the executive summary:

"A Carrington-level, extreme geomagnetic storm is almost inevitable (my emphasis) in the future. While the probability of an extreme storm occurring is relatively low at any given time, it is almost inevitable that one will occur eventually. Historical auroral records suggest a return period of 50 years for Quebec-level storms and 150 years for very extreme storms, such as the Carrington Event that occurred 154 years ago."

And:

"As the North American electric infrastructure ages and we become more and more dependent on electricity, the risk of a catastrophic outage increases with each peak of the solar cycle. Our society is becoming increasingly dependent on electricity. Because of the potential for long-term, widespread power outage, the hazard posed by geomagnetic storms is one of the most significant."

Which brings us to:

The Insurance Journal ran an August 2014 story titled *Time to Be Afraid — Preparing for the Next Big Solar Storm*, with an opening sentence reading, "The probability of a solar storm striking Earth in the next decade with enough force to do serious damage to electricity networks could be as high as 12 percent, according to solar scientists."

The article goes on to describe a solar storm in 2012 that produced a massive coronal mass ejection that was a 'near miss.' Had the pulse occurred a week earlier, it would have impacted the earth head-on.

Both of these stories are available at the links listed below these notes and I invite you to read them for yourself if you have any doubts as to the sources. I picked insurance industry sources as examples because insurers are noted for their unemotional assessment of risk. All the things I outlined in *Under a Tell-Tale Sky* regarding the vulnerability of our power grid are true. I could just as easily have cited any one of a hundred equally credible sources.

But what the heck is going on anyway? If our national leadership knows about the vulnerability of the transformers, why isn't the problem being addressed? Well, maybe it is. According to a March 2015 story in *Environment & Energy Publishing*, the Department of Energy is 'studying' the problem. However, I wouldn't hold my breath — they've been 'studying' it since 1990.

And at this juncture, I should point out that all the above references deal only with natural or solar threats to our power grid. The military is more concerned with the much greater potential for damage by an electromagnetic pulse (EMP) weapon, or cyber-attack, or a coordinated physical attack on critical transformers by terrorist cells. There are an equal number of disturbing studies from established, credible sources discussing this separate but similar threat, and some security experts consider it far more likely than a solar event.

Without flogging the deceased equine much longer, I will refer you to a November 2014 article in the *Business Insider*, in which Admiral Michael Rogers, director of the National Security Agency, admits China could shut down our power grid.

So there you have it. My biggest concern when I went into that doctor's office a few years ago was enduring a prostate exam, but you might say my horizons have broadened a bit. I started off more than a little skeptical regarding the entire 'grid down' scenario, but everything I've researched so far leads me to believe we are all much too complacent.

Don't get me wrong, I don't think you can live your life worrying about things that may never happen, and being prepared doesn't have to take over your life. That said, there are a lot of positive things that can spring from contemplating and preparing to live a simpler, less complicated life. Regular weekends in the woods can do wonders for your point of view.

So now you know why I now feel competent to write a postapocalyptic novel. I surely hope nothing like this ever happens, but everything I've learned has convinced me it's at least possible. How serious am I? Well, let's just say we now have our own little piece of wilderness and I'm starting to collect books with titles like *101 Delicious Possum Recipes.*

Sincerely,

Bob McDermott

Links to the Internet references cited in these notes are available below:

National Geographic - March 2012 - **Solar Flare: If Biggest Known Sun Storm Hit Today?**
http://news.nationalgeographic.com/news/2012/03/120308-solar-flare-storm-sun-space-weather-science-aurora

National Geographic - April 2015 - **Video - Solar Storm & Secrets of the Sun**
https://youtu.be/xew3KabTrAc

Lloyd's 2013 - 2013 - **Solar Storm Risk to North American Electric Grid**
https://www.lloyds.com/~/media/lloyds/reports/emerging%20risk%20reports/solar%20storm%20risk%20to%20the%20north%20american%20electric%20grid.pdf

The Insurance Journal - 2014 - **Time to be Afraid/Preparing For Next Big Solar Storm**
http://www.insurancejournal.com/magazines/features/2014/08/04/336115.htm

Environment & Energy Publishing - 2015 - **DOE Probes Need For Emergency Stockpile of Transformers to Power the Grid**
http://www.eenews.net/stories/1060014919

Business Insider - 2014 - **NSA Director: Yes, China Can Shut Down Our Power Grids**
http://www.businessinsider.com/nsa-director-yes-china-can-shut-down-our-power-grids-2014-11

Thanks!

There isn't any shortage of thrillers in the world, so I'm truly honored you chose to read mine and I sincerely hope you enjoyed it. I'm hard at work on *Pushback: Disruption Book 2* and will get it out as soon as I can.

While you're waiting (and if you haven't already read them) please consider my Dugan thrillers. The Dugan books launched my writing career, accumulating a combined total of over four thousand reader reviews while maintaining an average reader rating of over 4.5 out of 5.0 stars. Brief descriptions are on the following pages.

With that out of the way, let me take my marketing hat off and say I truly enjoy hearing from readers, so if you have questions, comments, or suggestions, let me know. Feel free to shoot me an email via my website contact page at www.remcdermott.com/contact.

And finally, independent authors such as myself live and die on the strength of our Amazon reviews, so for us they're a very big deal. But it's not enough to just accumulate a lot of good reviews, as factors in the Amazon quality ratings also include both the frequency and timeliness of those reviews. Thus a book with a lot of great reviews will tumble in the ratings if reviews don't continue to accumulate on a regular basis.

So the bottom line is, I regularly beg for reviews and appreciate every single one. If you're so inclined, please consider leaving a review of *Under a Tell-Tale Sky*.

On that note, and whatever your decision regarding a review, I'll close by thanking you once again for taking a chance on a new author, with the hope that I've entertained you at least a bit, and with the promise that I'll always strive to deliver a good story at a fair price.

Fair Winds and Following Seas,

R.E. (Bob) McDermott

More Books by R.E. McDermott

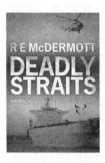

Deadly Straits - When very part-time spook Tom Dugan becomes collateral damage in the War on Terror, he's not about to take it lying down. Falsely implicated in a hijacking, he's offered a chance to clear himself by helping the CIA snare their real prey, Dugan's best friend, London ship owner Alex Kairouz. But Dugan has some plans of his own. Available in paperback on both Amazon and Barnes & Noble.

Deadly Coast - Dugan thought Somali pirates were bad news; then it got worse. As Tom Dugan and Alex Kairouz, his partner and best friend, struggle to ransom their ship and crew from murderous Somali pirates, things take a turn for the worse. A US Navy-contracted tanker with a full load of jet fuel is also hijacked, not by garden-variety pirates, but by terrorists with links to Al Qaeda, changing the playing field completely. Available in paperback on both Amazon and Barnes & Noble.

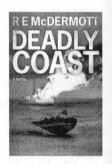

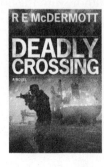

Deadly Crossing - Dugan's attempts to help his friends rescue an innocent girl from the Russian mob plunge him into a world he'd scarcely imagined, endangering him and everyone he holds dear. A world of modern-day slavery and unspeakable cruelty from which no one will escape unless Dugan can weather a Deadly Crossing. Available in paperback on both Amazon and Barnes & Noble.

Made in United States
Orlando, FL
12 October 2024

52566471R00211